GRADES OF EXECUTION

ANNE WERNER

DEDICATION

To my mother, who convinced me I could be like Elvis Stojko with enough hard work.

1

———

SOME PEOPLE DREAMT of defying gravity, but Satoru wasn't one of them. Defiance was a brave and noble quality, but it didn't equate with success. One could defy the rules but still end up punished for one's daring. Satoru recognized the power and dominion gravity held over Earth, and knew it wouldn't stand for insolence. It would prosecute all trespassers, thrust all sons of Daedalus back to the ground with their wings in flames, no act of brazen audacity would be stunning enough to earn an exception. So he had no plans to defy gravity.

He planned to murder gravity and leave its corpse in a ditch.

The music he'd chosen for that evening's free skate filled the ice rink, and Satoru's heart quickened at the familiar sound. He wasn't the only athlete practicing on the ice, but his world had shrunk down to the feel of his blade, and he didn't need to worry over the other bodies racing around. The right of way belonged to him, and sure enough, the other figure skaters cleared like water before Moses. Satoru turned around and stretched his leg behind him. No need to see, not when his intended destination was the air. The seconds stretched out as he tried to focus on his next set of actions.

And then it was time, and seconds sprung back like elastic. Sweet, blessed sky. One rotation, two, three, the pull of gravity trying to take away four, but no! Satoru completed the turn and slid out on that blade, beautifully balanced on the outside edge for just a moment, before he slammed his toe pick into the ground to jump back into the air where he belonged.

Four more rotations, a little harder this time, not as much air. He felt a little disappointed by that. Didn't the sky want him to stay? Well, the space above the rink had many skaters vying for its favor. Maybe it felt crowded. So Satoru took his four rotations and returned to the earth, coming out of the jump with his arms spread out in gratitude. He rode his landing blade for a few seconds before turning back to face forward, and the spell broke.

And to think he'd started out wanting to play hockey. Blasphemy. He flew through the rest of his program and sliced air with the final triple axel. By the time he skated over to the boards, he was grinning. "Kara Beth! That's clean! You owe me lunch!"

"The deal was a *judged* program. You skate clean tonight, then we'll talk." His coach shook her head. "But that quad-quad combo's getting so solid. I can barely believe it."

"What's not to believe? You doubt me?"

"After this? Never." She handed over a tissue box and Satoru gratefully took one to wipe his face. "How do you feel?"

"Good. I feel, like... just good. Everything's... smooth." He scrunched up his eyebrows as he tried to find better words. English wasn't his first language, and though he communicated well, his vocabulary wasn't as wide as he wanted it to be. But he never had a problem talking to Kara Beth. "Feels better than home practice."

"I like the sound of that." Kara Beth gave a few more observations while Satoru inhaled some water. There was always room to improve, always ways that he could be better, but most of his coach's comments were nitpicking at this point. They'd made huge strides over the summer and put together two competitive programs that fulfilled every ambition spawning inside Satoru since he was eight years old.

Well, almost. "I still think we should add double axel to flying sit-spin."

"I still think we should commit you to a mental institution."

"That means no?"

"That means stick to your program layout or I'll stab you with your own ice skates." Satoru couldn't remember the last time he felt so good about an upcoming competition. Practices had all gone well, with both his technical and artistic elements dripping in confidence, and the competitive figure skating season opened like a keg of dyna-mite. Enormous scores at his first event, even if he'd popped his new 4A into a triple. Satoru was still beating himself up for that. He hadn't trained so hard to master jumps and combinations that no one else could do, only to not do them when it counted. But his short program had been perfect yesterday, and he was determined to replicate that for the evening's free skate. By the end of the Grand Prix series, he'd be even better. By the World Championships, he'd rule Mt Olympus.

Once he'd caught his breath, he zipped out onto the ice again. The official practices were short, and there was no sense wasting time. He stroked a few laps around the edges of the rink, mindful of the other skaters but resisting the urge to make eye contact. Kara Beth called it the Competitive Cone of Silence, and a few tense interactions from his junior days taught Satoru to respect it. But if he had his way, he'd be commiserating with his fellow skaters both verbally and non-verbally, releasing pressure through his connections to human beings. He was a social creature in that respect, but an anomaly as an athlete, and his rivals liked to keep to themselves as it got closer to crunch time.

With some exceptions. "Would you pick up the pace, Miyazawa? The rest of us need to move around the rink, too, you know." Satoru had seen the skater from his peripheral vision, so it didn't come as a shock when Derek Donner of Great Britain sidled up and skated a slow semi-circle around him. "The last thing anyone needs is to trip over you."

"You have eyes to see me and move," Satoru said as Derek slid away, and he tried not to relish the flinch his next words earned, "So many carrots, vision must be *very* good by now." The reply came a few seconds later, when Derek threw out a 4T that furiously rejected the idea that someone could call it under-rotated. Satoru had to admit it impressed him; the quadruple jumps had always been the other skater's nemesis. Derek excelled in many areas and had a hydroblade that was downright legendary, but his quads were notoriously underrotated, to where the technical panel sometimes dinged him with two "carrot" marks and downgraded them to triples.

Satoru had accumulated a few carrots of his own over the years, so he knew the frustration. But he and Derek had a long history of barely restrained animosity, and just about any subject was fair game. At least, Satoru thought it was a game. He didn't actually hate Derek, and the feeling was mutual. Probably .

He questioned that when Derek came back across the rink with the look of charging death. No words passed between them, but that expression caused a chill to run down Satoru's spine. Not that it stopped him from hitting his own 4S with stunning quality, and a 3A shortly after. Nothing could intimidate him out of his beloved Axels.

His coach was less impressed. She had been speaking with one of the other skaters she managed, Eric Blaine, but looked over the eighteen-year-old's shoulder and beckoned Satoru with one disdainful finger.

"*Seriously?*" was all she said when he arrived, and that accented word was all she needed. Kara Beth had made an admirable attempt to learn Japanese over the years, and pretty much only busted it out when Satoru was in trouble.

"*I'm sorry.*"

"*Good.* Keep it off the ice. His coach can beat me up." She shooed Satoru and returned to her conversation with Eric, who looked between the two with some confusion. Across the rink, Derek was having similar words with his own coach, and Satoru felt the shame setting in. There was no point arguing that Derek had started it; Satoru should have known better. What if Derek felt goaded into that 4T and hurt himself on the landing, or if they'd been so focused on each other that they became a distraction, or collided with another skater? There were too many people on the ice and way too much at stake to behave so irresponsibly.

Satoru groaned to himself. Twenty years old, an Olympic medalist, world, national and Grand Prix titles, but he was still such a dumb kid. It would have been so easy to ignore Derek for five seconds. Now he was causing trouble to his colleagues, setting a bad example for the younger skaters and presenting a poor image of his country, his family, his skating club and his coach.

And his life was complicated enough without adding any more drama. Satoru skated for Japan, but he'd moved to America when he was a teenager to train under Kara Beth, and after seven years, some people wondered how strong his ties to his home country were. Insignificant people, ones who didn't know him, but Satoru had been changed by his experiences to where his family sometimes commented on how "American" some of his mannerisms were. Of course, trying to pass as a native of his adoptive home in Ohio was just laughable, so such comments left Satoru feeling lost. Forgetting to treat his fellow competitors with respect was like forgetting his hometown ideals, abandoning the values his parents raised him with.

He didn't want his brash behavior to reflect badly on his parents. They'd given up so much for his skating, and deserved a narrative saying they'd raised a son who was hardworking, kind and respectful. They needed to be praised for their sacrifices, not regretting that they let him out of the house. He didn't need anyone wondering if Kara Beth was a bad influence on him, either.

But that added another layer to his problems, because Kara Beth had outside commentary of her own. She'd been just twenty-six when she began coaching him, barely out of her own competitive career. Young, inexperienced, and it didn't help that Satoru came to her with a pre-existing knee injury that he'd hidden for the better part of a year, or that personal circumstances led to him living with Kara Beth until just this summer. She'd been his guardian, a surrogate parent in addition to a coach, and she answered for his conduct in the world as much as his own mother did, whether or not she wanted to.

Satoru thought finally moving out into his own apartment would fix some of that, but it just made things weird. Instead of being relieved of a burden, Kara Beth looked sad to see him go, and there was sometimes an awkward wall between them as they tried to navigate what they were to each other now that they didn't live in the same house. Kara Beth used to have the right to set rules and curfews, discipline him when he got out of line, and there was no separation between skating life and home life.

Not that she would send him to bed without desert over this, but the slip made Satoru feel murky all the same. The personal connection aside, his skating federation had recently been suggesting he make a coaching change, or at least a change in training location. Kara Beth's skating club was located in a small town in Ohio, far from the ample resources of the larger cities and more established coaches, and the woman herself was still navigating the world of coaching elite athletes. She'd only coached three skaters in her entire career: Satoru was first, then a French skater who joined the club a year afterwards named Damien Saint-Michel, and the new Eric Blaine. There were more experienced coaches out there, his federation reminded, with more connections and resources, who could challenge Satoru, keep a professional distance and not take selfies in the Kiss and Cry.

Satoru knew better. It killed him that Kara Beth didn't get the respect she deserved, even after she guided Satoru out of a dismal Junior's career to win every title available, and turned Damien into the French champion three years running. Even Eric, who'd only been with their skating club since the last season, had gone from sixteenth to seventh in the American men's division. The evidence should have ended the discussion, let alone the fact that Ranmaru himself couldn't have felt more loyal to Nobunaga than Satoru to Kara Beth.

He said that, but he'd just gone and embarrassed his beloved coach with barely a thought. Satoru cringed and tried to focus on his skating. Crossovers, mazurkas, mohawks, the sharp turns of direction matched the fury of his thoughts, which seemed to escalate so quickly after one negative influence. A moment of thoughtless behavior with his rival, and suddenly the floodgates opened to drown him in all the other flaws and worries he'd been trying to ignore. A dumb thing he'd said in yesterday's press conference, being aloof with a hotel employee, forgetting to call his mother on her birthday, each trying to chip away at his thoughts.

And the hits kept coming with every second. The countless English conversations he only half-comprehended, accidentally knocking over a water glass at breakfast, the missed calls from his older brother that he still didn't have the courage to return, he tried to dispel it all with a series of twizzles.

He marked out his cantilever without taking the position in order to give a wide berth around Alberto Casal of Spain. He bled his feelings through his feet, and felt his breath flow out of him in a soothing current as he regained synchronicity with the ice. There were plenty of stresses and flaws to disturb him, but skating was constant. Skating was his shield.

He looped a slow, deliberate rehearsal of his choreographic sequence once around the rink, then twice, and felt his tension carve into the ice with each step. There were no wild thoughts that skating couldn't calm, no pendulum swings of mood that a few good strokes couldn't control. His parents thought his boundless energy and need for people would be a good fit for soccer, basketball, and eventually hockey, but none of those team sports satisfied Satoru's need to move like a few solitary minutes on the ice. None of them provided an outlet for his anxious soul to transform into something greater than himself, body and heart finally united to create a whole being. Nothing else dissolved the weight of failure and disappointment and waste that hung on his slender frame and threatened to drag him straight through the cracks of the earth.

At the next break in the music, Satoru found his opening and set up for his Triple Axel. Once a jump that made history, now it was the least valued jump in Satoru's whole program. For all Satoru loved jumping axels, the relative ease of them grated on him, made him want to push his difficulty further. But when he said that out loud, Kara Beth launched into a tirade about hubris, physical limitations and "What part of a six-quad program isn't good enough for you?"

But she did help him train his dream jump. The rest was acceptable. For now. He turned his shoulders and took a step to flight.

As soon as his feet left earth, he knew something was wrong. That perfect connection to the ice and awareness of space had evaporated, leaving Satoru spinning in midair with no sense of where anything was in relation to his blades. He felt no confidence about where and when his foot would touch down, and that hesitation didn't help him hang onto the landing when his weight fell backwards over his heel. In the end, he over corrected and went tumbling.

For a second, he was too stunned to move, and let the ice carry him almost gently to the sideboards. Then he made impact and came back to reality. There was the embarrassment, of course, and the bruises, but what hit Satoru the hardest was the disbelief. He didn't fall. That was his biggest claim to fame. Undefeated for nearly three years since he won the last Olympics, all because he never fell in competition. And the Axel! The Triple Axel was not easy, but in the relative sense of Satoru's abilities, it was nowhere near his hardest element. He jumped axels for fun!

He looked down at the ice for a minute, and almost asked what it thought of the whole debacle. After a fall like that, he probably owed it an apology. Which was the attitude Kara Beth took when he checked in with her. "That poor rink, what did it do to deserve punching it with your butt? I hope it's okay."

By Satoru's count, the ice tended to get its revenge on skaters without help from sarcastic coaches. "Not sure what happened. Lost balance."

"You went up a little off-axis, too. Get your focus back and try it again." Satoru obeyed, but the second attempt was worse than the first, and now he had another massive bruise to add to the collection.

It was delusional to think the other skaters didn't see. Competitive Cone of Silence was still in effect, but Satoru could almost read their minds, the expressions were so obvious. *Don't look, don't look, stay focused-thank the lord above, he's human, maybe I have a chance of winning this-he's not getting up, what if he's hurt, should I say something-don't look, don't look, focus...*" In the stands, the paying public were whispering and had probably blogged and re-blogged that little splat all over the internet. By evening, the commentators would be debating whether it was a sign of things to come, the Olympic Champion falling off his own podium and bringing his reign to an end.

But Satoru couldn't fall from a height he hadn't really achieved. He got back up and did a few lazy strokes to get his feet back under him, but failed. The ice was sandpaper below him, grinding his blades dull and threatening to take blood if he touched his skin to it again. By the time he made it back to Kara Beth, the official practice was over and they had to clear the rink.

Eric had enjoyed a good run through, by the looks of it. The boy was brimming with all his cocky, teenaged joy, and Satoru felt a stab of jealousy when Kara Beth returned it. He smashed that down as soon as it came up. He'd felt the same things when Damien first came to train with them, and that turned out all right. A seven-year coaching arrangement wouldn't come apart because the rookie was having a good day.

Then again, after two catastrophic triples... He was still distracted when Kara Beth handed him his skate guards. "You," she snapped her fingers in his face. "Come back to earth. What happened on the Axel?"

Satoru winced. It wasn't that her tone was harsh, far from it, but the coach before Kara Beth had instilled such a sense of dread into the question that he was still suffering from the Pavlovian conditioning. "Don't know, just wrong." He ran a hand over his face to hide the fact that his eyes were burning. By now, the heat should have melted the rink into a swimming pool. "I don't understand, I get triple fine in combo!"

"Okay. Let's think about that. What's different?" When Satoru didn't answer right away, Kara Beth gave an exasperated sigh. "Try to breathe, kid. I don't have the muscles to carry you if you pass out." Kara Beth never used pet names with Eric, or called him 'kid', even though he was younger. Satoru liked the expressions of affection, but wondered if it wasn't a sign that she viewed him as more juvenile than his peers. She wouldn't be the first person to act like Satoru's maturity matched the level of his English grammar. "The combo's more complicated, so you're a lot more focused on your positioning than when the triple's by itself. So, think through it now. Where did it get weird?"

"I think maybe... too forward? On takeoff..."

"That's what it looked like from here. Your free leg was pretty wild, too."

"Shouldn't make mistake like that, too beginner," he mumbled, and Kara Beth barked out a laugh.

"It's a Triple Axel, there's nothing beginner about it! Honestly, Sato..." She shook her head, but her eyes were sparkling with affection. "Even the best fall sometimes. Don't stress out over it."

Satoru wondered what it was like to just tell yourself not to feel things and have that be the end of it. His brain was busy reminding him that one mistake meant maybe making the mistake again, then a third or fourth mistake and before he knew it, his coach would drop him and he'd never podium again and his family would lose the house. If he tried the jump again now, he wouldn't trust himself to land it, not with the way his eyes were stinging, and if he couldn't trust himself in practice, then how could he be trusted in competition?

He snapped on his guards and gathered his things, despite the fact that the world was so watery he could barely find them. The self-destruct sequence had already been activated, and there was no choice but to keep steering the ship until it went down. Hopefully, he could at least get out of the public space before he achieved full meltdown, not like any of the present company would be surprised either way. It just wasn't skating season if Miyazawa wasn't getting emotional about something.

As usual, Kara Beth understood. She waited until they'd left the arena to pull him to the side and let the line of people pass on by. Satoru wasn't sure how she kept the camera operators and representatives from the Japanese Skating Federation moving along, but somehow she managed that feat of wizardry. For him, though, her face showed nothing but kindness. "Honey, calm down. I'm not mad about the Axel."

Satoru didn't know how to explain that he knew. That he knew it, and for some reason his mind kept expecting it anyway. He kept projecting his own anger and self-loathing onto her, and it wasn't helpful or fair, but with the weight of the world title on his shoulders he just couldn't stop. Not when bad skating led to a score of other problems that neither of them could fix. And when it all came crashing down around him, he wouldn't even get to go home to Kara Beth making him a plate of Snickerdoodles anymore. "I know, but I'm mad about it."

"No, you're scared. You're scared that if you fall in competition, your skates will explode, the ISU will disband out of disgust and the Japanese flag will burst into flames. Astronauts will see your mistake from space and steer themselves directly into the sun." And that was why Kara Beth was the best coach in the world, the only one who could ever work for him. Satoru couldn't help the laughter bubbling up inside him as Kara Beth continued, "Tchaikovsky will rise from his grave and tear up the score for Swan Lake out of spite. Brian Boitano will personally make sure you're never allowed to do axels again. Skaters of all disciplines will burn their costumes out of shame. Rhinestone factories across the world will go bankrupt and all because you couldn't land a Triple Axel."

"You forget tissue industry," Satoru managed a weak giggle through his tears. "I fall on jump, world buys out supply, tissue crisis makes stock market into collapse."

"See? You're a long way from the Tokyo suburbs. The stakes are life and death out here!" She squeezed his shoulder, and it helped because Kara Beth knew those stakes better than anyone. The same pressure sat on her shoulders less than a decade ago.

Funny, how Satoru couldn't remember one instance where Kara Beth had broken out sobbing over a practice, but maybe she was just better at hiding from the camera crews. "I know I'm being over..." he forgot the word for 'dramatic', "... like, dumb, but I want to get it right."

"It's a long season, Sato. If things don't go perfectly today, we still have the NHK Trophy, and the finals. And Nationals. And then Four Continents. And Worlds..."

"Okay, okay. I know..." He exhaled, and Kara Beth waited, forever patient. "I know. But I think not everyone sees like that..." Everyone else demanded perfection, without excuse or compromise. Even if he had a flawless free skate that evening, the interviewers would all comment on how horrible his practice was and how did he manage to stop screwing up? *Yesterday's short program wasn't completely perfect, how did you find the courage to show your face?'*

Heaven forbid he actually stumbled on something. *'Lovely performance, inspiring how you pushed the boundaries of human capability, but let's talk about that one moment where you sucked.'* That's what the press would focus on, the fans, the sponsors, the skating federation, his brother, and the list went on.

But Satoru himself was at the top of that list, so maybe it was hypocritical to be bitter that everyone followed his lead.

Some days, his coach was the only one who thought it was okay to mess up, and wasn't that a reversal of expectations? Kara Beth searched his face and found the tiny slivers of doubt he was hiding. "If perfection's what you want, we can lower the difficulty. You don't need the Quad-Quad combo to win today. Lord knows that thing's more trouble than its worth." The second she said those words, Satoru's heart froze, but before he could form a protest, Kara Beth's lips quirked up into a smirk. "But that's not what you want, is it?"

Satoru didn't know how to respond. Having a perfect skate and winning was the right answer, the one people expected. And he did want to win. Every skater did, Satoru more than others.

But to hold back and not push his limits when he was capable of so much more? That felt like a lie, a photoshopped version of perfection. It mocked everything he'd achieved, and the goals he still dreamed of achieving. "No," he replied, gaining confidence. "Want something else." He couldn't quite put words to it, but it would be a skate that satisfied him, a definitive moment. A brick house was functional, society couldn't live without it, but humanity couldn't live without the Statue of Liberty, the Pyramids, or the Eiffel Tower. There were a hundred practical skates within Satoru, but he wanted to prove he could create a world wonder, and he thought he was getting close.

"Right. I know how much pressure's on your shoulders, and if you want, you can go out and make all those people happy. Give them the gold medal they want." Satoru's bitter thought was that he'd never make everyone happy, though he sometimes ground himself to hamburger in the attempt. "Or, you can give the skate you want. Even if it means falling along the way ."

The risk was never that he'd fall, and they both knew it. He could get up from a fall, try again, learn and improve. The actual risk was far greater, and not always definable. Medals and titles were just symbols of the real things he stood to lose, and Satoru wanted to curl into a ball at the thought of being brought down so low again.

He was a panicked wreck, but Kara Beth was calm. "Really, give yourself a break. I love your crazy jumps, but I don't love any of them if they make you miserable. A fall's all right with me if you come off the ice smiling."

Satoru grimaced. "Can't smile after fall, that's dumb."

"I don't know," Kara Beth sighed. She gave him a small pat on his shoulder. "Sometimes I think your best skate is going to come on a day when you don't win."

That was nonsensical. "I always win."

"Of course you do, champ," Kara Beth chuckled, and Satoru was pretty sure he was being patronized.

"Win is important, yeah, but need to do more. Not just because I like jump. I think, I only skate because others give, and I should pay back," he tried to explain his conflicted feelings, "But if that's all I care about, better to stop skating as kid, right? Be doctor, or something." Not that Satoru had the brains for it, but medical school might have been cheaper. "I have to skate. So skating should mean something."

"Okay." Kara Beth was frowning a little. Satoru wasn't sure if she disagreed or if he'd misunderstood the question. That happened sometimes. But as always, she somehow came up with the words he needed to hear. "Look, sometimes practice just goes weird. But you're the best skater in the world. And no matter what anybody says, a few falls won't change that. Not for me."

The best skater in the world. Satoru wished that were true. He wished he could look at the growing collection of trophies and see that for himself. He wished he didn't feel like he was running some elaborate con and needed to make good on his reputation before everyone realized the lie.

But when Kara Beth said it, he thought maybe it could be true someday. If Kara Beth saw him fall every day and still kept coming back, after staring down gravity in her day and going beyond simple defiance, if she said he was the best, it meant something.

And with her backing him up, Satoru vowed to take revenge on gravity before the day was out.

2

————

ON THE SHUTTLE back to the hotel, the Competitive Cone of Silence lifted, and Satoru welcomed the chatter. How well he spoke any language didn't matter, as long as he could sit in the atmosphere of friendship. And during competition season, it was especially important to remember each other as people, not obstacles.

He plunked himself down in a seat next to Alberto and spent half the bus ride discussing the future of Real Madrid before a shock of messy black hair popped up from the seat in front of them to interrupt. *"Excuse me, beloved and highly decorated champion, known for his extreme generosity-"*

"What do you want, Yukiya?" There wasn't actually a point in asking. The Japanese silver medalist was too predictable. Either he forgot his phone charger, again, or his seventeen-year-old metabolism was demanding to be fed. A spare charger wouldn't be of any use on the bus, so Satoru was already digging through his bag for granola bars before Yukiya finished his request.

"It's been, like, an hour since I last ate and I'm starving! You got anything edible? I think my stomach's gonna turn inside out!"

"Oh, stop whining, here you go." Satoru handed over two of the bars and Yukiya chirped back his gratitude.

"Thank you! Even though I'm totally going to destroy you tonight."

While Satoru rolled his eyes, Eric's head peeked over the neighboring seat.

His eyes danced with eager hope. "You have food?"

Satoru parted with two more granola bars with a show of incredulity, but he didn't actually mind. The food was there to share. He liked to make sure people were happy and taken care of. *"Haven't you two stopped growing yet? I don't know where you put all that food..."*

Ignorant of Satoru's words, Eric just mumbled his thanks around mouthfuls. "You're the best, thanks! I didn't think you'd have snacks on you without Damien around to force feed." He paused and looked chagrined. "Am I allowed to say that?"

Well, it wasn't as if the world didn't know. But Damien was touchy about the subject. "I think maybe you should ask him." It took Eric a second to realize that Damien was not there to ask and therefore that was the answer, but he got there and disappeared behind his seat with a sheepish nod. Likely, Damien himself probably didn't care that people acknowledged it, just the judging assumptions that followed.

But Damien was assigned to different stops on the Grand Prix, last week's Skate Canada and the upcoming Internationaux de France, while Satoru was given today's Skate America and then the NHK Trophy in Japan. They saw each other between their events, but they wouldn't be competing together until the finals. Damien was on his own in the food issue, and as much as Kara Beth tried, the reports from Canada last weekend had Satoru a little worried.

But it wasn't something he felt comfortable talking about with outsiders, so he turned to Alberto and changed the subject. "Hard ice today, huh?"

Alberto laughed and rolled his eyes. "Do they think we are a hockey team? *Dios mío*, I thought it might crack under my feet!"

"Might need hockey pads if I fall again," Satoru agreed, happy to commiserate over the ice conditions. "This is California. How do they keep so cold?"

"Aw, did the princess feel a tiny pea under all those layers of mattress?" Derek broke into the conversation, and Satoru turned around to face him.

"Please, not princess. I deserve be Queen. Besides, skate is job, of course we notice." Notice, even if he couldn't do anything about it. Every rink was different, and this ice was a bit cold and brittle for his liking. His skates didn't grip in quite the way he liked, but the audience wouldn't care, and neither would the judges. They'd only see his combination pass go down like a string of dominoes, so he had to adapt to the rink conditions. Yesterday's skate went off without a hitch, despite the chippy ice, and it certainly wasn't the worst he'd ever skated on. "You thought was fine?"

"Well, I wasn't the one impersonating a curling stone in practice." Ouch. But that was just how competitions went between them. Satoru enjoyed talking to people, Derek enjoyed throwing shade. So Satoru threw shade right back with the force of a ballistic missile and they both got what they wanted. It had been that way since their Junior years.

He used to wonder if he'd done something offensive or hurtful by accident. People often described Satoru as sassy when he spoke English, and back in the days when that English was on par with the average four-year-old, the direct approach sometimes left bruised feelings in its wake. But apologies didn't make the situation better, and when Satoru asked Kara Beth for advice, she told him Derek was probably just jealous and to ignore him.

Easier said than done. "Blame the ice if you want, Miyazawa, but the rest of us skated just fine."

"Then it's not you who nearly falls on face in step sequence? My mistake."

"I'd say pretty much all mistakes in that practice were yours."

"It is mistakes in competition that matter, not practice," Satoru grinned. "You want to talk about short program? I break world record, you nearly break teeth?"

"You'd never know it from the press conference." Derek straightened up and began imitating Satoru's accent. "'I do this wrong, and that wrong, everything is a failure...' Only you could hold the world record and act like you came in last place."

It was one of Satoru's greater flaws. He was trying to work on it. "Is this insult or to encourage me? Make up your mind."

"Enough of this, the subject bores me," Alberto jumped in before the bickering could escalate, and Satoru felt a little guilty to have made other people uncomfortable. "And to ruminate on mistakes is not healthy for any of us." The arguing was petty. Satoru would have to be more considerate in the future.

Derek seemed to be of the same mind and slunk back into his seat with a mumbled apology. Satoru echoed it, but the awkward air that settled troubled him.

In front of him, Yukiya turned back to look over his seat. He paused for a moment, regarding Satoru and company as if trying to puzzle out the exact context of all the English that had gone on around him. Then, he grinned and made a show of exaggerated bowing in all directions. *"Please excuse my countryman, he trains in America and it's kind of turned him into a weirdo. I swear we're not all like this..."*

Even though most of those words weren't understood by the present company, the sentiment was, and it broke the tension hanging over the area with healthy laughter at Satoru's expense. Satoru himself managed a few grateful chuckles as well, before reaching up to flick Yukiya in the back of the head.

SINCE THEY'D KILLED the conversation, Satoru opened his bag and started digging through it for a book. An awkward task, as they always seemed to sink straight to the bottom of his bag. But he found it in the end and settled back in his seat to read.

Skating didn't leave room in Satoru's life for college. Keeping up with the demands of high school and training had stretched him past his limits, and he decided university would burst the edges completely. Many of his competitors were students, some had even finished degrees and were considering further education, but Satoru didn't know how they managed. It was possible that they were just smarter than him, as Satoru had never felt he was intellectually gifted.

But he loved to learn, and what captured his interest the most was classical architecture. There was something about the way old buildings still held resonance after hundreds of years and changing styles that was inspiring. The genius of the designs, the effort of construction and the symbols these landmarks became to the world stirred something in his heart similar to figure skating, though he wasn't quite able to describe what the parallels were. But if he hadn't discovered ice skating and instead pursued an education, he thought he might be happy as an architecture historian.

Currently, his reading involved the Rouen Cathedral, a building that had existed since the late 4th century as a church, expanding to cathedral, and was once the tallest building in the world. Its height had been surpassed several times over, but the building hadn't lost its legacy or majesty. What it lacked in size was made up by its beauty and impressive array of massive bells.

Something in that spoke to Satoru. He was also intrigued by how many times the building had been attacked, ransacked, set on fire, and still restored to grandeur. Lightning struck the cathedral half a dozen times, and yet, it still held meaning to the city of Rouen, to artists like Monet, who created works of art after laying eyes on it, and to the musicians who made the cathedral's organ into one of the best and most renowned in France.

Nothing Satoru did was permanent. Someone would eventually surpass all his titles and accomplishments, and his minutes on the ice were so fleeting. He spent life as a cherry blossom, desperate to be the most beautiful it could be before nature forced it to wither and fall, forgotten among a thousand others. But it was human nature to want to create lasting beauty and fight against the transient nature of life. These buildings carried the hopes and passions of so many people long dead, and would take on more with each passing year. Satoru knew nothing about building things, but the idea still motivated him.

The shuttle finally pulled up to the hotel, so Satoru closed his book and tried to fit it back into his bag, now that he'd messed it all up looking for it. In the struggle, his hand brushed up against something unusual. Satoru paused, then pulled out the object. A frayed, hideous orange watch, held together with duct tape and faith, the face so caked with grime that it was impossible to tell whether it still worked. Upon inspection, it seemed the clasp had broken.

Alberto looked over. "Isn't that Saint-Michel's lucky watch?"

"Yes," Satoru said, frowning to himself. "It was missing."

"No way! You found the watch?" Eric turned in his seat and leaned over the back to see. "I hoped that would turn up! Damien was going crazy." He laughed, then paused. "Why is it in with your stuff?"

"I don't know. Weird." He noticed that both Eric and Alberto were staring at him. Even Yukiya, though he couldn't follow the dialogue, looked down with curiosity in his eyes. "What?"

But the answer came from behind. "Nothing," Derek drawled, "just that his precious magic watch has never been off his wrist since he was twelve, except to show up in your private skate bag during competition season. Nothing weird about that."

"Watch breaks all the time," Satoru huffed, shaking it a bit to emphasize the point. "He loses often." Satoru suspected that Damien's affection for the watch had a lot to do with nostalgia and the disgust it brought to Kara Beth, rather than any belief it was lucky. Keeping the accessory together was more trouble than it was worth, and since Damien won Skate Canada last weekend with no watch in sight, Satoru hoped that would be enough to let the trinket go.

"That, I don't doubt. It's the part where you ended up with it that's interesting. Sabotaging the lucky magic? Or do you routinely let him paw around your personals?" Derek raised an eyebrow with a smirk that was mostly joking. "Actually, with you two, I'm not surprised."

Satoru rolled his eyes. He was close with Damien, close enough that the space they shared was sometimes the subject of teasing.

They'd grown up together, trained together, and resembled nagging husbands complaining about who left socks in the locker room.

But no matter how close they were, Damien's watch had no business being near his competition bags, and Satoru pondered the implications of that as he returned to the hotel.

ONCE IN HIS HOTEL ROOM, Satoru rang up Damien. He tried not to tap his foot while waiting for the Frenchman to pick up. Eventually, he heard the click on the other end. "Hello? How is the competition going, my friend?"

Satoru didn't waste time with pleasantries. "I find your lucky watch."

"You did!" There was an explosion of grateful sounding French, or possibly overly florid English, it was hard to tell with Damien. Satoru tried to keep a lid on his impatience. "Where was it?"

"In my skate bag."

"How did it get there?"

"I'm asking you. Maybe snag on inside, but you shouldn't be in at all." Satoru wanted there to be an innocent explanation, because it seemed out of character for Damien to rifle through his things without asking, but his friend stalled in providing an excuse.

"I'm trying to think..." What was there to think about? Was Damien in the habit of opening his competitor's skate bags by accident? "Oh! Probably when I borrowed your iPod to take to Skate Canada!"

Satoru froze. "You!" He'd been looking for that all week! "Thief! Why you take iPod?"

"You said that I could! Remember, after my phone broke?"

"I tell you get new phone!" Satoru's mind instantly combed through the previous two weeks, trying to find any moments where Damien would have had the opportunity for this act of criminality. With the amount of time they spent together, it was certainly possible.

"But I was busy preparing for the competition, so you said I could take your music for the weekend. 'Help yourself', you said."

"I didn't! Why would I..." A sudden memory hit him, and he groaned. "I said you can borrow spare player!"

"Right. And I did not even scratch it, so what is the problem?"

"iPod is not spare player! iPod is iPod!" Satoru could have thrown his phone in frustration. "Phone is for competition, iPod for if battery dies! Spare player is the green Zune, or blue RCA! Those ones for people to borrow!"

"That is confusing. Ever think you don't need four different MP3 players?"

"Maybe you don't need watch?" Satoru threatened. "I can throw away." He blew his bangs out of his eyes while Damien let out a string of apologies. Some people soothed competition nerves with lucky watches. Satoru coped by being over-packed. Besides, if Damien was so attached to a stupid watch that didn't work, it shouldn't be so weird for Satoru to hang onto old electronics that still provided some use. "Player is not problem. Why you touch my competition bag?"

"You fear I unscrewed your blades or something?"

Satoru's response was a snort. "Is only way you win gold over me."

"Ah, the little flea draws blood with such tiny teeth! You win, my friend. The misunderstanding was mine, and I was wrong to assume. I apologize."

Satoru huffed. "Please remember, or I stop letting you to play my video games."

"The sanctity of your skate bag will never be breached again. How's everything going, otherwise?"

"Ice is hard," Satoru complained. "And Derek's skating good this year. I try to destroy him but I think he still make finals." There was a chance that their competitor would do poorly in the free skate, or possibly bomb his second Grand Prix assignment at the Cup of China and thus fail to get enough points to qualify for the finals in Osaka, but Satoru didn't see it happening. Which wasn't really a bad thing, since Satoru enjoyed seeing Derek at competition. Rivalry was a connection that didn't break easily. The lack of antagonistic banter would be refreshing, but he'd feel a tiny pang for Derek's absence at other competitions. "Please fight hard to get silver from him."

"Of course. To beat the English is a sacred duty passed down by my ancestors. I will prevail," Damien chuckled. "But how do you know I won't steal gold from you instead? I scored a personal best last weekend, and my quad loop is more solid than ever."

"Please, loop's so tilted you can see own reflection in the ice!" Satoru scoffed, but smiled to himself. He'd seen the results from Skate Canada, and had to admit Damien's improvement. When they met at the Grand Prix Final, Satoru might face his first real competition in years.

"It got a +2 Grade of Execution."

"Fans call it 'Leaning Tower of Pisa'."

"Only because you called it that first."

"Maybe," Satoru grinned, then grew serious. "You do great, but still tired by end. You don't eat, do you?"

"I ate just fine, mother."

"I'm serious, you need be careful!" Finding nutritious meals that Damien would deign to eat was almost a full time job. Satoru knew his friend couldn't help his lack of appetite, but it still worried him, to where he shoved food at the other man every chance he got. "I hear you pass out after. What happened?"

Damien sighed. "It's not important."

"Not important?" Satoru was incredulous. "Dami, I was scared! To pass out is always important! What if it happens on ice again?"

"We can't all be as perfect as you."

Satoru frowned, not seeing how he related to this issue. "Isn't about skating, is about eating!" he insisted. "Because skating is fine! You should beat me from day I was born! If you didn't always eat starving, you would!"

"*Pardonnez-moi*, I did not realize I had a new coach." Damien's voice had such a sharp edge that he could have skated on it. All the words Satoru had planned to say left. "You're such a little nag. You can't leave it alone for five minutes?"

The room felt suddenly tiny. Tiny and unfamiliar, and the

connection of radio waves and cell phone towers seemed more fragile than ever. Satoru was afraid to breathe, in case that link shattered and cut him off from his best friend forever.

He heard a massive exhale from the other side. "My, but I sometimes wish I could be rid of you..." What could Satoru say to that? He stared holes in the opposite wall in order to stop seeing his brother storming out of the apartment, his first coach's sneering disinterest, every mistake he'd ever made in competition...

"I'm sorry," he said after a few tense seconds. "You're right, I'm sorry. Isn't my job." But it was so frustrating to just sit back and watch. He knew Damien was trying, and he knew Kara Beth was helping, and he especially knew he wasn't entitled to know his friend's deep, personal secrets. But it broke his heart every time Damien's poor relationship with food kept him from his full potential. Last season, Kara Beth had actually ordered him to withdraw from the World Championships.

Maybe they weren't as close of friends as everyone seemed to believe. "I say too much. Sorry." He didn't even know why Damien had this eating disorder. It was nothing to do with weight or body image, but Satoru had never been privy to whatever the actual issue was. "But have to say, when I see things not right. Because friend is more important than not making mad." If Satoru said nothing and it resulted in Damien becoming seriously ill again, he'd never forgive himself.

Better to lose his friend like this than to the alternative. He waited out Damien's temper, hoping against hope, and was finally rewarded with a response. "...*non, Satoru, désolé,*" Damien muttered into the phone. "The fault is mine. You're a good friend to worry."

"I'm sorry," Satoru repeated, not knowing what else to say. It had nothing to do with their languages. If he were a better friend, he'd find the words and the gestures to make these situations right, but that wasn't his gift. Outside of skating, it seemed he couldn't do anything right. "Only want good things for you."

"I know."

"My fault I say like lecture. Don't mean to make mad."

"I wish you would not apologize so much to me, little duck. You will regret it when I eat all your food and steal your titles." Damien gave a soft laugh, but it sounded forced.

Satoru fidgeted. He heard a small beep, showing that he'd missed a call. When he looked at the screen, he saw it was his brother, and ignored it. "Do you want talk about what happened?"

"You would not understand," Damien muttered, and Satoru mustered a chuckle.

"I don't understand anything you say. That's why I'm so good at listen."

This earned a laugh from his friend, and he relented a little. "You remember my stalker? Henri? He came to the arena during the official practices."

Satoru frowned. He hadn't remembered the man's name, but the man had made a nuisance of himself in the past, hanging around their rink until Kara Beth threatened to call security. But though troublesome, he'd always been good-natured and harmless. "We don't see for whole year. I thought he give up."

"It seems his visa just expired. But now, it's renewed and he can follow me wherever he likes."

"He make trouble?"

"No!" Damien scoffed. "No, he just wanted to express his happiness that I had recovered after last season. To tell me I was an inspiration. That I was a strong and beautiful man, and his one true love." Damien's tone didn't convey whether that flattered or offended him.

But the silence stretched on, telling Satoru there were no more clues to be revealed. "This makes you not eat?"

"I said you would not understand."

He was right. "I'm sorry he make you have bad day."

"No, it is not the stalker's fault," Damien groaned. "He is confusing, but he does not tie my hands or hide my fork. This is my problem to overcome."

That sounded like an improvement to Satoru. In the past, Damien would have denied that there was ever an issue. "Please say if I can help."

"Ah, you already do more than enough, *cygneau*." That was a strange thing to say, as Satoru couldn't see where he'd done anything at all. Not that strange sayings were anything new. Satoru had once picked up a book entitled "How to Understand The French People" hoping to get insight into Damien's behavior, and finally had to throw it out in disgust. His friend defied all convention and explanation. That was the only truth he could cling to.

But Damien had something approaching warmth back in his voice. "Do not concern yourself with my anger. It means nothing, and never lasts. I apologize for my words to you."

"It's fine. You have stress."

"As do you. You should be more cautious about encouraging your rival. I am in a good position to beat you this year!"

If Damien was attempting to get back to his usual mood, Satoru could meet him halfway. He shook off any remaining unease, and said, "If you win Grand Prix over Axel and Quad-Quad, I give you Olympic gold."

"You must land such daring feats first, don't forget. Perhaps you won't, and I will break your world record?"

"Then I'll break it back." Things were just settling back into their usual pattern, when Satoru heard another beep from his phone. Even with a guess at who it was, he pulled it away from his ear long enough to see the caller ID, but wished he'd find a different name displayed. He didn't.

To say he didn't get along with his older brother was an understatement. They were family and Satoru loved Wataru, but their personalities were far too different to have much in common. Training kept Satoru living away from his family, which only compounded the issue. Absence made the heart grow awkward. The bickering children they'd once been weren't sure how to relate to each other as adults, and Satoru knew he could be hot-headed and say the wrong things at the wrong times.

But last time they'd spoken, Wataru told his brother to go jump in front of a train, so Satoru thought he was downright saintly by comparison. The thought of Wataru distracted him enough that he spaced out on Damien for a few minutes. "You don't agree? Is the thought so shocking?"

"What? I'm sorry, please say again?"

"Ah, it's not important. Is everything all right, little duck? Did I upset you with my earlier foolishness?" Again with the pet names. Kara Beth used them, Damien used them, but only for him.

"Why you call me ducks and things?" Satoru asked, deflecting from the question. "You don't with Eric." Damien's behavior with Eric was noticeably more formal, to where Eric found it cold and border-line rude. Satoru liked to think he'd ascended into a closer social circle that warranted first names and replacing handshakes with an occasional 'bise', but taken with everyone else's behavior, he wondered. "Do you all see me like child?"

"You are two years younger than I and I have no brothers to tease, so that might be inevitable. Have I bothered you? If so, I will stop."

"Well, no... don't." Satoru grimaced. He didn't want to say he liked it, that sounded even more childish. His parents were very loving, but hugging and saying 'I love you' wasn't a huge part of their culture, whereas Americans hugged everybody and the French seemed to throw out a thesaurus of endearments once they deemed you worthy. Satoru didn't consider himself deprived, but he liked the constant affirmation.

Still... "Just better not because you think I'm stupid, or something."

There was a hiccup in the connection as Damien burst out laughing. "What fool would think so of you? Certainly not I!" Satoru felt his cheeks burning a little, even as he felt relief. Would that his emotions could ever make up their minds for five minutes. "But I can tell there is more beneath the surface. What troubles you?"

Curse Damien for being so perceptive. He'd never been able to hide anything from his friend. "My brother keeps calling. Just now, and yesterday. I don't know why." Satoru flopped back on the bed, and turned his pleading eyes to the ceiling fan. "Should I answer?"

"He never says anything good to you."

"But if I don't, I worry all night," Satoru pointed out. Neither option left him with peace of mind. "Maybe is important?"

"A starving wolf is important, but you don't invite him into the house." Satoru furrowed his brows as he tried to make sense of that. "What could he say that cannot wait?"

What could Wataru say at all? The last conversation had left little on the table. Satoru groaned to himself. "He's my brother. I can't just ignore..."

Damien's disapproval was implied, but he merely said, "Do as you will. But whatever happens, do not let it trouble you. There is too much at stake tonight to let him fill your head with foolish thoughts."

"I know."

"And I apologize for what I said earlier. I don't ever wish to be rid of you. Your brother does not know the gift he has wasted." That startled Satoru, and he sat up straight.

"I don't know what you mean," he tried to begin, but Damien cut him off.

"That is clear. But someday you will, and might not need to ask why I drench you in so many affectionate names, hmm?" Satoru stared at his phone, not sure why he couldn't pull meaning out of that string of words.

"You don't make sense," he said at last. "You're strange man, use more words than you need, and you don't make sense."

"A pity. I shall just have to keep repeating myself until it sinks in. For now, I must go. I wish you a good skate tonight, friend."

Satoru returned the farewell. "I see you soon. Break iPod and I flush watch down toilet."

"I don't know why everyone thinks you're so nice..."

HE'D BEEN impatient for Damien to pick up the phone, but now Satoru wished the dial tone could stretch out to the end of eternity. He'd decided to be brave and call Wataru back, but when he heard the click of the phone picking up, his heart jumped into his throat.

"Hello?"

"Uh, h-hello," Satoru scrambled for words, never knowing how to start conversations with his brother. Usually he didn't have to. Wataru always had plenty to say. "Well, you've been calling... everything okay at home?"

"Yes, why wouldn't it be?" Wataru's answer was abrupt, and it grated on Satoru.

"I don't know, you never call me with good news. I thought someone might be dead."

"Don't even joke about that. And I call you with good news plenty of times."

"I can't think of a single one."

"That's because you've always got to be the victim. It gives you amnesia." He heard some rustling that might have been bedclothes. "It's way too early for this..." Satoru had a sudden insight into his older brother's mood.

"Sorry, I didn't even think about the time difference. What time is it in Tokyo? Ugh, I'm sorry..."

"Quit apologizing. Like you said, I just called you. I thought it must be a bad time, so I went back to bed. Not a big deal." Satoru apologized again, unable to help it. "I said it's fine. Quit apologizing for everything, it's annoying."

Satoru's mouth formed another apology for being annoying before he caught himself. "So... uh, what did you need?"

"Well..." Wataru hedged for a bit, long enough that Satoru thought he might have fallen back asleep. He almost hung up, before the other voice started up again. "I saw your short program yesterday. It was pretty good."

A world record score was more than 'pretty good', but it was still a compliment. "Thank you."

"That 4F was shaky, though. I thought you were going to work on that?"

Satoru grit his teeth. "I did." Hours and hours spent on that stupid Flip. "It's improved a lot since last year."

"Well, they don't give out medals for 'most improved', do they? But whatever, it's your time." Except it wasn't, that went unspoken.

Their parents made a lot of financial sacrifices for Satoru to skate, Wataru had given up going to his dream school. Skating time was precious, and it belonged to others as well.

Satoru felt the familiar sensation of pressure on his chest that ruled most of his childhood. "If you don't have anything important to say, I'm hanging up."

"No, don't," Wataru entreated with another groan. "I'm sorry. That's not what I meant to say."

"Oh? I can't wait to hear what you really meant."

"You know, it's hard enough to talk to you without all the sarcasm," Wataru growled, and Satoru sensed he was nearing the end of his patience. "Sometimes I think you misunderstand me on purpose."

Satoru hesitated, wondering if that was true. "Sorry. I'm listening."

"I just wanted to wish you luck in your free program tomorrow. Or, I suppose that would be tonight, for you."

"Yeah. Thanks." There were two events that decided the winner of a figure skating competition, the short program and the long, also called the free skate. Adding together both scores determined the winner. With breaking the record, Satoru had earned himself a nice cushion of points to land on if things didn't go his way in the free skate, not that he expected to need it.

Satoru felt a little guilty for being a brat if his brother had such good intent all along. Maybe he was a bit too sensitive sometimes, making drama where there didn't need to be. He waited through an awkward pause, then realized it was his turn to keep the conversation going. "Anything new with you?"

"Not much. I've started doing a lot more translation for the sports department at work. They have me traveling to events now, too."

"Really?" Wataru had always been good at English, and landed a job with a media outlet translating and subtitling interviews. It was impressive work, and Satoru was a little envious of his brother's skill. Wataru's English had been good straight out of high school and he'd become fairly proficient in Korean since then, while Satoru had been living in America for over half a dozen years and still needed help figuring out his phone bill. "That's great. Ever cover figure skating?"

"Yeah, but I wouldn't ever be the one interviewing you."

"What, they worried you'll lose your journalistic impartiality?"

"I think you're the one who should be worried about that." It was probably a joke. It was the sort of banter that brothers would have, the kind of good-natured ribbing that Satoru shared with Damien. But one could never be sure with Wataru's jokes. They always made Satoru feel unsettled, like maybe he'd misunderstood something. He couldn't claim he really understood Wataru on any level, unless he was yelling. That was easy enough to interpret.

"Well..." Satoru didn't know what else to say. Neither of them had said anything really important yet, they were just filling space.

His sister was easy to talk to. Satoru sometimes felt anxious about all the time he spent away from his family, and he'd moved to Ohio when his baby sister was still nine. These were her formative years, she was developing her personality by the day, and Satoru sometimes worried he'd come home and find they didn't know each other anymore. But Izumi was still one of his best friends, he loved to talk with her. Some of his fondest memories involved hanging out with his little sister .

He didn't know why he couldn't have that with Wataru. Their personalities were different, sure, but it wasn't like Satoru hadn't tried to be accommodating. When he'd first moved to Ohio, it had excited him to know his big brother was coming with him. The original plan was for Wataru to live and work in America with Satoru, getting some practical experience with his language skills and supervising his little brother during the long months of training.

It hadn't ended well. The culture shock proved to be a bit much for Wataru, and in hindsight, Satoru could forgive that. It hadn't been easy for him, either, but Satoru wasn't responsible for anyone but himself. It was a lot of pressure to put on Wataru at nineteen, and Satoru could also understand the frustration of giving up his expensive dream university for his brother's skating. Those sacrifices might have been willing in the beginning, but hardship turned the generosity into resentment. Minor irritations turned into burning flames of rage, and Satoru's dream of bonding with his big brother on this foreign adventure became a nightmare. He could understand it now that he was older.

But it was hard to forgive Wataru for leaving. Less than a year into the arrangement, Wataru decided he'd had enough, bought a plane ticket, and flew back to Japan without telling anyone. Satoru was lucky he'd woken up early enough to see the suitcases, but no amount of begging, pleading or sobbing would change his brother's mind. Wataru disappeared for two weeks, and Satoru's life was bleak, fearful agony. He was terrified to call his parents or tell his coach, but pretending everything was all right when he was only fourteen and couldn't read the bus schedule wore him down to bare threads.

Of course, his parents figured out what was going on and Wataru eventually came to his senses and went home. Kara Beth went far beyond her job description in helping the Miyazawa family figure out its internal issues and how to make the training situation work. In the end, she opened up her home and Satoru lived with his coach for the next several years. Everything worked out, more or less, and Wataru calmed down a lot once he was back in Japan and they lifted some responsibility off his shoulders. Their parents flayed him for leaving his little brother like that, but had to admit that stress could crack a person and make them behave irrationally.

Satoru could appreciate that on an intellectual level, but his heart couldn't forget. Doing so felt like conceding that Wataru had been right to leave, right when he'd said everything was Satoru's fault, right about all the charges he'd levied back then and still did, even though the supposed stress was gone. To forgive it felt like accepting that anyone could find him annoying and leave. Anyone who loved him might someday stop.

He wasn't ready to jump into that black abyss. "Well, if there's nothing else, I've got to go..."

"Wait, Satoru..." But even after saying that, Wataru paused. Satoru realized he was tapping his foot and forced it to still. "I'm sorry for what I said. I didn't mean it."

"What?"

"The last time you were home. I didn't mean all those silly things I said."

Silly things? Satoru couldn't believe it. But it was the first time Wataru had apologized to him without their dad around to twist his arm, unless Miyazawa Shinji had been lurking in the back of this phone call the entire time. "Sure sounded like you meant it."

"Well, I didn't!" came the hot reply, then another groan. "You're always like this! I said I was sorry! It's hard when your little brother's famous. That shadow of yours is difficult to live with."

Satoru wanted to ask what Wataru's excuse was before his brother got famous, but the words stuck in his throat. He *was* difficult. Didn't Damien just say so? Without meaning to, he'd provoked his friend to anger, and he did it purposefully with Derek. It wasn't like he was some saint inspiring goodwill everywhere he went. Even his close friends sometimes wished to get rid of him, so why was he so surprised that his brother felt the same way?

He forgave Damien for what he said. It shouldn't have been that hard to forgive Wataru. After all, Wataru and the rest of the family carried more and done without, all for him. If that burden sometimes got heavy enough to provoke an outburst, couldn't Satoru let it go? His brother was willing to apologize, he was trying.

So Satoru swallowed back the feelings of being fourteen and abandoned. "It's fine. I said some things, too."

"I know I haven't been the best brother over the years. We've both had our problems. But I'm going to fix that. Everything's going to be different, you'll see."

"Uh..." Satoru didn't know what to say. "That's... great. I'm sorry, too. I know I can be stubborn."

"It's in the past. Things are going to get better for us." There was a long silence while Satoru still struggled to come up with a reply. It didn't help that Wataru, in his usual way, didn't have an overabundance of warmth or sentiment in his voice. But it seemed sincere. "I should let you go. I just wanted to tell you that. Good luck with the rest of the competition."

"I... yeah, thank you," Satoru finally said. "It means a lot to hear you say that." Surreal, but as it sank in, touching. He wished he could say something worthy of matching it. "I've always looked up to you, you know. Even when I got angry, I never hated you."

"I know. Don't worry, it's going to get better from here on out," Wataru promised, then a yawn broke his words.

"You should probably get back to bed."

"Well, it's basically morning," Wataru groused, but agreed. "All right. Take care, Satoru. Stretch well, stay hydrated, all those sport things."

"I will, thanks. See you in a few weeks." They ended the call, and Satoru stared down at his phone for a few minutes. He needed the extra time to process what he'd just heard. Not only had he finished a civil conversation with his brother, but Wataru had apologized? And promised to be better?

Meanwhile, it was Satoru hanging on to grudges and refusing to forgive. He felt like an idiot. All along, he'd been hanging on to the past, and his brother just wanted to make the future a better one. Wasn't that worth a little forgiveness?

Well, if Wataru could make the effort, so could he. Satoru put away his phone with a lightness he hadn't felt in a long time. Things were going to be different.

3

———————

WINNING WASN'T EVERYTHING, so the saying went, but that didn't make it any less fantastic. Inessa Levi was no stranger to winning and didn't see any reason to stop now. It felt good to win, to see that number one next to her name, to hold flowers and medals and hear *'Hatikva'* played while they raised the Israeli flag into the air. But Inessa knew that there was a petty side to winning. She didn't like the superiority of saying she was better than the woman next to her, or that you could rank people's worth in numerical order. Every one of her competitors was a world-class athlete and all of them worked harder than the casual fan could fathom, but there could only be one first place.

And if Inessa was going to steal that one place, she wanted to make it mean something. The only one she could, or should, try to beat was herself, and she went into every practice with that in mind. She didn't fear what her competitors were doing, but celebrated their success and only focused on improving her own technique. If she faltered with something, she drilled it until she could never make the mistake again. If she was flawless, then she looked for ways to make her routines harder. It was a strategy that pushed her more than any rivalry could and kept her heart light when she bore the weight of expectation.

If she cared only about beating others, she wouldn't ever have tried to land quadruple jumps in competition. "You didn't even need it!" was the phrase Inessa heard most often, and currently being uttered by Amina Massot of Belgium. "Crazy girl! You didn't even need it to win today! How are we supposed to keep up with you?"

For a minute, Inessa thought Amina might actually be angry, and her face suggested dark thoughts of dragging Inessa from the hallway and into some private corner of the building to end the queen's reign. But then other emotions broke through, pride, incredulity and elation. "But, oh! It was powerful to see! I'll never forget that!" Neither would Inessa. She wasn't the first to land a quadruple jump in the women's division, not by a long shot, but it was still a rare feat. To push herself and the sport forward like that was worth more than simply scoring more points than Amina and the others.

She thanked Amina, along with the flood of others who came after her. It was especially gratifying to be applauded by her fellow skaters so quickly after the competition had ended. Inessa wasn't sure if she could have been in such a gracious and congratulatory place while still digesting the results, had they been reversed. Even if they agreed it wasn't everything, in their hearts, everyone wanted to be the winner.

"*Mazal tov.*"

Inessa recognized the voice and spun around with glee to face Satoru Miyazawa. "*B'Karov etzlecha!*"

This was about where Satoru ran out of Hebrew, and so switched to English. "You're amazing. Made history today!"

"Not really, girls were trying quads in competition before I knew what skating was!" Inessa tried to be modest, even if her heart was still doing fireworks. "It's hardly making history, I am just learning from it."

Satoru grinned. "Is still special." He withdrew a plush rabbit that he'd been trying to halfway conceal behind him and presented it to

Inessa. "For you. I wanted to throw on ice, but then you don't know it's me."

"It is adorable! Thank you!" Inessa squeezed the large rabbit and admired it from head to toe. She was extremely fond of rabbits, and her fans often threw plush bunnies on the ice after her performances, so she was developing quite a collection. More than she needed, and so, she gave many of the gifts to local hospitals or children's organizations, which brought Inessa an equal delight in them. This one from Satoru was exquisitely made, with the softest body, white fluffy tail and satin inside its ears. The final touch was a little skating costume and a pair of cloth ice skates. "You made this, yes?"

Satoru looked a little embarrassed, but nodded. "I hope you like."

"I love it!" Every stitch was perfect, each inch crafted with loving care, Inessa could see that. "You're very talented. You make your own skating costumes too, right? I heard you even did Damien's this year."

Satoru had been only blushing, but now looked mortified. "Where you hear that? Ugh, don't tell anyone! I help Damien but he *wants* sparkle like that! Not my fault he looks like disco ball!" As he ranted, Inessa tried to hide her giggles. Damien Saint-Michel's love of flashy costumes was no secret, and it looked like Satoru's more understated design sense couldn't tame it. "I try to give him dignity, he don't know what that means!" He ran out of steam when he saw Inessa laughing. "Please, don't tell world. I can't deal."

"Not a word," she promised, then hugged the rabbit close. "This is beautiful. Thank you." Satoru beamed, and looked about to say something, but must have changed his mind. He did lean forward for a friendly, one-armed embrace, and Inessa happily accepted that instead.

They'd met when Inessa was just thirteen, at a Junior Worlds Exhibition practice where both of them had won the event. They had little occasion to speak to each other before then, and wouldn't have succeeded if they'd tried, as Satoru's English was barely comprehensible and Inessa's was not much better. Both of them struggled to keep up with the choreographer's instructions, but thankfully, dance moves tended to be universal, and the whole diverse crowd managed.

Their first real meeting came at a point when the champions in each of the four disciplines would skate to the center of the ice and take their moment under the spotlights. The rest of the skaters formed a procession of two lines, and the pairs champions first skated between them, then the ice dance team. Satoru and Inessa were both single competitors, but the choreographer thought it would look nice if they came through the procession together. So they rehearsed it several times, coming through the line and then turning a slow circle on the ice while holding each other's hands like a school dance, before separating to take their individual moment in front of the crowd. Inessa's only thought in practice was making sure she screwed nothing up.

During the real thing, her thoughts were taken by the dim, blue lighting punctuated by follow spotlights, the music coming over the loudspeakers and the dozens of skating costumes that glittered in the dark like the night sky. It was a magical evening, and as she and Satoru passed through the two rows of skaters, the weight of winning the Junior World Championship hit her square in the chest, along with the fact that she was being escorted to the winner's circle by an attractive older boy who sparkled like some ethereal fairy.

Right before they separated, Satoru winked and blew her a kiss, and Inessa had been in love ever since.

They rarely saw each other outside of figure skating competitions, but being at the top of their respective fields, it was enough time together to develop a friendship over the years. They exchanged phone numbers and emails, and the friendship grew deeper as they both gained more proficiency in their common language of English.

But they weren't dating. A fact that was further emphasized when Alisha Brian of Canada came over to congratulate Inessa. "Sorry to break up the happy couple, I just wanted to say 'good game' before the reporters try to smother me again." Inessa laughed and exchanged praise and congratulations with the day's silver medalist, while Satoru looked worried.

"We're not couple," he was quick to insist, and Inessa tried to ignore the pang of disappointment. "Just friends."

"Yeah? I thought I was your friend. Where's my handmade plush doll?"

"Um..." Satoru blushed deep red and couldn't speak for a good minute.

"I forgot, you're married to your skating. You'll never look at a girl the way you look at a triple axel." Alisha teased him a few seconds longer, then moved on to a new topic, to Inessa's relief. As much as she sometimes wanted to grill Satoru and ask just what they were to each other, she was also afraid to have that serious talk about what dating would mean for two elite level athletes training in different countries. Satoru divided his time between his home in Tokyo and his coach in Ohio, while Inessa still had a year of high school besides training in Tel Aviv. Long-distance relationships could last, but the distance, the commitment to their training and the media that followed them were nothing to take lightly.

And of course, she was scared that if she asked, she might find out she was still blinded by those dazzling spotlights, and that magical moment belonged only to the past. For now, maybe it was better to just enjoy their friendship for what it was.

So she banished any lingering disappointment and focused on Alisha's next words. "Well, it's been a good night for the women's division. Our teenaged queen has raised the bar yet again, while my crotchety old grandma bones managed to fend off the rest of the horde, and we'll probably get to duel again at the finals, if neither of us chokes our second assignment. Battle of the Generations." Inessa tried to deny it, but Alisha was twenty-seven years old, an anomaly in their sport. Age was not kind to the female singles skater.

But Alisha seemed to get better with every year. Whether by her training regime, nutrition or just pure drive, she kept increasing her abilities and skills, her scores rising each season. There were a lot of young skaters posing a challenge as they came up, like Inessa herself, but no one could deny what Alisha had accomplished over the years. And it was pushing a lot of other skaters to try to match it. "You are still young, compared to Sokonthy."

"Oh, man, I still can't believe that's happening!" Alisha shook her head, sending her thin, dark braids swinging in every direction. "What am I gonna blame my falls on, when she's hitting a triple lutz at thirty-one?" Sokonthy Masters was a former American pairs skater, and a giant in that sport. She and her partner had won world title after world title, Olympics after Olympics, and were both missed when they finally retired. They spent a year skating professionally, but officially ended their partnership when Sokonthy became pregnant with her first child.

But now that child was celebrating a birthday, and Sokonthy wanted to get back into competitive skating again. This wasn't such a surprise, but her decision to come back as a singles skater broke the internet for a day. Inessa had heard of singles skaters finding a second career in the pairs division or ice dance, as the technical requirements were less focused on jumping elements and thus a bit more rewarding of maturity, but never had she heard of a skater going in the other direction, and certainly not at that age. Then again, for all people talked up the fewer jumping passes in pairs, most of the jumps they did do involved throwing a girl ten feet into the air, and those athletes came to competitions with bandages and braces like soldiers fresh off the battlefield. It took a special courage to join the competitive women's scene when Inessa was landing quads, but Earth had no more fearless creature than the female pairs skater.

Sokonthy's first outings had been successes, and her Grand Prix assignment at Skate Canada had netted her a silver medal. The scores weren't as high as Inessa's personal best, but still worthy of notice. "The way she's going, we'll probably see her at the finals, too. You're gonna have to beat up old ladies for your podium, Inessa." While Inessa laughed and protested, Alisha turned her attention to Satoru. "But for this weekend, we've only got the men to go. And I hear your free skate blows even Miss Quad Sal here out of the water."

"Not true, I make mistakes," Satoru protested, even as a confused little wrinkle appeared in his left eyebrow. Inessa had learned it was a sign he wasn't confident he'd understood what was just said. "Jump has all been trouble today, maybe Inessa should do for me."

"If Inessa does your Quad-Quad combo, I'm retiring on the spot," Alisha said with a roll of her eyes. "But good luck, Sato. I look forward to your demon jumps and world record shattering and whatever else you have planned out there. Peace." And she left the two of them with one last wave.

"I should probably go, too," Inessa sighed. After winning first place with such an impressive jump, everyone wanted a moment of her time. She wouldn't get to relaxing or celebrating until much later. "Thank you for the gift. I will be cheering for you tonight as well."

"Better not cheer too loudly," a British accent broke into the conversation. "Saint-Michel will get jealous if he hears he's got competition for Miyazawa's affection." Both Satoru and Inessa turned to see Derek Donner a few feet away, passing by the small press area with his coach and equipment in tow. The coach was doing his best to keep his charge moving along, and looked a bit exasperated when Derek started slowing his gait in order to more conveniently taunt his rival.

Satoru didn't seem to mind at all. "You're so worried about Dami's feelings, maybe I set you up? But I think he has too good taste for you."

"Is that supposed to insult me?"

"Not my fault you so bad at trash talk that garbageman won't stop by house."

"What does that even...? You-" Derek would have said more, but his coach was trying to shove him along, and Derek gave up. "You need help, Miyazawa!" he called as he continued on down the hallway.

"Yes, help, gold medal collection is getting heavy to lift."

"And may you be strangled by every single one of them."

Once he was gone, Satoru tried to put on an innocent face. "What?"

"You should be more careful with him," Inessa said, as diplomatically as she could manage. "It wouldn't be good to make him angry."

"Nothing to worry about, just how Derek is," Satoru insisted.

"Says rude things to everybody, but doesn't really hate." That may have been true once, but lately Derek seemed to have more bite behind his words, and concentrated all of that negative feeling on Satoru. Whether it was because Satoru had no problems countering the words and thus provided a safe outlet for jitters and tension, or whether Derek genuinely wanted to mount Satoru's head on a pike remained to be seen. Inessa's rivals were either polite or ignored her, so she had nothing to compare it to. Maybe it was a boy thing?

"If you say so..." She shrugged her shoulders. "I guess everyone is different. But be a little careful, please? I don't want anything to stop you from having a good skate."

"Nothing's going to stop me from good skate," he laughed. "But I've got to go now. Congratulations for medal." He blew a kiss as he left, and Inessa fell in love all over again.

THE TIME directly before a skate could be just as nerve-wracking as the program itself. Athletes stretched and warmed up with minimal privacy, and couldn't help but see their biggest rivals and what kind of day they were having. Intentionally or just by accident, the mind games started as soon as you set foot in the arena. For that reason, most of Satoru's competitors retreated into the Competitive Cone of Silence and tried to block out the world.

That was a strategy that didn't work for Satoru. Trying to ignore everyone emphasized the pressure. Kara Beth was indispensable in that regard, happy to tease or chat with him as he jogged, stretched and went through his various warm-up exercises. They sang along to the songs over the intercom, made jokes, and waved at anybody willing to interact. By the time they got the six-minute warmup on the ice, Satoru was usually in a positive headspace to compete.

But sometimes he had to share his coach with Eric or Damien, and that was annoying. He'd had many years to get used to it, and there were other people on his support team willing to help keep him out of his anxious head, but there was a childish petulance that still wished Kara Beth could focus all her attention on him. Especially since the people who constantly orbited him like the rings of Saturn, while exceptional in their own ways, were not friends, and couldn't duplicate what Kara Beth's presence did for him.

Sometimes Damien would talk or acknowledge Satoru during competition, and he had a prayer ritual that he didn't mind sharing, but Eric was aggressively determined not to engage with anybody. Yukiya was friendly and usually made some good-natured remark about destroying Satoru when they passed in the hotel, but kept to himself in the arena, and Alberto and the rest were much the same. Derek was more than happy to interact negatively with Satoru, and while it didn't really offend him, Satoru liked some positive conversation to balance it out.

So he was glad to see Alisha Brian still wandering the back-stage area, and even more grateful when she caught his eye and came over to where he was on the floor stretching. Satoru took off his headphones to show he was up for a conversation, and she eagerly dropped her gym bag next to his and plunked herself down on the floor. "How's it going, champ?"

"I'm good. What you do still back here? Not go back to hotel?"

"Nah, decided to stay and watch you boys skate. And it was Marco's birthday yesterday, so I wanted to drop off a gift." Marco Velásquez was one of the up-and-coming skaters from America, very talented, very friendly, and very eager to steal Satoru's first place medal if given the opportunity. Satoru would have to be careful not to leave any openings.

"Oh? I didn't know. That's nice," he said. He turned to stretch out his other leg, and Alisha mimicked the posture. "You finish skating, don't need to stretch."

"You sure? My old muscles ache just getting up from a chair. I should stretch these poor legs out whenever I can."

"Lie, you always look young to me."

"Flatterer. Now I see why you have so many fangirls." But despite her skeptic tone, Satoru could see she was pleased. Alisha made jokes to disguise it, but she was sensitive about her age and what it meant for her career. Still the reigning Canadian champion and still on an upward trajectory, but the younger girls were overtaking her on the international scene, and at twenty-seven, her body was slowing down.

Satoru couldn't remember a season without Alisha's bright presence. When he'd first made his senior debut, it was her brash and carefree antics that helped him handle the pressure and escape his own demons. She'd known that, too, seen the little boy shaking in his skates and decided it was her mission to make him laugh before the weekend was out. Satoru needed that and still did, from time to time.

"Congratulations again for silver today! Excellent skate!"

"Thanks," Alisha said, but there was a tension to her shoulders. A silver medal was nothing to be ashamed of, especially in any competition where someone landed a quadruple salchow, but at a certain point in one's career, it hurt to get anything less than first place. Alisha had many gold medals to her name, but not in recent years, even though she was exceeding her personal best. It was just a testament to the depth of the women's field that Alisha's monster scores still couldn't overtake the podium.

The thought must have been weighing on her mind, because Alisha said, "You know, a lot of people are saying this should be my last season." She tried to sound casual, but Satoru knew better.

"What? But you're so good!"

"Aw, you're cute. But good doesn't mean anything if you're not good enough." She grimaced. "I get sick of explaining to people why I'm still not first. Like, sheesh, I can't do anything about Inessa's quads. Sometimes I wonder what I'm doing all of this for." She paused for a moment, then fixed Satoru with a serious look. "What about you?"

"Huh? What about...?"

"Why do you skate? What does it mean to you?" The question was a simple one, but Satoru found he couldn't answer.

"I... don't know words to say." That was a lie. Words weren't the problem, but he hid behind the language barrier to avoid admitting that he was drawing a blank. Skating was important to him, but to distill those feelings down into a single sentiment was impossible. "I have to skate. It's... only option. Many reasons, but the answer's always skating." He tried to move the focus off of himself. "You shouldn't stop just for other people."

"Well, they're right, aren't they? I'm good, but there's a new standard for gold now, and it won't be long before I'm on the decline. Still," she sighed, "I'd like to push for the Olympics. I've never won that, and it's only the season after this one. Fourth times the charm, right?"

It still amazed Satoru that she'd been to three Olympic games. That was the longevity most skaters only dreamed of. He'd won his first Olympic outing and was planning to repeat the experience next season, but he couldn't say if he'd be able to manage that a third time at twenty-six, or if he'd even be skating a fourth games at thirty.

Then again, it didn't stop Sokonthy. "I think you should do! You're too good not to be Olympian. That's where you belong." Against Inessa, he doubted Alisha had a shot at first, but Alisha could still make a push for the podium. And regardless of the outcome, she'd done so much for the sport, she deserved to march into that arena with all of Canada cheering her on.

"You sure? It's over a year away. A lot can happen."

"Yeah, but good things happen, too," Satoru insisted. "You're fighter, I think maybe things change for you this season." Alisha looked a bit surprised, and Satoru wondered if he'd said the wrong thing again. Maybe she didn't want to hear platitudes from someone on top of the skating world, let alone someone biased in favor of her rival.

Then again, Satoru knew a thing or two about losing in his day, and failing to live up to expectations. "I mean, you still have more to give to skate. To make this far, you must fight to end, right?"

Alisha's face looked troubled, but eventually set in a determined nod. "You're right. To the end." She broke into a shaky laugh. "And what would I do if I wasn't skating? I've been competing so long, I really haven't thought about it at all."

"No? Even with school?" Satoru knew little about what Alisha was studying, since science involved a bunch of complicated English that was a headache to listen to, but he knew it involved chemistry, agriculture and emailing in a lot of reports and experiments. He wasn't positive, since he frequently mixed up the terminology, but he was pretty sure she'd actually finished her undergraduate studies and was pursuing a Master's degree. Or maybe it was a second bachelor's, but either way, it was impressive. "You're smart enough to do anything, I think."

"I think you're going to make me blush. Enough buttering me up, let's talk about something else." Satoru couldn't understand why she looked so sad. Maybe there was something in her life he wasn't privy to, or maybe the idea of ending her competitive career was that heavy of a weight. That future was a ways off for Satoru, but it would come for him someday, and he also had no clue what he'd do when that day came. Unlike Alisha, he had no talents to fall back on. So he changed the subject. "I'm excited for Exhibition later! We'll have cantilever battle in practice, right?"

"Boy, you gotta win this next skate before you think about challenging me!" But she threw out a wink before Satoru changed position in his stretch again, getting his nose as close to the floor as he could manage. He couldn't see if Alisha was matching him or not, but heard her voice slightly above him.

"Maybe we should have a stretch battle instead? Who has the best Y spin?"

The Y spin involved spinning in an upright position with one's free leg straight up in the air. Satoru winced, but mustered his bravado. "I accept challenge."

"Ha! Looks like I'll win something this weekend." He heard Alisha's clothes rustling as she stood up and lifted her gym bag, and Satoru sat up to face her properly. "Thanks for the talk, Sato. I needed that. Knock 'em all dead out there, 'kay?"

"See you later." Satoru smiled as he watched her go. It was weird to think about, but many of the faces he'd grown up with would retire after the next Olympics, and once they stopped skating together, they'd never see each other again. The world felt so small in figure skating, but once their lives revolved around other things, Satoru knew he'd discover what a big place planet earth really was. No more globe-hopping, and no reason to see the people who'd become his close friends. His only friends.

But that thinking was too heavy for right before a competition. Satoru banished it from his mind and resumed stretching.

4

———

KARA BETH BONOGOFSKI TRAINED CHAMPIONS. She'd once been a World Champion herself, and an Olympic gold medalist, but that was over a decade ago and the public had largely forgotten. She'd had the dazzling spotlight for a few beautiful moments, but more phenomenal skaters replaced her with even more impressive resumes. But that was life, and she didn't mind. Her reputation as a coach was in the public eye now, and with the way her three pupils were doing, it was hardly worth mentioning her past accomplishments.

But her students knew and never forgot. "I'm just saying you should bring back the bowl-cut bangs and sparkly scrunchies. And the poofy sleeves. The more embarrassing the fashion, the more likely you are to be immortalized forever on the podium."

"You're delusional, Eric..."

"It's like a driver's license photo! Or school picture day!" the boy insisted. "It's always when you shrink your favorite shirt or try a questionable hairstyle that, snap! Permanent reminder. And you had a million gorgeous skating outfits but the day you showed up looking like a psychedelic swan is the day you won Worlds!" Eric grinned, and Kara Beth's lip twitched. "Wear that fashion disaster to the kiss and cry and Murphy's Law dictates I'll win the Olympics so no one ever forgets."

"By that logic, it should be you wearing puffed sleeves and scrunchies. I can arrange it."

"No, because I'm gorgeous enough to pull it off. It's gotta be you."

Kara Beth allowed him a moment to preen, then brought the mood back down. "You know my teenaged fashion sense isn't your problem, right?"

Eric sighed and dropped his head. "I know..." He began undoing his skates so he wouldn't have to look her in the eye. "I shouldn't have messed those jumps up."

"Your jumps were okay. Not as clean as we'd both like, but you stuck the landings. I just want to know where those deep knees went during your footwork sequence. You should have got Level 4 on that." His short program wasn't up to par, and today's free skate wasn't any better. Not terrible, but he'd definitely choked under the pressure, and she wouldn't let him pretend he hadn't.

"I know, I know! I just..." Eric trailed off, out of excuses. Kara Beth took a seat beside him on the bench.

"You thought being at the senior level was just another competition, didn't you? I warned you about that."

"I don't understand. I never get nervous," Eric whined. "And I wasn't today, not until I was actually in the center of the ice and suddenly it was... I can't even explain, that's never happened to me before!" He put his head in his hands, leaving his laces undone and sprawled on the floor. "I'm in last place with an entire group left to go. That's humiliating!"

"Not really. There's some veteran skaters here, and it's your first time being invited to the Grand Prix. To hold your own against them is pretty impressive."

"Satoru would have won," Eric muttered.

"What?"

"Satoru would have won no matter what. Or Damien. They both were on podiums in their first senior season. And, like, every year after that. It's all anyone talks about." He was clenching his fists so tightly that his knuckles were turning white. "Why couldn't I do that?"

Kara Beth took a minute to gather her thoughts. Sometimes, being a good coach had less to do with knowledge or technique and more to do with saying the right thing at the right time. And with Eric, one had to balance the encouragement with the tough love. "Because Satoru shows up to the rink on time. Damien practices stroking until his feet bleed. The two of them wanted to win so badly that they moved to a foreign country and learned a new language. You've never wanted anything like that."

"Yes, I have!" Eric insisted. "Winning a gold medal is all I've ever wanted. Why else would I be here?"

Kara Beth tried not to smile, since that would just anger the boy more, but it reminded her so much of herself when she was just starting out. "Everybody in the world wants to be a gold medalist. But most people want other things more. If you're going to chase the podium, you've got to want it more than anything else on earth. More than breathing." Eric was quiet for a minute, and Kara Beth patted his back. "It's okay if your goals aren't the same as Satoru or Damien's."

"How can anybody's be? Even if I improve, so will they! It used to be a 5-Quad program was the outlier, but they've gone and made that normal! Their technical scores are already insane and the two of them are still pushing for more, Satoru's adding Tano variations to his Quads now!"

"You do know they'll have to retire eventually, right?"

"Damien, maybe. Satoru will never retire," Eric groused. "And in the meantime, my best score got beat by someone in the Women's division."

Kara Beth's lips quirked into a smile. "Inessa may be one rotation away from achieving actual flight, but she wasn't born turning quads. She's had that goal for years, and she sunk her whole life into working for it. You need to figure out what your own goals are. And stop comparing yourself to other people," she added. "It wasn't your best work today, but we can improve on that. We'll focus a bit more on the mental side of things when we get back to Ohio, okay?"

"Okay," Eric said, but without his usual conviction. Kara Beth poked him in the shoulder.

"And just so you quit idealizing him, Satoru's first senior trip to Four Continents was a disaster. He managed to get on the World podium later, but he's as human as the next guy. Trust me, if he can come back from that performance, you can come back from this."

"Is it really that bad?"

"Flubbed his opening jump, then tried to make up for it by turning his triple loop into a quad, which we did *not* practice beforehand," Kara Beth said, pressing her lips together at the memory. "He mistimed the takeoff and went careening into the boards, got into his camel spin late and didn't get enough rotations, and then tripped over his own feet in the footwork section."

"Yikes."

"You're telling me," Kara Beth laughed. The debacle had made her wonder if she was really cut out for coaching. The Japanese Skating Federation had asked themselves same thing. "But he got better. You will, too." She gave his back one last pat. "Speaking of Satoru, I've got to go take care of him now. Think over your mistakes today and what you can improve, but don't beat yourself up too much. I'm proud of you."

"Thanks, coach." She left Eric and jogged down the hallway to the rink, changing out of her American team jacket and into her Japanese one. With the final group about to do their warm up, the atmosphere in the rink was boiling. So many great skaters had taken the ice already, but the last six were the most likely contenders for gold. The crowd knew it, and so did the skaters, creating a pressure that seemed to push against the walls of the building.

And if everything with Satoru went as planned, they were going to blow the roof completely off. She found her star athlete over by the boards, and a sudden burst of nostalgia hit her. In their disastrous first season together, her little Satoru had been shivering with locked knees and staring at the ice like it was going to eat him. Now, he bounced from foot to foot as if he couldn't wait to be on it.

"Ready to do this, Sato?"

"Always ready." When he met her eyes, they both almost giggled with anticipation. Every competition was exciting, but Kara Beth hadn't felt so giddy since she herself was competing. Satoru's energy matched hers. "After this, you'll be so famous. Everyone will want that you coach them. You take new students and forget me."

"I can barely handle the three knuckleheads I've got." She gave him a light punch in the arm. "Keep your head on earth. We don't have this in the bag yet."

"Not yet. But I think good." He took a drink from his water bottle while they waited. "Everyone is scared of me. But I'm not scared. That's good."

"Yeah." He was correct in his assessment. When the skaters were allowed on the ice, it was Satoru everyone was glancing at out of the corner of their eyes, or trying to ignore. Tension and nervousness were nothing new, nor was it new to have everyone chasing after Satoru's lead, but today was different and they all knew it. They saw his quads, his axles and combinations, the difficult entries and arms over his head. They knew all the ways he could squeeze out extra points for spins and step sequences, and he'd spent all year taking his artistry, expression and other components to a whole new plane. And he'd been nailing all of it in practice, except for the weird fluke that morning. That 3A was a mischievous outlier, but Satoru had a clean run-through and Kara Beth had confidence the problems wouldn't repeat themselves.

Yesterday's short program beat the world record by 4.03 points. If he had a good skate today, the kinds he'd been having in practice, he'd set a total point record that would make the ISU faint. The kind of score that would redefine what the human body was capable of, and force his opponents to scramble just to keep up. And Satoru was still young enough to go higher before his career was over. By next year's Olympics, they'd be defying reality altogether.

The possibilities were enough to make Kara Beth drool. Plenty of skaters were driven to win, but Satoru was determined to push the sport beyond every limit, until the future generations of athletes were legitimate super humans. It was exciting to be part of it.

Which was ironic, since she'd never wanted to be a coach. Though she enjoyed teaching the occasional workshop, coaching wasn't something she aspired to, nor was it a profession she planned to continue once her current charges retired. Her dream was professional skating, and the year she'd retired, she'd bought an ice rink for the purpose of creating and developing shows. People would flock to her rink to see art on ice, and they'd tour the world to show all that skating could be. She'd restore American professional skating to its former glory, making it as big as the competitive circuit. Coaching didn't fit into that.

But Satoru won her over, and she agreed to help because she'd fallen in love with that crazy kid trying every wacky jump variation he could. It was a vivid memory for Kara Beth, the first time Satoru had asked her to be his coach. He'd been twelve, a local skater who'd signed up for a special workshop she was leading in Japan, and so got to perform in a group number during her show. Satoru was outgoing compared to his shyer peers, and they developed a playful friendship that transcended the language barrier. And then one day, he skated up to her with a fistful of pocket change and begged her for a skating lesson.

She didn't take the money, but she did give him a spin lesson. Then another, then another. On the last day of the tour, he delivered an obviously memorized speech about how hard he would work if she would become his new coach. She'd declined, and Satoru panicked. He began a new diatribe in Japanese, with raised voice and flailing arms, and his frazzled mother ran over and began apologizing that her son was making a public scene.

But somehow, Kara Beth understood the second speech better than the one in her native tongue. And though she'd never know just what moved her, there was something in Satoru's eyes that communicated deeper than words. A connection that caused her to prioritize teaching over her ice show dreams, and later, invite Satoru to live with her. He needed a coach, and for whatever reason, Kara Beth needed to be that coach.

After that, she took on Damien because he'd managed to charm her despite himself, and started coaching Eric because he reminded her of a tiny Kara Beth. A few others had approached her, but Kara Beth didn't feel that personal connection, that driving need that demanded she put her own activities on hold. And if she didn't feel that love and passion for her skater, then she'd rather be back performing in ice shows while she still had some youth left.

But her three boys had snagged her, and she loved every minute of their journey. Kara Beth was quick to admit she didn't know what she was doing in the beginning, but she thought she'd proven herself by now with the results. So what if she jumped and screamed on the sidelines like she was actually in the match? Her skaters thought it worked, and they were her boss, not the millions of YouTubers who thought they knew what a coach was supposed to act like. If she cracked jokes and hugged and loved her three boys like a surrogate mother, if she cheered when her skaters won and cried with them when they lost, why was that a bad thing?

The only person who had the right to give her advice was her own former coach. "Skaters come and go," he'd said, and it sounded pessimistic to Kara Beth. "It's a close partnership, but a job. They'll change coaches, change styles and eventually retire from that job. Don't get your heart broken over something that isn't personal."

Kara Beth got along well with her old coaches, but they weren't close. It had felt that way, back when she lived or died by her triple axel and the coach was the strongest ally in her camp, the one who challenged, pushed and praised her every day. They kept in contact, but now that Kara Beth was a little more removed from that life, the relationship had changed. She'd depended on her coaches once, still hoped they were proud of her, and now they lived completely different lives.

She'd die if that happened to her and Satoru. He wasn't just a job, the two of them shared something that went beyond a financial transaction. He didn't just skate at her rink, he'd lived in her house. Kara

Beth wanted to prove it's worth to the world. It was the same with Damien, and growing to be so with Eric. Those boys put their hearts on the line every day, and Kara Beth couldn't do less.

But everything had an expiration date, didn't it? Every summer, Kara Beth was reminded that Satoru had a real family back in Tokyo, one that would still exist when his skating career was over. And only a few months ago, he'd packed up most of his belongings and moved into an apartment of his own. It made sense that a young man in his twenties would want his independence, and never being able to escape one's coach was its own struggle, but that didn't make it hurt any less. She was constantly coming across items of Satoru's he'd forgotten to pack, potholders they'd picked out together, nicks in the walls from rearranging the bedroom furniture. Her streaming service kept recommending movies based on Satoru's viewing habits and it *ached*, even though she still saw him every day at the ice rink.

But she wasn't his mother. Her heart would break to lose Satoru, and she didn't even have a right to claim that pain.

The intercom announced each skater and their accomplishments, while Kara Beth set out Satoru's towel, water bottle and tissue box. Satoru wasn't overly picky with how he liked his things placed at the boards so long as they were accessible, but he did like the tissue box in clear view. The box itself was nothing special, frequently disposed of and replaced, in fact. But Satoru always taped photos of his three favorite skaters on the side, and the sight of his idols during competition helped him stay focused on his goals. There was Axel Paulsen, for whom the Axel jump was named, Surya Bonaly, a French skater known for her backflips and refusal to cow before expectations, and Yuzuru Hanyu, the first Japanese man to win Olympic gold in figure skating, twice. Satoru used to have a picture of Kara Beth on that box, too, but it disappeared about the time he moved to Ohio. When she asked him about it, Satoru just blushed and mumbled in a way that was too adorable for words.

Kara Beth arranged the items with care, straightening and smoothing things out, even though the extra fussing didn't really help anything. It was her need to control things, really, but she remembered when she'd been skating, and how nice it was to know everything she needed was in its proper place without having to think about it. Being a coach had taught her just how many things she'd taken for granted. Someone had always had her towel or water bottle within reach, someone always took her tissues and snack wrappers the second she was ready to discard them, her jacket and blade guards were always in someone's arms when not in use, along with her lucky plush Minnie Mouse. Now that she was on the other side, she realized she needed to send some overdue thank-you notes.

Beside her, Derek Donner's coach was organizing his skater's personal effects with the focus of a brain surgeon. He pointedly set the water bottle as far away from Kara Beth as possible. Derek and Satoru both clung to complimentary water bottles from an ice show years ago, garish pink things with lids that were notoriously leaky. Kara Beth had one from the same show, though it sat on a shelf in her office as a memento rather than see regular use. Satoru had landed his Quad Flip for the first time the day he received the item, and claimed if he kept it with him, he'd always remember the feeling and land the jump. Results varied, but he loved the thing, hypocritical as it was to have a lucky water bottle and criticize Damien for his lucky watch. Satoru always retorted that the water bottle got washed.

But since all those complimentary water bottles were completely identical, Satoru and Derek had occasionally gotten them mixed up. Once, Kara Beth had turned to speak with a trainer and turned back to see Derek in front of her, grabbing Satoru's water bottle and taking a long draught. Once he realized what he'd done, he did a spit take and pretended to gag for hours. It was an innocent mistake, but a distraction that neither boy wanted to repeat.

Satoru marked out the main beats of his program, turning singles on his double quad combo, then giving a 3A the full three and a half revolutions. It looked beautiful, with no evidence of the morning's fluke. No way he wasn't getting a +5 grade of execution on that.

But he seemed a little off when he slid up to the boards. She watched him wipe his face with a tissue and concluded that he did look clammy. Not good. "You coming down with something?" Satoru paused, and his eyebrows wrinkled in the way that indicated he wasn't quite sure what he'd been asked. "Do you feel sick?" she rephrased, and got a frown in return.

"I don't know..."

"Well, that's not reassuring." She leaned over to feel his forehead. Satoru typically ran at a lower body temperature when he was sick rather than burning up, and he did feel cool now, but it was hard to judge while standing in a skating rink and after he'd begun exercising. "How do you feel? Chills? Headache?"

"Cold hands," Satoru complained, and he pulled his forehead away. She let him, and he grabbed his water bottle. He took a drink and grimaced. "It's okay. Stomach wrong, but okay. Little blah, but okay."

"Wrong like pain? Or something else?"

"Um... like mud." Now it was Kara Beth's turn to wrinkle her eyebrows. "I don't know. It just happen." Satoru shrugged. "No big deal. Feeling weird but not bad. I don't notice during skate."

Kara Beth waved over Maureen Shibutani, her assistant coach. Maureen was a whiz with off-ice training, but Kara Beth hired her more for the woman's background in nutrition and her ability to speak mostly functional Japanese. Over the years, Damien and Satoru made sure the latter two skills were the more urgent. Yes, there were those among the Japanese Skating Federation within reach who could translate, but Kara Beth and Satoru preferred to keep things in their own circle when they could. It was one way they were similar as competitors; the more people involved in their lives, the less control they felt over their own decisions.

Maureen and Satoru rattled off a conversation, and then Maureen explained, "His stomach's a little upset, and he feels a bit achey, but just in the past ten minutes or so. It could be mild food poisoning, or maybe early flu symptoms. But he doesn't think it's serious."

"Oh, don't you?" Kara Beth raised an eyebrow at Satoru, who clasped a hand over his heart.

"I wouldn't lie!" he insisted, and pretended to be offended. "Remember, I'm the good kid!" Compared to Damien, who sometimes skipped three meals in a row and thought he could still turn quads, Satoru was more honest. He'd learned to be more upfront about his major injuries, and that made him infinitely easier to handle. "Promise. Swear on Surya Bonaly's backflip."

But honesty didn't mean he was a perfect judge of whether he should skate. Seven years, and Kara Beth still hadn't replaced the influence of Satoru's first coach, who pressured him to compete with a fractured knee for the better part of a year. Satoru wouldn't lie about his health, but he'd power through anything if he thought people expected it of him, to his own detriment.

Kara Beth hoped he'd gotten a better perspective on that in recent years, but she wasn't always sure. Still, today's mysterious illness didn't sound serious. "Okay, keep going," she sighed. "Tell us if you start feeling worse. You're fourth in the group to skate, so let's see where you are in half an hour."

"Not sick. I burn up germs with skating," Satoru grinned, and then took off for another lap around the ice. Kara Beth just took a deep breath and shook her head. This wasn't the best sign on earth, but when Satoru landed a perfect triple axel, she began to relax.

OVER THIRTY MINUTES LATER, the ice was clearing and Kara Beth and Satoru stood on opposite sides of the boards.

"Okay, almost time. How do you feel?"

"I'm focused. Ready for war."

"Good. You've got this. It's your dream program, three axel jumps." She saw Satoru try to hide a grin. "Hanyu himself could not skate them better."

"Shh, you disrespect God," Satoru giggled. His intensity and determination were as sharp as ever, but he was still loose and having fun. Exactly where Kara Beth wanted him. This long program was an aggressive piece, and Satoru took the role of a warrior. Kara Beth wanted him flying into his elements like it was the greatest battle of his life, but not like a shell-shocked soldier. A few smiles amid the warrior mentality was a good sign.

Because the pressure he was under would crush anybody, and her kid had a bad habit of ruminating over details that didn't matter. There was enough to think on without worrying about his scores or the stakes or the magnitude of what they'd been trying to achieve this season. There was no room to think of the judge's reaction, the crowd or his rivals. Just skating, just being his best. Nothing else needed to get in there.

The last of the flower girls stepped off the ice, her arms full of roses and teddy bears. Kara Beth kept her mind on the task at hand, and made sure Satoru did, too. "Who's your opponent?" As a skater, Kara Beth was urged to take acting classes to develop her performance skills, and while she hadn't taken to them in the beginning, she eventually saw a parallel in skating programs and performing monologues. Her teachers taught her to view those solitary endeavors as a dialogue, visualizing the other person as a force to push or pull against. It not only made for a better performance, but kept Kara Beth from over-analyzing the technical side of things.

And it was a perfect technique for Satoru. He'd been an emotional and passionate skater before he came to her, but those feelings were directionless. Making him create a character to play against had that passion transforming into works of art on the ice. It was that, rather than his jumps, that made him so intimidating to compete against.

"The ice," Satoru now replied, with no hesitation. "Ice is my opponent. We old friends, but betrayed. We have battle today." He still looked a bit off color, but had shown no signs of difficulty through his various exercises earlier. Kara Beth had to trust him on that, but she still worried. No one liked to compete sick.

Not like she'd never done it before. The unease she felt was probably nothing. "Then cut the ice with your blades. Dig into it with every step. Slice it deep when you take off, and gouge it on the way back down. Make it bleed."

Satoru raised an eyebrow. "Does ice bleed?"

"It will when you're done with it."

"Hmm..." Satoru took on a feral grin. "Ice is dead. I bring you back its heart."

There was a beat, and then the announcer's voice exploded over the intercom. "On the ice, representing Japan... Satoru Miyazawa!"

Time to go. Satoru leaned over the boards and looked for Kara Beth's bag. "Quick! You have pom-poms?"

Kara Beth sighed as she lifted two massive red and white cheerleader pom-poms, but the attitude was for show. She loved this ritual, and Satoru knew it. Even if it meant the other coaches laughed at her, even if Eric questioned her sanity. She gave the pom-poms a shake. "Ready? Okay! S-A-T-O! Take the ice and get the gold! Goooo, Sato!"

"Whoohoo!" Satoru clapped, looking for a brief second like the giggly little boy he'd once been. But then the years crashed back in a second, and a fiercely confident young man emerged from the wreckage.

A quick bow, a sharp push off the boards, and he was gone.

5

WHEN DAMIEN first arrived in America, he thought perhaps he'd gotten on the wrong plane. And it was possible, since he was familiar with English but hadn't made a diligent study of the language. That stopover in Toronto might have gotten him all turned around. But even when he saw the signs, even when he found his new coach waiting for him and everything in its correct place, he couldn't believe it was right. America in the movies looked nothing like Ohio.

Well, maybe in the old movies, when everybody farmed and highways weren't paved. But in this modern era, Damien felt like he was the victim of a practical joke. The skating rink Kara Beth owned was housed in a town nearly an hour's drive from Cincinnati, and when practice was in session, the number of skaters seemed to beat the number of town residents. When he worked up the courage to ask, "Do people really live like this?" Kara Beth just laughed.

Not that his home country of France didn't have rural areas along with urban ones, but the image Damien had always had of America was so different to his new reality. Where were the skyscrapers, the sprawling cities, where was the noise and colorful life? Kara Beth would say he was in training and should be grateful to be isolated from distractions, but Damien was seventeen at the time, and thought it would be fine if he got a little distracted. He wasn't especially social, but he liked activity and thought he'd be perfectly suited for the urban city life of LA or New York, the bustling, high-energy existences the movies promised. Millions of people providing stimulus to each other, while simultaneously ignoring any personal connection, it sounded like a paradise! He'd asked the then fifteen-year-old Satoru what he thought, since the boy was from Tokyo and had to be going stir crazy, too, but Satoru just flung out both arms and exclaimed, "Space!"

Over the years, Damien grew to love "Absolutely-Middle-Of-Nowhere, Ohio." It had its flaws, it's deficiencies, and its hard days. Rural areas came with a different set of stereotypes than urban ones, and sometimes his new home lived up to those in the worst ways. But it had its good points, too, and plenty of surprises.

And the town their skating rink called home, Granville, loved its skaters more than crops loved rain. "Everyone be quiet! Satoru's next!" The talking soon quelled, as the half of Granville that was smashed into an old barn waited for one of their favorite sons to take the ice. Satoru might skate under Japan's flag, but Granville would always claim him, and all Kara Beth's skaters, as their own.

It hadn't been easy to hook up the projector out here, or to access the live stream. They'd had to switch locations from a farm further down the road because they couldn't get the Wi-Fi to work. But once the feed was playing, the popcorn popped and everyone together, Damien was glad he hadn't bailed to go watch in the comfort of his apartment. Shared experiences were treasured ones, and the love the room held for the skaters, particularly the two Granville trainees, was palpable.

"Well, it wasn't Eric's best work, but he kept it exciting! I bet he comes roaring back for Nationals!" said the woman on Damien's left, a former ice dancer named Rachel Vines. She was a choreographer now, and assistant trainer at the Granville ice rink. Rachel had choreographed both Eric and Satoru's free programs, and Damien's short.

"Once you get on the Grand Prix circuit, it's hard to accept anything less, right?"

"Too true," Damien agreed. He still remembered what it was like to stand there with the best in the world, an atmosphere and a challenge so different from the other competitions he'd participated in. For the rest of the season, he doubled efforts to become the French champion so that he'd get sent to these major competitions again and again. "He will only improve as the season continues."

"You getting worried, Dami? He might turn into your competition!" a voice called from behind, and Damien laughed.

"The one I'm worried about is this fool!" He pointed to the screen, where Satoru and the rest of the group were finishing the six-minute warmup. "That is a man without limits. Gravity itself should be worried." There were nods from an Iranian family sitting nearby, though Damien wasn't sure how many of his words they really understood. The parents, at least, spoke little English, but were kind enough to pretend they did as an old woman talked their ears off because she was Russian and therefore a born skating authority. That entire group had met Satoru through his efforts volunteering with immigration services, and always came out to cheer at his matches, complete with signs, flags and noisemakers.

One skater from the adult classes plunked herself into a chair on Damien's right. "So, what craziness can we expect from Sato today? I haven't seen any of his run-throughs. Did he get KB's pass for the Jump-That-Must-Not-Be-Named?" She offered some of the freshly made popcorn, but Damien politely refused. The smell of the various snacks in the room was getting to him, and he couldn't open a window because they needed to keep all the heat in the building.

It didn't help his nauseous stomach that the smell of food was mixing with the smell of *barn,* but he knew his discomfort was largely mental, and he could distract himself until the problem went away. "As far as I know, he will attempt it today. But he popped it during the Autumn Classic, so Kara Beth does worry that he might be overtaxing himself this season."

A young man near the front of the room snorted. "Dude, he's

been overtaxing himself since he was born!" There was a burst of laughter, and then someone else asked, "What jump are you talking about?"

Damien twisted back in his chair to answer the older man, Alan Johnson, who had graciously provided his barn as the gathering place. "That would be the Quadruple Axel."

"Oh." The name meant little to Johnson, but he looked interested. "Is that hard?"

"Very," Damien replied, repressing the urge to say something sarcastic. To do so would go unappreciated by Johnson, but the 4A was so notoriously difficult, he could only speak of it in a hyperbolic sense. The idea of landing one at all, let alone in a competition program, was akin to stealing fire from Olympus. Axels were tricky jumps, and required an extra half rotation because of their forward takeoff, so the four and a half turns necessary for a Quad Axel was thought impossible for years, on the same level as quintuples. But the nature of sports was to challenge higher heights, be stronger, move faster and in the case of figure skating, achieve more revolutions in the air. Even the 4A had seen light in competition now, but rarely. The luster and awe were as potent as ever.

So of course Satoru would make it his life's mission. And he never did anything halfway. Damien had seen him training the thing, first in harness, then without, then in run-throughs. It felt like a game of roulette to watch, the risk of injury was so high, but it was Satoru's superior technique that allowed him to make this jump in the first place, and also help him land safely. No one else in the current field came close.

And Damien never would. He wanted to try, couldn't help the hunger he felt for it, but knew it was something he could never achieve. Maybe if he hadn't starved himself throughout puberty, but that was done now. He was lucky his body was as powerful as it was, able to get monstrous height on the toe assisted jumps and rival Satoru's stamina, but that 4A was asking a bit much.

It stung to see the ceiling above him, but Damien knew there was more than one way to grow. Just as grass found the cracks in the sidewalk, he'd found the openings where he could shoot forth and blossom, and was feeling more healthy than ever. It would be a fight to overtake his rival now that Satoru was bringing his 4A to competition, but Damien was prepared for the siege.

"Up next is a skater who's surely feared by his competition today. Satoru Miyazawa, in first after yesterday's short program."

"There he is with coach Kara Beth Bonogofski. A few spirited words before taking the ice." Those pom-poms. Damien used to hate them, or at least, he pretended to. But part of him secretly loved that his coach treated every competition with the gravity of a children's kickball game. She was more serious during Damien's pre-skate rituals until he caved and asked if she knew where to find pom-poms in France's colors. That year, she went to Nationals with her face painted the color of the French flag.

The room buzzed while two commentators discussed Satoru's planned events, not that Damien needed the refresher. He and Satoru trained together, even shared tips and pointers, and both knew enough about each other's programs to be wary. Which made competition season a bit awkward, when they both showed up to events and realized that they were on opposite sides now. But that was special, Damien thought, to have a rival that would help you achieve your full potential, even knowing that doing so might help them take you down.

"Looking at the planned program list, it's no wonder that he's the world champion. He's got five quads today, the best skating skills... he's been training that Quad Sal-Quad Toe combination and, can you believe this, a Quad Axel! I said last week that Saint-Michel might be capable of taking the Grand Prix this year, but I don't think Miyazawa's ready to step down!"

"Not only that, Marc, but Satoru's known for adding difficult features to his jumps. And I can't say this enough, but he has not lost once since winning Olympic gold. Barely even fallen. I won't say he's perfect, but I think we all know who's the boss here."

Damien smirked, and Johnson gave him a playful nudge. Satoru was good, no doubt about that. But Damien had been training with him since they were teenagers. He knew Satoru's weaknesses as well as his own strengths, and had built his programs with the sole goal of dethroning the king.

And Satoru wasn't the only one training crazy jumps. He could break all the records he wanted to today, but Damien was going to be the one taking gold at the finals. "Shh, it's starting!"

The operatic chords began, opening the free skate with musical drama, and Satoru's choreography matched that perfectly. His facial expressions were intense, he looked like fury incarnate out there on the ice. And he went into that elusive axel jump with such speed that Damien knew he'd land it without a hitch.

Except he didn't.

"What a shock! We rarely see falls from Miyazawa! But he's up, he's up!" Back into the choreography with barely a step wasted, but it was a clear break in the program and he'd lost time to build up speed for the combination. A botched jumping pass and the deduction for a fall, Satoru was going to hate himself later. *"He started out so strong. I did hope we'd get to see that Quad Axel today..."*

"Yes, but we forget sometimes how demanding these elements really are. The skaters make it look so easy, but they're pushing their physical limits to stay competitive. A program with this degree of difficulty can't be perfect all the time."

Damien wasn't sure what to think. Mistakes happened, even for Satoru, but this fall looked different from ones Satoru typically made in practice. If he had to guess, Damien would say his friend looked tired, but it was far too early in the program to be running out of stamina.

Whatever the odd fluke, Satoru seemed to find his groove again, and sailed into his next jump with determination. Damien realized what was about to happen a second before the blades left the ice, and he scrambled up from his seat to get a better view. *"Quoi?!"*

"I don't believe it! Absolutely stunning! Quad Salchow, with the Tano position! Needed that deep knee bend of his for the landing, but he did it!"

"Did you see that height?"

The commentators expounded on their admiration for the next several seconds. Some viewers didn't fully understand the difficulty, but applauded the jump nonetheless. "Ooh, very nice," an elderly grandma sitting in front of Damien clapped. "That was lovely."

It was lovely. And also staggering. Yes, Satoru had great jumps, getting height and speed other skaters only dreamed of, but that he could increase the difficulty further and do it so casually... *"Quelle surprise..."* When the camera panned by the boards, they saw Kara Beth screaming and waving her pom-poms in the air.

"Never thought I'd see the return of Tano Sal," someone groaned. "I thought he had a ban on that?"

Damien looked over at Rachel for the answer, who'd been quietly relishing everyone's reactions. "Kara Beth lifted it. He's been training that for a while. Didn't you know?" she asked Damien.

"He mentioned it, but I thought he was joking." In Satoru's junior days, before either of them had made the move to Ohio, Satoru added Tano and Rippon variations to all his jumps, putting his arms over his head in order to get more points on his Grade of Execution. The problem was that Satoru's jump technique was abysmal back then, so he usually ended up falling, driving those GOE points back down the toilet. Damien never understood why his old coach hadn't put a stop to it, especially after the kid tried a Quad Toe with a Rippon variation and broke his nose on the ice.

Once Satoru signed on with Kara Beth, the Tano was the first thing to go. According to rumor, the conversation was "Stick your arm over your head one more time and I'm shipping you back to Tokyo in a banana crate." And overnight, the skating improved.

On the screen, Satoru sailed into his crossovers, but when he came out and went into his Quad Flip, he looked a little wobbly. Jumps involving the right toe pick were more difficult for Satoru, and his technique on the flip was particularly odd. A past knee injury prevented him from learning it correctly in his youth, and the jump had been suspect ever since. Satoru once confessed that he sometimes brought his foot down and flashed back to his traumatic junior years, where he didn't have a leg, just a giant mess of pain receptors.

Today's attempt resulted in a very suspicious landing. *"A bit dodgy, but I think he got round...*" the commentators reported. "*The judges are definitely going to put that one under review, though.*"

One teenager who worked at the rink leaned over to Damien and whispered, "Do you think he injured something during the first jump?"

"Naw, his Flip's always been wonky," Rachel leaned over to disagree. "If it were up to me, he'd keep the flip as a triple, but you know Satoru..."

Damien wasn't sure. He was inclined to agree with Rachel, but Satoru was looking a little off up there on the screen. It was possible that he could have bruised something or pulled a muscle in practice, any number of things.

Or he could have just gotten cocky. "I think he's still got the lead, though," one of the younger students said. She pointed to the box in the upper left-hand corner that showed Satoru's technical points compared to the current leader. "See? He's pretty close, and still got a bunch of elements to go."

"Plus, he's leading after the short program," her friend agreed. "I bet he still wins in the end. Sato always wins." He probably would, but that wouldn't be enough for Satoru. To ask him to be 'good enough' was like asking him to drink antifreeze. He expected greatness from himself, and winning wasn't an accomplishment for Satoru if his program had a flaw. The pressure he was under was astronomical, but somehow the standard he'd set for himself was higher. Satoru was getting better about letting the failures go in time, but he'd been downright miserable to be around when they were kids.

"This thing you do, insulting yourself, it is not attractive!" Damien had told him, after Satoru won gold to Damien's bronze and still couldn't take a compliment graciously. By the time the celebrations were over and the two made it back to the hotel, he'd been ready to strangle the kid. "The insecurity and lack of confidence is not cute! You are behaving like a spoiled child!"

Whether Satoru understood all those words was up for debate, but he understood why he was being yelled at. He didn't care. "I fall. Have to work. Can't play like you." By the end of the night, Damien had tried strangling him for real, and they faced Kara Beth in the morning with black eyes and scowls. But over the years, the two grew to understand each other a little better. Satoru would be miserable for a few days, but he'd get over this latest disappointment in time. Probably by throwing himself into work with even more determination.

On the projector screen, things were not looking good. Satoru vaulted into another jump, and Damien knew from the takeoff that it would't land right. Maybe exhaustion or a minor injury, but his training partner was far from his usual standard. That didn't mean all was lost, and Satoru had saved bad jumps before. Even if he couldn't correct the position in the air, he still had magic to work with his core muscles to yank him back over his skates. The grade of execution would be clobbered, but Satoru would find a way to finish on his feet.

But this time, Satoru went straight down into the ice. He got up again, slower that anyone might have hoped, but after only a few seconds, abandoned the choreography. Satoru bent over and braced his arms against his knees.

"Do you think he's hurt?" The commentators wondered the same thing, and after a few seconds, Satoru changed direction and began gliding toward their coach.

He didn't make it. Less than ten feet away from the boards, he slid to his knees and threw up. Awkward laughter came from the commentator's booth. *"Well, that's rotten luck, but I guess it explains some things."*

"Poor kid. You just can't help getting sick. Might have been better to withdraw, though."

"Yeah, I pity whoever's got to clean that up!" Damien's heart cringed in sympathy. Sometimes the referee would allow an athlete to resume their program after a delay, but Satoru didn't look in any condition to continue, no matter how much time they gave. And with that, he'd effectively lose the competition. Even Eric would place higher.

At least he'd had the sense to get off the ice and not try more jumping passes, but Damien knew Satoru wouldn't see it that way. No, Satoru would see this as cowardice, and who knew how long it would take to talk him down from that ledge? He wouldn't consider this taking care of himself, he'd consider it betraying Kara Beth, letting down his friends and family, the fans, the ISU, the ghosts of figure skaters past. Their little Olympian would rather kill himself than leave the ice over a stomach bug with barely a minute left to go.

And yet, he'd done it. Maybe all of Kara Beth's assurances and lectures were sinking in. But Damien soon had a different explanation. *"Oh, my goodness! Marc, I think that's blood!"*

"What? Where- Oh!"

Pandemonium broke out in the barn. "He's bleeding! Did he cut himself?"

"No, look, it's on his mouth!" Satoru was retching uncontrollably now. Damien felt his own blood drain out of his face. "What's happening?"

"I don't know..."

Damien couldn't find the words. He saw Kara Beth on the screen, paler than he'd ever seen. The pom-poms lay forgotten on the ground, stepped on and kicked aside by the medical staff. Any face visible showed fear and bewilderment, adding to those emotions building in Granville. But the medics were there, they trained people for this, Damien told himself. They had resources and an ambulance, Satoru was in good hands.

Then the kid started convulsing, and all Damien's optimism shattered. He jumped to his feet, as if he could possibly get close enough to Satoru to help. No, he was stuck here in a barn, while his best friend bled and vomited his way around some unprecedented seizure. All Damien could do was offer silent prayers to God and try to keep breathing.

Satoru was carried out of range of the camera in a few seconds, presumably where he'd be swarmed by staff and taken to a hospital, but Damien couldn't calm his racing heart. He pulled out his phone to call Kara Beth, but then realized that she'd have enough to deal with without him distracting her. He couldn't bother her, but had to do something, talk to someone who was there, someone who might know more about what was going on.

His panicked brain decided on Eric. While he waited for the younger boy to pick up, Damien's eyes landed on the leader's score box, with Satoru's unfinished and significantly lower score underneath. For some reason, though it shouldn't have mattered at all, the sight made everything hurt all the more.

6

———

IN THE SUMMER after turning eighteen, Damien became obsessed with the idea of a male pairs tournament. "Can't you just picture the side-by-side quad combos?" he'd gush, and then go into his theory that throw quintuples were surely a possibility if they put enough practice into it. Kara Beth did her best to shut down that train of thought and redirect the energy into Damien's off-ice training, but it wasn't long before she showed up at the rink and found her oldest skater attempting to hurl sixteen-year-old Satoru across the ice.

Damien's logic behind this was that Satoru was the best technician he knew and "basically built out of drinking straws." Satoru hadn't actually needed much convincing to try the stunt, and tried to argue that it would help him master his inconsistent Flip, and Damien insisted it was all fair because he'd had Satoru try to throw him in a Quad Loop a few minutes before. Kara Beth lectured them for a half hour on their idiocy and thought that would be enough, until a few days later when the boys got it in their heads to try side-by-side spins.

Satoru travelled during his spin and his blade sliced a long gash in Damien's cheek. It ended up looking worse than it was, but Kara

Beth still blanched at the memory of Satoru's frantic yelling, the blood and the white knuckled drive to the emergency room. Damien, the little brat, had laughed the whole way and teased her about her sudden transformation into "Super Coach".

While there were many aspects of coaching that intimidated Kara Beth, especially in the beginning, injuries were the only thing that truly frightened her. Injuries were something she couldn't fix, she couldn't break it down and train the problem away. And maybe it was a sign she was too attached, but to sit by helplessly when her kids were in pain was too much to ask.

And so she put the fear of God in Damien and Satoru, if they dared put her back in this situation with one of their brainless stunts. It worked on Satoru, he'd been ready to flog himself at the first sign of blood, and even Damien seemed repentant. There were only a few stitches, but it was an effective object lesson for reckless endangerment.

It wasn't the most serious injury, or the most frightening hospital visit in her history of coaching those two, but it was the one that always jumped to the front of her brain. The repercussions had been so minor that it was little more than a humorous, if cautionary, anecdote around the rink, but it stoked a primal fear in Kara Beth that resurfaced every time she set foot in a hospital.

And those images filled her mind now. There was only so much she could do once the medical personnel took over, but Kara Beth itched to be at Satoru's side until he was finally pronounced healthy. Waiting had never been her strong point, and after seeing her skater's eyes roll back into his head, she felt that every second mattered.

But there wasn't anything productive for her to do. She wasn't family, not even Satoru's legal guardian anymore, so they forced her to sit and wait with Maureen until someone had an update. And all the while, Kara Beth sank deeper into her anxieties, praying that her boneheaded boy had somehow managed to hide a pre-existing but easily curable illness from her. But deep down, she knew this couldn't be a simple issue.

Those hopes plummeted further when the police arrived. With

little explanation, they surrounded her with an exam's worth of questions. What did Satoru eat or drink that day, what was security like at the event, did he have any enemies? They also seemed unusually interested in Satoru's water bottle. Kara Beth did her best to answer the questions, then finally got a word in edge-wise to ask what was going on.

But the answer felt unreal. "Someone poisoned Miyazawa." Kara Beth's thoughts swam, unable to find anything to anchor them.

Only one idea floated to the top. "Is he going to be okay?" Of course, the police didn't know. Their job was to gather evidence, and so resumed their questions. Kara Beth stared into the distance for a moment and wondered if she needed to call a lawyer. But then she remembered how frustrated the police were in procedural dramas when the witnesses didn't cooperate, and didn't every second count in a situation like this? She wished there was someone to direct her, and then remembered that was the point of lawyers, and so was back at square one.

The thought of calling someone reminded her that Satoru's family needed to be notified, and that broke her composure completely. She dropped her head into her hands and sobbed, and after an awkward moment, one officer guided her to a plastic chair.

But they didn't stop with the questioning. Even if their voices grew more sympathetic, the constant push to recall facts and details that hadn't seemed important at the time was excruciating to bear, and Kara Beth finally snapped her head up to say so. But as she did, her eyes fell on the water bottle in a plastic bag, the one the police were so concerned about its comings and goings.

"That's not Satoru's water bottle."

"What?"

"He wrote his name on the bottom. See?" There was no black sharpie spelling out 'SATO' on the cheap plastic. "It's not his."

But that didn't make sense. It had been with Satoru's things, Kara Beth had held that water bottle in her hands, she'd handed it to him during the six-minute warm up. "How did we wind up with someone else's water bottle?" Derek's coach popped into her mind; he'd been very obvious about preventing a mix-up, but what if that was the goal?

Meanwhile, the emergency room was still in a frenzy related to Satoru, and didn't seem likely to calm down soon. Kara Beth answered everything as best she could, but felt herself growing more and more detached. Someone tried to kill her skater, right under her nose. Satoru could be dying, and she might have handed the poison to him.

"Ma'am? Are you alright?" She let someone hurt her kid. And that thought was galvanizing. Kara Beth sat up straight again and faced the officers.

"I'll be all right when you figure out who did this!" And when they did, Kara Beth would bring the wrath of 'Super Coach' down on that unfortunate soul.

THE TANO SAL WAS PERFECT, as expected. As it deserved to be. Too long had Satoru's faulty body failed to realize the majesty of that jump, and now the specter of past failures could leave him alone. He had to finish the program. Even if he popped the combo, even if he made a poor showing, he had to at least finish. He'd make a try for the combo. It was just his stomach, not his legs.

And then the rink monster opened its jaws.

The teeth clamped around his middle; they pierced and tore, and Satoru scrambled to get away. He kicked with his bladed feet, clawed at the ice's surface with his fingernails, but the monster kept chewing. In the distance, he saw Kara Beth running onto the ice, her hand almost close enough to grasp his-

But then the monster swallowed him whole, and Satoru journeyed into the dark.

He woke up on the ice, with no Kara Beth in sight. But his old coach was back, demanding to know why Satoru had tried that stupid Tano variation after what happened at Lombardia? Didn't he know what an embarrassment he'd been out there? Satoru tried to ask for his real coach, tried to protest the man's presence, but his throat lit up on fire the second he forced oxygen through it.

He sat up and searched the rink, but the dialogue followed him. There were other skaters with more potential, why did Satoru have to keep wasting everyone's time? His coach was ashamed of him, his family was ashamed of him, did he think they would forgive him if he landed that 4S+4T? When his skating skills were so sloppy? How dare he ask for help after a display like that?

Satoru pushed himself to his feet, pushing through the crowd of faceless voices that had assembled. Old coaches, old spin technicians, old schoolteachers and classmates. He needed to work harder, juggle everything, answer the expectations, or they were through wasting their time on him. On the fringes of the crowd was Damien, and slightly beyond, Inessa. Satoru stumbled over to both of them.

His throat was too raw to speak, but he tried. The tears came, and painful wheezes, but no words, and the ones Damien spoke were incomprehensible. Satoru tried to say he didn't understand, tried to explain that he couldn't speak, but Damien's stream of words grew louder and faster, smashing into Satoru's head like a river and threatening to wash him away. Behind him, Inessa's language joined the cacophony, and he heard the voices of Eric, Alisha, and Alberto as well. Flashing cameras and microphones appeared, with more words that might as well have been gibberish for all the meaning they gave Satoru.

He whirled around, looking for a friendly face, a face that wasn't frustrated with him, a face that would speak something comforting. He turned to Wataru, who left. Turned to Yukiya, who pushed him down with eager ambition. Turned around again, and fell, the pain in his stomach was too great to continue...

He woke up again in a bed. A strange room, and he couldn't figure out more than that, since his eyelids were too heavy to keep open for more than a quick flutter. There was pain, but the sources were hard to identify, as every time he focused in, something else would flare up to steal his attention. First his stomach, then his arms, his ankle, then his stomach again, and his pounding head. He breathed, and his lungs tried to force glass up through his throat.

And yet, if he stopped focusing on it, stopped listening to his body's complaining, he found he could let it drift away into the back of his thoughts. A constant presence that didn't have to affect his performance if he numbed himself down to the soul, like his old knee injury had been in the days before Kara Beth.

He hoped he wouldn't be asked to skate like this.

With great effort, Satoru forced his eyes open for a bit, long enough to get his bearings, then closed them again. Something medical. Looked too established to be the medical facility at the ice rink, the brief image he'd snagged read more like 'hospital'. He must have fallen on the ice or something.

"Ugh, that's embarrassing," he mumbled, but the sounds scraped his throat and the result was a formless moan. But it startled him to hear a voice in response. A light touch on his arm accompanied it, and the fingertips were warm against his skin.

He didn't realize he'd been cold. "Mom?" he asked, working hard to force the speech out through uncooperative avenues, but the response was negative. Satoru wrenched his eyes back open in surprise.

For all the good it did. He was too tired to focus them, and even after several bracing blinks, everything still looked slightly weird in a way that Satoru was too tired to explain. But he recognized Kara Beth, and that was a relief, at least.

"*Hi,*" she whispered, and she looked tired. Tired and sad, but happy, too. A lot of emotions for Satoru's tired brain to analyze, and he squinted to get a better look.

"Hi," he replied. Swallowing made the problem worse, and he coughed a few times before squeaking out, "I'm sorry I screwed up. I didn't mean to..." He wanted to say more, but his throat wouldn't let him. He was already being punished for pushing it that far.

Kara Beth hesitated, then patted his shoulder. "*It's fine. Don't...*"

Satoru couldn't make out what she didn't want him to do. He grimaced and tried to sit up, but his muscles had no strength, so he gave up.

"I'll fix it at NHK," he promised. Whatever he'd done, there was always another chance, right? Kara Beth always said so. Falls weren't a big deal he could always try again. A skater was more than one performance at one event, it was a long season. He hoped she wasn't lying about that. "I'll get it right next time." He broke into a coughing fit, his throat and lungs didn't want to handle all that talking. Being sick was the worst.

"Don't talk now, honey, just rest until..." Kara Beth's words carried on, but become a string of sounds with no meaning. It confused Satoru at first, but then he realized what was happening and concluded he didn't have the energy for translation on top of everything, and went back to sleep.

But his dreams were full of ice.

TEXTS BOMBARDED Kara Beth's phone, most of which she didn't have time to answer. Satoru's family took priority. The media got a bland statement, and everything else could rot for all she cared.

But she made time to call Damien. His one text had politely asked for an update if she got a free second, and not to worry if she didn't. He was the only one to reassure her that everything would be alright, to thank her for her efforts, and then to wait patiently on the sidelines and not bother her again.

That deserved a reward, in her opinion. Damien picked up the phone with faint traces of panic coloring his otherwise unflappable composure. "What is the status of our little bird? I have been looking up symptoms on the internet for hours. I'm sure you can't tell me anything worse than that."

Kara Beth felt the universe laughing at both of them. "How about acute arsenic poisoning?"

There was a pause. "If you are making a joke, I will hang up on you."

"No jokes. It's looking like someone tried to poison him by switching out his water bottle. But he's going to pull through. We can be thankful for that, at least." Kara Beth didn't yet know what 'pulling through' was going to look like, but Satoru would live and that was the important thing. "It did a number on his system, so I guess the doctors are worried about any permanent damage, but everyone's already saying we're really lucky, so I'll take that as a good sign."

Damien didn't seem to share the optimism, but masked it with indignation. "Who poisons with arsenic anymore? Are we living in the 18th century?"

"That's the part that bothers you?"

"No, but it is the only part to which I can put words." She heard a thunk in the background, like a countertop had been struck. "Who did this?"

"I don't know. The police are still investigating." Kara Beth didn't know how they could, though. Many people involved with the competition had been questioned and fingerprints taken, the whole rigamarole, but the police couldn't possibly keep hundreds of people detained in California for an indefinite period. Most of the athletes and their entourages were flying home now. Eric had boarded a plane that morning. But if all the suspects flew to different points on the globe, how was anything supposed to get accomplished?

"This is insanity! How could someone get their hands on Satoru's water bottle in the first place? With no one noticing? It's always on his person and there's a crowd of people documenting his every move! You saw nothing?"

Kara Beth choked. "No..." The guilt that she'd tried to ignore came back in force. "I didn't see anything... But that might be the whole problem, that there's so many people around, anyone with a lanyard could have walked into the training area," she rattled off, trying to out talk the onslaught of emotion. "The press, the other skaters, their coaching teams, the medics, the support staff... Even if I saw someone walk up to him, I wouldn't have questioned it. It could have been someone standing right next to me during the warmup, all it would take was a second." Her mind flashed back to Derek Donner and his coach, with that identical water bottle that would have been so easy to switch... She'd mentioned it to the police, but hoped she was wrong. It was too horrible to think about.

"I can't believe this." Damien sounded like he wanted to throw something. "Why would someone do such a thing?"

"Your guess is as good as mine. Maybe one of his rivals is just that desperate to win? Or someone from their camp."

Damien muttered back some foul-sounding French before switching back to English. "I don't know what to say. Have you talked to Satoru yet?"

"A bit. He's woken up, but hasn't stayed awake long." Poor thing looked like he'd aged fifty years since the competition started. "But that's probably for the best. They've got him on dialysis now and you know how he is about needles. The more he sleeps through that, the better."

Damien barked out a laugh. "Yes, I'm sure he's not pleased. How long do you think, before... that is..." Damien's tone grew unusually hesitant, but Kara Beth knew what he was asking.

"Will he be able to skate again?"

"I know the little duck will pull out all his feathers until that's assured."

"Don't I know it," Kara Beth laughed, but it was painful. "As far as I know, yes. It sounds like exercise can only help his recovery. But I don't know when he'll be turning quads again. It's just a question of when he can get back on the ice, and how long he takes to get back in shape for heavy training, then we'll have a better idea. But the doctor said he's a lot healthier than he has any right to be after a dose of arsenic." She grimaced. "Sato still thinks he's competing at NHK Trophy in two weeks."

"God help that poor boy."

"Yeah, I don't know how to break it to him. But it's not crazy to think he might finish out the season, we just have to see how things go."

"In that case, he's won."

"Hm?"

"Why else would someone kill him, if not to become the new men's champion? But Satoru is alive, and will return for the Olympics next year, if not this year's World Championship? He has foiled the evil plans."

Put like that, it sounded like a victory. But Kara Beth wasn't so sure.

"I guess we'll see."

SATORU BLINKED a slushy dream out of his eyes and was back in the hospital. There was a nurse nearby, and he inclined his head to ask a question, but fell asleep midway through his sentence, and said nurse was gone by the time he woke up.

He drifted in and out like that for some time, shifting through a string of dreams and realities that were equally exhausting and blended together in a way that Satoru stopped trying to question. Sometimes his mother was there and he talked to her, sometimes he realized halfway through the exchange that it had to be a dream, but he kept talking anyway. Sometimes he felt Kara Beth's fingers carding through his hair, and he wanted to open his eyes and tell her he wasn't a kid anymore, she didn't need to try so hard. Taking in a stray skater was one thing. Staying up with him when he was sick wasn't what she bargained for. Making him soup and wrapping him in comforters and watching movies on her couch was never in the job description.

His mother didn't raise him to be such a nuisance. But the physical touch was soothing, and everything else in his body ached. Might as well enjoy those small actions that made him feel special and wanted. He could work out whether he deserved them later.

His consciousness floated back to the surface when he felt the touch leave him. He opened his eyes to the hospital room he didn't recognize and squinted at his surroundings. The only familiar thing was Kara Beth, who plastered on a tired smile when she saw him awake. "Good morning."

"Morning." Satoru wondered just how early it was, as the lighting in the room was so weird. Or maybe his eyes were just tired. He closed them for a minute. "Was I dead? It kind of feels like it."

Kara Beth laughed, but more for the release of tension than humor. "It think like that. A bit. But not."

Why was she talking all strange? Satoru wrinkled his nose as he tried to figure out what was weird. "I don't remember what happened. Did I fall in the free?" He opened his eyes again, but Kara Beth looked apologetic.

"Sorry, kid, I don't know how to answer that."

It took Satoru a minute to process that. It finally hit him that Kara Beth had been speaking Japanese to him earlier. Weird. She hardly ever did that, since she was kind of terrible at it. It was nice of her to try, though.

He tried to rephrase his question in English, but his brain didn't want to switch. Like being a kid again, having to think his thought and then translate it before saying every little word, a laborious and time-consuming task. He pushed through with an easier question. *"You stayed?"*

"Of course." That was nice. She wasn't his guardian anymore, she didn't have to do that.

Especially since she had other students to worry about.
"What about Eric?"

Kara Beth looked puzzled. *"He and his parents went home already. The competition's over."*

"Oh." In the back of his mind, that meant something to Satoru. But he couldn't focus on what. Just communicating in English was giving him enough of a headache. *"I do okay?"*

"Let's worry about that later. Just rest now. Once you're stable, we can get you back to Japan for recovery. Your parents will be relieved to have you home."

"Yeah... I miss them," Satoru offered, and Kara Beth patted his knee.

"I know." She said something more, but Satoru didn't catch it, and decided it didn't matter.

"I'm tired," he yawned, and hoped that wasn't too rude. The

hospital walls were already melting away into the ice rink back home, and though it made little sense to fall asleep in his skates, he gave into the exhaustion while Kara Beth chuckled in the background.

7

____

"**B**ETTER BRACE YOURSELF, HONEY."

That was the warning. Satoru wanted to know what happened back at the rink, why was he in the hospital and how soon could they get those tree trunks the nurse called needles out of his arms, and all Kara Beth said was, "*Brace yourself.*"

'Brace' was an interesting word and made for a more interesting phrase. It was one thing Satoru loved about English, that it was so full of metaphor and vivid imagery down to the most common phrase. Words Satoru heard every day took on new meanings as he learned the full definitions behind them, and he valued that exploratory aspect of language acquisition. When he'd first heard that line of syllables, he'd learned to associate it with something unpleasant about to happen.

Now that he'd looked up the verb 'to brace', he knew a tsunami was coming.

The first wave involved police. Because they'd been waiting to question him and couldn't waste any more time now that he was cognizant. Where did he go all weekend, who did he talk to, did anyone threaten him, where was his water bottle at all times? It seemed someone switched his water bottle for one spiked with arsenic, and that was why he got sick on the ice, but Satoru couldn't come up with any answers how or why someone would do that. Sometimes it felt like his brother wanted him dead, or at least to never be born, but this went a bit beyond sibling rivalry. He was a professional obstacle to the other male skaters, maybe even a personal annoyance to some, but no one hated him enough to kill.

Or so he thought. Now he had to list everyone who might have gotten close enough to switch out his water bottle or had access to his possessions. Kara Beth, Maureen and the rest of the team who supported him, staff at the hotel... Possibly Derek or Alberto, Eric or Yukiya, but Satoru didn't see how he wouldn't have noticed them, and by that logic they might as well question the whole arena. Anyone with a talent for pick-pocketing who'd gotten close to him in those crowded hallways could have been the culprit.

His tongue tripped just before Damien's name. Damien was over at his apartment all the time and had rifled through his skate bag, but that was nearly a week before Satoru left for California, and he was reasonably sure he'd had the correct water bottle when he'd boarded the plane. Even if he hadn't, he'd refilled the bottle several times, but was only poisoned the day of the free skate.

Also, it was Damien. Satoru's brain refused to even think about it. In the end, he decided not to bring it up.

It was bad enough puzzling out who in his acquaintance might have just tried to kill him. As the second wave hit, he wondered if he shouldn't have just died and let them win. That was what his liver and kidneys thought, and Satoru would have happily amputated those organs and stomped on them for such betrayal, if the doctor didn't think recovery possible. Recovery came with conditions, since some of the organ damage wasn't reversible and might continue to deteriorate with age. Satoru would probably be looking at renal failure at some point in his life, but since it wasn't an immediate concern, Satoru let that drop. He was having trouble concentrating with the hemodialysis needle sitting in his vein like a knife waiting to stab if he let his guard down. Which wasn't even the only needle or tube tying him to the bed, but he could only handle one of those things at a time.

And then there was his stupid heart, which had apparently decided that if everything else was giving up, it could just do its own thing for a bit. It was back to a regular rhythm now, but the doctors wanted to monitor that. Satoru also needed to submit to tests and prodding to check for nerve damage and the state of his muscle control, and then he'd gotten a case of pneumonia after his stomach decided the only way to get rid of the poisoned water was to vomit the stuff into his lungs.

The report of his wrenched ankle was almost laughable after that. But despite the relief at having something normal to concentrate on, the news jolted Satoru back to the one thing that mattered. "When can I skate again?"

The doctor looked perplexed when the translator finished. *"What?"*

"I'm a competitive figure skater. I've already missed days of training, and it's less than two weeks until my next Grand Prix assignment, and..." He trailed off as reality hit him. Skate America was over, and this had forced him to withdraw. He'd effectively lost the event and earned zero points towards advancing along the Grand Prix. Even if he sold his soul for the right to skate at NHK in two weeks, first place would only net him fifteen points, and he needed upwards of twenty-four to even hope. He wouldn't be going to the finals.

His Grand Prix title was already lost.

"I... uh..." The rest of the room faded away, and Satoru couldn't focus on anything but his hand twisting up the thin excuse for a blanket draped over his bed. The right hand only, his left arm still had a needle in it large enough to knit a sweater and he couldn't risk moving that.

His right hand, though, that couldn't stop moving. The restless energy had to go somewhere. The last time he'd lost a skating competition, the last time he hadn't made the podium, he'd been...

And suddenly, he couldn't breathe. He clapped his hand over his mouth, not because that would actually help the problem, but because he was sobbing with such gasping force that each wheeze threatened to heave his lungs out of his throat. He felt every muscle shaking, his eyes bulging out and pouring fluid over everything, and a mace had somehow got lodged inside his chest cavity.

Nothing he did would make this go away. It wasn't an injury he could power through, a personal problem he could cast aside. He couldn't try harder and be better, because he'd already failed. The medal, the title, the prize money, lost. His family, his coaching team, Japan, all disappointed. He'd flown so high, but missed the goal, and now he was screaming towards earth from the stratosphere.

He didn't notice when Kara Beth replaced the doctor, but when he did, the shame doubled. Once again, he was caught in all his lies, a terrified, sobbing mess forced to confess his shortcomings.

"I'm sorry! I'm sorry, so sorry, I didn't mean to..." All he could do was cry. Show remorse, because there was no fixing this. Kara Beth had spent so much time trying to teach him. She gave him a home, picked him up when he fell, just because she believed in him. And this was how he repaid her?

And his family? How many extra hours had his parents worked, how many things had they gone without, how many of Izumi and Wataru's dreams were thrown away just so Satoru could lose the Grand Prix? "I'm sorry, I'm sorry!"

"Kid, calm down. Look at me, okay? There's nothing to be sorry for, got it?" Satoru tried to deny it, tried to explain that this was all his fault, didn't she understand what happened, all the ways he'd failed, the repercussions that would come from this? But Kara Beth persisted. *"It's not your fault, Sato. Calm down. Everything's going to be fine."*

"No, I didn't mean to, I'm sorry..." Satoru wasn't sure what he was saying anymore, but it didn't matter. Kara Beth tried to hug him, but Satoru held her at arm's length. No matter how much he craved the comfort, he didn't deserve it after this, and he still had a needle in his arm, didn't anyone realize that was still there? But if he weren't tethered to the blood-sucking tube of death, he'd have run from the room and launched himself off the nearest terrace, jumped into the ocean and begged the sharks to eat him, anything to escape the crushing failure he was staring down.

He couldn't understand the words Kara Beth said, too distraught to process English, and it was clear she didn't appreciate the magnitude of this catastrophe. But sooner or later the reality would sink in for her, too. She'd realize what a wretched being she was looking at, and that would be it. Because everyone left in the end, be it coaches, friends or family. Sooner or later, everyone realized Satoru was not worth their time.

"Hey. Not so bad. Calm down." Satoru blinked to hear his native tongue coming from Kara Beth. It was surprising enough to yank him out of his mental tailspin. "No sorry Satoru. Everyone happy alive. No angry." She moved to the other side of the hospital bed so she could rub his shoulder without disturbing the arm that could not be jostled under any circumstances. "We love. Doctor say okay. Skate again. Is okay ."

Satoru felt the breath returning to his lungs, and some measure of calm and reason, but things were far from okay. The tears still flowed without restraint. The long-term effects of this disaster still loomed on the horizon, both physically and in terms of the skating season. But he let his coach's reassurance wash around him like the tide on the beach, smoothing even the roughest rocks into sand. "I'm sorry," he said when he could speak again. "I'm sorry for everything." He felt himself getting worked up again, and Kara Beth tightened her grip on his shoulder.

"It's okay. All okay. Don't worry." That was like telling the moon to reverse its orbit. But Kara Beth's broken words were soothing, and Satoru felt the hysteria leave him, to be replaced by the quiet guilt that would slither through his heart and strangle him in the night.

"I won't make the finals," he whispered, hating how the words sounded out loud. He didn't know if Kara Beth understood, but she didn't have to. She'd surely figured it out by now. "People all over the world bought tickets for me. They saved all last year to fly to Osaka and see me skate, and I'm going to ruin their vacations." His jaw trembled, and he tried not to freak out again. "My sponsors support me so that I can get them exposure at these high-profile events, the Federation supports me so I can go represent Japan on these world stages. My family gave up everything so I could skate and now I can't make good on it."

As always, Kara Beth seemed to understand without translation. *"Hey, it is not your fault, got it?* Sad okay. We don't worry that. Happy alive. That's all."

"Why?" The word nearly left Satoru, but he stopped himself. It sounded pathetic to say.

But if he wasn't skating, he truly didn't know the answer.

SATORU DIDN'T KNOW why it took so long to notice. Maybe it was the pain or the exhaustion stealing his focus. Maybe it was his poor brain trying to juggle medical information and police questioning and all the stupid English coming from people he didn't even want to talk to. Thank goodness Kara Beth had locked the media out, because if one of them came barging in with a microphone, Satoru might have exploded. As it was, the only thing that kept him from curling up in the fetal position was the fact that his stomach had been turned inside out and then braided into a rope used for bungee jumping.

But finally, it struck his overloaded little brain that he couldn't see properly.

And that was enough to throw everything else to the side. Satoru sat up in his hospital bed, staring at a picture on the far wall. It was only ten feet away, but he couldn't make out the image. He thought it might be a landscape. The odds favored that guess, but he wasn't sure. When he craned his neck to see into the hallway, he thought he saw a human head bobbing above what might be a desk, but he couldn't make out the face, the gender, or even really confirm it was a desk he was looking at.

It was the flowers that tipped him off. Several of his friends had sent flowers or balloons as get well gifts, including one potted plant that Kara Beth hadn't managed to remove before Satoru noticed. It was an old superstition from his hometown, one he'd never believed in, but one look at that death plant trying to take down roots in his hospital room, and he suddenly believed with his whole heart that those things were bad luck. And while logic defended the poor thing by pointing out the damage was done long before its arrival, Satoru blamed it for everything. Until the police caught his poisoner, he had to blame somebody.

The stupid flowers were gray. Gray, some sick yellows or a muddy green. Satoru had felt a lingering sense that something was weird for a while, but thought that was to be expected, given everything that happened. How could he narrow the undefined weirdness to just one thing? But now, he knew the problem. If someone was going through the trouble of sending him flowers, they'd probably choose ones that looked nice.

It was more than just bad lighting or drab hospital gowns, more than asking Kara Beth when she'd dyed her red hair dark brown, only to get a blank look in response. No one with any sense would send him gray roses, that was for sure. Roses came in red, pink, maybe yellow or white, but never grayish-brown. And he never used to squint to see objects across the room. The more he paid attention to his surroundings, the more Satoru was sure something was wrong.

Trying to say that out loud nearly broke him in two, but the doctors didn't even seem surprised. They ran him through a bunch of eye exams and told him he'd need prescription glasses, and that he was now colorblind. No one but Satoru thought that was a big deal. How the eyes related to his renal function, he'd never understand, but apparently a severe battle with poison could have left him fully blind, so the doctor thought he was getting off easy. Over half the world's population wore glasses, they were easy enough to obtain, it was hardly debilitating. His new deuteranopia would present some chal-lenges as he learned to navigate a world where red and green looked basically the same, but wasn't he lucky it hadn't been worse? He could have died, this was a small sacrifice by comparison, right?

Yes, Satoru nodded his head in a daze. So lucky. What else could he say?

He spent the rest of his day trying to decipher that dumb picture on the far wall until Kara Beth produced a phone. His mother was calling, and did he feel up to talking? Satoru knew then he was the worst son in the world. Calling his parents and letting them know he was alright should have been his first action, not sleeping the hours away or staring into space he couldn't even see. How could he be so inconsiderate?

Kara Beth must have read his mind again, and told him she'd been keeping the Miyazawa family updated, but that wasn't much relief. Satoru should have done it himself. But he did want to hear their voices and accepted the phone with gratitude.

The first sounds were pure cacophony, as all four Miyazawas tried to shout into the receiver at once, but the noise eventually pared down to just his mother. "I'm so relieved! We were all worried about you!"

"Yeah, sorry," he coughed. "I should have called earlier, I'm sorry."

"There you go again," his mother sighed, then turned her head to address the others. "Can you believe this? Barely out of recovery, and the first thing out of his mouth is an apology." Her voice came back to full definition with laughter in the background. "Don't be sorry for anything, just focus on getting well again! How are you feeling?"

"I... don't know." The obvious answer was "horrible", but he couldn't say that. It would just make everyone feel bad, and anyway, he was so *lucky*, right? "They keep poking me with needles, but other than that, I guess I'm alright." Sick, hospitalized, colorblind, near murder victim, how was he supposed to process all of that at once? And in the meantime, there was the status of his skating career to figure out.

"Well, don't you worry about anything, Satoru. Everything's going to be fine, and we'll get you home as soon as possible, okay?"

"Okay." That was one good thing. He'd get to go home and spend time with his family, not that he was going to be much good to them like this. "I can't wait to see you."

"Oh! We miss you, too!" His mother's voice broke, shocking Satoru. "I was so scared! I don't know what we'd do if we lost you!"

Satoru didn't know how to respond to that. "Um, thanks..." He hadn't meant to worry anyone. But he'd missed the real drama, unconscious while he hovered between life and death. If he hadn't been so careless, he'd have noticed that someone had switched his water bottle. He should have checked that, it would have only taken a second, and prevented so much. "You don't need to cry, Mom." He tried to fake a laugh, but his throat was still irritated. "Come on, that's supposed to be my thing."

His mother's laugh was genuine, at least, but he could still hear her pain. "I just don't know who would do this to you."

"Me neither." Across the room, that dumb painting still looked blurry. He could make out a splash of blue in the image, and everything else was a mess of gray and greenish yellow. If those were the colors the artist intended, Satoru would never know. "It's weird to think about..." But he had to, didn't he? It couldn't have been a stranger, only a friend could have gotten so close. Someone in his life was a liar.

But what could he have done to be hated so much? Winning? Seemed like he ticked people off no matter what he did. "Satoru? Are you still there? I can hang up if you need to rest."

"No," he snapped back to the conversation. "Sorry. I am kind of tired." So ridiculously tired. "But it's good to hear your voice." And what was he going to do otherwise? Lay in bed and try not to think about the needle in his arm? Count all the colors he couldn't see? "How is everyone at home?"

"Us? Oh, we're fine. Nothing exciting to report." There was some chattering in the background, and his mother scoffed. "I'm not saying that."

"What?" Satoru asked, and after another weak protest, his mother gave in.

"Izumi says you owe her 1,000 yen and don't think this gets you out of it." That made Satoru burst out laughing, even though his body wasn't quite on board with all that movement.

"Trust me, I'm thrilled I'll get to pay her back." Good for Izumi, she always knew how to break through his moods. "It's the first thing I'll do when I get home."

"The first thing you'll do is rest!" Right. Because he sure wasn't going to be preparing for the Grand Prix. "I know you're not one for taking it easy, but you'll do as your doctor says, understand?"

"I promise," Satoru said, though his mind was already trying to figure out if he could be back on the ice in time to enter some of the Challenger Series.

His mother must have heard the tone in his voice. "I know you're disappointed, but your health is more important."

"Yeah, I know, I just hate this," Satoru mumbled, then cringed. He sounded so whiny. Wasn't the gift of life enough? He had to be more grateful.

"Is there anything I can do to make it better?" His mother's voice was sympathetic, but Satoru couldn't form an answer. "Your father or I can fly out there."

"No, don't," he was quick to protest. They'd move him back to Japan once he was stable, once his kidneys ended whatever vacation they were taking and got back to work, so there was no point wasting time and money on a needless flight. "I'm really fine, just cranky. You don't need to worry."

"I'm your mother. I'll never stop worrying about you, Satoru." He almost cried then. Mothers were selfless, and his more than most. And he couldn't pay any of that back as a helpless invalid. "But I know you. You always want to be on the move. Take care of yourself, and you'll be back on the ice before you know it."

"Yeah," Satoru sighed, but it wasn't enough to be back on the ice. He needed to be back on the podium. People would object if he said so out loud, tell him they'd support him no matter what and results didn't matter, but Satoru had lived through the reality. He couldn't bear it if that inky stain spread far enough to corrupt his mother.

He'd have to get back in shape as soon as he could. "Thanks for calling. And for everything. I'm really grateful."

"We're always thinking of you, Satoru. All of us." She passed the phone to his father, and Satoru shared similar sentiments with him. Then Izumi had a turn and filled her time with terrible jokes, and even Wataru had a few uplifting words. But none of it could fully distract him from the fire that seethed inside him, the desperation to make up for lost time.

It was fine, though, to have the fire burning. He could surpass limits, he could bury mistakes with greater successes. His body could recover, his eyes could adjust to this blurry, yellow-gray world, and Satoru would triumph in the end. It was just a moment that he'd have to sit in the shame of defeat, but he'd be back on the competition circuit and paying back the expectations of all who believed in him, putting the Japanese flag back in the sky.

But then he realized he couldn't see the color of his own flag, and he broke again.

8

EUROPEAN ARCHITECTURE COVERED a wide variety of styles and time periods, but the one thing it all had in common was stone. It drew Satoru to that continent and history more than any other, finding some resonance in people without modern tools hewing blocks out of pure rock and building religious structures all the way to the heavens. Artistic pieces that demanded blood and sweat to build, and created a permanent expression of feeling and devotion.

Not that other types of buildings weren't impressive. The beauty of Japanese pagoda temples could take Satoru's breath away, especially knowing that most Japanese houses in the modern era were only built to last thirty years. That something made of wood could still stand after several centuries was astounding, and showed the love and care of those surrounding the structure. Still, there was something mind-boggling about a culture that imagined cathedrals that touched the clouds, spires and majesty worthy of their God, and built their ambitions out of heavy rock. If he had a time machine, he'd love to go back and meet one of the first people who looked at a mountain cliff and saw it as a canvas.

American architecture fell somewhere in the middle for Satoru. It was a young country, and while there were many styles cropping up over the decades, it had yet to find its iconography in the same way people recognized the styles of Imperial Russia, Aztec ruins or Grecian cities. Even their Statue of Liberty had been a gift from France.

To build something like Rouen Cathedral meant an entire society had to come together with a similar vision. And preserving relics like the Ginja temple needed an entire region of united effort. America's history of immigration and diverse freedoms meant it still had many varied influences and disparate visions. It was too early for wonders like the Taj Mahal.

And yet, America sometimes reminded the world that it was capable of greatness on all fronts, and built something that could stand with the Eiffel Tower and Colosseum. For Satoru, the Empire State Building evoked feelings of ambition, hope, and desperation. They constructed it during the Great Depression, a time when many people didn't have homes or food. And yet, when the country was at its lowest, someone felt their vision of the then-tallest building on earth needed to be realized.

Who knew what the Empire State Building's legacy would be in the coming generations, but Satoru knew what it felt like to be desperate, and to feel behind the rest of the world. To have dreams and desires that reached higher than human hands could build, and the unrealized glory destroying him from the inside out, demanding he build no matter what the cost. "And it's still the site of the longest survived elevator fall, seventy-five stories!"

"No one cares, Satoru."

"But isn't that crazy? That had to be terrifying! From that height, you'd probably feel like you did die."

"I just said no one cares." Wataru looked like he might jump off a building to escape the chatter. "Stop spouting facts to impress people. It's juvenile." He turned back to his computer desk with a scowl. "Just stop talking in general. Your voice sounds like an eighty-year-old man."

Satoru made a face and returned to his book, but not without hiding a cough. Bed rest was the worst. He would have happily left Wataru in his precious solitude if he could, but Satoru didn't ask for the stupid pneumonia. He didn't ask to be poisoned. Nor did he want people hovering over him like he was an invalid. He wanted to be back in his routine, skating and training for the next competition. To be stuck in his old room with Wataru, sleeping most of his days away and bored all the rest of the time, it was torture.

But his brother was right, he did need to lay off the chatter. His throat would get more irritated, he'd have a coughing fit, and he'd already finished his glass of water, which meant he'd have to ask Wataru to get him a new one. And then his brother would sigh and grimace and be all dramatic to prove what an inconvenience Satoru was, but the minute he got called on it would insist Satoru was crazy and making trouble. Of *course* Wataru would do anything to help his sick brother, how *hurtful* it was to say otherwise.

If the two of them were near the Empire State Building, Satoru would pick it up and hit Wataru with it. He sunk back down into his mess of pillows and leafed through the book he was reading, or trying to read. He needed to hold the book a little closer to his face to compensate for his poor vision, as they hadn't picked up his new glasses yet, and the book was in English, a bit too technical for his skill level. Satoru had been nervous when he picked it up, but thought it would be good to challenge himself, and he'd managed to enjoy it so far. He frequently needed to look things up, but Satoru was following the history of the Empire State Building and making new discoveries, so he felt proud of himself. Reading in English used to be too much of a headache to be fun.

But whatever progress he'd made, he still wasn't fluent, and a roadblock was inevitable. He read over a passage several times to glean meaning from context and tried mouthing the offending word, but had to concede defeat. He reached for his phone, only to find the battery had died, and that forced him to call the last resort. "Big Brother? Can you help me with something?"

"What?" His brother sounded irritated, but turned around. "I am busy, you know."

"It'll only take a second. Does *"lightning"* have to do with lightning, or light conditions, like fixtures and things?"

Wataru wrinkled his brow and looked exasperated. "Say that word again?"

"*'Lightning'. Like, lightning rod.*"

"I can't tell what you're trying to say. Your accent's terrible." He grudgingly got up from his chair while Satoru's cheeks burned. "You can't figure it out from context?"

"No..." He showed the book to his brother, and Wataru skimmed over the paragraphs. "I'm just not sure. I thought this was talking about thunderstorms, but this part here is talking about the building lighting up in different colors for holidays, so..."

"Yes, that's the point of separate paragraphs, to discuss different topics," Wataru patronized, then pointed to the words in question. "Lightning rod. On a building to protect it from lightning and ground the electrical charge. 'Lightning' is spelled with an 'N' here, 'lighting' isn't."

"Yeah, I know that," Satoru muttered. He thanked Wataru, but couldn't bear the condescension on his brother's face. "It's just those words are so similar. *Lightning* and *lighting*, and then *lightening*..." Not to mention, 'lighting' could be both a noun and a verb, while 'lightening' could refer to color, brightness, or weight. "When people talk, the words sound almost the same. It's easy to forget which one to use and the meanings and how to spell..." He trailed off when Wataru started laughing.

"You're so lucky you can do sports!" He smiled, but that superior smile that Satoru hated. "Don't worry, not everyone's cut out to be a scholar."

Satoru grimaced, then buried his head back in his book. He hated that evil trio of words. Every time he heard one of them in conversation, his comprehension fell to pieces trying to figure out which meaning it was. Trying to ignore it and latch onto other words in the sentence didn't work; his brain hit *"light"* and refused to go farther. Having to use one of those words himself was even worse, with him stumbling and stammering his way through the thought, trying to do some mental acrobatics just to figure out which syllables he needed and what order they were supposed to go in to convey his meaning. And if he had to conjugate negatives or past tense on top of that? What a nightmare.

Needless to say, he defaulted to *"lights"* whenever he could, bad grammar or no. *"Good lights"*, *"bad lights"*. *"More light"* or *"not light"*. *"Use lights"*, *"stop lights"*. He could get away with that most of the time, but now and then he had to describe the natural phenomena in the sky, and then he fell apart.

"Aren't you ever going to take an English class?" Wataru continued as he returned to his computer. "Start making a serious effort? Really, it's got to be so frustrating for your coach."

"Kara Beth understands me just fine." Most of the time. Satoru had been making a serious effort at English for seven years, what more did people want from him? "I'm a lot better than I was."

"And you still need help reading a children's book."

"It's not a children's-"

"Forgive me. Junior high level."

Satoru wanted to keep arguing, but Wataru was right. He closed the book and pressed the cover against his forehead, as if he could bleed out all of his angry feelings and let the pages absorb them. "I'm not trying to insult you, it's just the truth."

What truth? That Satoru was an idiot? That he was only good for skating? He knew these things already. "Thanks for the help," he ground out. "But please keep the commentary to-" A tickle hit his throat, and he fell into a coughing fit.

"See? I told you to stop talking, you never listen."

Satoru would have glared, but he was busy trying not to choke on his own uvula. Sometimes he wanted to hit Wataru hard enough to make his nose come out the back of his skull. After a minute or two of extended wheezing, he finally croaked out a request for some water.

"It's right there."

"Huh?"

"Beside you. I already got you some water." Satoru blinked, but sure enough, there was a glass of water by his bedside. And Wataru wasn't at his computer, but sitting next to Satoru's futon. He gulped down some water and let it soothe the fire in his throat, before asking, "When did you do that?"

"While you were hacking up your lungs." Wataru raised an eyebrow. "Did you think I was going to just sit there and watch you suffer?"

Yes. That brief period they'd lived together in America supported the idea. Wataru had no bedside manner, he didn't like touching people, he hated Satoru. If Satoru was sick, he got his own cold compresses, made his own soup, took his own temperature, because no way was Wataru coming within a meter of that disease factory. And all the while, his brother would complain that he needed his sleep, he couldn't get sick because he had a job and Satoru didn't understand what the real world was like. Sick or healthy, life with Wataru was walking on eggshells, one wrong move, and Satoru would be...

... what? Dead? Someone had already tried to do that. Satoru allowed that fact to sink in. People hated him. Someone wanted him dead. Someone hated him that much, and Satoru could never make it right.

"What's wrong? Are you crying? Stop that." But Satoru couldn't help it. All his life, he'd been so nervous about doing or saying the wrong thing, disappointing people and making them mad. Afraid he'd let loose the monster in his brother, in his teachers, his old coach, so afraid of their wrath, and now it was no longer hypothetical. Someone wanted him taken out of this world, and nearly succeeded.

"Hey! Hey, come on, you can stop crying now." Wataru looked so confused and helpless. "Can you breathe? What's wrong?"

"Nothing," Satoru gasped, getting the coughs under control, but not the tears. "I'm fine!"

"Clearly not." Wataru looked offended. "You really need to stop the sympathy crying. Grow up."

Sympathy crying? Satoru wanted to strangle him. "If I'm such a baby, why don't you just leave?"

"Because this is my room, for starters."

"It's our room!" Satoru yelled back. "Both of ours! We share it."

"Hmph. For now. You don't live here, remember?" And that stung, to be reminded that Satoru was a guest in the house that raised him. A sick, troublesome guest.

The tears doubled. "Then why don't I just leave?"

"Like that? You can barely crawl to the bathroom." Wataru rolled his eyes while Satoru seethed. "I don't know what's wrong with you, but calm down. Get some sleep, and maybe you'll be more rational when you wake up." And he returned to his computer, leaving Satoru to stew.

Satoru flopped back against his pillows, seeing only rage. "You must have been so disappointed when I didn't die."

That got a reaction. Wataru went stiff. "Excuse me? What did you say?"

He didn't dare respond. Satoru knew he should have kept that thought to himself the moment he'd said it. Of course, by then it was too late.

"You," Wataru said, slow and measured, "Shouldn't say things like that. It's so out of line." There was a pause, as if he was trying to find the best way to yell at Satoru. "I'm sorry about Ohio, all right? A thousand times sorry! I made a mistake, I was wrong, and I'm sorry!" Wataru got to his feet, fists clenched. "At what point are you finally going to let it go?"

"Maybe when you start acting like you mean it," Satoru couldn't stop himself from saying.

Dark clouds gathered around Wataru. "You know, I hate sharing the room," he growled, "and we have nothing in common, but I was trying to make the best of it. I thought if you were ever around for longer than a day, if you ever stopped skating for five minutes, maybe we'd find something to bond over. Maybe I'd have a real brother instead of some stranger who drops in a few times a year." The thought overrode Satoru's anger, if only slightly. He'd wanted the same thing for so long. "But if you want to be a brat about this, fine! Enjoy your new room. I'll bunk with Izumi."

"No, wait!" Satoru groaned, now feeling guilty. "I'm sorry, I shouldn't have said that. I'm just... frustrated." And scared. And angry. He was every feeling on the spectrum, happy to be alive, resentful of everything that came with it. "You're right, I'm being a brat, and I'm sorry."

Wataru looked him over, then calmed down as well. "I'm sorry, too." He didn't look especially sorry, but at least he wasn't yelling anymore. He sat down beside Satoru's futon. "Before all this happened, I said things were going to get better. I meant that," he said in all seriousness. "It is going to get better."

"Okay." Satoru didn't know what else to say. He'd like to believe it, but they just kept falling back into their old patterns. Maybe they were just too different to ever be real brothers.

After a minute of silence, Wataru picked up Satoru's book and handed it to him. "So, Empire State, huh? Learn anything interesting?"

"Huh?"

"Tell me about it." He leaned back, and Satoru's hands gripped the edges of his book for a lifeline.

"I thought you said no one cares."

"Maybe someone does. A little." Wataru shook his head. "I've got stuff to do, but I can take a break for a bit. Tell me what makes your building so important."

They were too different. There was no way Satoru could come up with any fact to interest Wataru. But his brother was asking anyway, giving him his time. Maybe things didn't get better overnight, maybe Satoru needed to give them a little time to build.

"Well, every year they have a race and athletes run from the ground to the 86th floor. The record is nine minutes and thirty-three seconds."

"It always comes back to sports for you, doesn't it?"

COMPETITIONS WERE STRESSFUL, but the exhibitions that followed were joy. As much as Damien loved the feeling of pushing his limits and raising the stakes higher, it was a relief to go out and skate a program that was just for fun, he could play around and enjoy the art of skating, turn some triples instead of quads, and show off some of his skills that weren't given point values in competitive arenas. After a weekend where everything revolved around winning, it was a gift to remind everyone that skating and sports were supposed to be enjoyable.

That felt especially important at this time. Damien went out and skated his playful show program under the spotlights, clapped and laughed alongside his fellow athletes and posed for all the pictures, but his heart never settled. For one person in their elite circle, it wasn't enough to stand in second place, or fulfilling to cheer others on. If not here at Bordeaux for the Internationaux de France, then elsewhere in the world was a contemporary that didn't feel uplifted in celebrating the talents of others. Someone in his acquaintance thought winning was the only value in a sporting event, and would kill in order to have it for themselves.

Because why else would someone harm Satoru Miyazawa?

The boy had his flaws, but none worth killing over. Damien rode the shuttle back to the hotel, the exhibition lights fading into the background, and felt his mood darkening. One of their friends was a liar.

But who? How was anyone supposed to get to the bottom of things when there were so many suspects and all of them fluttered around the globe like leaves on the wind? He wanted to believe the police were doing their jobs, but he just didn't see how anyone could track Satoru's poisoner under these conditions. A crime like that deserved to be punished.

"Whoa, watch where you're going, Dami!" Damien snapped out of his thoughts and realized he was in the hotel lobby, and had nearly knocked over Clara Bertinelli. He'd made it off the bus on autopilot, and only now noticed his surroundings. The young ice dancer from Canada didn't seem offended, and teased, "You're so lost in thought, we'll have to send a rescue team after you!"

"Sorry."

"No big. But since I have you, a bunch of us are going out to celebrate. Wanna come?"

Damien hesitated. Going out usually meant food. Which meant smells and sights that disgusted him, even if he wasn't eating. And it meant constantly refusing the meals and drinks shoved in his face, or having to explain that he wasn't hungry and then enduring the looks from people who thought he should eat anyway. It was easier to just go back to his hotel room and avoid all of it. "Thank you, but no. I think I'm just going to rest."

"Aw, please, Dami! We hardly ever see you anymore!" Her brother and dance partner, Mark, joined Clara, and the pleading continued in stereo. "Join the party?"

"Yeah, we haven't caught up in ages! It won't be the same without you. We swear it's not just 'cause we need you to translate the French menus for us," Mark added with a grin, and Damien laughed.

"All right. For a while, at least." The Bertinellis were ecstatic, and after everyone changed and deposited their gear in their rooms, the group crowded into a small restaurant down the street. The wait staff gave them a large enough table to accommodate the skaters, but the seating arrangements became a game of musical chairs as people travelled from one end to the other to have conversations with everybody.

Besides the Bertinellis, the party also included Sokonthy Masters, a former pairs skater turned singles despite being thirty-one and the mother of a toddler, Mariah Birch and Emil Reich, a German pairs team who were extremely happy Sokonthy had switched disciplines, and Inessa Levi, the reigning ladies' champion. Rounding out the party was Sione Tulafono, a man who dreamed of being the first Samoan to win an Olympic medal for figure skating, and he was known as much for his skating as for hugging people with the power of a two-tonne truck. "Damien! It's good to have you back! Congratulations again, my friend!"

"And to you," Damien said, once his ribs recovered from the impact. "Your skating is masterful, as always." And it was; Sione was built with the dimensions to succeed in American football, tall and broad. But he worked hard to keep his body lean, and sunk all his free time into ballet lessons and *siva* in order to get that large frame to move with grace. Adding in the natural gift of his leg muscles, and Sione was a force to be reckoned with, though learning quadruple jumps had been a challenge for him.

Some thought he might have been more successful as a pairs skater, as he wouldn't need the quads and could make use of his impressive strength for twists and throw jumps, but Sione remained a single's skater. Whether that was just his dream, or due to the lack of Samoan female skaters to be his partner was never said, but either way, the financial side of figure skating had always been Sione's greater challenge. His country had little in the way of ice rinks or skating programs, and it was an uphill fight to get to represent them on the world stage.

But here he was, among the elite. "A good night for both of us! Silver's not a bad color on me, and God above, it's so good to finally see you back in gold!" Damien was a little taken aback, even though he was used to Sione's effusive compliments. "We've all waited way too long for that!"

Weren't competitors supposed to push you down the stairs? "It's kind of you to say so…"

"Kind? It's fact!" Sione boomed, his voice not knowing how to communicate at any other decibel. "It was only a matter of time. Much as I'd love to take the gold back home, it's better to know you're healthy again."

Damien really didn't know what to say, and so just thanked him. He wasn't used to such compliments outside of Satoru. Despite knowing Sione to be honest, if overly grand, Damien's brain tried to convince him the words couldn't be sincere. He was far too used to lies and pretty words that concealed a hidden agenda. But the gregarious nature of Sione was born from an innocent appreciation for the entire world around him, and Damien wished he could be more like that himself.

And Sione was correct; it was good to be healthy again. "My accomplishments are nothing compared to the Bertinelli twins," he deferred to Clara and Mark, who beamed at the well-deserved praise. They weren't actually twins, but triplets. They had a brother who also took skating lessons from an early age, and pursued ice dance along with his siblings. He and his partner had won Canadian Nationals the previous season only a few tenths of a point over Clara and Mark.

Damien thought there must have been some awkward family dinners after that, but the teams of Wah/Bertinelli and Bertinelli/Bertinelli were surprisingly free of drama in public. He only wished his own family could put aside their egos so easily. "To reverse the gender roles on the lift was very daring," Damien said, speaking of the traditional practice of the male skater lifting the woman off the ice. In ice dance, the rules allowed for the female to lift the male, and Clara and Mark were taking full advantage this season.

"Got to set ourselves apart somehow," Mark laughed, and nudged Clara. "And why should she get all the glory? I want to fly, too." The choreographic lift where Mark flipped over Clara's shoulders nearly stopped Damien's heart when he saw it.

"Isn't it great to be a skater now?" Sione asked. "It feels like we've entered an era with room for all kinds of skills. No mold's guaranteed to win, and we'll all leave our mark. I feel blessed."

Damien couldn't do anything but agree. In the men's discipline, the quadruple jumps were still necessary, but they weren't the only achievement. Amazing things happened when a skater looked at some of their other skills and maximized them. Even Satoru, who seemed to have mastered everything, could have his podium shaken if one focused on their own strengths and attacked them with the same level of drive.

But it reminded him that there was someone out there who didn't agree, who thought the only way to win was to push others down. It cast a shadow over the party atmosphere for Damien, an extra guest at the table that could be ignored but not silenced.

Even so, he was glad he hadn't spent the evening alone and brooding. Despite the occasional reminders that there was something sick in the world and the abundance of food that sometimes turned Damien's stomach, the gathering did lift his spirits. He even managed to nibble on an appetizer. The Bertinellis were right, it had been too long since he'd talked to everyone. After withdrawing from Worlds last year, he'd unconsciously retreated into the hermit-like behavior of his teens. It was easy to forget how much he enjoyed socializing when his stomach preferred to take the path of least resistance. But in stepping out of his comfort zone a little, and not letting his health problems dictate his life, he could fill his world with good friends and shared experiences, rather than isolation.

He had Satoru to thank for that. They weren't friends in the beginning, but that shrewd boy figured out why Damien refused everyone else's invitations to hang out, and decided it wasn't acceptable. And like that, Damien had a fifteen-year-old shadow inserting itself into his life, demanding Damien's presence with little to no words. Satoru dragged him along through all his activities, and introduced him to his friends until they became Damien's as well. "This Dami. He come with us," he'd say in a tone that was both affable and non-negotiable. "Nice guy. You'll like." Satoru joked, smiled and charmed his way through every barrier, and Damien benefited by association until one day he realized people were still talking to him when Satoru wasn't around.

All those years before Ohio, and Damien never realized he was lonely. He picked at the lucky orange watch that Kara Beth had returned to him, reflecting on his last conversation with Satoru. He wished he'd said something more meaningful.

"Hey, Damien, whatcha staring at?" He realized he'd let his attention wander, and craned his neck to see Sokonthy Masters calling to him from further down the table. "Quit spacing out on us! This is a party!"

"I'm sorry. I've been guilty of that a lot today."

"I'm sure a champion's mind is full of heavy thoughts, too big for us mortals."

"Oh, stop," Damian scoffed, while Sokonthy changed seats to continue their chat more conveniently, "As if you weren't also standing proudly on your podium."

"On it, but silver isn't gold, little boy. I couldn't break Levi." But

Sokonthy didn't seem bitter. "Still, I'm going to make the Grand Prix Finals. This old lady can still fight!"

Damien shook his head. "With you and Alisha out there, maybe people will stop putting so much emphasis on age."

"Don't I wish. On the other hand, it means there's no expectation on me, I don't have to prove anything, total freedom. I'm just in this for the giggles."

"I don't believe you. But it's good to enjoy something other than winning." He picked at the tablecloth to avoid looking at the messy plates. Food was unappetizing enough, but the smeared remains of it were vomit inducing. "I wish more of the world would think this way."

"Hmm. You're definitely not happy enough for a guy who just won gold in front of his home crowd. What happened?"

"Nothing. Not to me, at least." He sighed, but decided he could tell the truth to Sokonthy. When it came to figure skating, she had seen it all. "My entire senior career has been spent chasing Satoru. That I have not been healthy enough to challenge him is no one's fault but my own," he said with a wry look at the bread basket beside him. "But this year has been different. I was excited to finally face my rival with the best that is in me. Now I am a worthy competitor, and he will not be at the finals."

"That's too bad."

"It's no accident!" Damien reminded, though he supposed there were no words weighty enough to express remorse. He lowered his eyes back to the tablecloth. "It will be a lonely Grand Prix without my friend beside me."

Sokonthy made a noise of sympathy, then leaned in close. "I heard it was another skater," she whispered, glancing furtively to the side. "Someone in the competition poisoned him. Switched out the water bottles. That true?"

"So I hear." They fell silent for a moment, but it was only a matter of time. It was the question on everyone's mind, and certainly the one on Damien's for the past several days. Ever since he stepped off the plane and realized that everything was the same as every year before, and someone had gotten away with attempted murder.

Sokonthy took the leap. "Who could have done it?"

"I think the results from Skate America provide a list of suspects," Damien made a face. "Derek has wanted to take Satoru down for years. And Yukiya, without Satoru, he becomes the new Japanese champion. Marco Velazquez is good, but he has never been on the podium on a stage like this. Now that Satoru's out, he might scavenge enough points for the finals. There's no shortage of motive."

"But would they?" Sokonthy asked, and Damien faltered. "I can't see any of them going so far as to murder. Even Derek."

"We see these people a few times a year," Damien reminded. Bonds were forged quickly in intense situations, but competition was still war. "How well do we really know them?"

"This is the question we all ask," Inessa interjected, and both Sokonthy and Damien were surprised to find her listening in. Inessa just rolled her eyes. "You talk too loud."

"Yeah," Clara said from the seat next to her. "You want a private gossip, get a room." She leaned in to join the conversation. "You've talked to Satoru, then? Do the police know anything?"

"I think if they did, the media would be on it in seconds," Sokonthy answered for Damien, and he agreed.

"I've not heard of any new discovery. But I do know that Derek has dragged that same cheap water bottle to every competition, and it is suddenly absent this weekend."

"Have you told the police?"

"Of course," was the dark reply. "For all it is worth. That trinket is easy to obtain, and the reasons to dispose of it are plausible. All he has to do is deny it."

Clara looked thoughtful. "But wouldn't it be too obvious? I mean, yeah, Derek benefits, but he's got to know that if he kills Satoru, the whole world's going to be looking at him. He's already taken a huge hit in the press, even his British tabloids are giving him the side-eye."

"Since when does Derek care what people think? It's not like the tabloids can arrest him."

"I still think we assume too much," Inessa disagreed, and put forth her own idea. "The Japanese men have many contenders for silver. Many skaters, but only a few spots on the world team. Satoru has said Nationals sometimes feels like The Hunger Games. People would give anything to secure one of those spots."

"So, who, Yukiya? That little cinnamon roll?" Sokonthy shook her head. "It's a stretch, even if he had opportunity and some motive."

"I don't mean Yukiya," Inessa said, now sobering. "Just because skaters play fair doesn't mean our Federations do." Silence fell over the table.

Damien wasn't sure if they were more frightened by the audacity of the idea, or the plausibility. But Inessa hadn't said her words lightly. "Politics and lobbying are one thing," he finally said. "Even bribing judges, I will believe. But murder?"

"And to take out Japan's biggest athlete right before Worlds is terrible business sense," Sokonthy added with a callous practicality. "Our placement at Worlds determines how many athletes each country takes to the Olympics, and they need Satoru to win this year so they can get maximum slots. Yukiya and the second stringers can't fill those shoes by themselves. They'd be throwing away everything, and no petty problem with Sato's worth that, if one even exists. I'd kill his coach first, she's the one they're always iffy about."

Damien shot her a look that could pierce titanium, but had to concede her point. "But if some other country was weary of Japan's dominance, that could be motive. Japan loses their three slots, another country moves higher up in the ranks?"

"Yeah, but can England even make use of that?" Sokonthy countered. "Derek's the best they've got, the guy under him barely passed the technical requirements to enter Worlds last year ."

"Same for Sione," Inessa said, but dropped her voice so that the skater in question didn't overhear. Though he seemed too absorbed in his conversation with Mark, Mariah and Emil for it to be necessary. "He skates quite well, so Western Samoa will get two slots, but they don't have enough skaters to take advantage of it." Nobody brought up France's stake in the events, to Damien's relief.

But Clara looked uncomfortable. "Guys, I just realized we're talking about the people who rule our lives trying to kill us. Does that scare anyone else?" They all shared grim looks around the table, but it was Inessa who answered.

"Whether an individual or organization, it doesn't matter," she said, and Damien noticed her fingers had been twisting the edge of the tablecloth. "Since Satoru was hurt, I have been scared every day."

9

SATORU WAS NOT a fan of his new glasses. Izumi told him he was being a baby, and should be glad he matched the rest of the family. And he had to give her that; it was stupid to complain when his mother, father and both of his siblings all wore glasses, but that didn't mean Satoru was used to them. They slipped down his nose sometimes, and he had trouble finding them in the morning. They made weird indents on the side of his nose and the back of his ears.

He also wasn't sure what color they were. When he'd gone to pick them out, he'd mustered some enthusiasm for looking at the frames, and found a stylish pair in an elegant, soft gray. When he showed them to Izumi, she wrinkled her nose and asked why he was going with "traffic cone orange"? Satoru dropped the frames and told her he'd wear whatever she picked out. He thought the result was black, but he didn't dare trust anything anymore.

The glasses were also a problem for running. Satoru finally had enough strength to handle jogging around the block in the mornings, but the glasses bounced with every step. They fogged up in the cold air. He had contacts as well, but he wasn't sure if he'd ever get used to them.

But he had to get used to a lot of things. Satoru entered the family house and removed his shoes, grumbling when his glasses immediately turned into white clouds. He resisted the urge to take them off and hurl them down the hall, and instead wiped them on his shirt. There was no reason to get so angry at such a small thing, and after all, he was *so* lucky.

So lucky to run for five minutes, then spend the next half hour catching his breath. He sat down on the stairs while the world spun, praying that he could get back to basic functionality before anyone noticed how much trouble he was having. The doctor cleared him for light exercise, but also warned not to push himself too hard, and his mother wouldn't find his current state of misery within those bounds.

But he couldn't keep waiting around, either. Satoru eventually got his breath back and staggered to his feet. He was about to go upstairs, but heard a sound from the spare room and turned. His father had spent the past few years carving out half of the storage room to claim for his hobbies, since their mother had taken over the balcony garden and just about every other room with her plants.

Satoru peeked in to see what his father was working on. Miyazawa Shinji built miniatures in his spare time and had a steadier hand than a surgeon for tiny details. The storage room was full of small shrines and pagoda temples, villages and cityscapes. He made them out of whatever materials were handy, often snatching cardboard or paper out of someone's hand before it went into the recycling if he liked the look of it, and he would transform it into a work of art. Bits of metal or screws, splinters of wood or plastic containers, all of it found a second life as a miniature.

Izumi always insisted they should begin a side business selling these creations, and their father did cave every few years and set up a booth at a street festival to clear out some space, but he otherwise kept his collection to himself or gave them as gifts. He preferred making traditional Japanese buildings, but occasionally dabbled in something more modern or further from home. He had a replica of the Sydney Opera house high on a shelf, complete with tiny posters advertising Pavarotti, and in the corner was a two-foot tall rendering of Notre Dame de Paris, a birthday gift for Satoru that would have sat in his apartment now if they were brave enough to ship something so fragile by mail.

It bothered Satoru that his father worked so hard on something that his son was rarely around to enjoy. But every time he thought of having it shipped, he remembered how callously airport workers tossed bags into the luggage compartments. They'd surely use more care if the package were marked 'fragile', but Satoru couldn't bring himself to risk it. His father pointed out that Satoru wouldn't be competing forever, and the miniature cathedral could safely wait until he came back to Japan and put down roots. So it remained in his parents' house, watched over by his father, until the day Satoru had a home of his own.

But it still bothered him. One more way he didn't show appreciation, and would have to make up for once he turned professional. One more reason he had to get back on that podium and prove it was all worth it. One more reason to give up his secondary home on the other side of the ocean.

He leaned against the wall and watched his father meticulously twisting and gluing tiny bits of pink tissue paper to a tree that appeared to have been crafted from the remains of an old toaster. The inner coils had been twisted and reformed into branches and roots, the cord had been stripped and the wires wrapped around a bolt to form the trunk, the whole of which was mounted on a cardboard base. Next to the tree, the metal shell of the toaster became the reflective pool of a pond, with a family of little paper ducks swimming on the surface.

The pink tissue paper was being turned into cherry blossoms, but Satoru noticed that one of the handmade blossoms was glued onto the cardboard ground. "Why isn't it on the tree with the rest of the flowers?"

His father didn't look up from his work, but smiled to himself. "Does the blossom stop being beautiful just because it separates from the tree?"

"I guess not," Satoru considered. He wasn't sure if there was supposed to be a metaphor in that. "They don't last too long, though."

"And so man invented art." His father gestured for Satoru to take a seat on a nearby box, which he did gratefully. Once around the block, and his legs still wobbled ten minutes later. "How are you feeling?"

"Better, I guess." He felt like screaming, or drowning himself in the bathtub. The only thing that helped him hang onto his calm was the promise that he could get on the ice tomorrow and try a brief stroking session. "It feels weird to just laze around the house all day. I don't know what I'm supposed to do."

"We need to get you a hobby."

"I had a hobby. That's the problem." And with skating largely absent from the picture, Satoru was confronted with his deficiency. Without skating, he contributed little to the world, a parasite. "I tried to go volunteer at the community center yesterday, but just walking there wiped me out. The kids wanted me to play basketball, and I had to take a break every other minute." Not to mention that once people realized it was *the* Miyazawa Satoru in the building, he created a brief commotion. But volunteering was a good way to fill his time back in Granville, so he'd thought he could do something useful at home. "I get tired so easily now. When I sat down to help a guy from the Philippines with his job application, I nearly nodded off a few times. I felt so bad."

"I'm sure he wasn't offended," his father reassured, though Satoru doubted it. Hopefully, the man got the job despite Satoru's questionable help. "You've been sick. This exhaustion won't last forever. In the meantime, try something less taxing. What about sewing? You seem to have a talent for that."

"I wouldn't call it talent." And the problem wasn't finding something to keep himself occupied during the day. He needed something with purpose, a reason to validate his continued existence. "And no one really needs anything."

"No one needs these trinkets of mine, but I make them anyway." His father took one of the tissue paper blossoms and carefully twisted it closed. He tore off a corner of a flyer with a bold green pattern and wrapped it around the outside, then took a pointed tool and pushed the edges of the paper into a smooth position. "Izumi would worship you if you made her a new dress."

That was an idea. Something that would make his family members happy filled the need in Satoru, but his mood didn't lift. After all, it only fulfilled his short-term problem. Even if he returned to competitive skating soon, and even if he could recover his former skills, he'd have to stop someday. Like Alisha, he'd eventually have to face the possibility of retirement and decide what he was going to do with the rest of his life. A hobby wasn't going to cut it. Maybe he'd find a career as a professional skater, but he couldn't do that forever, either. What remained after that?

And where would he live? Tokyo seemed the obvious choice, but Satoru had seen so much of the world, could he really settle down to one area? It wasn't 'home' in the same sense of the word, but Satoru had grown to love Ohio. Especially that one little house in Granville... How could he just cut Kara Beth and the others out of his life?

His phone buzzed, shaking Satoru out of his thoughts for a moment. He held it out and tilted the screen, then let it go to voice-mail. But his father noticed. "Who was that?"

"Damien."

"Oh, how is he?"

"Good. Winning everything." Satoru slumped a little further. "I haven't really talked to him since it happened."

"Why not?"

"I should be congratulating him. He's doing so well right now. Like, the best in years," Satoru emphasized, "But all I can think of is how I'm losing the Grand Prix. Why would he want to talk to someone so selfish?"

"I'll bet he thinks the same thing about you, in some of his prick-lier moods." There might have been truth to that. His father glued the latest blossom to the tree, the green paper turning it into a premature bud. It looked out of place in the explosion of proud blossoms.

"What's wrong with that one?"

"Blossoms don't all bloom at the same time. Nature works on its own timeframe, not ours," his father said, moving on to the next, normal tissue flower. "It'll fulfill its ultimate destiny in time."

"To be pretty for a second, then fall and get crunched by a thousand shoes," Satoru muttered. His father turned sharply. "What? That's the metaphor, isn't it?" The cherry blossom bloomed for such a short period, then disappeared. The beauty was stunning, but couldn't last, and so became a symbol of the precious and transient nature of life. But a fall from grace was still a fall, no matter how pretty you looked on the way down.

"You're very pessimistic lately."

"Sorry." Satoru mustered up a little chagrin. "I'm just frustrated."

"I wonder why." They shared rueful looks. "But things will be all right in time."

Satoru wasn't so sure. "I feel like I got robbed. Everybody jokes that I'll be competing till I'm an old man, but the truth is I only have so many years at this. I can't turn quads forever, so time is precious. Even if I'm capable of competing past the next Olympics, that doesn't mean I should."

"What would stop you?"

"I have to start paying you back."

His father snorted. "We're not destitute. Things were tight for a few years, but your skating pays for itself now." Yes, between sponsors and prize money, he was doing well, and he still taught at Kara Beth's rink sometimes. But that wasn't the point.

"Yeah, but-"

"Money isn't important, Satoru. Even your skating isn't." His father put down his work, as if aware that he'd just uttered blasphemy. "Your mother and I only care about who you are as a person. Nothing makes us happier than having a son who is honest, hardworking and kind. For that, we're proud of you." It was high praise, and the words were a relief to hear, but Satoru felt guilty as well. He wasn't always on point in the kindness department. If his parents saw him sniping with Derek, they probably wouldn't be so proud of him. Their patience with him would wear out before the convalescing was over.

But he couldn't find a way to explain the turmoil he still felt, so he stayed quiet as his father resumed work on the cherry tree. With its boughs full of branches, it was really taking shape. It wasn't realistic, but there was still a living beauty crafted from the man-made materials. His father transformed junk and garbage into something that lasted, and etched out an image of transience before it could fade. It both inspired and frustrated Satoru. All life was short, and if that was the destiny of everyone, then was it wrong to want to be the brightest, pinkest blossom on the tree? Or was he just that desperate to pretend he was relevant?

His father continued to add small touches here and there, further elevating the project. "You know, metaphors mean whatever people want them to mean. The cherry blossom isn't about transience at all, but permanence."

"How so?"

"The point of the blossom isn't to be admired, but to bear fruit or seeds. The petals fade away, but the essence of the flower lives on, and eventually becomes a new tree, and flowers again." His father smiled to himself, but kept his eyes on his task. "It never really dies. It comes back after every winter, and makes more flowers, and more seeds. The cherry blossom isn't a temporary beauty, but one that's lived since the creation of the earth, and will outlive all of us."

"I guess that's one way to look at it." It was an interesting thought. The blossoms faded, disappeared for a while, but were never truly gone. Just reincarnated after a period of rest. Like he was revived at the end of every summer, taking the ice in full bloom.

But the winters were brutal, whatever time of year they arrived. Satoru leaned on the craft table and sighed. "Or it's just a tree."

"Maybe. I suppose they don't really care about being poetic. Still, this tree was born because of a fallen blossom like that one," his father said, pointing to the lone flower on the cardboard ground. "What a fool that tree would be, to feel ashamed that it was once a flower in the mud."

Satoru rested his head on his arms, a clumsy action with his new glasses in the way. But he found a new appreciation for the frames that provided some barrier against the atmosphere that stung his eyes and made them water.

"Thanks," he whispered into his elbow, and half-hoped his father didn't hear. If he did, the man only acknowledged it by gluing another blossom on the tree.

CUP OF CHINA was the absolute worst. Not in terms of skating-that had been amazing. And Shanghai was a beautiful city. The weather had been great, the event ran smoothly, and all four disciplines performed well. Everything that had to do with the locale and the actual business of being on the ice had been an exceptional experience.

It was the press conferences that ruined everything. "Has competition changed for you since the incident at Skate America?"

Isaac Bertinelli stared into the flashing lights and wondered if all the camera shutters had distorted the sound. He looked over at his ice dance partner, Hser Nay Wah, but she'd been done with the press conference since it began, and once the words left the journalist's mouth, leaned back in her chair and gave up all pretense of courtesy. On his left, Bronze medalists Ellen McGregor and Graham Bartholomew were deliberately not making eye contact with him. He turned to Chen Huan and Song Min on his right, who had just finished listening to the Chinese translation. Huan's eyes widened, and she mouthed to Isaac, "You first."

As the winners, Isaac and Hser Nay were expected to have the first response of the group, which was the only downside of that gold medal. He never knew what to say in interviews. Hser Nay always knew what to say, but it was generally a bad idea to let her talk. She spoke her mind and had no tolerance for questions that were too personal or mundane in the extreme, and would respond with her undiluted and scathing thoughts. Normally his girlfriend was quite sweet, but when that patience ran out, she had no problem telling the world about it.

So Isaac was on his own. He doubted it would help, but he tried to cut the question off at the knees. "Hser Nay and I weren't at Skate America. So we can't compare." When he leaned back from the microphone, Huan and Min were glaring at him. They didn't speak a lot of English, but they didn't have to in order to realize Isaac had thrown the bomb towards them and ran.

But they recovered quickly. Their answer translated to, "Our job is to skate each program to the best of our ability, so we try to keep our focus on the event." They answered without actually saying anything, leaving Ellen and Graham to try their escape.

It was even shorter than Isaac's response. "Our program stayed the same." After a long pause, Ellen just shrugged.

"Nothing to add."

Isaac hoped that would be enough of a clue that nobody wanted to talk about this. Of course, every skater had thoughts about the events surrounding Satoru Miyazawa, whether it was outrage at the crime itself, fear that the same thing could happen to them, or anger at the ways the situation was handled or not handled. But there were better places to express those thoughts than at the medalists' press conference for ice dance, and some thoughts were too personal to be shared with strangers. For Isaac, who'd known Satoru since he was fifteen, the topic was way too sensitive for a reporter just trying to make their headlines.

But the press didn't take the hint, and the next one knew better than a yes or no question. "The events of Skate America were shocking, to say the least. Describe the effect this crime has had on the skating community and on competition in general."

That was followed by, "Do you feel the competitive environment encourages rivalries and acts of violence?" and "Talk about the pressure put on elite athletes to excel. Do you think the emphasis is more on winning than sportsmanship?"

It wasn't long before Hser Nay couldn't keep up her illusion of a cute, demure little ice princess. "What a stupid question."

Isaac winced, but didn't stop her. It had been a long competition, and an even longer press conference. He sat back and let his partner go nuts. "Of course there's pressure to win! When was the last time we got medals for sportsmanship? The bottom line's always about winning, otherwise you just have an expensive hobby. I mean, yeesh, everyone still grills us if we wobble at World Team Trophy! Like, you all tell us to have fun and skate nice with the other kids, but no one means it. And you're suddenly going to pretend all the politics and lobbying is a surprise? Give me a break!"

Graham let out a soft laugh, though Ellen looked like a deer in headlights. Hser Nay continued with a disdainful look at all the camera flashes. "And don't act like you guys have nothing to do with it. If you cared about sportsmanship over winning, you wouldn't be asking so many questions about why we didn't win, do we secretly hate the guys who did win, whatever. Or you," she suddenly pointed at a reporter in specific, and Isaac realized too late where she was going with that. "Kentwall Sports Magazine? You covered the Grand Prix last year. I remember you wrote that piece trying to make drama between Isaac and his siblings. Where was everyone's sportsmanship then?"

The press conference finished shortly after Hser Nay finished up her tear, and Isaac was only too happy to get out of there. The room was twice as loud and seemed to have four times as many cameras as when they started. Poor Ellen still looked shell-shocked by Hser Nay's candor, but Huan and her partner honored it with slow claps and matching smirks. Isaac put a hand on Hser Nay's arm to soothe her agitation, but it wasn't until they'd left the building entirely that she regained any semblance of good humor.

They walked down the Shanghai streets, hand in hand, until Hser Nay finally exhaled. "I'm sorry."

"No, you're not."

"Well, I will be once that press con goes viral." She pursed her lips together. "I can't stand public speaking."

"I know. It's more stressful than the free dance."

"It's like, the one time someone asks something unique, and it's still dumb. What are they expecting us to say? If we wanted to share our opinions on that, wouldn't we have done that by now? It's not like we just put our brains in cold storage until someone comes along and asks what we think."

"What brains? We are jocks," Isaac pointed out, earning a scoff. He gave her shoulder a soft bump with his. "They're just doing their jobs. Something interesting's got to go in those papers."

"Then they can write about our skating," Hser Nay snapped. "We spent forever trying to raise the level of that serpentine sequence, no one wants to talk about that? They could ask about our training regime, our off-ice work, anything related to what we're actually doing out there! I don't want to talk about which of our friends might be a killer, not in front of strangers."

"Yeah." Isaac also didn't want to share his thoughts with someone searching for a soundbite. Even so, if he kept those thoughts in his head forever, he'd explode. "But the competition has changed, hasn't it?"

Hser Nay hesitated, but nodded. "I can't explain why. Skating is still the same, warming up is the same..." But maybe someone would spike your water bottle if you looked away too long. "I can't believe whoever did that is going to get away with it."

"They're not going to-"

"It's been weeks!" Hser Nay interrupted. Her walking slowed to a complete halt, and Isaac stopped beside her. "What are the police even doing? Can't they get a fingerprint, or DNA, or something?"

"I'm sure they're trying."

"Trying isn't good enough!" She pulled her hand away from Isaac's. "Not a single lead? We don't even really know why this happened! Maybe someone else could be next? This is stuff we need to know!"

"You think there's other targets?" Isaac asked, surprised. "What would be the point of that?"

"I don't know, what's the point of killing Satoru?"

"To be the men's champion?"

"Over Damien's dead body," Hser Nay retorted. "And if we live in a world where he's actually behind this, I don't even want to be alive."

"Ditto." Isaac reached out and took a lock of Hser Nay's black hair, curling it around his fingers. "It's gonna be okay, Hser," he told her with a peck on the nose. He gathered his girlfriend in his arms, and she slumped against him.

"I just want things back to normal. I want Sato back, I want this guy behind bars..." She sniffled and rubbed her nose against Isaac's shoulder. "I'm sick of all of this."

"Me, too. But it's out of our control, so you have to try to keep your chill." He could tell she didn't accept that answer. "What could you or I do about this?"

Hser Nay froze, then pulled out of the hug with an incredulous look on her face, that quickly morphed into a look that Isaac knew he needed to worry about.

"You know, that's the first good question anyone's asked me..."

BEFORE ISAAC KNEW IT, he was reunited with the teams of Chen/Song and McGregor/Bartholomew in Hser Nay's hotel room. Alisha Brian was there as well, being their only fellow representative of Team Canada not otherwise occupied. There were over half a dozen computers between them, and five sets of confused eyes. "What exactly are we doing?"

"We are going to catch that would-be murderer on tape," Hser Nay declared. She organized a bunch of pens, post-its, and notebooks in front of everyone. "Someone switched out Satoru's water bottle for one filled with poison, and we're going to find them."

"How?" Alisha asked, and Chen Huan followed the question with "What?"

Isaac wasn't sure he got it, either, but he tried to explain. "There's always a bunch of cameras on us at competition, right? Maybe someone saw something."

"Well, yeah, but don't you think the police thought of that?" Graham asked, while Huan and Min put their heads together and started whispering in Chinese. "I bet the first thing they did was request the footage from security."

"Yeah, security," Hser Nay rolled her eyes. "But what about the five thousand fancams that were going on?"

That gave everybody pause. "Marco Velázquez sometimes records videos for his website, and Amina Massot's got her vlog. I know Eric Blaine took a ton of pictures of his first time at the Grand Prix," Isaac listed. "There's a lot of eyes backstage that the police might not have thought to look through, or even had the time."

"And there'll be multiple recordings of the open practices," Graham said, as the room started to realize all the resources available to them. "Probably one from every imaginable angle."

"Exactly. Figure skating fans are nuts, and Sato's top dog," Hser Nay explained. "Every time he steps out of his hotel room, someone's trying to get a picture or video. They want to know what he eats, how he stretches, what his coach is like, what stuff he brings to competition. I bet we can track that water bottle through the entire weekend if we look hard enough."

"We make timeline?" Min questioned, looking hesitantly around the group for confirmation. "Internet find Satoru's bottle?"

"Yes!" Hser Nay cheered, and Min and Huan looked relieved to be on the same page as everyone. Hser Nay mimed holding water bottles in each of her hands, then switching them around. "We'll catch the bad guy on video!"

"That's a lot of work," Ellen said, and Graham agreed. "We're talking thousands of pictures and videos to go through, if we can even find the right ones."

"I know, but we have to be a little careful," Isaac cautioned. "After all, the culprit might have been another skater. We don't want this guy to get wise and start covering his tracks."

"But we've got no motive to hurt Satoru. We can't compete in the men's division!" Hser Nay finished. "Not a single one of us benefits from hurting him, so we're the perfect crew to do this job!"

"When did we turn into the Scooby Gang?" Alisha muttered, but adjusted her laptop anyway. "Good to know all those Agatha Christie novels of mine will be put to use." Hser Nay ignored her comment and pressed on.

"I'm going to make an online document we can all access," she said amidst a fury of typing. "And we're going to piece together a complete schedule of that water bottle's comings and goings. We'll find everyone who touched it and the exact moment it got switched with the fake."

"And if that exact moment didn't get caught on camera?"

"We'll still have a list of who was acting suspiciously, and who lied about their whereabouts," Hser Nay replied, then cracked her knuckles. "Let's get moving, shall we?"

10

———————

KARA BETH often communicated with Satoru via email when he was in Japan. Video chat worked well too, when available. Without the visual cues, it was harder for them to understand each other over the phone, and Satoru's English was infinitely better with a few minutes to proofread. They both checked their email often enough that there usually wasn't a problem with delays.

But now and then, something would come up that had to be dealt with face to face, and Kara Beth knew that moment was coming long before she got the email in all capitals, "CALL ME AS SOON AS YOU WAKE UP!"

She turned on her computer and adjusted her webcam, dreading the conversation she was about to have. "Hello, Satoru."

Her student was too polite not to return the phrase, but he wasted no more breaths before airing his grievances. "They make me to withdraw from Nationals!"

"Yes, I know," Kara Beth sighed. She rubbed at her temples a bit. Technically, no one could *make* Satoru do anything, but governing sports bodies had enough power that a strongly worded suggestion was almost synonymous. "I heard earlier."

"And you don't do anything?"

"What do you want me to do, Sato? You're in no condition to compete."

"I will be!"

"No, you won't." He was actually glowering at her, but Kara Beth refused to be cowed. "Don't you still have pneumonia? And a sprained ankle? I know you've been pushing yourself way harder than you should be- don't deny it, I know you too well- but you're barely able to handle easy stroking. Forget jump practice."

"I'll be better by competition. Help me convince them."

"There's no way. Nationals are just before Christmas, and you can't go from hospital discharge to quad rotations in a month and a half. Your doctors and Federation doesn't think it's healthy for you to compete now, and I agree with them."

"Federation just cares about look good!" Satoru snarled. "They don't care about me before, why start now?" That caused Kara Beth to sit up straight in her chair. Not because of the sentiment, because every skater felt objectified by their federation at one point or another, but she'd never heard Satoru say it out loud before. He was a snarky little imp sometimes, but he toed the line around authority. For the Japanese Skating Federation and the ISU, he was all bows, deference and agreement.

Even Satoru had to have a breaking point, but Kara Beth was a little surprised to find it here. Maybe it tapped into a larger issue he was having. "Well, even if you don't agree with their motives, they're still right. Your body needs more time. Jumps are risky elements, and I don't want you rushing yourself into those quads. What if you break an ankle and have to sit out Worlds? Or crack your head and end your career forever?"

"That's not... triples are fine! Can beat Yukiya like that. Have to try!"

"You're missing the point, Sato."

"Have to try!" he insisted, knocking his fist lightly against his computer desk in agitation. "I miss whole Grand Prix, and it's *home!*

Even if I don't do like normal, I have to go!" He dropped his gaze and mumbled, "Even if I don't win, have to go, everyone expects..."

"You can't put yourself at risk just because people expect it," Kara Beth said, trying to be kind. "Japan will forgive you if you can't skate this one time."

Satoru raised a disdainful eyebrow. "Japan forgives. People don't." He groaned and ran his hand through his hair. "I don't. Federation thinks about pretty skate for advertise and things, and put on best face of country, but Nationals is more. And I don't be in Japan all year, so I think means more to me." He shook his head and spoke with more deliberation. "No, I don't think. It means more. Means everything. Is important to my skate and even if I can't be best, must give what I can. I have to go," he pleaded, and Kara Beth wanted to take his side.

But reality wouldn't and they had to admit that. "I know this is important to you, and you're frustrated," she said, "But you'll hurt yourself if you try to get back up to speed in time for Nationals. This isn't the time to take risks."

Satoru's look was one of pure heartbreak. He opened his mouth to say something, but then shut it again. Kara Beth could tell from his expression that he couldn't find the words. She wasn't sure if there was anything she could say to make it better, but she tried to empathize. "I know you're under a lot of pressure. But right now, all that pressure is coming from you, do you understand? Your Federation's giving you a break, your family is grateful for the chance to pamper you. Everyone understands you need to rest, and nobody expects you to move at a pace faster than you can handle. Can you try to be that understanding with yourself?"

She remembered him crying in the hospital about the Grand Prix, overwhelmed by the thought of all the people he was letting down. It was a dark echo of all the times he'd broken down under the pressure of competitions, the nights following a bad skate where she wasn't sure how low spirits could sink. He'd never disappoint anyone like he disappointed himself. And trying to convince Satoru of that was a workout.

It was easy to say Satoru was stubborn, and he was, but Kara Beth had spent enough time with him to know that wasn't the problem. "You don't owe the world anything. The Grand Prix will be back next year, along with Nationals, and I know you'll get back to doing everything you love. It's not like it was in Juniors."

Satoru snapped his head up from where it was downcast, then swiped a quick hand across his face. "Feels the same. Feels worse. Like Juniors and Wataru and mono at same time."

"I believe it. But remember what it felt like to skate on that knee injury? Do you want to put yourself through that again?"

"No..." His face had gone white at the mention. "But not skating is bad, too..."

"I know." Kara Beth wished they didn't have computer screens separating them. She wanted to reach out and hold those thin shoulders that thought they needed to carry so much. "It's the worst feeling in the world. But you're more than your skating, Satoru. And not one of us values your skating ability more than we value you."

There was a pause as Satoru processed those words, and then he gave up pretense of not crying. "Why you say things? You know I'm baby."

"Because you need to hear them. Hang in there, Sato. It's tough now, but everything's going to be okay." They shared a few more words, including several assurances that the JSF was still considering Satoru for the Four Continents and World Championships, health pending, and then they ended the call. For a minute, Kara Beth sat in front of her computer with eyes glazed over, her fingers locked and supporting her chin. Satoru was an independent adult now. And if he needed help, he was an ocean away with his actual family. He was still her student, but he wasn't her kid anymore. He had to find his own way.

That pain in her heart would go away once she accepted that. Maybe.

But Kara Beth felt drained, and it still showed when she met Damien at the rink. "My goodness, what Zamboni has run you over?"

"I'm fine, just a little worried about Satoru. I talked to him this morning, and it looks like he's not adjusting well to captivity," she sighed, and Damien clucked his tongue. "The JSF suggested he withdraw from Nationals."

"Ah, you brave woman. I could not face him in such a mood." Damien finished lacing up his skates and got to his feet with a resigned smile. "But I cannot say the news surprises me. He couldn't possibly be back to full form in such a short time."

"That's what I said. He might put in an appearance at Four Continents, though." Before taking the ice, Kara Beth paused to look over Damien. "How are you doing with all of this?"

"What?" Damien looked confused by the question. "I don't understand."

But her skaters were suffering from an outside force that Kara Beth couldn't protect them from. Or, rather, hadn't protected them from. If she'd have taken one look at the bottom of that stupid water bottle, they'd all be breathing a sigh of relief and leave the nightmare in the past. "It rattled a lot of skaters. Some are calling for extra security at events, or threatening to boycott competitions if Satoru's poisoner isn't found. And the media might as well write their Christmas bonuses early." She tried to phrase her worries delicately. "A lot of it is at your expense."

A haunted look passed over Damien's face, and Kara Beth knew he was more affected than he let on. "I am hardly concerned by what some website writes about me. And my job is to skate. Save your worry for Satoru. There's no telling what crazy ideas he might concoct in order to skate at his Nationals."

"Okay," Kara Beth said. Damien was tough, a strength forged from years of insensitive commentary about his weight issues. Still, being accused of attempted murder was a heavy blow to anyone, no matter how disreputable the source of that idea. And as the favorite to fill Satoru's shoes, there was always the possibility the culprit would set their eyes on him. "But tell me if something bothers you. This is scary for everyone."

"I know." Damien skated a few lazy loops onto the ice, then

slowed. He glided back to Kara Beth, his face more serious. "Actually, there is something that worries me."

"What is it?"

"I know Satoru will resume skating in time, but until then, I am the favorite to win."

"It's a lot of pressure," Kara Beth agreed, but Damien shook his head.

"No, I am not concerned with this. The pressure is nothing, I have worked my whole life to win. But skating is Satoru's entire purpose for being." From Damien's pained face, Kara Beth knew what his question was going to be. And she knew she didn't have an answer.

"Will he forgive me when I take his title?"

WHEN INESSA FOUND out about the plan to scour the internet for backstage videos of Satoru's now-infamous water bottle, she was furious. Not because she thought it was a bad idea, but because she hadn't been invited to join.

"Sorry, I just didn't think you'd..." Hser Nay trailed off, and Inessa grew impatient. Her phone plan was accommodating of international calls, but one didn't stay up late to call Canada only to listen to dead air. Ellen McGregor had let slip that this little project was in place when Inessa had been up in London to work with their mutual choreographer, and Inessa had been stewing ever since. Since Hser Nay was the ringleader, she was the one who would face her ire.

"Didn't think what? That I would want to help? That I would care?" She willed her voice not to crack, even as the familiarity of the words struck her. She'd said them to her parents before, assistant coaches, myriad people only a few years ago, when she'd discovered in the worst way that her former coach had been diagnosed with cancer. Old Muhlenberg, the stoic man who kept all his thoughts to himself, came to lessons and competitions without ever an indication that he was sick, until the one day he couldn't hide it anymore. Most of his other students had been told, but not Inessa. She was just a little girl, everyone said. They didn't want to scare her.

As if seeing him collapse and rushed to the hospital with no explanation hadn't been equally traumatizing. Seeing Satoru being whisked off the ice similarly had sent Inessa back to that mindset temporarily, and she'd clutched her new plush rabbit in fear until word came back she wouldn't lose yet another important person with no warning. She felt having information and honesty would have been easier on her, rather than feeling like the entire world around her was as two dimensional and easily shredded as paper.

There was a moment or two of static silence, before Hser Nay replied with all of her blunt honesty.

"No, I keep forgetting you're not twelve, so you weren't on the radar. Like, I just didn't even think of asking."

Inessa hated the answer, but Hser Nay was probably the only person to tell the truth on that matter. "I am not some child to be protected, or too foolish to keep a secret."

"I know, sorry. You just look young... You're right. It's not fair. I'm sorry." Hser Nay seemed sincere, but Inessa still fumed. Did even her friends see her as a little girl, not to be taken seriously? To be shielded from hardship and left out of important plans?

Though Inessa had to admit, she was a good four years younger than Hser Nay, and they weren't exactly close. She'd call Hser Nay a friend, but an acquaintance might have been more accurate. Still, she was *Satoru's* friend, so it hurt not to be asked, or to be viewed as an adult in her own right. She was eighteen, she deserved to be treated with some modicum of maturity .

So she thought. Even Satoru kept his true self hidden from her.

And her fellow skaters seemed to think her nothing more than a jumping pixie. But the good thing about Hser Nay was that she was as willing to change as she was blunt. "Well, to make up for my gaffe, want in now? I can forward you the info we've already gathered." And just like that, the insult was forgotten, and they began discussing the particulars of the scheme.

It was going better than anyone expected. In such a short time, they'd been able to track the infamous water bottle's arrival to the competition, and determine that it must have been switched out long after arriving at the venue, but before Satoru had changed into his costume. "That's probably nothing the police don't know," Hser Nay admitted, "But there's only two five-minute pockets left where none of us got eyes on the water bottle. That narrows things down. If anyone's alibi doesn't match the video, we can know that, too."

"I am impressed," Inessa said. "I think we should also make a list of anyone we know who could obtain arsenic."

"Huh? That could be anybody. Can't you buy it online from a chemist or something?"

"Yes, but that is something that would leave a record." The police surely had means of investigating that, and Inessa had no doubt their first item of business was looking into who in Satoru's acquaintance purchased arsenic in such a way. "I'm suggesting we search for someone who could have obtained it in a manner that wasn't suspicious. A student, or someone with a chemist in their family. Even if they don't have the motive, they may have a connection to the person who does."

Hser Nay chuckled. "I like how you think. We should have brought you in from the start."

IN THE PROCESS of cross-referencing all the videos, one unknown man kept popping up. A young man, probably close to Hser Nay or Damien's age, wearing a blue suit jacket and a beard. In all the videos, he was hovering around Satoru's general area, and when Inessa put out a message to the group, they all reported back that they'd noticed him, too. Alisha thought she'd seen him in person, but had thought nothing of it at the time. "I mean, if I can't remember that much about him, he probably wasn't doing anything weird."

None of the behavior seemed suspicious, but Alisha didn't recognize him as being part of someone's coaching team or federation, or having given the man an interview. And since no one else could, either, the picture began to look odd. He had a lanyard, but the angle of the videos made it hard to see, so it was difficult to say if he had legitimate business in the mixed zone or not.

He must have, to have been there so long without drawing the attention of security, but he still seemed to spend an awful lot of time in Satoru's orbit. And that was a worry for Inessa. "If this stranger is acting on someone's behalf, how will we find out the real criminal? There will be no motive." If any of the suspects had asked someone else to do the dirty work for them, how would they trace back to the truth? It meant the possibilities went beyond those skaters, coaches and others present at Skate America, and their attempted murderer could have been anyone or from anywhere on the planet, something the gossip media had already been postulating.

When presented with that possibility, Hser Nay looked grim. "We'll have to hope we can find a connection somewhere." But the girl was prepared "to go full Nancy Drew on this", and Inessa shared the same drive. Though it made her wish she'd swiped her mother's collection of Batya Gur and Ora Shem Ur to study. She didn't know what their next step should be. They'd amassed so much information, but could do nothing with it.

Inessa plunked her elbows on the desk and gazed at her computer. Something felt odd to her, a fact she'd forgotten, or a puzzle piece that needed to be turned upside down to fit. But every time she cast her mind back to that awful day at Skate America, her brain zoomed in on Satoru being carried off by medics. Her eyes watched each shaky phone video until her eyes glazed over. She'd watched Satoru for hours, and he never made contact with this stranger.

And then, struck by both inspiration and boredom, it entered her head to stop watching Satoru. She started focusing her attention on what others in the video were doing. Yukiya Minami, Alexi Buryakov, Coach Bonogofski...

Within fifteen minutes, she was calling up Hser Nay. "I may have an idea..."

11

———

SINCE THE GRAND Prix finals were being held in Japan, it was easy for Satoru to take the bullet train from Tokyo to Osaka and join the festivities. He hadn't wanted to be a bother or a distraction, but he wanted to see his friends skate, and if he knew that if he didn't come down, most of them would add an extra day to their weekend and descend on his house.

Besides, Izumi was begging for someone to take her to the Finals, even if her brother wasn't competing and even if she technically hadn't finished her schoolwork like she'd promised. Satoru thought their mother was going to blow a gasket, but she'd allowed Izumi to go anyway. She seemed to think family time was more important than school these days.

And so, all three Miyazawa siblings prepared for their getaway skating weekend. Izumi was a bundle of energy straight up until they boarded the bullet train. But somewhere between Tokyo and Osaka, her mood did a complete 180-degree turn.

Satoru couldn't figure it out what turned his sister from an enthusiastic neutron star into a sullen lump of furniture in less than an hour, and Wataru was no help. He didn't exactly radiate warmth and confidence, and his attempts to coax information out of Izumi would have been hilarious if she didn't look so miserable.

But after a series of monosyllabic responses, Wataru gave up and retreated into his own wall of unapproachability. The torch fell to Satoru. As they walked from the train station to their hotel, Satoru let himself fall behind Wataru to where Izumi was dragging her feet. "Everything all right with you?"

"Fine."

"You sure? That smile of yours doesn't seem fine."

Izumi looked up and glowered at him, no evidence of a smile in sight. "It's none of your business."

"Okay, you don't have to tell me. But can I give you a hug anyway?"

"What? Why?" The shock on her face almost made Satoru burst out laughing.

"'Cause I'm your big brother and I want you to feel happy."

Izumi still looked at him like he'd grown another head. "No way. It's dumb."

"Okay. But if you change your mind, I'm right here."

"Weirdo." But after a minute, slowed her shuffle to a stop. "Whatever. Fine," she allowed, with all her teenaged disdain. "You're so American now, what's with that? My boyfriend didn't even hug me in public."

Satoru gave his sister a quick squeeze, but didn't miss the use of past tense. "Didn't? Did something happen between you two?"

Izumi chose not to answer, which spoke for itself. "Okay, enough being creepy. Let's get going before Big Brother forgets about us."

* * *

THE ORIGINAL PLAN was to get to the hotel, settle in, and watch the parts of the competition they didn't have tickets for on television. For Wataru, that was amended to "bury himself in his work laptop and do his best to ignore his siblings." But Satoru and Izumi expected some of that, since Wataru didn't especially enjoy the sport of figure skating. "It's one thing if you're competing," he eventually confessed to Satoru. "Otherwise... I don't really care." It surprised them he even wanted to come on the trip, but sibling bonding trumped being slightly bored for a few hours. Or maybe he was just there to shadow Satoru and reassure their mother, but it was nice to have him along either way.

But with Izumi's mood, the plan changed. Satoru convinced his brother to put away work for a bit, and the two of them took Izumi out to dinner. There wasn't much they could do about the boyfriend issue, but a little attention and pampering would cheer her up. More than that, getting out of the hotel room gave Izumi a chance to save face, at least online. A little encouragement was all it took to coax the phone out of her purse, and the selfie narrative detailed what a great time she was having in Osaka without some stupid boy, even if those exact words were never spoken.

After that came shopping, and Izumi dragged her brothers to every music or electronics shop in the area. Satoru watched her drool over amplifiers and turntables and a bunch of other equipment he couldn't identify as genuine enthusiasm crept back into her face. Mission accomplished.

Wataru thought so, too. "You're better at this than I am," he observed quietly, as their sister discovered some junky box and decided it was the greatest treasure ever. Satoru was surprised and thought maybe he'd misheard, but Wataru elaborated. "I'm not good when people are upset."

"I'm really not, either." He knew what Izumi liked, but that didn't mean Satoru had any confidence in his actions. He hadn't known if Izumi would want to be cheered up, or if she wanted to have a good sulking cry session, if she wanted comfort or advice versus her brothers just ignoring the issue. "Normally I just annoy people. But all we can do is try, right?"

"I guess." Wataru pressed his lips together in a wry smile. There was no one Satoru annoyed more than his brother.

Satoru couldn't help but fidget at the reminder. "I think that it's fine, even if we screw up sometimes," he said, unable to stop his mouth. "Better to make someone mad at us than let them think we don't care." It was what sustained his friendship with Damien through the occasional fight. Even if he was afraid of saying the wrong thing or pushing too hard, he had to find the courage to speak anyway. Because good friends didn't let each other waste away, anymore than good brothers sat by and let their sisters suffer a broken heart.

"And that's why you're the favorite." Wataru turned to fiddle with some indecipherable equipment, leaving Satoru to wonder if that last comment was meant in bitterness or not. "By the way, I'm part of the media team that's going to be covering the Four Continents Championships in Beijing. You're still planning to compete there, right? If you're healthy enough."

"I will be healthy enough," Satoru said, because there was no other option.

Wataru just shrugged. "We'll both be pretty busy, obviously, but if you want, we could meet up there..."

Satoru paused. "You want to?"

"Well, we'll actually be in the same country for five minutes, it would be stupid not to try and see my little brother." For a second, Satoru thought he'd misheard, and waited until Wataru turned around. His brother saw his expression and frowned. "You okay?"

"Yeah," Satoru quickly jumped in, just in case the window of opportunity slammed back shut. "Yeah, that would be great!"

"All right. I'll get back to you on my schedule and we'll work out the details."

"Okay," Satoru replied, still dazed. He wondered if their mother had put Wataru up to this. He was distracted when Izumi rushed up to him with some piece of electronics he couldn't make heads or tails of. There was a strange style of keyboard, and several knobs, dials and what looked like head- phone jacks. "What's that supposed to be? Half a piano?"

"It's the Concertmate MG-1!"

The words meant nothing to Satoru. Nor to Wataru, who gave a few seconds of pretending to be interested and knowledgeable, then shuffled off to look at something else. Satoru sighed. "It's an instrument?"

"Yeah, it's a synthesizer, but better than that toy I have at home! The bass sounds are great." Izumi placed it into Satoru's arms so she could inspect it more thoroughly. "You can do some really cool things with it, plus it's vintage!" She winked. "I'd sell both my hands to have this in my room!"

"Then how would you play it?" Izumi ignored him and dragged over the shop owner so she could test out the device, and spent the next twenty minutes churning out bizarre and unnatural sounds that nonetheless blended into a musicality of their own. Satoru couldn't say he followed anything Izumi was doing, despite her explanations, but he liked the sound. Wataru looked like someone had run their nails over a chalkboard, but tried to plaster on something that could be interpreted as a smile. He soon disappeared to wait outside the building.

But eventually, Izumi had to separate herself. "It's a little out of my price range," she admitted, and Satoru wasn't sure if she or the shopkeeper were more dejected. But he doubted Izumi had ever looked at her boyfriend the way she looked at that synth.

"I can buy it for you," he offered, and Izumi was floored.

"Really! Oh, thank you, thank you! Wait, no, it's way too much..."

"Not really," Satoru insisted. "It's not a problem at all."

But Izumi sobered up all the more. She bit her lip and kicked her shoes against the floor. "I know you're just doing all this stuff to cheer me up. You don't have to try so hard."

"It's not just about that. I want you to have it, if it's important to you." He poked his sister's cheek until she smiled. "You should get to chase your dreams, too."

"Well, then I accept." She was pleased, but still subdued as the purchase was finalized. "At least you think it's important. Wish Tomo did."

"Is that why he's an ex-boyfriend?"

"Pretty much," Izumi grimaced, and leaned against the counter, while the shopkeeper went into the back room to dig up some auxiliary cable Izumi insisted she needed. "You know that show I'm doing next weekend, with my friend's band? He doesn't want to come. Says he's busy."

"That's too bad."

"He's had weeks to make time, and I've been to every one of his stupid baseball games!" Izumi moped. "Wouldn't even give me a fake excuse, he just doesn't think this is more important than video games or whatever. So we fought." She made a face, to hide how her jaw was trembling. "He's so stupid."

"Sounds like it." Satoru tried to sound sympathetic, and less like someone who might stalk a high-schooler and throw him off a building. "You'll find someone who'll appreciate it, though."

"Will I? Mana from school said guys don't like girls to be too good at stuff. Like it's intimidating if the girl's more popular than they are."

"That's definitely not true. It's not!" Satoru repeated, when Izumi still looked depressed. "That's egotistical. Your boyfriend should want you to be your best self." At that moment, the shopkeeper returned, and Izumi took the cable while Satoru got to carry the synthesizer.

He almost dropped it when Izumi asked, "Do you want Inessa to be her best self?"

"What?"

"Don't play dumb, the entire world knows you like her." Izumi rolled her eyes. "So? She's got to be pretty intimidating. Are you okay if she gets more popular than you?"

Satoru was still a little shellshocked by the question, but his mind did run through Inessa's impressive reputation, which was so grand it couldn't even be exaggerated. She was smart, beautiful, capable of amazing things with little to no ego marring the achievement. Sometimes it was hard to face her after his own mistakes or choppy English speeches.

"We're not dating," Satoru said. Izumi didn't look like she believed it.

"But you like her."

"We're just friends. But yeah, I do want her to be her best..." He hesitated, knowing he was saying too much, but if it helped Izumi... "I wouldn't like her so much if she didn't give her best to everything."

"Hmm." Izumi smirked a little bit. "So you'd date her even if she won more medals than you?"

"I'd date her if I felt like asking her and she said yes," Satoru said with a bit of edge. "But that's none of your business. Keep your mind on your own dating life." He adjusted the synthesizer in his arms. "A guy should think you're as important as your brothers do. If not, he's not worth the effort."

Izumi gave that some thought, and the two walked to the front of the store. When they rejoined Wataru, he stared and dropped his jaw a little. "Are we supposed to haul this thing all the way back to Tokyo?"

12

***

AMIEN DIDN'T EXPECT to get emotional upon seeing Satoru. Outbursts of tears were his friend's signature trait, and the shock of Satoru's hospitalization had worn off over the weeks.

But one look at Satoru's thin, pale frame and owlish glasses, and Damien barreled through the intersection, kissed both sides of his friend's face and then clamped his arms around him as if to prevent the wind from taking him away. How close he'd come to losing his best friend forever hit him like a punch in the gut, somehow more powerful than it had been when Satoru's life was actually in danger. "How did you end up skinnier than I am? Do you not listen to your own lectures?" Was this how Damien looked to other people? So sickly and fragile?

"They don't let me eat, then pneumonia," Satoru complained, with a bit of an awkward laugh. He patted his friend on the back. "Is okay now."

But it wasn't, so Damien didn't let go. That wasn't exactly the custom in Japan, and he knew Satoru cared a lot about other people's opinions. But Damien also knew Satoru craved physical affection, and being as that wasn't the custom in Japan, probably hadn't been hugged nearly enough. So he squeezed tighter and tried not to think of how little he'd been able to do for his friend since this happened.

After a second, he felt Satoru patting his back. "I don't go anywhere, Dami. Still here."

"Thank God for that." There was a time in Damien's life that he hated God. And everything else. It was hard to cultivate patience when one lived in a perpetual state of starvation and shame. Lashing out became a habit, and by the time he was eighteen, the only thing that filled the void.

In hindsight, he realized the one he was truly mad at was himself. But at the time, all his rage was for the God who let him be born with a senseless aversion to food, demanding yet distant parents, and a wealth of natural talent that he couldn't take advantage of. He built up walls between himself and the rest of the world, pushed away the few who tried to reach out, and then complained that they left him to live that wretched existence alone. If God was all powerful, why could there be no miracles for him?

But God had already given him a miracle. Damien didn't realize it until he was nearly nineteen, but it came in the form of a skinny teenager, and God couldn't be blamed for Damien's lack of attention. Satoru was hardly a saint, but he was a gift, and one that continued to show up on Damien's doorstep during his lowest moments. Even if Damien could convince Satoru his presence wasn't welcome and his entire existence hated, Satoru would still check up on him. Until Damien was better, he'd said.

Damien would never be 'cured', but neither would Satoru's attention end, and Damien almost heard the voice of God come into his apartment and say, *This is your miracle. Why do you not treasure it?*" In that moment, Damien saw through his own wretchedness, saw through Satoru's determination, and realized that if he took care of the gift he'd been given, he'd find the end to his misery. Damien cherished his friendship with Satoru from that moment on.

"I'm fine now. Be back in Ohio soon," Satoru said as they finally broke the hug. "You can stop worry."

"If only it were so simple, little duck." Behind Damien, Sione cleared his throat.

"See, this is why everyone thinks you two are married."

Satoru rolled his eyes, and they joined the rest of the group. The original plan had been for Damien and Inessa to meet with Satoru on their off-day between the short program and the free skate. The lunch party soon expanded to include Satoru's sister, Sione, Alisha, Sokonthy, Yukiya, Hser Nay and all three Bertinellis. Satoru said he was eager to hang out with everyone, but seemed a little over-whelmed on the phone. He kept mentioning that the two ice dance teams would compete that evening and that he didn't want people to feel obligated. Knowing how Satoru was, Clara called him up and assured him the meeting time didn't interfere with any official prac-tices or preparation, and that the diversion would be welcome.

"We're not going to be eating anything weird, are we?" Issac asked as he looked over the menu.

"Like greasy burgers and fries? No, they don't serve here."

"That's not what I meant!" he protested, while everyone else cack-led. "I just can't read the menu, and I don't need my stomach freaking out right before a competition!"

"If your stomach doesn't freak out over *poutine*, I can't imagine anything in this country's gonna kill it," Sokonthy said, and then laughed at Issac's pained face

"Please, Satoru, just tell me if there's anything on the menu I'll recognize!"

"Baby," Hser Nay grinned. "The minute this competition is over, I'm going to introduce you to *natto*." Izumi looked up at the word and made a face, causing Issac to pale a few shades.

"Don't worry, I find you good food," Satoru promised, though he had a bit of a smirk. He was more sincere when he looked at Damien. "If you want, I tell you what's good, too."

"Please. I yield to your expertise." Damien didn't feel hungry, and doubted that would get any better once he was assaulted with the sights, smells and textures of unfamiliar foods, but he trusted Satoru to find something that wouldn't make him hurl. He sat back while Satoru made his selections to the waiter without consulting him.

Yukiya cast an odd look at the two of them, but Sione laughed aloud. "And he orders your food, too? Damien, how did you live without Satoru to run your life?"

"I didn't." Next to Damien, Satoru raised an eyebrow. But Damien couldn't say more, and he refused to take the words back. He'd nearly lost Satoru once, without saying anything. Given this second chance, he had to make sure he said more. Satoru had to know his own importance, had to know how much Damien appreciated him, before another day came where Satoru left and there was no chance to speak.

But identifying all those sensitive things and putting words to them was something Damien struggled to do with his therapist, let alone in mixed company. So he let the words land with all the weight of a brick, then changed the subject to something easier. As with eating, he couldn't swallow the whole refrigerator from the beginning. He could only do his best whenever possible, and try to do more the next time until it became habit. Someday, he would be able to thank Satoru properly.

For now, he just tried to be good company, which was significantly harder once the food arrived. Even though he'd been preparing himself mentally, the sights and smells still overpowered his senses, and Damien dropped out of the lively conversation in order to stare at the tablecloth. Sooner or later, people were bound to notice. "You alright there, Damien?"

"I am fine, just eat your tentacles."

"What?" Issac gave an audible groan. "Oh, wow! Hser, we have to skate later!"

"I eat octopus all the time! Just because your palate has the radius of a teaspoon doesn't mean mine has to!"

From across the table, Sokonthy took on a wicked grin and held up something that appeared to be slathered in orange mayonnaise. "Sure you don't wanna try this, Damien?"

"Absolutely not." This was why he hated going out. "Keep your culinary abominations to yourself."

"Be nice," Satoru chided, and Damien winced. Hopefully his

friend didn't take it as a personal slam against his culture.

But if he did, he was more than capable of payback. "We can't all eat snails out of dirt like France." Damien tried not to moan, while Satoru focused on the meal being set before him. "Is okay. I know you. We share this."

He divided a bunch of small bowls and plates, and Damien forced himself to at least appear interested. They were mostly recognizable: some white rice, miso soup, tofu and some crispy meat pieces Satoru identified as chicken. The main dish was a hot noodle soup in a large ceramic bowl. "You know *udon*, I make you once. Nothing weird."

"Thank you, duck." His stomach curdled at the sight, but he forced a few grains of rice into his mouth. "You are a treasure." Satoru beamed, which overrode Sione's good-natured smirk.

SATORU WOULD NEVER TELL ANYONE, but one of his fears was of not being missed. That his presence was tolerated, maybe even pleasant, but not sought after. He worried that he'd be forgotten without making much of an impact, and that fear extended to both the individual level and the larger scale of his place in history.

So it made him happy that Kara Beth still kept chopsticks in her silverware drawer, "just in case." He was glad his parents still held on to his childhood mementos and kept his pictures around the house. Damien's use of pet names that designated Satoru somehow separate from all his other friends was a relief. But in the back of his mind, Satoru still feared, and the recent hospitalization only emphasized how precarious his situation was.

All his friends wanted to know how he was doing. What had he been up to in his forced vacation? And Satoru didn't know what to say. He couldn't talk about skating, he'd done so very little of that. A lot of reading got done, but the table would be bored to tears if he started expounding on how many times the Empire State Building had been struck by lightning. He'd been able to make it out to the community center and put in some volunteer time, but he didn't really do anything important there. Nobody would care about the cool embroidery stitch he'd found online and tried on the new dress he'd made for Izumi. The dress was cool, but the minutia of sewing was kind of boring.

Satoru did nothing important, not really. And sitting around the table with so many of the people he loved and admired, he felt small to talk about his silly hobbies, his strange and useless interests. They all acted excited and interested, but Satoru was sure it was just politeness.

He steered the conversation back onto his friends, because it was more interesting to hear about them. Sokonthy was building a family, that was so much more valuable than any hobby of Satoru's. Alisha didn't just read about things that interested her, she experimented and wrote papers, chased the new discoveries that would someday be put in the books Satoru read. Sione was blazing all sorts of trails in his home country, his sister was making such strides with her music mixing and creating wonderful things for others to enjoy, while Inessa was finishing her last year of high school and contemplating all her options, still finding the paths to her passions. Everyone was so driven and talented, so important.

He felt like an impostor anytime someone's eyes were on him. "But it's such a beautiful dress!" Inessa gushed, which caused Izumi to beam and Satoru to suddenly need a glass of water to cool his head. "You have a real talent for this!"

"Thank you," Satoru said, and tried not to look as awkward as he felt. "Was fun to do. Would like to do better, though. Better technique." Izumi would kill him if he started pointing out all the flaws in the dress he'd made for her, flaws she claimed only he could see. But Satoru knew they were there, which meant others could see them, and he wanted everyone to know he was aware of them. If people thought he didn't know his own deficiencies and limitations, that would be humiliating.

"The rabbit you made for me was adorable, and I still can't believe you make your own skating costumes." Inessa looked a bit shy. "Would you consider making one for me? Next season?"

"What?" Satoru's heart beat wildly, and his brain started picturing all manner of chiffon and lycra draped over Inessa's form, but he managed to wrench control over his mouth. "You want I do... but will be Olympic year!"

"I think you'd come up with something amazing." Inessa looked sincere. Was she delusional? "I would pay you, of course! I don't expect you to do it for free!" When Satoru still didn't answer, she looked away. "If you have time, I know you will be busy with your own training."

"That's not..." Satoru swallowed. He would love the chance to design and create a costume for someone so beautiful, and Inessa's programs were artistic, the process would be a pleasure. "Not really good enough to make for other people..."

"Nonsense, your costumes always look brilliant! And you did Damien's."

"I only help, remember?" Satoru grimaced, and Damien leaned over to add his two cents.

"Yes, and I promise, Inessa, he is the wrong person to ask if you want to sparkle."

"This new strategy for win? Blind all judges?" Satoru asked darkly, and Damien just laughed.

Inessa picked at her food, and her smile looked a little fake. "It is fine if you don't want to, Satoru. I am sure you are busy enough without one more worry."

She looked so disappointed, though, and Satoru found he couldn't stand to be the cause of it. "I do want to do. But I think I can't. I don't..." His throat felt suddenly tight. If Inessa had asked a few months ago, Satoru would have jumped at the chance, insecurities or no, just to see her happy. "I... I don't see colors now."

"What?"

"I'm colorblind." He gestured to the dress Izumi was wearing. "Don't know what colors that is. She pick it all out." Satoru just cut the pieces and followed the pattern. Izumi told him it was mostly apricot with a pale purple lace, but it looked gray and blue to him. He wasn't even sure what colors his own clothes were. "Like, can see some colors, but not others, make a lot of mistakes. Twice I eat lemon instead of orange," he tried to laugh, aware that the table had drifted into silence. "So... maybe I can't make."

He couldn't bear Inessa's stare. "Really?" she finally asked, and the word hit like a dart.

"Yes. Since poison." He shrugged, faking nonchalance. "Small thing. Lucky it's not worse." So, so lucky. Someone tried to murder him, he could have died. Since he lived, he had to be happy about everything else, right?

Nearby, Yukiya was realizing something serious had been said in the English half of the party, and was trying to catch up. Izumi looked up from the cat videos she and Clara were watching, and the rest of the table slowly brought their various discussions to a halt.

Satoru wasn't sure what was worse, the silence, or the words that inevitably followed. "Did you just say you were colorblind?"

"How long has that been going on?"

"Is it permanent? How does poison screw up your vision, anyway?"

"Is everything black and white now?"

Satoru did his best to answer quickly and change the subject, but his friends only leaned in closer. Damien reached over and put a hand on his arm, and Satoru almost wished he hadn't, because he could feel his internal waterworks starting and if people kept acknowledging his feelings, his body would follow suit. No way was he crying in front of this crowd, not today. Not over something so small.

"So, how does that work? If you can't see a color, is it just blank?"

"Hard to explain. Kinda grays and yellows, red and green doesn't see right, so those look wrong." His lips twisted, and Satoru fought them for control. "Not so important. Ice is always white. I can see that." And what else mattered? Did Satoru need to be greedy, and demand more? He didn't need colors to skate, he didn't need senseless hobbies, he didn't need perfect health. He didn't get to demand friends and happiness and fulfillment. All that mattered was getting those high scores and gold medals, delivering dazzling, perfect skates in front of the crowds when it counted. That was what he sold his life for and decided was worth making his family miserable over, so he needed to get back to doing that as soon as possible. It was stupid to cry over something that mattered so little.

But when a pair of dark arms encircled him from behind, Satoru almost lost it. "Just ignore me, it's fine," he growled, and hoped it didn't sound too much like a whimper. "Isn't big deal, just ignore."

"How could anyone ignore you, Sato?" Alisha squeezed him tighter, and Satoru angrily blinked back the tears that were threatening to fall. He was always getting emotional and crying, whether he was happy, sad or afraid. "I'm so sorry."

Not today. "Is tiny thing. Not worth big deal." He pushed Alisha's arms off of him. "Don't want talk about this. Today supposed to be fun."

"Okay..." Alisha went back to her seat with a concerned look, and seemed guilty. Satoru felt much the same. He didn't want to hurt her feelings, but if he kept talking about this, he was going to melt down right there in the restaurant.

But just because the topic ended didn't mean the mood shifted. Everyone could see he was upset, that he was a mess. He was bringing down the whole party, after everyone had taken time out of their day to come see him. Now they surely wished they'd done something else, prepared for the competition, maybe just hung around the hotel. Anything had to be better than this.

He could feel the eyes on him, Inessa's most of all. Those pretty brown eyes, they used to be so rich and vibrant, but now he couldn't see all the shades that gave them their depth of color. Satoru didn't dare raise his head, not until he could get his weakness under control. He owed Alisha an apology, and the rest of the table, but he couldn't get his mouth to work.

Somebody had to say something. They couldn't spend the entire afternoon miserable because of him, someone had to take control and- "Satoru? Yo, Sato!"

Satoru wrenched his head up at Sokonthy's voice. He peered down the table at her. "Yes?"

"How do you say 'snot' in Japanese?"

The whole table barked out laughs. Satoru wrinkled his nose. "Why you want say that?"

"To change the subject." She leaned back in her seat, with her usual grin on her face, unaffected by whatever expression Satoru was wearing. "I'll teach it to my kid, all the other moms at daycare will hate me. So? How do you say 'snot'?" And the more Satoru stared at her teasing grin, the more the surrounding people started giggling, the more he found his own mood lifting.

"*Hanamizu*," he said, and found the strength to smile when his little sister looked mortified.

"Nice!" Sokonthy clapped, and repeated the word a few times, while Yukiya and Izumi shared a look of confusion that Satoru was all too familiar with. But now the table was back to its jovial state. Satoru's brief burst of negativity had been overturned.

If Sokonthy could diffuse tense situations so easily, she was definitely cut out for motherhood. She waved at him again from across the table. "Hey, one more! Teach me one more!"

"What immature thing you want now?" he asked, not that Sokonthy looked ashamed.

"Immature? Me? Never!" She clutched her chest in mock offense. "No, just tell me how to say 'Everybody loves me and I want a hug!'"

That was too deliberate. Satoru swallowed. "You play game with me."

"Always." There was a sincerity in Sokonthy's playful eyes. "You play, too. Come on, teach me."

He couldn't. It was presumptuous. Narcissistic. Greedy and demanding and weird, and no one really wanted to, and he was probably going to cry if he didn't stop thinking about this soon. Wataru's complaints about "sympathy crying" echoed in the back of his head.

But then he caught Inessa's eyes. Beautiful Inessa, smiling at him in eager anticipation. "Please, Satoru, this sounds like a wonderful game. Teach us how to say the phrase." How could he refuse her?

So he told Sokonthy and was immediately smothered by a mob of skaters. If any tears sneaked out, nobody noticed, and Satoru would never admit to it.

13

WITH A LONG, rectangular table, it was impossible for everyone to face each other in conversation, so inevitably, people in the party would occasionally switch seats or scoot them closer to who they wanted to speak to. That suited Inessa's needs perfectly. When Clara flagged Izumi over to watch another video on her phone, Inessa took her vacated seat so she could now face Yukiya.

But then, she balked. She didn't know what to say, or how to say it, but couldn't back out now that she'd gone out of her way to sit down. As the seconds ticked on, Yukiya's friendly face grew more expectant, and Inessa still couldn't bring herself to begin. She didn't know how to grill anyone for details.

But Inessa had watched fancams for hours, and Yukiya had talked to that stranger in the blue suit jacket, the one no one could be sure if he belonged in Satoru's space. Yukiya might have been the only person to exchange words with him, as far as Inessa could tell, and might be the difference in deciding whether this man was unrelated or someone the police needed to look into.

And Inessa was determined to ask. But she could barely ask Yukiya for directions to the bathroom. She had to have this conversation before the week was out and any natural way to broach the topic was squandered. Yukiya probably had nothing to do with the crime itself, but she had to treat him like a suspect. After all, she didn't know that he hadn't been involved in something sinister to get his coveted information, or if the real culprit was watching to make sure no one looked too deep into their activities.

Crime shows made it all look so easy. "*Hey, Yukiya? How weekend?*" She'd attempted to learn some Japanese after becoming friends with Satoru, and no one else in their band of detectives had any better experience with the language except for the pairs team of Naka-maru/Sanda, and they had some feud going on with Yukiya over a childhood incident and didn't feel comfortable implying they knew someone involved in Satoru's attempted murder. Neither did Inessa, but somehow the task had fallen to her.

So she tried to grease the wheels with small talk. Simple sentences were the best she could do, but Yukiya seemed pleased by the effort. He rattled off a response that went over Inessa's head, save for the word "*great*", beaming all the while.

Inessa hoped he'd keep the attitude through her next question, but she doubted it. "*Is good, yes? Not Skate America. That bad, right?*"

The look on his face was so bewildered, Inessa wished she had a camera. Meanwhile, Satoru had heard her words and had whipped his head around fast enough to break his neck. Yukiya gathered enough wits to stammer out, "*Yes...*"

Inessa's cheeks burned, but she pressed on. "*Before skate? See someone backstage?*"

"*Uh, I don't really know what you're talking about...*"

"*See man? Talk him? Before warm up?*" In the back of her mind, a voice screamed at Inessa to abort, but she'd already gone this far. She fumbled a bit to find the picture of the stranger on her phone, stumbling over her words along the way. "*Something strange seeing?*"

"*N-no. At Skate America, you mean? I didn't talk to Satoru, I was just focused on the competition. I didn't really talk to anyone but my coaches...*"

"*No? I see talk man.*" While Yukiya gaped, Satoru stood up and left his own chair, coming over to stand behind Inessa.

She wanted to sink underneath the table, but it was far too late for that. Satoru folded his arms and leaned on the back of her chair, then rested his chin on the top of her head. He held that position until Inessa felt brave enough to tilt back and meet his gaze. "Hello..."

Within Satoru's eyes were a thousand expletives. "Hello." Inessa couldn't ever remember being so scared of a smile. It didn't get any better when that mouth started spouting one of her ancestral tongues. *"What's happening?"*

"When did you learn Russian?" her timid voice asked in an effort to deflect, though Satoru's expression showed he wasn't distracted.

"I sometimes volunteer with community center. There's cute old lady, she immigrate from Russia, good chance to practice."

Inessa hadn't known that. Satoru did a lot of impressive things that he never told anyone about. He didn't think too highly of himself or brag about his good deeds, which was one of the many things Inessa loved about him. "Your accent is not bad."

"Spasiba." And with a glint in his eyes, the subject was over. "You have interesting conversation here. I think you don't know good words to say. Can I help?"

Yukiya looked relieved, and across the table, Hser Nay had clued in to what was happening and looked horrified. Inessa gave up and nodded. This wasn't getting any less awkward. "I was asking him about Skate America."

Satoru quickly translated, not like Yukiya needed it for that, then glared down at Inessa. "Why?"

"Because... we're trying to find the person who hurt you."

"We?"

"Our friends. Other skaters." Satoru looked stunned, and while Yukiya didn't understand a lot of English, the word 'skater' crossed the language boundary. He looked up and down the table in a mix of incredulity and, strangely enough, admiration. He said something to Satoru, who looked troubled.

He motioned for Inessa to scoot over so he could share some of her seat, and ignored whatever rant Yukiya was currently going on. It didn't look especially heated, but Inessa hoped she hadn't offended him too badly. "I don't want to make bad feelings between friends, Inessa."

"Of course. But the police haven't found the person, and everyone is scared. We want to do something."

"You think him?" Satoru asked. "Think he tells lie?"

"No," Inessa replied, and shot a reassuring look across the table to save Yukiya's perception of the situation. "I just want to know what he saw that day, where he went. We're making a timeline of everyone who talked to you before you skated that day."

"Timeline?"

"Yes, from all the cell phones cameras. The mixed zone and a lot of the warm-up areas are completely covered. There's even a couple selfies from the locker room."

"You see everything," he marveled, that confused wrinkle back in his eyebrow. His voice was suspicious, but more as if he didn't believe his comprehension skills than not believing Inessa. "From people's phones?"

"Almost everything. People post all sorts of videos online."

Satoru looked stunned to hear it. But if the knowledge that he lived in more of a fishbowl than he'd thought disturbed him, it quickly faded. "You can see who switch bottle."

"That is the hope. We can at least see who is not where they said they were. And I think Yukiya saw something that does not fit with the rest of the evidence." Or maybe he was covering for something. That went unsaid, but Satoru seemed to know anyway .

"I see." He filled Yukiya in, and the boy calmed down with more information. "You interrogate in public place? With terrible Japanese?"

"It's not an interrogation, I was just asking," Inessa whined, but Satoru just laughed at her in a mirthless way. It had been foolish, though Inessa didn't know when else she was going to get a chance to talk to Yukiya, and everyone else at the table was absorbed in their own conversations. But with Satoru laughing at her, she wanted to rewind the past ten minutes and not even bring it up.

"I want you stop, Inessa." Satoru would have continued, but then

Yukiya broke in. *"Are you serious?"* Yukiya gave a reply that Inessa didn't understand, and Satoru looked visibly angry. *"I don't like this."*

"Okay. Go. I say alone," Yukiya said in his broken English, with grim determination. Inessa looked between the two of them for an explanation.

"What's going on?"

"He wants answer your questions," Satoru grimaced. "Wants to help."

"Is that not good?" She didn't understand Satoru's attitude, but he eventually put his head in his hands and groaned.

"You two make more trouble without translate. Fine. Ask questions quiet and don't scare friends anymore." His expression was very pointed, and Inessa felt chastised.

"Right..." She pulled up an image on her phone of the man in the blue suit, and asked Yukiya if he'd seen him. While Yukiya was looking over the picture, Satoru leaned in and whispered, "Who else knows you do this?"

The puff of air tickled over her ears and neck, and Inessa almost couldn't see straight, let alone think. But she wrestled her thoughts back from fantasy. "Nakamaru and Sanda. About four ice dance teams. Everyone at this table, except Sione and Damien. Well, not Izumi, either. We've not told any men's singles. Yukiya must keep quiet, just in case."

"Lots of people," Satoru murmured, and it again sent chills up Inessa's spine.

"It was a lot of work. And everyone wants to help. But we are careful about who to trust."

"Not that careful," Satoru pointed out. "Worst interrogation ever. Anyone can hear. Never put you on crime show." He almost said something more, but then Damien stood up from the table and excused himself. For a minute, Inessa was scared he'd overheard their conversation, but he didn't send any looks in their direction, so she thought they were safe.

"You alright, Damien?" Sione asked, and upon inspection, Inessa thought the French skater looked a little green.

"I need some air." He said nothing further and left for the bathroom. After a minute, Satoru sighed.

"Sorry, you lose translator. Good luck," he said, and he left as well.

Yukiya handed back Inessa's phone, and they were left to muddle out the results on their own. *"You know?"*

"Yes." Yukiya said something that went over Inessa's head, and so, had to put his high school English classes to work. "Volunteer rink. Help me stuff. Damien's boyfriend."

Inessa stared. "But Damien doesn't have a boyfriend. You sure you didn't misunderstand? *Is mistake?"*

Yukiya responded by dragging out the word "boyfriend," with relish on every syllable. "Man say that," he added in English with a shrug."Secret?" Inessa didn't know what to say. She wouldn't have thought so, but Damien wasn't obligated to tell her things. Yukiya frowned, puzzling through something. "Boyfriend, scandal. Here. Maybe France, too."

"Well, I guess he's entitled to a secret romance," Inessa allowed, but Yukiya shook his head at her tone. "What is it?"

He seemed frustrated at the inability to communicate. "Sato-kun. Damien. Like boyfriends."

Inessa shook her head. "Not really. It's just a joke people make. *Joke. Friends. Just that.* They're more like brothers."

"They're close," Yukiya replied. *"To a secret boyfriend, I bet it doesn't look like a joke, whatever the truth.* Kiss Sato-kun. Hide boyfriend?"

There were a few moments while Inessa's brain caught up with the unfamiliar words. But then, despite the language barrier, she understood Yukiya perfectly.

"Yes, I would be mad enough to kill..."

14

D AMIEN TRIED, he really did. He went grain by grain, crumb by crumb, drop by drop, knowing that it didn't matter how slowly nutrition made it into his system as long as it got there without disturbing his stomach. He took deep breaths, kept his eyes off everyone else's plates, tried to focus on the conversation rather than the food, but all the tricks were in vain.

The nausea was first, and that could be ignored for a bit. It was a physical reaction, but based on mental stimulus, he hadn't actually eaten something that would make him sick. Damien talked himself through the sensations and feelings as he'd done many times before, determined not to be beaten.

And for a while, it worked. He could laugh and joke with Sione, tease Satoru every time they caught him staring at Inessa, and provide sarcastic commentary as Izumi, Hser Nay and Sokonthy tried to teach Issac proper chopstick technique. Despite Damien's queasiness, the day was proving to be a good one.

But then the pain hit. And Damien tried to talk himself down from that, but it grew too great to bear. He feared that if he didn't throw up all over the table, he might actually start whimpering. His body felt chill, his hands trembled, and it became difficult to focus on anything but his misery.

Which was the cue to make his exit. He escaped to the restroom where he could be alone and away from all that wretched food. Damien leaned against the counter and tried to breathe through the feelings. Without the stimulus, maybe the symptoms would go away and he could rejoin his friends before long.

He should have expected one of his friends not to wait. Satoru entered the restroom not a minute after Damien, and joined him by the counter. "Sorry you don't feel good."

"I'll be fine in a minute," Damien said, closing his eyes. He felt Satoru shifting next to him, and felt guilty. "You should be out there with everyone else."

"I don't mind. If helping, I mean. Can go if I make worse."

"Never worse," Damien chuckled. "I just don't like to bring the party down. You are welcome to stay, little duck."

They stayed like that for a minute or two, before Satoru broke the comfortable silence. "At hospital, inside is like pain all the time, from poison, so they don't let me eat. Just tubes. When I can have water again, hurts so much. Food is worse. I almost tell them take away, but then I think you'll make fun of me, so I eat."

Damien felt a smile stretch his face, despite himself. "I would have made fun of you."

"I hope that's not how you feel always."

"I'm sure it's not as severe." Seeing Satoru out there vomiting on the ice was chilling, even before the blood. And then the seizure... Though in a discussion with his therapist, Damien had realized that many of Satoru's symptoms and consequences mirrored ones that Damien either faced now or would face in the future, if he didn't change. They had poisoned Satoru with a heavy metal, Damien poisoned his own system with poor nutrition, and the body reacted in a similar fashion.

It wasn't fair that an innocent had to suffer more over things Damien had largely inflicted upon himself, but it redoubled his resolve to stick to his diet. To relapse would be an insult to his friend, and after seeing some of the damage on Satoru, frightening.

"Must be bad, or you wouldn't have problem," Satoru said, and Damien opened his eyes to find him twisting his hands. "I don't know anything before. Now, I think you must be very strong. More than me." He gave a weak smile. "Maybe I think before I nag."

Damien opened his mouth to speak, to say that Satoru had more right to nag him than anyone, and thank God he did, or Damien might not be around to have this conversation, but the bile suddenly rose in his throat and he pitched himself towards the nearest stall. For a minute, his world was nothing but heaving, all the hard work of eating erasing itself before his eyes.

What was the point of forcing himself to eat, if this was the result? That was the argument he'd used as a child to escape the dinner table. He would just throw it up later and be sick for the rest of the night, better to avoid the awful experience and not waste food. Such words usually got him in trouble, especially before his parents realized he wasn't just being obstinate.

His stomach gave him a short break, and Damien laid his forehead on his arms, panting for breath. He felt his body trembling, and tried desperately not to scream. He had worked so hard, and here he was again, on his knees and shivering while his own vomit stared him in the face. There were no words to describe the shame.

Luckily, Satoru didn't need words. He rubbed circles at the base of Damien's neck and waited out each wave of nausea, even as the smell turned vile and the action was little more than dry heaving. He ran some paper towels under cool water for Damien to clean his face, and never once said a word of disgust or reproach.

Finally, Damien was able to speak, if not stand. "You don't have to stay with me while I'm sick in a toilet."

"Is what we do," Satoru shrugged. "After Olympics, I owe you for life." Damien snorted at that. The last night of any competition was one for reveling, and none more so than the four years of pressure building to the Olympic Games. Satoru had gone into that competition with a millstone around his neck, and celebrated its release by getting drunk off his eighteen-year-old head.

Damien had been called to the rescue and smuggled Satoru into the French side of the Olympic village in order to avoid Japanese media, but never got the full story on how his normally responsible friend ended up drinking his weight in vodka. Satoru wasn't at his most coherent that night, but apparently the Russian bobsled team was involved. "Friendship isn't about who owes what. But if it were, yes, you would be deep in the hole for that."

"Wish I could make go away. Is bad this time, isn't it?"

"Not especially worse." Damien looked into the toilet bowl and tried not to think of all the lectures from his old school counselor on the dangers of bulimia meant to scare him into healthy eating. "But I have grown accustomed to keeping my dinner down, so it seems more out of place." He flushed the toilet and then pulled down the lid so he could sit somewhere other than the floor. Satoru stood, nodding like the mother hen he was.

"Yes, you look better now. More healthy." He gestured to Damien's frame and managed a grin. "More healthy than me right now."

"That would be a first." But yes, Damien was clinging to an acceptable body weight, and the face that looked back at him in the mirror didn't seem so close to death. He barely recognized himself these days, and the visual evidence of his accomplishment helped push him through the times his stomach didn't want to cooperate.

Which made it all the more humiliating to stumble now. But Satoru didn't share that opinion. "I'm proud of you, Dami. Maybe you don't need, but I am. Happy for you." He looked away, suddenly shy. "Like skating, I think. Fall isn't good, but doesn't mean you should feel shame. Try hard things means fall sometimes, and you do hard things every day."

Damien swallowed, again struck with the thought that he was witnessing a miracle. "Never think that I do not need you, *cygneau*." He didn't know what else to say beyond that. Someday he would, and maybe then he'd be able to bring forth a miracle of his own. And by now, he was sure that God expected this of him. He'd learned a lot about Satoru that one night at the Olympics... "I'm sorry to always cause you such worry."

"Is fine. I make worry, too." Satoru grew suddenly morose. "Media is not nice to you right now."

"Ah." It wasn't something Damien wanted to think about, and he tried to block out memories of the hurtful words. And the signs that sometimes waited for him in a crowd. As if he could ever do something to harm his friend, or didn't deserve to enjoy his own accomplishments. "You heard about that?"

"It's hard to miss. I'm sorry to give you trouble."

"None of this is your fault, Satoru. Do not blame yourself."

"I can't blame anyone else," Satoru whispered, and Damien felt his heart breaking.

"The police will find the culprit. There is no reason to take the punishment yourself."

"I know. Everyone is so good. But I feel..." After a few distracted gestures to conjure words from air, Satoru gave up. "I don't feel like me. Or, like, me is ... not what I thought."

"There is no worse feeling in the world," Damien agreed, getting to his feet. "But for both of us, these trials are short."

He and Satoru left the stalls, the latter with a confused look. "Come, let us put on smiles for our friends and rejoin the party. Such tiny moments do not define us, *oui?*"

"Tiny? Dami, you deal with this whole life."

"Do I? The burden seems to be lifting already." He patted Satoru's cheek, smirking when the younger one pulled away. "One day you will see these times with a new perspective, little duck. Then you will grow to love your strange feathers."

"You talk so strange, worst English ever. Only understand half you say," Satoru grumbled, but both he and Damien wore smiles as they walked back to the group.

LEAVING THE RESTAURANT, Satoru took special notice of Isaac and Hser Nay. He saw the rehearsed ease in how they handled their bill, shared looks and smiles, and the way Isaac held the door open and let his hand fall to the small of Hser Nay's back as she passed through. They were so close, and Satoru envied the lack of physical or emotional space between the two.

"Is very nice, to be close like that," he couldn't help but say, and only realized after the fact that he was talking to Inessa. He hoped she didn't read too much into that.

But she didn't have any monumental reactions, and just nodded her agreement. "They are a cute couple. But Hser Nay is impatient waiting for Isaac to propose." She waved at Hser Nay, who had turned around at the sound of her name, but hadn't heard the rest of the conversation. Inessa waited until she turned around to say, "If he doesn't hurry, she might just do it herself."

Satoru didn't think that was such a bad idea. There was nothing more intimidating than asking a girl to commit herself to you. He was happy to protect, provide and all the other responsibilities society expected of him, but it would be much better for Inessa to do her own asking. After all, it made more sense for someone so perfect and self-assured to seek and choose her own boyfriend, not wait for whatever inferior basket cases scrounged up enough courage to approach her first.

But that wasn't the custom, and no matter how society changed, rituals still had meaning. "I hear he makes plan this year. He tell me after Worlds, so they're not distracted."

"He's been planning since the last Worlds?" Inessa shook her head. "That long?"

"No, um... Today he tell me..." Satoru's face burned. Past tense was such a pain. He needed to be more mindful of that, so he didn't screw up something really important. "Today he say... said... he will ask... after Worlds. So not distracted now with wedding plans."

"Ah," Inessa said. She didn't comment on how Satoru's brain had nearly turned into a pretzel trying to get that sentence out. He was grateful for that, as it was so embarrassing to have someone call attention to his poor English. On the other hand, sometimes he wished people noticed when he managed to employ a new word or a particularity tricky conjugation. No one was going to give him a gold star for something the average five-year-old could manage, but a little acknowledgement would be nice.

How had Inessa gotten so good? Satoru remembered a time when her English was as bare as his, but she'd somehow become nearly fluent while Satoru still struggled to put together broken sentences. And he'd been living in America since he was a teenager! Was he that stupid, or was Inessa a genius at everything she did?

Yesterday's conversation with Izumi sprang to mind, whether he'd be intimidated if Inessa was more successful than him, and Satoru almost laughed. It was a dumb thing to be jealous about. "But Issac's silly. He's more distracted to not ask."

"This is true," Inessa laughed. They had drifted towards the rear of the group, able to speak freely without risk of alerting Hser Nay, not that she was completely oblivious of Isaac's intentions. Asking was just a formality, the last step to making what existed between them official. "Here is a thought: If they do get married this year, and Hser Nay joins the Bertinelli family, will the Olympics see two Canadian teams named Bertinelli/Bertinelli?"

"Poor press, they're so confused already!" Satoru laughed. "Hope she never changes name!" Surely she wouldn't change her professional name, there was enough potential for mixups as it was. Clara once told him of an occasion where she and Mark had shown up to an ice show, only to find the producers had thought they were booking Isaac and Hser Nay. It was disappointing and embarrassing for all involved.

"Would you ever be an ice dancer?" Inessa asked. "Or pairs?" Satoru had thought about the question often. When he was young, many girls had approached him to be their partner. There were disproportionately more female than male skaters to begin with, but especially in dance and pairs, and many girls joked that any man with a pulse could make the cut. And back when Kara Beth was just an idol on a pedestal to him, he sometimes entertained fantasies of asking her to skate pairs with him once he was old enough to join the senior ranks. Even so, Satoru hadn't been persuaded or even bribed into switching. Both disciplines had their attractions, but he paled at the responsibility. He sometimes developed joint programs with Kara Beth or other skaters for ice shows in the summer, and had a pact with Damien that if they both medaled at the next Olympics that they'd choreograph their own victory tour to celebrate, but those were all in fun, no scores and far less pressure.

"I'm bad with own mistakes. To let someone else down in big competition, I couldn't deal. And pairs?" He shook his head, "If I drop you on lift, I couldn't live."

Inessa raised an eyebrow. "You automatically assume we would be partners?"

"Uh…" Satoru sputtered, while Inessa just laughed at him. He didn't dare mention all his dreams where they were ice dancers, gliding across the ice with their bodies always sharing a point of contact. Everything was soft and smooth, he could reach out and touch her hair, caress her face, lift her off the ground and let the world see her fly. Sometimes those fantasies were triggered by watching an ice dance competition, which was just awkward if the Bertinelli siblings were involved. "Is just example…"

"Of course." She was still laughing at him. He wanted to crawl into the gutter and die there. "Well, if I were to try pairs, I'd want to skate with you. You're the only one who could keep up with me. Side by side quad sals?" she suggested with a mischievous smirk.

"Would be amazing." Satoru agreed. "But I think dance. More footwork. I like better."

"Okay. It is settled," Inessa declared with a little skip in her step. "When we have done all we want as singles, we will be an ice dance team."

Satoru paused. "This is joke, right?"

"It doesn't have to be."

He hesitated, but then decided she couldn't be making real life plans. Not based on him, in the middle of her own shining career. "Is joke. I wouldn't be good partner for you."

He felt uncomfortable when Inessa fixed him with a piercing look. "Who told you that you are not good at things?"

"What?"

"I have noticed you for many years. You are very unkind to yourself. It's unattractive." Satoru blanched and turned away, but Inessa continued speaking. "When someone needs help, you are the first we all think to ask. When someone does something well, you are the first to praise. But when that someone is yourself, your voice is full of hate."

"That can't be right," he spoke to the sidewalk. He started to walk a little faster, but Inessa kept pace.

"Perhaps hate is too strong a word," she agreed. "But I watch you, always. You only express pride over skating. And even then, when you are happy and jumping to the sky, you still are cruel over mistakes." Satoru felt his breathing coming in shallow, and his pulse speeding up. Why did words have such power over him? "Who was it that told you to be this way?"

"I... don't really..." He wondered if his face looked as bewildered as he felt on the inside. All his words had collapsed like a tower on fire, he couldn't find the right ones in the wreckage. "You ask strange question."

"Maybe. You don't have to answer."

Satoru almost snorted. No one ever meant that, or they wouldn't bother asking. "Then I say no."

"All right." There was a moment of silence, but Satoru knew it wouldn't end there. What surprised him was Inessa's reasoning. "I know the Satoru you want me to see is not a complete picture of my friend. I feel I do not know you so well at all." The panic hit Satoru like an air-raid siren going off in the night, but Inessa was now the one awkward and quiet. "I can't help but want to fix that."

He stopped walking and faced her, feeling a strange mix of anger, guilt and desperation all at the same time. The sensible thing to do would be to tell her it wasn't any of her business

But no one had ever accused Satoru of being too sensible. He swallowed, and fixed Inessa with the most commanding look he could. "No one has to say I don't be good at things. I know this." The look in her eyes made his insides twist, and he couldn't stand up to it for longer than a second. He shoved his hands in his pockets and resumed walking. "We fall behind friends. Waste too much time here."

"This is what I mean! It makes no sense, you are so talented," Inessa said as she jogged a few steps to reclaim her place at his side. "You speak many different languages."

"Just Japanese, really. Not even that, I do bad in school."

"You're speaking English now, you were speaking Russian earlier, you have learned a few Hebrew phrases, and I know I've heard you speak French to Damien," Inessa listed off, and Satoru couldn't figure out why this was so important to her.

"Just some words, is very bad. Not fluent, even English is hard for me."

"But you can do it. And you know a great deal about architecture, too."

"I like, but don't really know..."

"More than some. You make skating costumes. I cannot do this. I pay a lot of money so others can make them for me." Was she going to lecture him the entire length of the street? "But you can make clothes and dolls, all manner of things. It is a skill."

"I'm not so good. Others are better." He was flattered enough to blush, irritated enough to yell. But above all else, confused. The conversation was one of the most uncomfortable he'd ever been in, he felt like a charlatan being exposed in front of the world. The Wizard of Oz as that dog was pulling back the curtain.

Why did Inessa get joy from dismantling him? Even now, she teased. "Must you hold the world record for your skills to matter? Just because you are not in first place doesn't mean it is no accomplishment." But Satoru couldn't match her chuckles.

"This intervention, or something?" he growled, and Inessa crossed her arms, becoming irritated as well.

"No, but it is so frustrating to compliment you. This part of you is ugly. I feel like I have offended you somehow."

"You don't." Except she kind of had, though Satoru couldn't explain how. It was stupid to be mad that she wanted to say nice things about him, but he didn't know how to convince her that her pretty words weren't true. "Not offended, but why we talk about this?"

"Because I am sick of a life with cardboard cutouts instead of people!" She sounded distressed, and Satoru slowed to look at her properly. He didn't understand what she meant about cardboard, but Inessa looked upset and he'd put that look on her face, so he tried to understand. "Everyone sees me as a little girl, they must not disturb my play. So they will show no depth, never let me past their surface. There is nothing behind the pretty picture."

Satoru still didn't understand her cardboard metaphor and how that related to pictures, but that and the word 'depth' conjured up the image of an empty box, and his shoulders tensed. Was she upset to find there was nothing more to him underneath the veneer of good skating? Was she hoping he would prove her discovery wrong? "I know you're not child. Your life isn't happy play."

"Exactly. You understand," Inessa said, "Or I thought you did. After Coach Muhlenberg died, you were the one to call me. You stayed up all night to hear me cry." It was difficult to do. Satoru hadn't been able to think of a single comforting thing, and he was too far away to do anything of value. But he tried to be there for Inessa while she grieved her late coach. "You let me cry and be vulnerable. I have always been able to share my burdens with you. But you will not share with me? This is not friendship."

That hurt. "You act like I have sad childhood, big tragedy."

"Do you?" And those words managed to stab something in Satoru that he thought had already been killed several times over.

She was going to wear his poor heart down to shreds. "You very strange today. Ask strange questions." He tried to glare, but his heart wasn't fully in it. "Bad at spy, Inessa, please stay skater ."

"I'm sorry. It's just that you seem so open and honest, but I don't actually know anything about you. I don't know what makes you upset, or how to make it better. I only know your reflection, the same you everybody sees." Yes, that was kind of the point. Didn't everyone want to present their best self to the world? He wasn't trying to deceive her, but there wasn't anything else in his cardboard box, so wasn't it better to just keep the lid closed?

Was she mad he turned out to be so empty, or mad that he didn't try harder? When he didn't say anything, Inessa sighed. "Well, I think you are pretty wonderful. I hope you always know that."

He could almost hear Wataru in his brain. "*If she could see what a brat you are at home...*" Satoru hung his head and tried to clamp down his feelings of guilt. It would be easier to just walk away from this conversation. But Inessa was right, and friends shared their burdens. It was the same sort of sentiment he used to face Damien with, and still felt unsettled that there was a side of his friend he knew nothing about. Satoru knew first-hand how painful and cruel it could be to care for someone and be held at arm's length.

And would he really be telling her anything Kara Beth hadn't already figured out? Anything he hadn't already told Damien during some meltdown or tantrum? Maybe if he explained why he couldn't accept compliments, she'd stop overdoing it, and they'd both be happy. It was clear Inessa needed more from this friendship, so the burden was on Satoru to rise up or let it end.

If there was a chance to keep Inessa in his life, he had to do it. He'd already lost too many hours of his life imagining what their future children would look like.

He took a deep breath, and tried to keep his voice steady. "Growing up, I want to do a lot of things. But mostly skating." He still remembered his first lesson, his first spin, his first toe loop. Skating beat out every other pursuit. "And that's hard, takes time and money, family makes a lot of sacrifice. So have to prove sacrifice is worth it, as kid. You know, if not going to be much, maybe don't need so many lessons. Maybe don't need new skates." He looked over at Inessa, to see if his words were tracking. "Have to prove I want and will work hard. You understand?"

"Yes." Of course she did. Every skater did. It wasn't cheap to be elite, and there was no outside financial support in the beginning, if one got lucky enough to be granted some as they ascended the ranks.

Satoru nodded, and continued. "But other things, still have to do.

Like school. So that's hard. And chores, can't stop doing because training, not fair, right?" Wataru and Izumi threw fits every time Satoru got to duck out on a cleaning project for lessons. Sometimes it escalated to fights and they all got in trouble, but they were right, and it wasn't fair. "Can't only do stuff for me. So, there's pressure, and no time. Have to be good skater, and good student, and good person, can't give up one. And then, everyone say you're too serious, relax." He rolled his eyes, earning a laugh from Inessa. "When do I relax? When there's so much to do?"

"People are silly," Inessa agreed, and Satoru thought 'silly' was a nice way of putting it. But sometimes he wondered if the problem was really with him, and other people could stand up to the weights placed on them. Every skater talked of similar burdens, but none seemed to be buckling under the pressure in the same way Satoru did. No one else melted down over mistakes, and they managed to find pride in their silver and bronze medals, their personal bests that included the stray flaw.

He couldn't. "My first coach is... awful man. So I change, move to America. Very expensive. Brother can't handle. More training, school by distance, now I need job..." He sighed. "I try to do my best. But best isn't good enough."

Inessa chewed at her lip. "How do you mean?" It wasn't enough for her to understand.

"Say I'm good at languages? But I can't say words I need. I can't understand person who needs me hear." Like now, trying to explain his complicated soul to a girl he wished he was good enough to love. "Sew good, I'm happy, cheaper than buying, but not like professional. Always must fix, before audience see. Know about buildings, but can't get job with just reading. Even skating, I do so well, make new record, but still mistakes and everyone angry. Why can't you do clean? Why don't you try harder? Best is never good enough."

It didn't matter what form the criticism took. Whether it was Wataru, yelling that he didn't give up going to the University of Tokyo so Satoru could goof off during practice, or his mother kindly asking if he would like to try some other sport or club next fall, it was all the same. The federation representative who asked if he was finally ready to challenge himself with a more experienced coach, the reporter who wanted to know why he'd landed his 4F so many times in practice only to two-foot the landing at the one moment it mattered, or the young fan with the poster begging him to break his own world record again, and disappointed when he fell a few tenths of a point underneath. The friend who stared back in utter confusion and the woman at the DMV who was sick of trying to find words dumb enough to explain whatever paperwork Satoru was supposed to be signing. Kara Beth and her kind suggestions that he was overworked and needed a break, even though the goal was still so far. The world resounded with the refrain that Satoru was failing to meet expectations, and all he could do was try to keep up.

He extended his hands in a weak shrug. "Now, best is really not good enough. You try to be nice, but I can't pretend I'm better than truth."

Inessa gazed back at him with her sad, brown eyes. Eyes that Satoru couldn't really see anymore. "I think you lost sight of the truth a long time ago."

Each step felt like he was dragging a bus behind him. He shouldn't have said anything, he'd disappointed her as well. "I don't mean to make frustrated," he apologized. "But..."

"You are under a lot of pressure. I see." Inessa exhaled. "And I don't mean to upset you. We can talk of something else." When she faced him, there was a smile on her face. "I like your sister. She is very fun."

That cheered Satoru up, enough that he could let the previous conversation drift into the background. "I worried she don't find someone to talk to. Glad she have fun with everyone." Ahead of them, Izumi was laughing with Clara and Hser Nay about something, though Satoru was clueless as to what.

"Cat videos are the international language," Inessa giggled. "You two get along well, I see."

"We do," Satoru agreed. "But if she knew English, she probably say embarrassing things about me. Little sisters have to, is rule."

"That's why I am an only child," Inessa grinned. "But you probably do the same thing to your older brother, right?"

The mention of Wataru caused all that weight to settle back into Satoru's heart, so close to their last topic. He fidgeted and took too long to give a carefree reply that Inessa picked up on his shift in mood. "Is something wrong?"

"I..." He debated, then decided it would be impossible to pretend. "My brother, we don't get along. To have little brother is annoying, we don't like same things." Satoru shrugged. "Think we're too different to get along."

"That's too bad." Inessa looked very sympathetic to hear it. Satoru wondered what her perspective was as an only child. "It must be hard."

"Sometimes." But Satoru couldn't pretend he didn't share any blame for it. "I think childhood is hard for him. Parents give more time to me and skating, don't have money for things. He gives up much and feels not important. I would hate, too."

"He blames you?"

"Yes," Satoru answered without thinking, then waved his arms in protest. "He's not wrong. I'm not perfect, do many things to make mad. Very annoying little brother." He tried to smile, but Inessa didn't take his words as a joke. Like before, he felt a strange need to explain, even though his mind warned him not to be so personal. "You ask why I don't say nice things about me? This is why, because to let me skate, everyone gives up so much, so I can't just laugh about mistake. Is insult." Satoru grimaced at the thought that even now, he was goofing off with his friends when he needed to be building his stamina back up. "Wataru says too much and too loud, in the past. Because he's frustrated. But he's not wrong. Just other people are nicer."

"I see," Inessa said, in a tone that suggested maybe she'd seen something Satoru hadn't wanted her to.

Which made no sense, since he'd told the truth. "He isn't bad person, don't think that," Satoru said, and hoped he hadn't given that impression. Much as Wataru frustrated him, he didn't deserve to have his little brother spreading bad words to others. "He's good brother to me and Izumi. I'm just bad for family."

Inessa looked depressed. "Satoru, please don't ever say that again." She said no more, and Satoru gaped all the way to the intersection where he and Izumi would part ways with all the skaters.

He exchanged farewells with all of his friends, but the back of his mind was still trying to process what he'd messed up. Inessa wanted him to disclose feelings, and he'd been honest, hadn't he? How dare she make him put his worst qualities on display and then act like he'd done something wrong?

Or maybe the result had been even worse than she'd expected? This was why he should never ask her out. Inessa deserved a boyfriend who wasn't afraid to peel back the surface layer. Friendship was already a better gift than he deserved, let Inessa find some tall, dark Israeli man who shared her religion and language and wasn't struggling to pass all the minimum bars of human expectation, rather than get stuck with Satoru just because he'd be the first one to ask.

Despite these negative thoughts, Inessa had a smile when she said goodbye, if her eyes were a little less jovial than usual. "You know, I would still like it if you would design my dress next season. If I am to claim my first Olympic title, I would like to look my best."

That wasn't what Satoru expected to hear. He almost pointed out that Inessa's logic was the exact reason she should ask some professional costumer, but in light of her previous words he kept his mouth shut. "I don't see colors, remember?"

"I know." Inessa smiled at him, but it was so serious. She suddenly looked far older than eighteen, more mature than he was. In an instant, Satoru saw her as a woman, as a rival, as a bride, an ice dance partner... And he was so caught up in that bizarre bout of time-bending fantasy that he didn't register that Inessa was stepping into his personal space.

The kiss was quick. A small peck on the lips, and then Inessa stepped back. If one blinked, they'd have missed the whole thing.

And yet, Satoru felt like he'd been ripped in half. One side of him was plummeting down to the pavement and never seemed to hit, as if looking up at Inessa from the ground, with the sky spinning and maybe he was also upside down. The other half of him was stuck on the fact that Inessa didn't need to get on her tiptoes to meet his lips, of all the dumb things to be fixated on, and couldn't get past the disbelief that he was that short.

As for Inessa, she remained cool and perfect, as always. Her smile was the same serious one she'd been wearing a second ago, her gaze far more confident than that of a high school girl.

"Make me something that looks beautiful in your eyes."

Satoru couldn't remember if he agreed to the job or not. But Inessa skipped off with a grin, so he must have. Either way, Sione was whistling at him and laughing loud enough to draw every eye in the city. Izumi all but collapsed in a fit of giggles, Yukiya looked mildly uncomfortable with the public affection, and Damien offered up a slow clap with a mocking twist of his lips. The girls all swarmed Inessa and started up a stream of whispers and sneaky grins.

The one half of Satoru was panicked and mortified, still wondering when he was going to make contact with the concrete. But the other half of him was working its way to some different emotions. Inessa had made her choice.

He was probably going to die before he got himself together. But Satoru could say with good authority that it wasn't the worst way to go.

15

DAMIEN DIDN'T DISLIKE press conferences, but he was always worried he'd say the wrong thing. He admired people like Hser Nay, who faced the media with complete candor and carelessness. But Damien was a little too aware of how thoughtless words could hurt and was careful not to reveal something that could be easily spun out of context.

On the other hand, there were many things he wished to say, but could not. He knew his personal trials were an inspiration to some, and that there were young people in his situation who needed a role model to show them it wasn't hopeless. To sweep eating disorders and their effects under the rug would do the world no favors, but Damien wasn't sure he had such courage yet. It wasn't even an issue of fearing the backlash, the sway of public opinion, as much as he just couldn't bring his heart to speak certain things aloud. And the same held true for many other topics.

So he was in a strange state of not saying what needed to be said, and possibly saying something unnecessary that could be taken out of context. Like the time he'd mentioned that he and Satoru used to share hotel rooms in their teens whenever possible, and somehow didn't convey that the primary motivation was to cut down on travel expenses. The gossip columns ran wild with the story of their teenaged romance and caused them both a lot of unneeded trouble. Damien's parents didn't find it amusing, not like it was their business to be offended. The one whose life might suffer real consequences found out through the gossip rags, and even though he'd lost a sponsor over it, just laughed it off with an irreverent text: *[You forgot to tell me I sleep with you! Was I best night of your life?]*

But there had never been a class or manual on how to deal with the press, not even any advice, before they suddenly shoved him in front of cameras as a young teen. Kara Beth had made up for that a bit when Damien came under her tutelage, since it hadn't been so long ago that she'd been in his shoes. "You're not obligated to answer anything," she reminded him now, as they went through the mixed zone. "If you don't want to talk, don't. They can't publish silence, so they'll come up with other questions to ask if you don't say anything, you don't have to fill dead air for them."

"I know, I know," Damien muttered, but he still dreaded the sight of cameras and handheld recorders. Now that he was away from his safe ice rink, he wasn't nearly as brave. And this year, the questions might be more personal than ever before. Satoru wasn't here to steal all the attention, and there was a very uncomfortable reason for that absence.

He could visualize the questions without needing to hear them. They would start small. *"Is the atmosphere of the training rink different without Miyazawa? Has this accident affected your training?"* Then, they would get a bit more ambitious. *"Does your coach have more time for you in Miyazawa's absence? How did you feel to hear this had happened to your rival?"* And before long, they'd be downright impertinent. *"How much of your current success is because of Miyazawa's absence? With him out of the competition, do you think it's finally your chance to win?"*

There was one question no one asked yet, but Damien feared it was only a matter of time. Logic and decency had never held the media back before, and why should they start now? There were people around him whose job was to act as a buffer between himself and the press, but there was only so much they could do, and Damien feared what would happen if someone finally crossed the line and asked that one question.

"You going to be okay, there?" Kara Beth murmured, her hand snaking up to rest on Damien's shoulder. He nodded a reply, but didn't trust himself to speak. His job was to skate, he could focus on that. One step in front of the other, until he reached a safe distance from the cameras. Let him skate and finish his primary job, then the ocean of journalists and photographers could descend upon him.

They made it safely out of the public eye, but the tidal wave hit him in the locker room. Yukiya Minami was glaring daggers at him, with no attempt to conceal it. After a few minutes of tumultuous seething, he faced Damien with resolve. "Hello."

Damien was a bit thrown. None of his competitors ever talked to him so close to the competition, save for Satoru, who'd have been nearly bouncing off the walls by this point. Competitive Cone of Silence, as Kara Beth called it. He doubted Yukiya was planning to wish him good luck. "Hello. You are doing well?"

"How is boyfriend?"

That was the last thing he expected to hear. "Pardon, but I do not understand you."

"Boy~friend."

"Again, I don't understand." Damien could only respond with a helpless shrug. "I am not dating anyone at present."

"Liar."

That caused Damien to pause. It also drew the attention of the other skaters in the locker room.

"Meet boyfriend. In California. Grand Prix America."

While Damien stared, Aaron Leval of the United States broke Competitive Cone of Silence and slung an arm around his shoulders. "Saint-Michel, you have a boyfriend? You didn't tell me you were seeing anyone!"

"I am not seeing anyone. Nor would I tell you if I was."

"Aw, you're such a snob." He ruffled Damien's hair, earning an expression of extreme disgust for the effort. But it only seemed to brighten Aaron's annoying smile all the more. "Well, if you don't have a boyfriend, that means you're still on the market-"

"No."

"You didn't even let me finish my sentence."

"I am reasonably sure I didn't need to." Damien shrugged out of the embrace, and Aaron just laughed at him. So he turned his attention back to Yukiya, who was growing increasingly more furious for some unknown reason. "There must be some misunderstanding. As I said, I don't have a boyfriend, nor do I know anyone in California." The real question was why Yukiya seemed to care so much.

"I meet. He say me boyfriend-"

"Well, it is not true. Though I don't know why you are so upset about it."

"Yeah, as long as he's single, there's still hope!" Aaron chimed in, and Damien groaned.

"Please, enough!"

Yukiya reached his limit, and burst out, "He backstage! California! Near Sato-kun! When poison bottle!" That caused a hush to fall over the locker room, and Derek and Sione, who'd been trying to ignore the conversation, now stood at attention.

"Hold up, mate," Derek said, looking troubled. "Are you saying you saw the person who poisoned Miyazawa?"

"Don't know. But there. Always, whole time. On video. Your boyfriend."

The words were nonsensical. But Yukiya was absolutely serious, and his face had a look of vengeance about it. While Damien tried to figure out what parallel universe he lived in, Sione stepped forward. "What video? Who is this man?"

"Yes, that is what I would like to know," Damien agreed, but the only person listening to him was Yukiya, who was growing more livid with the lack of answers and inability to communicate.

"He hurts Satoru? Tell me!"

"How should I know anything? I don't even know who we are talking about!" Damien yelled back, but the fury and desperation in Yukiya's eyes were ones he knew well. Since the day the tragedy happened, he'd had those feelings also, and no place to direct them. "I do not understand what you're saying!"

"I ask boyfriend hurt Satoru! Because you!" And that response was a stab to the chest, even though it couldn't possibly be true.

God above, he thinks I had something to do with this...

Not that anyone cared about the truth. Derek looked between Damien and Yukiya with growing disgust. "This is some Tonya and Nancy level intrigue right here. But it makes sense, doesn't it?"

"What makes sense?" Damien sneered. "I've no boyfriend, no idea who Yukiya is talking about, and I certainly would never ask someone to hurt others for me!"

"No? You prefer to do your dirty work yourself?"

Sione stepped in front of Damien before he could launch himself at Derek's throat. "No one's accusing you of anything," he lied, even with Derek snarling in the background. "But maybe there's a connection. Yukiya's right, it is weird." Behind him, Aaron nodded.

"You got a crazy ex or something? Someone who'd want to see you win?"

"Jealous," Yukiya added his input, looking like he'd only just managed to dig that word out of his subconscious. "Jealous of Satoru. Always touch and cute names."

Derek snorted, and Damien shot him a glare. He should have expected as much from Derek, but to have earned Yukiya's suspicion was a crushing blow. Did his character hold no weight against this stranger? "There is no ex. I don't know who this person is."

"Maybe it's not now, like, from a few years ago?" Aaron prodded, but Damien grew impatient.

"There is no one," he growled, a little embarrassed to admit it. "No boyfriend, no girlfriend. I can't think of anyone who could claim such."

"Really?" Aaron seemed incredulous, which only soured Damien's mood further. "You've never dated anyone? Like, ever?"

"Pardon, but my romantic life is none of your business." He crossed his arms and glared at Yukiya. "You mentioned a video. Can I see this pretender?"

While Yukiya dug into his pockets for his phone, Derek got more bold. "It would make sense, though. I can't think of anyone who'd want Miyazawa gone more than you. And now it seems you've had a secret boyfriend placed in the perfect position-"

"How dare you!"

"As if you haven't been saying the same things about me!" Derek challenged, and Damien had to admit, he felt a bit of guilt at the realization.

But not much. "You have never liked Satoru. How many times have you tried to bully him out of your sight?"

"As a joke!" Derek scoffed. "He returns it just as hard! We're fighting for the same podium, but you, you've got that and a coach to fight over. He disappears, and suddenly you're the favorite to win the Grand Prix? Can't say the timing isn't suspicious."

"I'm sure the timing is coincidence," said Sione, though he looked disturbed. Damien's heart sank at the thought that even Sione might view him in an unfavorable light.

And then a paralyzing thought: What if Satoru believed these rumors?

"Yes, coincidence, Sione," Derek sneered. "The fact that Saint-Michel may have a connection to the event and gains endless benefits if Miyazawa disappears is complete and utter coincidence."

Damien's eyes narrowed. His entire slender frame shivered, which could only reflect a fraction of the dissolution inside. "You know I gain no benefits from Satoru's absence."

Aaron cleared his throat to break the stoney silence that followed. "Come on guys, calm down. We're not accusing anyone, just trying to get to the bottom of this weirdness."

"You all say no one accuses me, but I feel a lot of hostility in this locker room," Damien grumbled. He crossed over to Yukiya, who had produced a screen cap of the person who started all the trouble. "Let me see that."

"You know?" Yukiya asked, and Damien was all set to deny it and put this entire conversation to rest.

But the words died on his lips. He did know that person.

16

———————

"ON THE ICE, representing France! Damien Saint-Michel!" Damien took a deep breath and skated to the center of the ice. While the entire men's division whispered about the open door left in Satoru's absence, Damien had four minutes to slam it back shut.

And maybe four minutes to lose his best friend, but he couldn't think about that now. Damien settled into his opening pose and waited for the music to start. He had worried for a moment that he wouldn't be able to skate today, since the police had taken so long with him. But he couldn't have let that wait, not after finding out his stalker had been present when someone poisoned Satoru.

It seemed unbelievable, even now, but Yukiya's video, apparently courtesy of Inessa Levi, didn't lie. Henri Petard of Belgium, the stalker whom Damien had just seen a week previous at his own Grand Prix event, had apparently flown down to California to stalk his rival. And while Henri had always seemed harmless, if a tad obsessive, this was crossing a line.

Damien couldn't say the young man had it in him to murder. He was the type to make handcrafted banners and shout from the stands during matches, or send thoughtful letters after Damien's withdrawal from World's last year. Even when he'd shown up at Skate Canada, sneaking into the backstage area without permission, the biggest trouble he caused was a heartfelt declaration of love. Damien's feelings about love were skeptical and confused, but it was hardly threatening.

Of course, now that he was stalking Satoru and claiming to be Damien's boyfriend, all bets were off. To pose as a volunteer at the event, and then hover around a person who was nearly murdered? It was more than a little suspicious. Damien thought it would have been better for Yukiya to have taken his discovery to the authorities from the start, rather than confronting him in the locker room right before a competition, but the kid idolized Satoru, and fear made people do foolish things.

Unless it had been his intention to shake Damien before the competition? To throw suspicion on him and turn the other skaters against him in order to take attention away from Yukiya? It would be a smart move, were Yukiya the culprit, to distract everyone from his own considerable motives and greater opportunity...

Damien shook his head to clear it. Yukiya was unworthy of such suspicion, even if he had just made Damien's life difficult. The competition had become a minefield in a few short weeks, with everyone distrusting the person next to them. Damien doubted Yukiya really believed him guilty of the attempted murder, but the younger boy definitely looked at him with skepticism, and that hurt. Sione and Aaron hadn't outright accused him, but Damien could feel that something had changed, and so had Nikolai Baratynsky when he'd walked into the locker room and after five seconds of taking in the atmosphere, asked who had been exiled to Siberia.

That was what awaited him when he got off the ice. All the media speculation, the tabloids running wild with theories, the rooms that became just a little quieter when he entered, the hidden glances people shot at him from across a crowded hall. He was the favorite to win the Grand Prix, not because of his own considerable accomplishment, but because his greatest competition had been poisoned. And no matter what the truth was, no matter what investigations were conducted, the narrative would always show that Satoru nearly died and Damien benefitted.

For now, though, he could only do his job. On the sidelines, Kara Beth stood at the ready, still as they waited for the music to begin, pom-poms waiting with the same anticipation as the crowd. But Kara Beth gave more support than all of them put together. "You're strong," she told him before he took the ice. "In ways you weren't even a year ago. You can make it through this."

And he would. There were skaters who thought Satoru was unbeatable, but Damien thought they were idiots. Yes, Satoru was intimidating and all the other superlatives, but not unbeatable.

He did agree that Satoru's level of ability was frightening. The men's division had been spooked ever since word got out that his Quad Axel was consistent enough for competition. A lot of skaters decided that chasing him for gold wasn't worth potential hip replacements at twenty-five, and Damien could respect that. It took a special insanity to be a world-class athlete, more so if Satoru was eating Quad Axels for breakfast.

It was those trying for the world podium and Olympic glory Damien couldn't understand. Why push yourself so far and endure such hardship, only to look at your competition and give up? What was the point of striving to improve if you believed that the limit was already reached? Particularly since Satoru looked through limits like they didn't even exist. If he could break them, so could someone else.

Chords from the musical "Notre Dame de Paris" filled the arena, and Damien couldn't help but smile at the memory of how he'd fought for this music. Not against his choreographer, though the man had thought the piece a little too on point. *"Yes, Damien, everyone knows you're French..."* Kara Beth had only sighed and said, *"Well, at least you're out of your punk rock phase..."*

But Satoru had thrown a little tantrum when he'd heard the news. "I wanted music!" he insisted and tried to claim he'd put it forth as an option to Rachel before Damien met with his choreographer and therefore had dibs. Damien responded that he was Parisian and not only qualified, but obligated to skate the piece. They took their argument to Kara Beth, who told them if they took dueling "Notre Dame" programs to Worlds, she expected a raise.

In the end, Damien won, but now and then Satoru would swipe his game controller or throw socks at him and say, "That's for Notre Dame." It was all in fun, though. At least, Damien thought that. But if Satoru's petty side ran deeper than the surface, he'd find out by the time the program was over.

He built up all the speed he could muster, sliding into his 3-turn and backward onto his left outside edge as he came down the rink. The 4Ltz was his best weapon on his quest for the top of the podium. Damien had a plan for this program on paper since he was nineteen. When he'd shown it to Kara Beth, she'd laughed.

"Ambitious, but you can't do that," she told him. "Nobody can."

"Not now," Damien agreed. He knew his body wasn't in the best condition at the time, and it was a struggle for him to keep up with the diet Maureen laid down for him. People had not yet succeeded in some of the combination jumps on his program list. "But skaters are pushing the sport as we speak. I know Satoru has been working towards a Quad Salchow-Quad Toe combo. He has learned the Quad Flip, backloads his programs, and is training the Axel. In a few years, this program layout won't seem so bizarre, will it?"

Kara Beth agreed after some thought, but still looked skeptical. "Do you realize how hard you're going to have to work?"

"You think I'm not capable?"

"I think it's going to take a lot of changes to your lifestyle." Damien expected as much, but still swallowed some pride to hear it mentioned aloud. He'd have to eat. Multiple times a day. "And I'm a little concerned about your obsession with Satoru's training."

"It's not an obsession," Damien insisted. He'd looked out onto the ice, where Satoru was going through his stroking exercises. Even now, Damien still remembered the focus in the other boy's eyes. "It's not about Satoru, exactly. But he is the one winning the race. I can't wait until he decides to stop running. I must run faster." Satoru was the new standard, consistent enough to always be on top of the podium.

It wasn't personal, but the bar Damien needed to jump over had a face and a name, and he tried to explain that to Kara Beth. "I want to win the world championships before I retire." He pointed to Satoru. "That is the world champion. I won't win gold until I can be a few steps ahead of him."

Kara Beth agreed, but she issued a warning. "I'm not picking favorites. My job is to coach you to be your personal best. How the placements shake out is up to you and the judges."

"I understand," Damien said, and he did. There wasn't a secret or conspiracy that he needed to keep from Satoru, nor did he want their coach to neglect one skater in favor of the other. But if Damien's personal best happened to one day exceed the reigning world champion's, that was a worthy goal. And to do that, he needed to look beyond the present.

But futures inevitably became the present.

English adapted Notre Dame de Paris as "The Hunchback of Notre Dame", but while that change shed more light on Victor Hugo's plot, Damien found the original title more accurate. The characters and the situations within the novel all revolved around the cathedral in Paris, and it was the star of the book. One of Hugo's goals had been to increase appreciation of gothic architecture, and wrote long passages detailing various features of the building, regardless of whether it furthered the story. That was probably Satoru's attraction to the music, loving old buildings and Notre Dame in particular.

But other aspects of the story commanded Damien. Grandeur, glory and meaning falling into decay, human virtues at war with human vices, and most of all, the way people could accept a status quo until the world around them warped into something unrecognizable. And once their eyes had been opened, would they rally to reclaim what was lost? Fate, destiny and determinism were powerful ideas, and though Damien didn't believe they and free will were mutually exclusive, he did believe in a greater power and purpose, and that some things were meant to happen.

In today's case, dethroning the Grand Prix Champion.

Satoru seemed to be a master of jumping passes, but his biggest weakness was his quadruple Flip. It was a jump with a higher point value, which shot Satoru's score up, only to then drop a few points on the Grade of Execution, the evaluation of how well he'd done the jump. Damien suspected the problem went beyond physical ability, and that the mental trauma of his first coach carried over. "Knee healed, but hard to tell at first," Satoru once confessed. "They worry I don't skate again." He didn't say much more. Damien guessed it was too painful to remember .

Satoru kept his Flip jump out of stubbornness, because the younger skaters were coming up with their Lutzs and he needed those higher base values to keep his lead, but it was common knowledge that he hated it. Damien suspected that as the Quad Axel, worth even more points, became more and more comfortable, that Flip would start to disappear.

And Satoru hadn't done a Lutz jump since he was a teenager. So as daunting as the Quad Axel was, that left two highly valued jumps that made only shaky to non-existent appearances in Satoru's programs. As far as base values went, it wouldn't be hard to train those jumps and thus make up the gap.

Of course, that was easier said than done. A four quad program was no easy feat, though becoming more of a necessity as the years went on. Satoru could handle five, would do more when he could cram them in around the rules, but there was still a wide point difference between a more difficult jump done poorly and an easier jump done well.

Moreover, Satoru wasn't oblivious to the threat flips and lutzs posed to him, and knew that he'd have to make up the points elsewhere. So he cultivated his skating skills, and the judges rewarded his speed, transitions and choreography. His components scores received high nines in all categories, and even the occasional ten out of ten. His spins and footwork sequences consistently got level fours, and fans had suggested the ISU should consider changing the rules to allow for a level five.

It made Satoru look unbeatable, yes. It seemed like one could push themselves to the brink and risk injury learning the high risk jumps, only for Satoru to make up points in another area and still walk away with the medal. But looks were deceiving, and Damien wasn't ready to give up so easily. To achieve Satoru's level, one had to attack from several angles.

The music of "Notre Dame" swelled like the voices of an angry mob, and Damien's Lutz rose above it as a destroying flame, lifted by the transcendent chords. He landed with all the ease of ash on the wind, barely a disturbance as he touched the ground. Damien still felt full of energy, more than enough for the task ahead.

On the ice, his next jumping pass was coming up, and he let the music reach through him and down to his toes and fingertips. Each transition was given due attention, he could get high marks for Program Components, too. A little diligence, and the goal was in sight. How could people be so content to accept Satoru as unbeatable?

They'd let him win for too long. Somehow, they'd all become complacent, waiting for Satoru to slow down, to fall, to hold himself back, sitting comfortably on their silvers and bronzes and minor competitions while the gap grew larger. It was easier to tell oneself that Satoru was just special than to jump off that lofty tower with him. Easier to say that they were still working hard, they just couldn't compete, and never seeing their own stagnation.

So Damien had cast his eyes over Satoru's beloved quad-quad combo. It was an ambitious undertaking, and a revelation of ability, but not unsurpassable. Two quads in the same combination was Satoru's act of defiance, a way to keep developing a property that had already been built too high. The legendary status of the jumping pass was intimidating.

So it was more of a personal message than a practicality that Damien began training his own special combination. A declaration to Satoru that he'd finally arrived, he could meet his rival on an even playing field. It didn't have to make sense beyond that. But Satoru would understand, and so would every skater that came after them. The both of them were still human, but anything was possible.

If the skating world was Paris, then Satoru was their Esmeralda, the shining standard of what they all wished to be. Talent, grace, kindness and integrity, the jewel of their community, and she'd been taken from them. Someone broke the rules of the sanctuary, someone coveted his brilliance and cheated, and now they saw the world around them differently. They saw the flaws in their surroundings, the flaws in themselves, and they weren't content to accept that anymore.

Damien hadn't needed the catalyst, but it was time to storm the cathedral. He steadied himself, then launched into a combination of his own. 4F+3A

It wasn't a surprise decision. Satoru knew Damien was working toward it, had cheered him on, in fact. Many skaters did ambitious combination attempts in practice, even if they weren't serious about putting it in competition, just to test their limits. Doing them together posed a challenge, but that was where Damien's real advantage over Satoru came in.

Physique. Satoru was 5'5 and built like a twig; he couldn't muscle his way through anything. Despite all efforts, Satoru remained lithe and weightless, which had its own advantages, but Damien, when he remembered to eat, was stronger. His genetics gifted him with more muscle than his rink-mate, and he hadn't spent years learning bad habits from skating on a fractured knee. It was both a lucky and a cruel reminder that if Damien had gotten help with his food issues as a teen, he surely could have flown even higher.

But as for the present, it wasn't hard to see Satoru training his 4S+4T and decide to attempt his 4F+3A alongside him. If well done, it could easily compete and there was no way Satoru was pulling out the strength to add difficulty midway through the season.

Especially not this season. Esmeralda was the finest girl in France, for so many reasons, and she didn't deserve her ending. That was out of Damien's control. The only thing he could control was himself. He landed his Flip, feeling the drag pulling him down, then used all his strength to turn and vault back up for the Triple Axel, the first time he'd attempted that pass in competition. A feat of strength, but he made it around and landed with the crowd roaring so loudly that he could barely hear his music.

If Satoru was Esmeralda, Damien was Quasimodo. Deformed and isolated, afraid of being mocked for his ugliness. Even when attention was meant in kindness, he couldn't stand the constant refrain of "too skinny, why don't you eat more, it can't be that hard." Having to constantly assure people that yes, he did eat, please leave him alone, or admit that he hadn't and somehow bear up the shame made the life of a shut in look appealing. It made it easy to look at the skaters ranked above him and think, "I'll never do that, I can't help it," easy to settle where he was and give up ambition, squander talent and push others away.

But Esmeralda showed kindness to the monster. She saved his life both physically and metaphorically, and Quasimodo's better qualities found their way to the surface. They were a strange friendship, and one that wasn't perfect, but the gratitude and loyalty Quasimodo felt for Esmeralda overcame his aversion to leaving the cathedral. When she died, he stayed by her until his own life ended, and the skeletons crumbled to dust when they were finally separated.

Irony was a powerful force in Notre-Dame de Paris. Quasimodo would do anything to protect Esmeralda, but mistakenly fought her rescuers and helped her enemies. Esmeralda trusted people who wanted to use her, was lied to and tricked, and eventually hanged for no crime other than being brilliant. Damien couldn't rewrite the ending of the tragic tale, but he hoped the consequences in his own life would be less dire.

The air rushed through Damien's hair during a spin sequence, before he launched himself into the most vigorous and majestic footwork his choreographer could throw at him. Who was beside Satoru during all of those stroking sessions, matching him blade for blade? Who lapped up Kara Beth's spin lessons with the same eager eyes? Damien could admit Satoru was the superior skater, but he was close enough to kick at Satoru's heels. There wouldn't be enough of a point lead to make up for Damien's technical content. Paris was burning, the peasants were storming the cathedral, good and evil were warring in the streets.

But oh, determinism. Fate. Damien could skate with all the spirit of revolution, but he would lose Esmeralda in the process. He never wanted anyone to hurt Satoru, shrank back from the thought of the vile deeds done to him, but the narrative had been screaming towards this end from the beginning. If he won the day here, Esmeralda would die, and his friend would forever see him as the monster that cost him everything.

But how could Damien do anything else? How could he not fight for the worthy causes, defy the oppressive limits set down by others? This was determinism, a series of circumstances that could only result in one outcome. The pretty building, a structure that told him to believe, to aspire to greater things, to exercise his own divinity and hope, it had distracted him. Even though stories had a predetermined ending.

But that building still held meaning to Damien. So he threw himself into his last combo with faith that there was a higher power above everything else. A guiding hand that accepted tragic endings, but still inspired humanity to rise, be better, to take leaps of faith. If that building had any resonance left, its bells would shout the grand plan that brought beauty and justification out of tragedy.

Damien pulled on the rope and let the tower ring. The combination was hard, but he exited the jump with almost more speed than he'd started.

The ending might be set, and might even be tragic, but Damien wasn't a victim of fate, with no control over his future. He wasn't content to sit back and accept circumstance, not anymore. He couldn't control the direction of the story, but he would own his place in it.

He would be the World Champion. Satoru was one person who'd convinced him he had the skill to get there, one of the few that made Damien believe he was more than ambition and an eating disorder. Each jump and spin reinforced the tragedy of this skate, the anguish his friend would feel at coming in second, at a time when his own abilities were bound and locked in prison. Each transition reinforced the rightness and inevitability of this skate, for it was time that someone looked at Satoru's accomplishments and mustered the bravery to join them. Maybe Satoru would be proud of him, maybe he'd be jealous, most likely both. But it was hard to keep a close friendship under these heightened circumstances, and as Paris descended further into chaos, Damien feared that this year, with the challenges they faced, it would be too much for their skating family to bear.

But whatever Esmeralda thought of her death, Quasimodo would be by her side until their bones were ash.

IT WAS, in short, the most impressive skate Satoru had ever seen.

The quad-triple-axel was especially thrilling and set Satoru's blood on fire. He couldn't wait to get back to Granville and try to beat Damien at his own game. And the artistry! The personal interpretation was intense and heartbreaking. The crowd rose and fell and even cried, all as one. Much as Satoru wanted the song initially, Damien was born to skate this music.

All of it would have been impressive for any skater, but doubly so because it was Damien. This was the first time Satoru had seen his friend finish a long program without bracing himself against his knees and heaving for breath, collapsing to the ice like a wet noodle. It seemed to mock everything else he'd achieved with the skate, but Satoru was most impressed to see that his friend looked healthy. Damien finished that skate like a champion.

He was so absorbed in clapping and cheering that the idea of scores didn't enter his head until Damien and Kara Beth were settled in the Kiss and Cry, blue, white and red pom-poms shaking in triumph. Each awful rhinestone on Damien's bedazzled outfit hit the spotlight and probably blinded the poor camera operator, but Damien and Kara Beth had never looked happier. The antics were endearing, but the two of them stilled as the screen lit up, ready to see the numerical result. And the cruel reminder that these performances had a point value sent Satoru's mind into calculations. Lutzs were worth more than Salchows, and Damien had two, the Flip combo, that spin...

The feeling of dread hit him just seconds before the combined score was posted on the jumbotron. When it did, the arena exploded. Damien started shrieking enough to be heard all the way back in France and maybe blew out one of the nearby microphones, but Satoru couldn't make a sound. He never should have returned that stupid watch. Next to him, Izumi clapped and whistled. "That's so high! Close to your best score, huh?"

"It's higher," Satoru said.

"What?"

"It's higher than my best score." His best score, which was also the world record. Izumi didn't seem to appreciate the full meaning of that, and when the cumulative score was posted a second later, her cheers for Damien grew even louder. Damien himself might have shattered glass. But Wataru knew.

Satoru didn't dare look in his direction. The arena's noise and adulation grew as the announcer repeated the score and announced the creation of the new world record. Izumi jumped up and down while Satoru forced his hands to move, to beat together in some show of support, but he was losing the sensation of touch from his wrists down to his ankles. Damien just broke his world records in both the free skate and the overall score.

On the screen, Damien was the picture of joy, still screaming, triumph on every inch of his face. He hugged Kara Beth, then kissed her, made the crowd clap for her. And she returned the applause to Damien.

And why shouldn't she have clapped? She was training the new Grand Prix champion.

"Hey, are you okay?" Izumi finally noticed he wasn't quite as enthused as he was a few seconds ago. She also seemed to have realized that breaking a record left sharp pieces that could fall on people. "Are you... mad?"

Satoru snapped on a smile, the same one he pulled out for press conferences after two-footing his Flip. "I'm fine. That was pretty amazing, huh?"

"Very nice," Wataru clapped, and the sound sent shockwaves that threatened to turn Satoru's brain to mush. "He's been working hard."

"I know, right! Congratulations, Dami!" Izumi jumped for joy, not noticing she was out of place next to Wataru's subdued clapping and Satoru's stilted panic. "I've never seen him skate like that!"

Satoru had. In practices, on good days, but the consistency had never been there until now. Damien couldn't get his eating under control to the degree necessary to sustain those abilities over a full season. But things had changed, just like Satoru hoped they would. This was what Damien was meant to be, his best self that he'd always been just shy of reaching.

He'd spent years waiting to see something like this. So why wasn't he happy?

"I need to go." He stumbled out of his seat and pushed his way down the aisle, muttering some excuse about needing the restroom. Izumi was incredulous, since there was still one more skater left to take the ice, but Satoru didn't care. The arena was stifling, he needed to get out before he stopped breathing, or something worse.

Away from the cheers, away from the crowds, from any prying eyes that could see the breakdown he was about to have. Satoru staggered down sets of stairs and turned into hallways until he found a place secluded enough to stop. The glasses were an unexpected privilege, in that they disguised him. Between the frames and the weight he'd lost in the hospital, the casual observer wouldn't easily recognize Satoru.

And he didn't need anyone snapping pictures of him while his life was getting upended. Satoru leaned against the wall and put his head in his hands, sucking air through the fingers to calm himself. For weeks, he'd been trying to get used to the idea that he was going to lose the Grand Prix championships. Now that the moment had come, he felt the loss as acute as a black hole, the gravity of absence crushing his bones. Nationals would soon follow this, and maybe more losses if Satoru couldn't get back to peak condition. And what was he without his titles and world records?

And entering into that line of thought was Wataru. Satoru heard the footsteps and looked up to see his brother. "You followed me?"

"Of course. You seemed upset."

"Upset?" Satoru scoffed. "Why would I be upset? I just needed some air. The rink was stuffy with all those people."

"Sure." Admitting his jealousy out loud would make him the worst kind of person. Not that Wataru didn't know how hard it had been to set those records in the first place, or the expectations that came with it.

Wataru didn't offer any of his commentary now, but he looked disappointed all the same. "Well, you look upset. Try not to make a scene."

"Yeah, I wouldn't want to embarrass you, or anything!" Satoru said. He kicked the back of his heel against the wall, his body full of tension.

Wataru moved to stand next to him. "You're not going to watch the last skater?"

"No," Satoru grumbled. "We already know who's going to win. Nothing's going to beat what Damien just did."

"It's not all about winning." When Satoru had only a look of disbelief for his brother's hypocrisy, Wataru continued, "And you'll miss the interview and medal ceremony if you don't get back in there soon."

Satoru grimaced. "I can't. Not right now."

"What do you mean?"

"Are you dense?" No, Wataru was too smart for that. Did he want Satoru to admit his failings? Confess that he couldn't go out there and watch someone else get awarded all the things he'd worked for, when he could barely land a single toe loop? Reveal that he couldn't handle someone else being first? Satoru hung his head, the weight of failure hanging around his neck like a medal of solid lead. "Whatever you came to say, I don't want to hear it."

"Hear what?"

Satoru snapped his head to the side, glaring. "Your usual lecture on how much ground I have to make up this season. I know. I already know I'm behind and everyone invested so much in this season and every second I'm off the ice is a disappointment." He swallowed, suddenly feeling thirteen again, having traveled thousands of miles and uprooting his brother, only to still fail. "I know Mom and Dad didn't work those extra jobs so I could sit around all day, and you didn't give up Todai for someone else to hold the world record."

"I wasn't going to say that."

"Then what?" Satoru balled his fists. He felt like punching something, but if it came down to his knuckles versus the concrete wall, he'd lose. The anger kept him from sobbing, but just barely. "You think I don't feel bad enough already?"

He wished Wataru would have a reaction, or else just leave. His brother only furrowed his brows in confusion. "You're whining over some dumb thing I said years ago?"

Satoru sputtered. "Years-? My whole life, what else have you ever said? Just that I'm selfish and awful and I can't even make good on the stuff I keep taking from you guys!" A splash of water hit his fists, and Satoru realized he was crying openly now. "Ugh, I'm sorry, okay? I'm sorry this happened, but can't you give me five minutes before you start?"

"You think that's why I'm here?" Why was Wataru playing dumb?

"What else would you be here for? To tell me it's okay? 'Cause it's not," Satoru spat out, but it felt watery. All this blubbering, he must look like more of an embarrassment than ever. "I know it's not. You've never pretended just to make me feel better. Why start now?" He swiped at his leaking eyes, but still wasn't used to the glasses being there, and nearly knocked them off. "I'm sorry, is that what you want to hear? I'm sorry I can't live up to you, I'm sorry I can't make everyone proud, I'm sorry I'm petty and awful and sorry I keep giving you reasons to hate me!"

"Why are you always so sensitive? I've barely said anything." The words caused an anguished scream to tear out of Satoru's throat, and he slumped back against the wall, hands covering his face.

"Just leave me alone," he whimpered. What could Wataru possibly say by now that Satoru didn't tell himself?

But Wataru didn't leave. And when Satoru raised his eyes to the world again, he found his brother with his hand stretched out.

It hovered in the air, hesitant. A silence fell between the two of them as they each debated whether or not to acknowledge the strange gesture. It looked like Wataru had stopped midway through some attempt at comfort, but Satoru couldn't fully believe that, since his brother had never done so before. Wataru barely touched him if he could help it. But the hand lingered, maybe six inches from Satoru's shoulder.

And then it made contact.

It was the most forced and stiff action of Satoru's experience, and enough to push him over the edge. He descended into full sobs, managing a half-hearted, "go away" before speech failed him entirely. Through it all, Wataru kept up arrhythmic, awkward pats on his shoulder. "You think I hate you for losing the title?" He asked, and his voice was almost soft.

Satoru didn't speak. He couldn't, and wouldn't have dared if he could. Wataru just kept up his weird patting that wasn't in the least bit comforting, and took out his phone with his spare hand. "You don't have to go back in. I'll stay out here with you," he said, as if that was ever something he'd been willing to do. As if his little brother wasn't making a public scene, as if they might be sharing a moment of affection for the first time in their entire lives. "I'll let Izumi know to meet us here when it's all over."

Satoru watched him type nonchalantly with his thumb, still keeping up the irregular beat of awkward touches. Wataru said nothing more, and fell completely silent once the phone was back in his pocket.

For several minutes, nothing happened. Then Satoru gave up. He buried his face in his brother's collarbone and sobbed.

And Wataru let him.

17

———

SATORU WAS aware he was ruining the trip. He tried not to, tried to put on a cheerful face and pretend he was just tired, but his lack of enthusiasm was dampening the mass of fireworks that used to be his sister. After a night of such great skating, including new world records and new Grand Prix champions, she was over the moon.

She managed to recognize that maybe her brother was taking that hard, but in her defense, she couldn't do anything about it. "Well, if someone else had to win, aren't you glad it was Damien? You are happy for him, right?"

"Yes," Satoru replied, because it was the only right answer. But he didn't dare face his friend, not even with cell towers between them. He ignored Damien's texts and phone calls, the invitations to come over to his hotel and join the post-competition revelry. There was even a message from Kara Beth, "just checking in", and Satoru let it sit in his inbox without even reading it.

He flopped down on the hotel bed as one more text came in, another entreaty from Damien. *[Please? We are not complete without you!]* Satoru tossed his phone to the mattress and wondered if he'd ever been that heartless. What gave Damien the idea that he'd be up to celebrating his own defeat? This wasn't some children's baseball game, there were real consequences on the line.

"You're thinking too much," Wataru said, and tossed a pillow at Satoru's head. It landed on his face with an oddly comforting weight.

Satoru left it there for a minute. "You don't even know what I'm thinking about."

"Please, Satoru. Everyone knows what you're thinking about." That caused Satoru to wince, and he rolled his head over to face Wataru on the other bed. Izumi pretended to be ignoring the conversation in favor of choosing a channel on the television.

"Sorry..." Satoru sat up and clutched the pillow. Izumi flipped through the channels, scrolling past anything related to the Grand Prix, even if her face betrayed that was all she really wanted to watch.

"It's awful now, but I dunno, this could be good for you," she said with a shrug. Satoru made a strangled noise. "Not that someone trying to kill you is a good thing, but you always seem to do your best skating on days when you don't win."

There was a bit of silence while both brothers stared her down. Wataru cleared his throat, but said nothing. Satoru threw the pillow at Izumi. "What does that even mean? Aren't days when I don't win the worst skating? Besides, I haven't lost in over two years." Until now. Now, he might find himself losing quite a bit.

Izumi shrugged again. "It's just something people say about you." Well, that didn't make any sense. But it reminded Satoru of something Kara Beth once told him. Izumi returned to her channel flipping, and the Grand Prix seemed to be on every network she scrolled through, news anchors commenting on Damien's performance and Satoru's convalescence, wondering if the latter had competed, would things be different?

And that was a question that haunted Satoru. He could crunch numbers all day long, but he just didn't know. If his free program had been able to develop according to plan, with that beautiful Quad Axel, maybe Satoru would have broken his own record before Damien had the chance to. Or maybe Damien was through enduring silver, bronze or less when the world knew he deserved more. Maybe this would have happened regardless, maybe this was just the opening Damien needed to prove himself. But either way, things had changed, and there was no going back.

Because that score Damien posted was nothing to be trifled with. And whatever might have been had Satoru been healthy, Damien's skate was the first real competition he'd had in ages. Satoru would have had trouble going against that under regular circumstances, but now he had to pull up to that level from behind. There was no more room to fall, no more freedom to fail, then learn, then grow. To fall on a jump now could cost him first place, or the whole podium with the way the rest of the competition stepped up that night. To falter on one edge could be the difference between a Japanese World Champion or a French one. And no one was going to tell him it was all right that he lost the title to his friend. The voices of his Federation filled his ears, the ones that asked him if he wouldn't rather train with a more experienced coach, in a bigger city with more resources, anywhere but on the same ice as his greatest competition?

It was all so deafening; he didn't even hear the knock on the door. "Hey, big bro! Inessa's here." Izumi mouthed the word 'girlfriend' as Satoru passed, and he jabbed her with his elbow.

Though she'd been invited inside, Inessa didn't venture far beyond the entryway. The weight of several conversations hung between them, the Grand Prix win Satoru needed to congratulate her for, the costume she had hustled him into making, the sudden kiss of yesterday that they still needed to talk about. But Inessa began another topic entirely. "Were you not invited to the party at our hotel?"

It took Satoru's brain a moment to interpret Inessa's unusual word order, especially after speaking nothing but Japanese all day. Like Damien, Inessa's English was strange, sometimes reversing the sentence structure or throwing in negatives that weren't actually useful to the sentence. "I'm invited," he said, not sure if "yes" or "no" was the appropriate answer in that case. "Not going. Busy."

Inessa looked over his shoulder to where Izumi had finally picked a television program, a late-night variety show hosted by her favorite boy band. Wataru's head was buried in his laptop. Inessa raised her eyebrow. "How the burden of activity must crush you."

Satoru's mood was not conducive to translation, and getting to the end of a sentence starting with "how?" only to find the question a statement and also sarcastic just ticked him off. "You want say something, say. I'm tired." He belatedly tried to keep the sharp edge out of his voice, but wasn't quick enough. Inessa looked a little startled, and a small movement from Wataru on the other side of the room reminded Satoru that his brother could understand every word they said. He softened his tone. "Maybe isn't good day for me to go party."

Inessa hesitated, then nodded. Her posture shrunk a little, wilting, but it almost made her more compact, like a runner taking position for a race or a fighter before a match. She was such a contradiction, and Satoru could never decide if Inessa was an easily crushed flower that hid thorns for protection, or slicing steel disguised by a sheen of velvet. He'd known Inessa since they were young, and he'd watched those two disparate natures grow more pronounced as she aged. Now, on the verge of adulthood, those two sides of her personality seemed to be at war. She could be gregarious and outgoing, or timid and hurt by harsh words.

While also being brave enough to show up uninvited at his hotel and confront him with his faults. "Good day or not, a friend would make the effort."

Satoru's insides bubbled and simmered, both in contradiction and guilty agreement. "Damien should enjoy medal. Doesn't need more."

"How can he enjoy anything?" Inessa asked, throwing her arms in a shrug. "When everyone says he only achieved this because you were not there?"

"That's not true," Satoru scoffed, but Inessa fixed him with one of her serious looks that transcended her age.

"You know the world as I do," she said. She added weight to each of her next words. "It is all anyone says."

Satoru digested that, then swallowed. "I can't. It's his moment, should be happy. Not cheering me up." He grimaced to hide the shame that threatened to overtake him. "Maybe better I don't go. Everyone forget about me. Just focus on champion."

"You're so strange." Inessa shook her head. But there was a smile on her face. "Okay. We won't go to the party. But I am not familiar with Osaka. Show me around?"

"I think you skate in Osaka as much as I do," Satoru answered, buying time while his brain made up his mind. He wanted to stay in the hotel and sulk, but he also wanted to spend time with Inessa, though not while he was demonstrating the ugliest aspects of his character. Then again, if he sulked all night, Wataru and Izumi would probably kick him out...

"Okay, we go. I get coat," he said, and ignored Izumi's deliberate winking.

THE AIR WAS cold and brisk, but wet. It was one thing Satoru liked about Ohio, that the air was dry. The snow piled and the air froze his insides during the thick of winter, but that same intolerable temperature kept the snow from melting and soaking through his shoes and pant legs. In Tokyo, the air was humid and his hometown rarely got cold enough to keep the snow from turning to mush the second it contacted anything on earth. If he even looked at some snow, that slush would soak his pants all the way up to his knees.

Osaka was even worse. Just cold enough to turn the rain to snowflakes, not cold enough to keep them from turning everything into a soggy mess. But somehow Inessa kept her boots looking immaculate. And the sparse, fluid snow charmed her. Satoru knew this wouldn't have been the first time she'd seen snow, but Inessa said it was a rarity for her back home and she was happy her winter sport got to have the appropriate ambiance.

The snow did nothing for Satoru's mood, but the rest of the city pulled out all its sparkle, and the views helped. Even if some of the colors were lost to him, he could still see the contrast of light and dark. He couldn't decide if he would call it beautiful or eerie, with the wash of yellows and greens shining against the black night, but it was striking.

"Look at all this," Inessa breathed as they stood at a window in a shopping plaza overlooking the busy streets and glowing halo of electricity surrounding Osaka. "I love cities at night. They are like something out of a fantasy."

Or a nightmare, Satoru wanted to say, but it would have killed Inessa's mood. And knowing that she still saw beauty in a world that he couldn't see anymore gave him some hope. Maybe he could trust in the other things she saw. "Very pretty."

Inessa gazed happily for a few more seconds. Moved by the light displays, she asked, "Are the Olympic Ceremonies everything people say they are?"

Satoru closed his eyes and remembered. "They're more."

"I can't wait. If I make the Israeli team, that is." She winked at Satoru, and he couldn't help but laugh.

"Yes, will be so hard for you to do."

"A lot can happen in a year. But the Olympics will be held in Germany. The first time in decades," Inessa trailed off, then stepped back. "You know, my grandparents were German. Russian before that. They fled to Germany for a better life, but it didn't go well for them. My mother was born before the wall came down, and she can still remember those times. I think life was very difficult for them, because they've never said anything nice about Germany."

Political strife was so prevalent in the news that it almost had a numbing effect, at least for Satoru, who was lucky enough not to have such personal experiences with war and its accompanying griefs. That said, war had scarred his country, and it was not lost on him that Japan was still answering for its own war crimes. He was never sure what to say in such matters. "Hard, I think, many painful feelings."

"I don't doubt," Inessa sighed. "It seems every border in Europe has a story of my family fleeing it." She wrung her hands a bit, possibly from cold or as a nervous gesture, her breath ghosting in the cold air as she looked over the twinkling lights.

She seemed far older than eighteen at that moment. "Germany is many things to me. But when I skate, Germany is sweet Anna Stein, who competed with me today. It is my old coach, Muhlenberg. Germany is all the fans who throw flowers after my performance, the volunteers who make sure I can compete easily. Because of skating, I own the flags of countries who oppressed my ancestors, and I think of my friends whenever I see them." She tucked a stray lock of blonde hair behind her ear, then looked up at Satoru with a sheepish smile. "Maybe sports won't change the world, but I dream to go the Olympics and see a different Germany than my family saw. Maybe they can see it, too."

Satoru couldn't help but smile back. Though he couldn't put it into words, he'd always thought there was something important about the way so many fans brought flags to international competitions, one for every skater. Japan had many tensions with its neighbors, but when he saw an arena of Japanese fans cheering as they held up Chinese or Korean flags at the NHK Trophy, Satoru thought there might be hope for the future.

"It's a good dream, Inessa." He smiled, and the silence between them was too comfortable to break. But Satoru knew he had to, there was too much to sort out between them concerning kisses and costumes, and they had to talk about it before Inessa got on a plane to the other end of the world. "You think about program for Olympics? Is still far, but..."

"Romeo and Juliet," Inessa declared, without a second of hesitation. "I have always hoped to skate this free program. But I have not fully chosen the music yet."

"It's beautiful for you, costume will be fun to make," Satoru agreed, then continued in a more hesitant voice, "Do you have Romeo?"

"You tell me," Inessa challenged, and that was it. There was no subtle way to ask the question, or cool way to broach the subject. He'd just have to come out and say it.

Given that Inessa had been as obvious as humanly possible, he wasn't sure what he was afraid of, but it was still intimidating. "You have time for dating? In middle of season, and then Olympics?"

"It will always be something," Inessa sighed. "If not skating, then university, or work, or family responsibilities, any number of things. I will always be able to make excuses for why I can't do something. But if I accept excuses, I cannot have a full life. I could not achieve quadruple jumps." She winked. "Besides, if I wait around for the perfect timing, my Romeo might fall in love with someone else!"

"That won't happen," Satoru declared, then blushed when he was caught. "I'm busy, too. And far away. We need focus on skating. Lots of reasons why maybe shouldn't date now."

"Do you love me?"

Satoru felt his breath catch in his throat. Why was it so hard to answer? Inessa gave him the easiest pitches possible, so why couldn't he take a step and swing?

The seconds dragged on, and he could feel her impatience. "I am not offended if you don't," she said, with a cross face, "But do not treat me as some child too young for the conversation."

"I'm sorry," Satoru said on reflex, then gulped. "I, ah..." There were a million reasons a relationship between them couldn't work out.

But no one could accuse Satoru of having common sense. In the back of his mind, he thought of how angry he would be if someone his age thought of romancing Izumi, how he was always saying or doing the wrong thing in Inessa's presence, how his priority was competition and it would always be that way until the day he retired...

He ignored it all. "I want you to be my girlfriend."

The words gave Satoru a thrill he hadn't expected. A voice inside still screamed that it was presumptuous and arrogant to ask, but Satoru kept reminding himself that Inessa kissed him first. "If that's okay."

Inessa giggled, but her smile could have parted the clouds. "It is very okay." She clasped her hands behind her back and stepped close to his side, back to being a bit girlish. "We are official now?"

"Um... I gue-Yes," Satoru said, willing himself not to faint from the weight of that. "Yes, official." He gulped, but was determined in his next step. "That, uh... that mean I can kiss you now?"

"I wish you would," she grinned. Carefully, as if doing this wrong would somehow end the dream he found himself in, Satoru leaned forward and pressed his lips to hers. It was only afterwards that he realized he was in a public place and people might talk, but then decided he didn't care if he offended anyone with the display. In fact, he soon didn't care about anything but the feel of kissing Inessa.

There was an ache when they finally broke apart, but Inessa soothed it leaning in to rest her head on his shoulder. "Thank you. This has been a very good weekend for me."

Satoru didn't answer, but put his arm around her and just breathed. No Grand Prix win could ever compare to this.

18

THE MILK in Satoru's fridge had completely spoiled when he returned to his apartment. He hadn't expected to be gone for more than a week at Skate America, but the plans changed, and all his non-perishable foods had turned into disgusting messes. If he'd have been thinking, he could have passed his keys off to Kara Beth or Eric to take care of that while he was away, but the thought hadn't crossed his mind once. The fruit was the worst to look at, but the smell of milk hit him the second he opened up the refrigerator. He didn't even like milk that much, mostly just used it for baking, and now it was stinking up his home.

It wasn't the welcome Satoru had hoped for. And it was no different at the Granville Ice Rink. The first thing he saw upon entering was the banner heralding Damien's win at the Grand Prix. That it hung next to Satoru's myriad own accomplishments didn't lessen the blow, and Satoru wasn't sure if the sight hurt more than the realization of how petty he was. But either way, he couldn't look at it, and kept his head down as he headed to the locker room. People stopped him at every step. The hockey teams, the rink employees, people from town who knew he was coming back and stopped by to say hi. He had to stop for Yosephina and Sandy, two junior figure skaters that he'd helped mentor, then for old Ksenia Grinkova and the Ditta family, whom he'd helped settle into Granville when they'd all first immigrated, and all the kids working in skate rental. Every person he passed offered cheerful and exuberant greetings that Satoru deflected as politely as possible. He loved all the people here from the bottom of his soul, but he wasn't in the mood to talk.

It didn't stop Damien. The French skater stepped in front of him before he could escape and refused to move until Satoru gave in. "Welcome back. It is good to have you with us again."

Satoru choked out a "thank you", but that was all he could manage. Damien fidgeted in front of him. That garish orange watch peeked out from under his sleeve, and his friend scratched at it. A nervous tick, one he'd always had, but most people didn't notice.

"How was your flight?"

"Long." Satoru tried to slink away, but Damien again blocked his path. "I need get to lockers."

"Are you avoiding me?"

"No," Satoru lied. "Just in rush."

Damien frowned, but his eyes hid a fear that broke Satoru's heart to see. "You haven't spoken to me since the Grand Prix."

"We talk now."

"This isn't talking." That hurt. Satoru wasn't sure if he was angry or heartbroken, but he knew he wanted to be left alone. "I'm busy person. Doesn't new champion have lots others to talk to?" he replied, and might have sounded more bitter than he wanted to, because Damien's face fell like a stone dropped off the Empire State Building.

After a long wait, Damien let out a sigh, "So, you are mad." Satoru wanted to say that was ridiculous, but the lie wouldn't leave his mouth. Confirming it sounded petty. So he stayed silent, while Damien shrank deeper into himself. It made Satoru feel like such a bully.

He'd pictured this scenario a thousand times, knowing it was only a matter of time before Damien achieved his full potential and claimed first place for his own. In his mind, Satoru always saw it as a joyous occasion, a true battle of skating masters, with no regrets when they crowned the winner. He knew it would hurt to come in second, but he'd assumed that his best friend's victory would be something to celebrate. He also assumed Damien's victory wouldn't result from the complete upending of Satoru's life.

Was that all, that Satoru had been denied the chance to meet Damien on the ice as an equal? Was he just upset that he'd been attacked and robbed, rather than having the honorable match he'd pictured?

Or maybe Satoru wasn't as good a person as he'd thought. But Damien had been coming in second, third or even fourth to Satoru for years. Had he been hiding feelings like this all along? Satoru winced at the thought. He should have been more considerate in the past, he probably owed Damien an apology.

And yet, he still couldn't bring himself to say anything. Damien broke the silence for him. "I did not mean to hurt you."

Well, of course. Satoru never thought he did. That was the worst thing about the entire ordeal, that it wasn't personal, that the only person he could be mad at had no face and no name.

"Please, Satoru. Say something."

"Why? If I mad, you mail back gold medal and records? Lose next match on purpose?"

"Well, no..." Damien stammered, "Not that." Good. Damien earned those, he deserved to enjoy them. Satoru was glad, somewhere in the depths of his heart, that Damien wouldn't give up his goals so easily.

"Then why care if I mad? You win, you be proud. Can't do anything else." He couldn't admit to being hurt and he couldn't deny it, but that wasn't Damien's problem. He'd skated well, he deserved to hold his head high and celebrate no matter what ungrateful wretches grumbled in the background. That was life. You couldn't make everybody happy, and as much as Satoru tried to, he'd learned that sometimes you had to be brave and push forward on the important things. The world hung gold medals that felt like millstones, but you couldn't let the weight stop you from skating.

Damien regarded him with a solemn expression. Of the two of

them, most people wouldn't call Damien the vulnerable one. And yet... "You know I am not as strong as you." He spread his hands, helplessly. "Please. I could not bear to lose a friend, even to gain the world. What must I do to make it right?"

Satoru clenched his knuckles to ride out the onslaught of feeling. He turned his gaze to the floor, but couldn't stop seeing skinny, teenaged Damien in front of him. Little Damien, who sometimes felt like a younger brother despite being older, whose arrogance only disguised how much he hated himself, who pushed friends away because he wouldn't know love if it punched him in the face.

Satoru's feet moved without prompting. He stalked to his friend with the force of a torpedo and clamped his arms around Damien. "You don't lose me," he growled into Damien's shoulder, letting his emotions bleed out with the words. Something that was both rage and love, but still impossible to pinpoint. Satoru couldn't describe it, but he couldn't stop it, either. "I only want good things for you. Always. Happy you do good, happy you win, not mad at you." His mood was black and sharp, but it would cool in time. The problem was never his best friend.

It hurt, but there was something satisfying about having this conversation, like a cold compress on a feverish forehead, or maybe like lancing a boil. Part of Satoru wished he'd gotten over himself back in Osaka and just celebrated with Damien after all. It would have been awkward and bittersweet, but there wouldn't be the question of regret.

"I'm sorry we cannot both win first place all the time," Damien said when he returned the embrace, and he sounded like he meant it. But that wasn't how winning worked.

"Next time you medal, I be on podium next to you," Satoru promised, and Damien pulled back in a fit of laughter.

"You are going to French Nationals? My, but they are getting lax in their registration process!" The reminder of Nationals caused a spike of bitterness to lodge itself in Satoru's sternum, but he tried to keep his face from reflecting it.

"You know what I mean. We both get medal at Worlds. I give real challenge then."

"I don't doubt it," Damien agreed, and his eyes swam with both laughter and trepidation. "I plan to win the World Championships this year. Don't make it easy for me."

The usual banter felt cautious, like laughter at a funeral. But it was there. Satoru forced a smile. "Don't cry when I ruin plan." Because he loved Damien, but the winning streak stopped here.

THE TECHNICAL AND artistic aspects of competitive skating tended to go through cycles. New elements would be attempted and physical boundaries pushed, and there would be a period where skating skills and artistry seemed to take a backseat as everyone coped with the new physical demands. Sometimes this led to changes in the scoring system, but over time, the new generations of athletes would come up having trained the more difficult elements and be able to grow their components along with the athletic marvels, and the sport would find balance again. Until someone raised the technical difficulty yet again, and the cycle continued.

Now, with the Olympics less than fourteen months away and the clear favorite knocked from his pedestal, the men's division found themselves in the middle of an arms race. Kara Beth knew her skaters too well to think it wouldn't affect them, and started preparing herself for layout changes, substituting elements or reworking choreography, and how to convince her charges when enough was enough. Especially the latter, in the case of Satoru.

She didn't doubt that Satoru had been keeping up his practices in Japan, or at least trying to. Even so, she knew not to expect elite athletic mastery after such a disruption to their routine, and was planning to ease her student back to form over time.

Satoru had a different plan. He threw himself into jumps like nothing had changed, but didn't land a single one of them. Kara Beth winced with every attempt. "Enough, Sato. Keep going like that and you'll break something."

"I know how to do-"

"Yeah, but you won't right this second. The last thing you need right now is to pull a muscle." Or worse. She skated a slow circle around him, taking in his physical condition. He was looking better, even more than when she'd seen him at the Grand Prix, but his chest heaved with exertion and his breath rattled. And there was a little timidity concerning that wrenched ankle, even if it had healed. "Sounds like you're still a bit sick."

"Just cough. Pneumonia is over."

"Even so," Kara Beth shook her head. "Go easy on yourself for a bit, okay? No quads."

"But I-"

"Trust me, this is not the day." Forcing him through such high-risk elements when he wasn't at his best was a recipe for injuries.

But she didn't expect Satoru's flaming anger. "When is day?" he snapped, then caught himself. "Think I wait long enough to skate."

"And if your body says to wait longer, we wait longer," Kara Beth replied, crossing her arms over her chest. Satoru mimicked the gesture, though his tone was a bit more reigned in.

"Ankle is healthy to skate. Doctor agreed."

"But that doesn't mean you can just throw yourself into quad rotations after losing months of training."

"Not months. And I'm fine now."

"You're not, Satoru. And it's not just because your mind excepts things your muscles might not be able to deliver right now." Kara Beth sighed. Satoru waited for her to elaborate on those other reasons, but she didn't. "There's plenty of other things to work on without risking your health. Trust me on this. You'll be back to flying in no time."

Satoru's face didn't agree, but he finally grumbled back, "Fine." They resumed practice, but the more Kara Beth watched him skate, the more she worried.

And she didn't find any relief from that in Damien or Eric. The first was showing all the signs of having skipped breakfast and the previous night's dinner, and the latter boy was only half focused on his crossovers, stopping every couple minutes to check his phone. "Little twerp," she muttered under her breath. She'd never had an issue about cell phones or other distractions on the ice until Eric arrived, because Satoru and Damien were both so driven and travelled too many miles to waste their rink time. But Eric was still a teenager and prone to losing focus. Kara Beth wondered if she should confiscate the phone, though it made her feel like an elementary school teacher.

That feeling doubled when she suggested to a pale and shaking Damien that he break for lunch and got an earful of attitude. "Ugh, I can't do this today," she moaned, rubbing her temples. "I just taught a class of actual five-year-olds this morning. Why are three of them still hanging around?" Damien looked miffed at that, but Kara Beth didn't care. "French Nationals are in less than a week. If you wanna botch that after winning the Grand Prix, just get off the ice!"

That got through to Damien, and he responded with a meek apology before heading off to find sustenance he could stomach. Kara Beth watched him go, then made a mental note to have a proper chat with him later. The sass and childish resistance was beneath him, but stress could aggravate Damien's issues with appetite, and Kara Beth decided long ago that dealing with that was part of her job. Lord knew Damien had enough to be stressed over right now.

But that could wait until he got a little food in him and was a bit more relaxed. Kara Beth turned her attention on Eric for his lesson. "So, who're you texting? Hot guy?"

Eric blushed at having been caught, but shook his head. "Marina Little. She needs a partner for pairs and keeps asking me." He left it there, and Kara Beth had to wait a while before deciding he wasn't going to give an end to that story.

"Well?" she asked. "How did you reply?"

Eric shrugged. "I skate singles. I don't know anything about pairs."

Kara Beth hesitated. "If you wanted to, you could learn. Don't let that stop you." At that, Eric snapped his head up.

"Why?" he demanded, but more confused than forceful. "What makes you say that?"

"Just that you're capable of anything," Kara Beth laughed. "And you look like you're having more fun when you're with people. Not that you can't get that in singles skating, but you could do well with a partner, if you wanted it."

Eric considered that while he put his phone back in his bag. "Maybe. But I don't think that's really what I want."

"It doesn't have to be." Kara Beth said that easily, but she thought Eric wasn't as sure as he made himself out to be. If he was, he wouldn't still be continuing the dialogue with Marina. "Either way, it is practice time, and you are definitely not warmed up."

"Oh, come on," Eric muttered, but pushed off from the boards with the impression of buckling down to work. But after a few crossovers, he stopped and circled back to Kara Beth. "Can I ask you a question?"

"Sure."

"Do you think I could ever win the Olympics?" That gave Kara Beth pause. She felt it her duty to answer Eric honestly, but the answer wasn't on the tip of her tongue the way it was with her other two skaters. When she'd met Damien, she knew he was capable of medaling at the Olympics. She'd been less sure about Satoru; that had been a fifty-fifty split between becoming a three time Olympic champion or killing himself on his stupid Tano Sal. With Eric, she'd never had that definitive picture of his future in her mind.

But that wasn't due to lack of potential. "I think you could be good enough to go," Kara Beth replied after some deliberation. "Not next year, unless you really put your nose to the grindstone. But the cycle after, you'll be twenty-three. If you keep on your trajectory, you're definitely capable of medaling at Nationals and putting some pressure on the top guys. I can't say more since we don't know what competition you'll be facing. A lot can happen in four years." Her face grew serious. "That said, keeping your current work ethic probably won't be enough. If you want to win the Olympics, you've got to make training more of a priority."

"Right..."

Kara Beth saw his face, and grew sympathetic. It seemed that practice time was going to turn into discussion time, but sometimes that was necessary. "Look, you're not less of a person if training doesn't come first. The world needs more than figure skaters to keep running. And winning doesn't taste so sweet if you lose something else in the process." She thought of Satoru and hoped Eric didn't realize she was referring to him. But she wouldn't have been the first person to be afraid of the toll skating took on Satoru, or afraid of what would happen to him when that competitive career ended. Much as she'd like to see a bit more effort out of him, Kara Beth didn't want that life for Eric. "You just need to decide what you want, and commit to that."

"I just..." Eric grimaced and turned a slow circle on the ice. His posture was terrible. Kara Beth almost corrected him, then decided it wasn't the time. "I don't want to get to the end of this and find it didn't matter. Like, telling people I used to figure skate but I never won anything important, so the conversation just gets awkward. Or working my butt off and giving up so much to place eighth at the Olympics. No one remembers those people. Just gold through bronze." He shrugged. "Satoru gets to be cool because he wins. Me, I'm just a gay kid in a gayer sport."

Kara Beth wasn't sure which part of that to address first. "You compare yourself to Satoru a lot, don't you?"

"Hard not to. He's our Olympic Champion." Eric's expression soured. "Everyone worships the ground he walks on. Even my mom says I should watch what he's doing and be more like him."

It did seem like something Eric's mother would say. Kara Beth tried not to wince. The woman had good intentions but was a little too invested in her son's career, something Kara Beth could relate to with her own mother. And like Eric, she'd been lackadaisical when it came to her training, until her father forced a family chat and they ironed a few things out.

She didn't doubt Eric loved skating, any more than she doubted her own love of the sport. But Kara Beth suspected a great deal of that love was buried underneath his mother's micromanaging, and Eric wouldn't blossom until he realized that for himself. "Sometimes it's useful to have examples or an ideal to shoot for," Kara Beth said, deciding that for now she could only lead the proverbial horse to water, "But trying to model yourself after someone else never works. You can only ever be yourself."

"That's not so great when everyone on earth wants to be him," Eric pointed across the ice to Satoru, who had just two-footed out of a triple axel. "Honestly, it's kind of a relief not to have his shadow hanging over us all season." His face immediately went white. "I didn't mean that! Not how it sounded, I swear! Obviously, what happened to him was bad!"

"Uh huh..." Kara Beth felt at a loss. She shook her head and tried to steer the conversation back somewhere helpful. "You say everyone wants to be Satoru because he wins a lot-"

"Not a lot. He wins all the time!"

"So everyone wants to be the World Champion. Who do you think he wants to be? Who's his ultimate idol?"

Eric rolled his eyes. "I don't know, Yuzuru Hanyu?"

"Close, but no. Try again."

"Axel Paulson, inventor of the Axel jump?"

"Another good guess, but no." That stumped Eric, and he narrowed his eyes as he thought, now intrigued. "No more thoughts?"

"Plushenko? Boitano? You?"

"Ah, flattery." Kara Beth shook her head. "The answer's really going to surprise you."

Eric crossed his arms. "But you're not going to tell me?"

"No fun in that." She skated backwards and beckoned Eric to follow. "We've chatted enough for this practice. But you should ask Satoru that sometime. Maybe then you won't put so much weight on first place."

Eric looked about to say more, but Kara Beth shook her head and clapped her hands. "Come on! You don't pay me to stand around! Time to work!"

19

GETTING to do run-throughs again was a blessing. Practicing strokes and elements individually was important, but after being forced off the ice the way he had, Satoru felt so directionless. Running through programs gave him an endpoint, a goal to work towards and gauge his progress against. Skaters universally dreaded run-throughs, but they were a key part of training, and how Satoru achieved the consistency he was known for. He rarely fell, never lost, because he trained like he competed, so every day he wasn't in that regime felt like he wasn't training at all.

That, and he loved his programs. His short was from the ballet "Giselle", a haunting dance to the death that a grieving Prince shared with his deceased love. Satoru and Kara Beth had choreographed it together, finding ways of moving to reflect the *pas de duex* even without a dance partner. Satoru thought there was something poetic about an absent Giselle, a representation of how she and her Prince now lived in two different worlds. To Satoru, that absence was the real tragedy of death. It came to everyone in the end, and whether there was a heaven or reincarnation, he couldn't say, but the simple separation was real.

It was something he'd been thinking about more recently, as he noticed his parents aging, as more skaters he'd grown up with retired or stopped bouncing back from injuries, and especially since nearly dying himself. Death and whatever came after were abstract, but not seeing the people he loved was relatable. Some day he wouldn't be able to call home or get on a plane and return to his family. He'd like them all to live forever, but odds were he'd have to say goodbye to someone. And knowing they wouldn't be there when he turned around, knowing he couldn't ask for advice or tell jokes or give gifts on their birthdays was more frightening than disease or peril. As for his own death, he'd nearly lost his connection to everyone in one fell swoop. Whatever awaited after death, he'd have been alone, and that was worse than any karmic judgement.

In a metaphorical sense, he'd face something similar with Kara Beth. She was over a decade older, and would be forced to stop skating programs long before Satoru. Her triple axel, the jewel in her competitive crown, was no longer part of her arsenal, and she'd eventually lose her other triple jumps and more flexible spins. In time, stamina would suffer, maybe arthritis would kick in, she'd eventually have to give up show skating, and Satoru knew she agreed with him that not skating was a form of death. It was natural, but it hurt Satoru to think of the day when there was no Kara Beth to skate with him.

For Satoru's short program, Kara Beth was his Giselle. Sometimes he visualized Inessa, but it was usually Kara Beth. There was nothing romantic about it, but he'd fallen in love with her skating ever since he'd seen his first competition on television. And after meeting her in person, seeing her skate from less than twenty feet away, that love transcended hero worship into a real connection. He joked with her, trained with her, even lived in her house. Unlike Satoru's other idols, the connection between them wasn't one-sided or abstract.

And how he loved to skate with her! If anyone loved show skating more than Satoru, it was Kara Beth, and developing programs together for summer ice shows was a joy. Her purpose in buying this ice rink had been so she could have a place to develop world class skating shows, creating a sort of skating Cirque du Soleil, or icy Disneyland. She was always trying to rein him in and be practical as a coach, but they shared the same sense of adventure and desire to wow the crowd, and when competition season was over, playtime began. Their official first meeting was during the ice shows and workshops Kara Beth did in Japan as a younger skater, when she raced Satoru around the rink during downtime or accepted his shy petitions to teach him.

Of course, their unofficial first meeting was at the World Championships, one of the years Kara Beth won the event and inarguably the best free skate she'd ever delivered. They held the competition in Tokyo, and Satoru was lucky enough to get to work as a flower boy, clearing the ice of gifts between each skater. To get within feet of so many incredible skaters was memorable enough, but after Kara Beth's title-defending free skate, it was life-changing. He only knew about three words of English at the time, but one of those words was "Amazing," and he tried to tell Kara Beth so as he passed her on the ice.

He wasn't supposed to bother the skaters while they were competing, but he was so overcome watching her skate that he couldn't help himself. And Kara Beth must have been pretty emotional herself, because she burst into triumphant tears and hugged that little flower boy hard enough his eyes nearly popped out.

Satoru wondered if Kara Beth remembered that, or if she knew it was him. He never asked, just in case the truth tarnished the jewel of a memory somehow. But now he got to skate every day with his childhood hero, to where she became some nagging sister/parent/teacher hybrid and was all the more magical for losing her pedestal. And like Giselle in the ballet, who had a weak heart holding her back from dance, Kara Beth was slowly falling victim to the chains of mortal existence. Each moment to skate with her was precious.

The short program they'd made for competition was beautiful. Sad, ethereal, and maintaining a connection to a dance partner that only Satoru could see. It was a shame that Satoru had only gotten to perform it twice this season, but he'd make sure it got its due glory at the upcoming Four Continents Championship.

First came the opening choreography, Prince Albrecht entering into the domain of the Willis, jilted brides doomed to dance forever after their death and take revenge on men who crossed their path. His rival in love, Hilarion, was forced to dance with the spirits until he died, just a scene earlier. But love would guide Prince Albrecht as he took the hand of precious Giselle, now a spirit herself, and his companion in this fateful *pas de deux*.

The opening jump was a Quad Flip, not Satoru's most reliable jump. But what was reliable about the world of ghosts and spirits? In a dance where he was fated to die, how could he be expected to be powerful and confident? Did life give one a choice of the trials they would face, allowing mortals to choose the challenges that came easily to them? No, death and the unknown were frightening, and any claim to face such other-worldly powers otherwise was a sham. Triumph or failure, the 4F marked Satoru's descent into the underworld.

Of course, Kara Beth still had him on stupid training wheels. She wasn't letting him turn anything above three rotations, even suggested he pop the flip into a double for the day. Satoru obeyed, and had to admit that his horrible Flip technique wasn't at all helped by all his time away from the ice. But it wouldn't get better by ignoring the problem, and so he transitioned out of the jump with a bit of attitude coloring the steps. It was a quality that had never been present before, but wasn't entirely out of place. In the ballet, the Prince had lied about his nobility to the peasant Giselle, hiding his true identity and betrothal to another bride. He hadn't meant to hurt her, but as with all lies, Giselle found the truth in the worst way, and it was what led to her death. There had to be some bitterness towards those who were so cruel to his love, and self-hatred for his own foolishness. Maybe even to Giselle herself, for misunderstanding his intentions and taking things so seriously. Pain sometimes manifested as anger, and not every step in the dance of love could be a happy one.

So if he gave Kara Beth a look as he passed her by the boards, it wasn't personal. Just artistic interpretation. He entered into his spin sequence, letting the entire rainbow of diverse feelings fill him down to his fingertips. Each movement had meaning and purpose, each muscle helped to tell the story of tragedy and true love.

Until he coughed. A horrible, wet thing that threw Satoru off balance and out of the spin. He scrabbled back to his feet and back into the choreography, cursing himself. There would be time to cough or sneeze when the run through was over, but he needed to get through the program no matter what. Even if his throat tickled, even if his cheeks burned red.

At the rink side, Kara Beth looked concerned, a question on her face, but Satoru let his skating answer for him. He wasn't stopping, not now. The judges wouldn't let him stop and do the program over, they wouldn't care if he had a coughing fit in the middle of a performance. They hadn't let him redo the Grand Prix after an outsider poisoned him, so they weren't going to cut him a break over an internal virus.

He had to focus. He had to be so strong that nothing could take him down, strong enough that his own body couldn't even hold him back. If someone tried to kill him again, Satoru was still finishing his skate.

With that thought, he stumbled on a Mohawk. Stupid mistake, beginner level. Satoru corrected his balance and dismissed his thoughts, bringing them back to Giselle. He skated this piece as a man looking for redemption. He'd been a foolish child in Act I, not considering the consequences of showing such attentions to Giselle while betrothed to another. Cocky and brash, he'd hurt an innocent girl, but there was no way to take it back.

Giselle, now one of the Willis, would be justified in taking his life. Let the Prince dance himself to death; he deserved it after such betrayal. Satoru threw himself into what should have been his Quad Tano Sal-Triple Loop combo, but was today ordered by his coach to be a pair of triples. But as originally planned, it was an act of passion, the embodiment of helplessness and guilt, as he literally danced himself to the edge of mortality. The short program was a tricky game, because it was more limited in its requirements than the free skate, and in a deep field, one tiny error could be the difference between first and seventh place. The difficulty and visual display of the jump, performed well and timed right with the music, usually put him a few points ahead of the pack.

But mercy would not be found in those bitter spirits, and neither would absolution, no matter what he jumped. The choreography was fast and furious as the dance drew to its close. His death was imminent, and if he was going to depict death by dancing, Satoru had to pull out all the stops in his footwork. In doing research, Satoru found that Albrecht's variation in Act 2 was considered one of the more demanding male variations in ballet. And he'd watched videos where the strength and flexibility were beyond Satoru's comprehension, for both Albrecht and Giselle. Either of those dancers could give Alisha a run for her Y-spin and some of those leg extensions were breaking the rules of gravity. Demanding acting roles, while demonstrating flawless technique.

Like skating, every aspect of the performance had to be perfect. He'd taken many ballet classes over the years, as well as other dance training, but he didn't just want to portray a ballet dancer on ice. He wanted to capture the spirit of that discipline, the energy and effort, and translate that into his own world. For dancers, they lauded Giselle as their Hamlet, and Satoru had to meet that bar with his best skills.

So he needed to do something unexpected, something better than convention. It was common practice to end programs with a spin sequence. It made the most logistic sense, as spins were fast and dramatic, and jumps, for all their wow factor, were exhausting. Putting one in the second half of the program earned more points for that reason, but muscles grew more tired with every passing second. Satoru imagined other sport disciplines were similar; the first hurdle of the sprint was probably an easier jump than the last one. Once the halfway mark passed, the bonus points went into effect on jumps, but there weren't any real benefits to be gained by where in the second half those jumps went. Best to get them done earlier, while the legs still had some strength, and finish the program with a climactic build of footwork and spins.

But this was Giselle. After watching dancer after dancer execute ridiculous feats of strength with flawless, jaw-dropping beauty, Satoru no longer cared about the best course of action. He convinced Kara Beth that he should end his short program on a triple axel. "Land jump, big chord, the end," he'd said with excitement, convinced this was the best idea he'd ever had, better than the quad-quad combo.

Kara Beth had taken some convincing. "First of all, you're crazy. Second, what are you trying to prove? The ISU doesn't give points for audacity."

Satoru didn't know what 'audacity' meant, but he knew he disagreed. "Points for skill. Interpretation. Judges reward with GOE and components." The argument did sway her a little, but the thing that really convinced Kara Beth was when he promised, "It will look so cool."

And that was why she was his coach. Not everything in life had to make sense, not all of it had to have a point value. In a world governed by justice and retribution, Giselle would show mercy. She would spare Albrecht's life, even though she could never be with him again, though her soul would never find peace. She stood up to the queen of the Willis, guarded Albrecht until morning, when the spell broke and the dance ended. Albrecht would find freedom in the Triple Axel, but there would be no Giselle when he landed.

Satoru prepared himself for that final element. The difficulty was less in doing the jump so late in the program, though that was tricky, but in coming to a complete stop immediately afterward. A skater ideally exited a jump with the same momentum they entered with, but Satoru's plan was to have the jump's exit be his final pose. So this plan of his had taken some practice. He could land the jump successfully, but stumble immediately after, and how embarrassing would that have been in competition? Kara Beth came up with the idea to glide to a stop rather than a sudden brake, and the ending image developed into a nice picture of the prince reaching out for a Giselle that could not stay with him.

But not today. Today, Satoru botched the takeoff and came down with a painful splat on the ice. He didn't bother getting up right away, since the program was now over. Just gave the ice a half-hearted punch and moaned to himself. Axel jumps were his favorites. He practiced them the most and hardly ever fell. He couldn't understand why he was screwing them up now, and didn't really want to think too hard about it. The whole run-through had been shaky, wobbling in one of the spins and feeling like he couldn't find his feet. It had been such a relief to be able to do full run-throughs again, but this couldn't be all he was capable of.

He got up before Kara Beth worried about him. She didn't look angry, but definitely troubled, and Satoru found he couldn't account for his performance or make excuses. "Well?" he asked in a weak voice.

"Well," Kara Beth repeated, and there was a tiny twitch at the corner of her mouth. "Far from your best, but considering we weren't sure if you'd be able to compete at all this year, I'd say you're in decent shape. We'll get those elements back over the course of the season and have you back to full form for the Olympics next year."

Satoru blanched. "No!" he exclaimed, just loud enough to startle himself. "That's not plan! Plan is go hard this season, build new skill so *better* by Olympics!"

The look on Kara Beth's face was both bewildered and pitying. "Sometimes plans get derailed. I can't just whack you with a magic wand and make everything good." She was about to say something more, then closed her mouth and thought better of it. She waved him out onto the ice. "Don't worry, I still plan to work you hard. We can start with your spin combinations. That last one travelled all the way back to Tokyo."

Satoru's shoulders fell, but he followed her instruction. What else could he do?

INESSA'S cute voice hummed through the phone speaker as Satoru finished his tale. "Yes, stumbling on a spin? This is horrible, I must now break up with you."

"Don't make fun!"

"You put too much pressure on yourself. What is important to you, Satoru? Will it be lost with one spin?"

Satoru swallowed. His mind said yes. It told him that this one spin, that one jump, it was all a thread that would unravel the whole tapestry he'd been trying to weave. And yet, Inessa kept trying to convince him of something different.

When it came to skating, hadn't Inessa seen his best and worst? "The important thing..." His friends, his family, his new girlfriend, weren't those the relationships that really mattered in life? Medals and trophies kept those precious things in his life, or so he'd always thought. But maybe his perception was limited? He was dating Inessa, and Wataru spent time with him of his own accord, all without a Grand Prix medal around his neck. Damien and Kara Beth hadn't changed just because Satoru hadn't trained for a few weeks, his family didn't forget him from competition to competition, the evidence was always in front of him. Satoru pushed his glasses up his nose and adjusted his phone a little closer to his ear. "You are my important thing."

He could hear her smile through the phone. "Well done. You will lose nothing." He heard her sigh. "And really, you skate your best without winning."

"What does that mean?" Satoru asked, growing more exasperated the more he heard this. "Last time I don't win, I skate horrible!"

"I don't mean it literally," Inessa replied, "Rather, that to see you skate is like to catch lightning in a bottle."

That word! Satoru tried to parse out, "Lightning in a bottle", but came up short. Was this the thing that came with thunderstorms, or the thing that happened when you flicked a switch? Or metaphorical light? Or weight, the opposite of heavy? He *knew* this, he did, why did his brain always short circuit any time he heard one of those evil trio of words spoken?

And bottles? A shining bottle, a thunderstorm in a bottle, a floating bottle? "On a good day", that meant a good thing, so a bottle used for lighting up a dark space? Nature's electricity in a bottle? Was this an idiom for lightbulbs? Special lightbulbs?

But since Inessa was still talking, Satoru accepted it as a compliment and filed it away for later. "There is a risk the whole bottle will explode, but it remains on the right side of danger."

"Right..." Some things, he was never going to understand. "Thank you for talk, Inessa. Sorry to give you my stress."

"It is no problem," Inessa replied, and the two of them slipped into silence for a bit. Satoru watched the other skaters looping around the rink and wondered what the scenery looked like on Inessa's side of the conversation. She'd said she was just walking downtown, and Satoru tried to picture the look of the buildings, the sounds of the street, the curve of Inessa's shoulder as she pressed her cell phone against her ear...

A whole world away, with her own life and her own problems. "How is teacher? Does it get better, or...?"

"No! He's so frustrating!" Inessa complained, and began detailing a list of woes concerning one of her teachers that Satoru only half-followed. The specifics escaped him, but he understood Inessa felt her teacher didn't respect her intelligence or maturity, and also that nothing would stoke the fires of Inessa's wrath faster than treating her like a child. "He thinks he's so important, that he understands the world and no one else can have an opinion! He has only left this country once! I have been to six different countries this year! Why do my observations mean nothing?"

Satoru wasn't sure, but it sounded as if Inessa's comments had been dismissed in a group discussion. "Are you able to get different teacher?"

"No, I am stuck with him until the year ends! Do I not do assignments like other students? But to him, I am just a little girl with a head full of air. I look young so I cannot comprehend. I travel and miss classes, so I must be stupid, even though my scores are among the highest! What must I do to be taken seriously?"

"You are serious," Satoru reassured, though he stumbled a little on his phrasing. "You are... a serious thing, not a child. We see it."

Inessa grumbled a little. "Sometimes it feels like only you." She sighed. "I'm sorry. It's a small thing to complain about, but..."

"It bothers you. So it's important." Everyone had their own struggles that were precious and meaningful, if only because they were theirs. Satoru had feelings he wasn't comfortable sharing, as surely Inessa herself did. Maybe as they grew closer, that would change?

It was scary to think about, but he liked the idea in theory. Or maybe not, since he and Damien were close and still kept things from each other. He trained on the same ice as Eric every day, but still had no clue what was going on in that kid's head.

"How do you say, 'I love you' in Japanese?"

"Hmm?" The question had been a little garbled by static, but even had they been speaking face to face, it would have taken Satoru by surprise. "We don't really say..."

"You don't have this phrase?"

"Well, we do, but..." Satoru pursed his lips as he tried to explain. "Say other things, to mean love. Not like English where say all the time..." And not just concerning love. Satoru had found most English-speaking countries to be uncomfortably direct with their words, compared to his home country. Now that he was used to it, he found it exciting, but in some things he'd always be traditional. Love wasn't expressed in words, but in the way his parents worked to support his skating, packed school lunches and kept the house in order. Words could be doubted, but actions didn't lie.

"Ah. My father is like this as well," Inessa said with a knowing air, and then she giggled. "But I am like my mother. I like to hear it said."

Satoru paused for a minute, then breathed out the phrase. He couldn't deny that girl anything she wanted. "*Aishiteiru.* I love you, Inessa." It sounded weird at first. Bold and intimate and somehow echoing like a thousand drums.

And also wonderful to hear. "And I love you. *Ani ohevet otcha.* Even when you make silly mistakes on your spins."

Those words made him happy in the moment, and he tried to block out the part of his mind that questioned and analyzed them under a microscope. But Inessa was intelligent enough to see through him, and kind enough to not lie about what she saw there. If everything around Satoru was changing, from the field of men's figure skating to his own eyesight, maybe it was time to trust an outside perspective?

He couldn't help but laugh. "You're always cheering me up. I need give you real date soon."

"You need to give me a dress for next year. Don't forget, I employ you, now."

"Demanding. Maybe I drown you in sparkle like Damien." He laughed to himself. "No, I already start drawing. Beautiful dress, promise. Perfect Juliet." Satoru described some ideas he was working with, as best he could without visuals, until Satoru's break was over. For the first time in his life, he felt reluctant to get on the ice. "I miss you."

"I miss you."

"I miss you more than skating."

There was a beat, before Inessa burst out laughing. "Ah, that is a declaration of love if I have ever heard one! So romantic! Say it again, no one will believe me!"

Satoru grinned, even though the tips of his ears were blushing. He decided to ignore the time for once in his life. "I love Inessa Levi more than Quad Axel."

"Oh, my beating heart!"

Kara Beth caught sight of him, raised an eyebrow, and then began a pantomime of looking for her lost third skater, which caused Damien to chuckle so hard he nearly collided with Eric. Satoru stuck out his tongue at both of them.

"I talk to you again soon, okay?" he promised Inessa. "Be happy, please. Teacher doesn't know you, what he thinks isn't important."

"I do feel very happy, thank you," Inessa replied, and Satoru thought he heard her smile widen. Funny how his stress and problems seemed so much more manageable after one phone call, even though his skating hadn't improved over the last ten minutes. Inessa sounded like the call had given her a similar effect. "Promise you will get out of your own head for a moment? The world does not turn on the success of your axel jump."

"I promise," Satoru replied, before ending the call with another hesitant, "I love you." It felt less awkward this time, and he returned to the ice with a smile.

Even when he two-footed his triple axel, the smile didn't leave his face.

20

GIVEN SATORU'S TRACK RECORD, Damien wasn't looking forward to life after Japanese Nationals. At that event, Yukiya Minami not only won his first title, but landed his first Quad Lutz in competition. The news blew up all Damien's social media feeds the second that boy's blade hit the ice. And it was beautifully landed, too, fully rotated with great flow and speed on the exit. From an objective point of view, it was a masterpiece, and Damien was impressed.

No one had to ask if Satoru had seen it.

In the same week, Aaron Leval added a fourth quad jump to his program layout, and shortly after, Derek Donner announced he was planning to attempt a five-quad program at British Nationals. Within the week, Sione Tulafono posted a video of himself doing a 3Ltz-3Lo-3T combo, though he didn't reveal whether he planned to add it to competition later in the season. When videos of a young Latvian skater attempting a Quad Axel in harness started circulating, Damien prepared for the worst.

It was bad enough that Damien had been marinating in his own sour moods, which justifiably caused Satoru to be testy in return, but there would have been trouble even if Damien were a pillar of positivity and support. His friend could be unbearably moody when he got negative GOEs in competition, so there was no telling what the atmosphere would be like after Yukiya Minami claimed the title of National Champion and broke the five-year streak of his predecessor.

But when Satoru showed up at Damien's apartment to carpool to the rink, he was in a surprisingly good mood. Still with his annoying habit of pushing food on Damien like a mother hen, and a bright smile that made the actions tolerable. It wasn't until Satoru ran a red light and nearly got them taken out by a semi-truck that Damien saw the tension broiling under the surface.

Satoru skidded to a stop on the shoulder and began cursing at his steering wheel in his native tongue, while Damien offered a quick prayer of gratitude for their continued existence on the earth.

"The red light is on the bottom, the green on top," he reminded his color blind friend, for all the good it did now. "Would it help to stick a note on the dashboard?"

"Fine, fine," Satoru muttered, which translated to "I'm not processing English right now and I don't care, so shut up." Damien thought the attitude unbecoming, considering they both could have died, but he supposed he might have been embarrassed, too.

The tension eased with time, only for something else to stir it up. When they arrived at the Granville Ice Rink, they found two police officers on the premises. A package had arrived from Damien's stalker, Henri, and Kara Beth thought it best to be cautious. In the end, the package only contained a handmade Christmas ornament and a love letter, but it might as well have been anthrax for the effect it had on Damien. He didn't know if the police could track Henri's whereabouts from any hidden evidence on the package, but he wished them luck with all his heart.

"You think he really do crime?" Satoru quietly asked as they removed their skate guards.

"It seems unlike him. But I can't say I really know this man." Damien's stomach twisted with the words.

Satoru nodded, then slipped onto the ice with a quick apology for asking. As if Satoru was in any way at fault for this. But though he threw himself into jumps with a bit too much intensity, the atmosphere between the two of them was more calm than Damien had any right to expect. He felt balanced on a blade's edge, the winds too frequent to truly hold his stability.

These feelings had come before, in hard times that he and Satoru weathered together. But this time, his friend found some sort of calming source that was keeping him close to center. One that wasn't Damien, and wasn't one he could share.

Damien doubted it was as simple as a new relationship, but when he saw the look on Satoru's face as he was on the phone with Inessa, he knew it played a factor. A few jokes from Kara Beth could diffuse Satoru's agitation, and even a call from that demon Wataru was putting his friend in a good mood these days. Love, in all its forms, could do amazing things.

So why was Damien such a wreck?

"What could you possibly have to talk about?" he finally commented, after seeing Satoru happily chatting into his phone with his brother, *again.*

"He's my brother," Satoru replied, and it just enraged Damien more.

"He has never acted like one. Now you give him all your time?"

The look in Satoru's eyes was curious, and something else that made Damien feel small. "People can change," was all he said, and Damien stalked off in order to avoid thinking too much about that.

As he warmed up on the ice, he felt everyone's eyes on him. The attention on him had increased with both the events of Skate America and the Grand Prix Finals, but today's visit from law enforcement ramped things up tenfold. And none of that attention was positive. Whispers, frowns and suspicious glances followed him with every stroke of his blade. Satoru pretended not to notice, Kara Beth kept up an aggressive positivity, but it wasn't enough to let Damien ignore his surroundings.

Especially when Eric was being a little brat and cutting in front of Damien's jumps. "Would you stop that?"

"Or what? I'll taste a new flavor in my water next time I break for lunch?"

He was too shocked to say anything in his defense.

DAMIEN HADN'T READ the love letter sent him, content to let the police take it as far away as possible. But he was sure it said nothing he hadn't heard before. Declarations of love, an insistence on Damien's perfection no matter what he weighed, a promise that if Damien would just let Henri in, he'd show him what it was like to have a real family.

When the time came to break for lunch, Damien threw his sandwich in the trash.

Damien couldn't explain his unique eating disorder any more than the doctors could. They diagnosed him with Avoidant/Restrictive Food Intake Disorder, which seemed to just mean they couldn't classify him as anorexic or bulimic, and if medical science couldn't figure out what was wrong with him, Damien wasn't sure how he was supposed to do anything about it.

But knowing himself to have a disorder, he couldn't explain why he didn't have the common sense to avoid heavy exercise after not eating for over a day. Or why he felt compelled to hide that fact.

So when he found himself blinking spots as he slumped against the rink boards, he knew it was no one's fault but his own. But as with most things, it was difficult to swallow.

"You need a break," Kara Beth said, and Damien turned away so as not to see the disappointment he knew was there.

"I am fine."

"You're not," his coach returned in a tone that could have cut diamonds. "Take a break. Eat something. And then, you and I are going to have a chat with Maureen."

"But-"

"Damien." That voice forced Damien to look up, forced him to meet Kara Beth's eyes. And what he saw was worse than disappointment. "I don't know what to do for you. But I can't watch you hurt yourself, okay? If we can't deal with this, then maybe you need something longer than a lunch break."

The implication stung. But Damien knew she meant it. Kara Beth didn't make half-hearted ultimatums. He withdrew from World's last year because she told him it was that or lose her as a coach, and Damien didn't doubt she meant every word.

And he didn't want to lose her now. So with meek obedience, he got to his feet and glided to the edge of the rink. His mind swam with guilt, embarrassment, resentment and worry, with nutritional stats playing ad nauseam against the rising men's technical scores. He'd just won Nationals; he should have been better than this. Damien took a seat on a bench to unlace his skates, where Satoru was already passed out on his back like a piece of cooked asparagus. Damien tried to ignore the other man's gaze on him, but couldn't ignore his words.

"You okay? Leave ice early..."

"The usual," Damien grunted. Satoru needed no more explanation. He gave a knowing nod, then rested his head back on the bench. His arm flopped to the side, indicating a backpack.

"There is rice for you here. No salt. No flavor. I think it won't bother you too much."

Damien grimaced, but accepted the offer. "Thank you." It seemed Satoru had forgiven him for his harsh words earlier. He always did.

He opened the backpack and found the plastic container holding the rice in question. The thought of eating it made his stomach seize all the more, even though he knew that Satoru had practiced long and hard to master cooking food with a minimal chance of upsetting Damien's system. But that was part of the problem, too. Satoru was reportedly a decent cook, but had wasted his time and talents on this? He certainly would have no need for this packing material disguised as rice, should Damien not consume it all.

Guilt and pressure made for terrible spices. Damien poked the grains around with a fork to stall. "Why are you out here?"

Satoru blew his bangs out of his face in a huff. "Stamina still problem. Need break."

"Hmm." They were in the same situation, then. Little children held back from a playground, having to accept their parents knew best. Damien still had yet to eat a bite, but was aware of Satoru's eyes on him, even from the other's sprawled position on the bench. He cleared his throat and changed the subject. "You hear about all the mid-season layout changes?"

"Everyone get steroids for Christmas?" Satoru griped, with a face that almost made Damien laugh. "They call me crazy... You make change too, don't you?" His face had a mock accusatory glare, and this time Damien did crack a smile.

"Maybe."

"Hmm..." Satoru scrutinized him, then waved a lazy hand. "Doesn't matter. I'll be back soon. Show who's boss." But even though his tone was playful, his eyes never left Damien. The reluctance to eat a single grain of rice had not gone unnoticed. "... I have juice in fridge. Do you want?"

"No, thank you. I'm..." Damien almost said, 'not hungry,' but dodged the pitfall. "Let me give my stomach a minute to settle. I feel nauseous," he excused. "When it passes, I'll eat." He wouldn't.

Satoru looked skeptical. "I don't think that's how it works. I have cracker."

"Thank you, but not now. My stomach really doesn't feel good."

"You always feel bad. Have to eat anyway," Satoru argued. "Then it goes away."

"Or it doesn't, and I end up regurgitating everything back onto the ice!" Damien snapped back, but tried to rein in his temper. Everyone worried about him, and he knew their intentions were good. This was no one's fault but his. Still, Satoru just didn't understand! "Not an appealing concept, is it?"

At Damien's sneer, Satoru wilted a little. Even so, he turned his head and mumbled, "Supposed to eat anyway." Damien felt his teeth grinding.

"Thank you, broken record, but I'm serious." He gestured at the rice, possibly the most inoffensive food ever created, but couldn't mask his disgust. "Even looking at this is enough to make me want to vomit!"

Satoru frowned and pushed his new glasses up his nose, then grumbled something in his native tongue. Without knowing the language, Damien still knew that he needed to be offended.

So he gave back some offense of his own. "Have you spoken to Yukiya lately? I'm excited to skate against the *new* Japanese champion." Satoru's glare could have curdled milk, and he hissed out something that Damien didn't know. "What was that?"

Satoru sat up, and Damien could tell that he was searching for the right words, but that somehow made it more threatening, every second holding off the promise of a dangerous conversation.

And then, Satoru found what he was looking for. "Coward."

Damien felt the blood rising to his cheeks. "Care to repeat that?"

"Yeah. *Tu es un lâche.*" And with that, the last friendly feelings were gone. Damien hurled the container of rice to the floor to splatter all over Satoru's feet, but all that hot rage didn't mitigate the return sentiments from his training partner. "I say again, forever! Coward!"

"What would you know about it?" Damien seethed, and he balled his fists so hard his nails might have cut his palms. "You can't even skate right now!" His barb had nothing to do with the current discussion, no logical contribution to the argument. It was only said in order to hurt. To distract the enemy by kicking at their own open wounds.

And he'd hurt Satoru, but hadn't distracted him. "I know!" his friend snarled back, and Damien nearly shrank before that look of utter contempt. "I can't believe you break my world record."

If he wasn't so angry, Damien might have listened to the voice in the back of his mind screaming at him to stop. But the angel on his shoulder was never as loud as the devil, who told him that this was how all human interaction was destined to end up and why friendship was such a stupid thing to live for. "How dare you!"

But Satoru did dare and came back with more cutting words. "Coward. Maybe get sick? So what?" He threw his arms in the air in a show of exasperation. "*Maybe* throw up in front of everyone? *Maybe* TV see and show whole world? *Maybe* lose big medal? Poor Dami, no one understands!" The words had such bite, more than Damien was used to hearing from Satoru, and he had to resist taking a step back. Satoru shook his head.

"You feel sick for maybe half hour. Embarrass won't hurt you. Bad organs hurt you, like kidneys, like brain and heart, like eyes!" He pointed to his new glasses with vehemence as the implications hit home, but still wasn't done yelling. "Not eating is just like poison. And you're scared to embarrass? You die for that? Maybe don't skate again, for that?"

He waited for an answer, but Damien was hard pressed to give one. Satoru's outburst of feeling had highlighted the situation in a way no one had managed before. Nevertheless, Damien felt compelled to cry out that it wasn't the same, wasn't that simple, and Satoru didn't understand. Even if the end result was the same, and perhaps Satoru understood some things better than Damien.

After a moment with no response, Satoru gave up. And that hurt Damien more than the yelling. "*Mou ii...*" he said, turning on his heel, "If you don't care, maybe I stop, too."

And Damien couldn't think of a reason to challenge that.

21

THE SNOW CRUNCHED under Satoru's feet as he walked, each step meeting a moment of resistance as it met the untouched frozen surface, before caving to his weight in a bunch of icy shards and granules. They hadn't had good snow-ball weather, something constantly lamented by the younger skaters who made up the local hockey teams, though some of the more rambunctious boys had tried throwing chunks of ice at each other until their parents made them stop. The air had been unusually dry of late, and the temperature too cold, resulting in snow that wouldn't pack but would melt just enough under the sun to create a hard coating like the surface of an ice pond. It was painful to play in, and no fun for any of the local children.

Satoru didn't mind it, at least not for the moment. Snow could be aggravating, but it was too cold and dry to soak his pant legs like it did back home, and solitary walks in the snow-covered world gave him a chance to think. Of course, when the weather was warmer and the snow a little better, Satoru would sometimes chase after Damien and force him to build a snowman or something. Not that Damien was likely to say yes these days.

"I did try to tell you. Maybe he's feeling jealous?" Wataru posed, and the phone echoed for a moment due to the bad connection. The slight delay made the conversation awkward, but talking with Wataru was always awkward.

But they were getting better, Satoru was glad to acknowledge. That they were talking at all was improvement. "Jealous? Of what?"

"Well, you've got a girlfriend now, and he's always been a bit weird with you..." Satoru sensed where he was going with that, and rolled his eyes.

"Damien and I are friends. I didn't think you were the type to spread rumors."

"Not rumor, observation. I don't think the guy's ever looked at me without glaring. He's dependent and you're clingy, but now you've got a girlfriend to focus on. It's only natural that he'd be moody about that."

"I don't think that's it..." Not that Satoru felt comfortable talking about Damien's issues with Henri in detail, or that he really knew what they were.

Wataru seemed to sense Satoru's unease and sighed. "Maybe you're right," he said. "Maybe it's just a cultural thing with Damien, and I don't get it. But I know how easy it is to hurt you." Satoru almost missed a step, but kept listening. "This co-dependent rivalry situation of yours can't hold. When the pressure hits its breaking point, it'll all blow up in your face."

"You're wrong," Satoru said, and wished it didn't come out as a whisper. "Not everything breaks."

"Let's hope so." Wataru's voice was unreadable, and it made Satoru fidget.

"Well, thanks for letting me rant. I hope I didn't keep you from anything."

"No, I was getting a little bored with this project I'm supposed to be working on. I needed a break." The little bell above the shop door jingled as Satoru entered the grocery store, and he gave a small wave to Carlotta Alvarez behind the counter and mouthed out a cheery "Buenos Dias!"

Carlotta, the matriarch of seven children, all of whom Satoru had taught a skating class to at least once, began clapping excitedly and motioned for him to come over. "Sorry, just a second," he told Wataru, then curiously approached the front counter. *"Que?"* Carlotta rattled off a long string of Spanish, then ducked under her counter to produce a wrapped gift. "For me? *Gracias!*" Carlotta explained what it was and offered thanks of her own, which Satoru tried to deflect with his shaky Spanish. But he beamed as he accepted the gift, and Carlotta then waved him off as she attended to a customer.

That few seconds of interlude got a reaction out of Wataru. "Since when do you speak *Spanish*? At least, I assume that's what that was," he said, and Satoru blushed.

"I don't, not really," he said with embarrassment. "I just know a few words..."

He could almost hear the way his brother pursed his lips, the same way he used to when Satoru fell on his Triple Salchows. "That was not a few words," he said with a bit of a growl. "What did she say?"

"Um, like, 'Hope you had a Merry Christmas', 'glad you're feeling better'," Satoru said, scuffing his boots against the tile of the store. "She's really grateful for all the help I gave her daughter when she was trying to pass her novice freestyle test and so she knit me a scarf, I think she said it had the Olympic Rings on it..." He winced under Wataru's silence, somehow more deafening than his words, but wasn't sure why. "I'm just paraphrasing. It's not like I could actually translate..."

"You really are impossible, aren't you?"

Satoru could have asked what that meant, but decided it was better not to. Instead, he unwrapped Carlotta's present. He was right, there were Olympic Rings. "It's not like I really know anything, it's just that she doesn't speak much English so I can't help but pick things up," he tried to explain. "And some parts of Spanish are kind of like French, so it's easier to understand her, I think. I definitely couldn't conjugate verbs or anything, I can barely do that in English."

"You don't have to apologize," Wataru grumbled, in a tone that made Satoru feel like he definitely needed to apologize about something. "You're just being you."

Satoru was too scared to ask what that meant. "I'll still see you at Four Continents, right? You still planning to go?"

"Yeah. Forward me your schedule once you know it, we'll do lunch or something."

"You sure it's okay? I know you have work and I don't want to get in the way of that..."

"Would I suggest it if it wasn't?" Wataru made an exasperated noise, and it made Satoru defensive, if only out of habit.

"I guess if it doesn't work out, I could just make a trip to see you," he blurted out, then felt awkward. "I mean, if that's okay? Hang out even if we're not working, if you want.."

"Yeah, why not?" Wataru made a distracted noise, and Satoru thought he heard a voice in the background. Maybe a co-worker. It was probably time to wrap this up. He was a little disappointed by the nonchalant response, though. Until Wataru's voice got a sudden injection of playfulness. "After all, I'm kind of starting to like you."

While Satoru tried very hard not to fall over himself, Wataru continued, "Try not to take everything with Damien so seriously. You don't need any extra stress."

"Don't I know it," Satoru agreed, before they ended the call. One person in the world tried to kill him, but there were so many others who'd stepped up to offer love and support.

If Satoru could just keep breathing, he might make it through the season. A shadow crossed his path as he wandered the aisles of the grocery store, and Satoru stepped out of the way.

"Hey, don't ignore me!"

Satoru looked up in surprise. Though they weren't friends, the face was easy enough to recognize. Even though the beard had been shaved off, Satoru knew Damien's stalker at once. Henri Petard.

"You... the police are looking for you." He shrugged out of the man's hand and tried to make eye contact with Carlotta, but there was a Christmas display blocking his view of the counter. That thing should have been taken down by now, just his luck. "You're not supposed to be here."

"What are you talking about?" Henri shook his head and glared. "I need to talk to you."

"Don't want to. Stay back," Satoru warned, even though it was him stepping away. Henri followed, and since Satoru couldn't easily escape the situation, he decided conversation might be his only recourse. "You follow me to Skate America, why?"

Henri didn't answer, just looked Satoru up and down with searing disdain. "Look at you. Why does everyone think you're so special? You're not good enough for Damien. You think he'd ever fall in love with you?"

It was the last thing Satoru expected to hear, but not entirely unsurprising. "I don't date Damien." As far as Satoru knew, Damien never dated, wasn't sure Damien had ever been in love. He seemed to have enough of a problem learning to love himself. "Nothing to be jealous of."

"Spare me. You're always clinging to him, even at competitions. It's disgusting!" Satoru tried to step to the side, but Henri grabbed his shirt collar. "You're the last thing Damien needs!"

Trapped, Satoru raised his voice loud enough to be heard by the other customers in the store. "Someone call police, there is dangerous man here-mrph!"

Henri clapped his hand over Satoru's mouth and shoved him up against the aisle. Several cereal boxes tumbled to the floor as he hissed, "I have as much right to be here as you! More right! I'm his boyfriend, and no skinny little brat is going to come between us! Understand?"

Satoru wasn't sure where to begin untangling that, but he'd have said anything Henri wanted if it would have gotten the other man to let him go. He struggled for a bit, only to find himself more pinned. If he lived through this, he'd have to congratulate Damien on his choice in stalkers.

He finally yanked his head away enough to cough out, "I don't date Damien! Promise! Let me go!" By now, the other customers had noticed the commotion and assembled. A few were calling for emergency services and one of them had drawn a gun just in case Satoru forgot he was living in America.

Satoru couldn't say it made him feel any safer, but the man's firearm did catch Henri's attention. He released Satoru with a hard shove. "You should have died. You ruined his life, you know that? Stay away from Damien!" As if Satoru was the stalker. "I don't want to see you near either of us ever again! Got it? Or else!"

But it was not to be, as several angry Granville residents soon accosted Henri, followed by the actual police. Without really comprehending, Carlotta whisked away Satoru to a back office to be plied with warm coffee and cookies until the police were ready to take a statement. The rest of the evening passed in a blur, and Satoru's only clear thought was that his brother was wrong and there was no way he couldn't take this seriously.

22

———

T HE WEEK ENDED with Henri's arrest, and it was a great relief to Satoru. And to Damien, though the agitation between the two was still palpable. But it didn't affect their training much, and their attention moved on to other things.

Such as the arrivals of old friends. Alisha Brian and Amina Massot had both flown in for a long weekend, though not together. Alisha to do some work on her program with the choreographer, Rachel Vines, who'd also choreographed programs for Satoru, Eric and Damien, and Amina was working with Kara Beth on improving her spin technique. Given that Granville wasn't a huge figure skating hub, it was a welcome surprise to have friends passing through. "Alisha! You don't tell me you're coming!"

"Satoru!" Alisha clamped her arms around Satoru, then looked him over. "I expected to find you bouncing off the walls after so much time off competition, but you look almost normal! When was the lobotomy?"

"Huh? I'm always normal!" Satoru protested, only to prompt a snort from Damien.

"He seems calm, but I still find scorch marks from where his glare has melted holes in the wall."

243

"What you all talk about? I'm fine," Satoru grumbled, but accepted the light ribbing. "Amina is here, too! How long you in town? You have time to hang out?"

"Yes, and please, there's nothing to do in this little podunk town," Alisha bemoaned. "If you all don't entertain me, I'll be so bored."

"It's not so bad," Satoru began, but Damien cut him off.

"Yes, it is." Nonetheless, they made plans to spirit Alisha and Amina away from their hotel rooms that evening to enjoy some of the local winter festivities. Damien left soon after that was settled, probably to find the French-speaking Amina and finally have a conversation in his native tongue, and Alisha turned to Satoru.

"Really, though. You look better than when I last saw you. I'm glad."

"Thanks," Satoru said. "I feel better." As good as could be expected, considering.

Alisha returned his smile, then pulled him into another spontaneous hug. "I guess that's something to be grateful for, at least." And for the first time, Satoru didn't feel resentful about that sentiment. Alisha let him go, then looked over her shoulder. "So, I hear they caught Damien's stalker. The one from Skate America? Is this over, then?"

"How you hear that?" Satoru asked. "Didn't think it made big news."

"You underestimate your star power," Alisha tsked. "I read a thing online about you getting threatened in a grocery store. There wasn't much to tie it to what happened in California, but..." But the connections were too obvious to ignore.

Satoru felt uncomfortable, but tried to give a casual shrug. "Not sure, they say. Still looking for evidence." Henri definitely had motive and some opportunity. Satoru looked over at Damien's retreating back and frowned to himself. Damien was extremely moody whenever the subject was brought up, and while he didn't avoid Satoru, things weren't the way they'd once been. Hadn't been since the Grand Prix, if Satoru was being honest.

So Alisha's next words surprised him. "You and Damien seem pretty cool, considering."

"Not Dami's fault," Satoru said, and he still believed that, but the way Alisha bit the edge of her lip ignited a slight flare of doubt.

"Yeah, I believe that, too," she said, but each word felt more like a question. "But how much of that is just hope?"

IN JAPAN, it was a social obligation to take the juniors in one's circle under your wing and mentor them. This also tended to include treating said juniors to meals. Even though other countries didn't always have the same customs, Satoru still tried to develop those habits as he rose through the ranks as a skater, to pay forward all the help he'd received along the way. He gave advice to Yukiya, Eric and many other young skaters, took them out to eat, whatever he could do. He knew all too well the feeling of being overwhelmed or adrift in a new environment, and having a good *senpai* to look to could mitigate that feeling.

But Satoru hadn't considered that as a gay teen, Eric might see Satoru's attention and paying for dinner as an attempt to flirt.

"And then I had to be like, 'No, seriously, dude, I'm not into older guys!'"

Eric finished his tale to the sound of Alisha Brian's howling. She poked Satoru's elbow. "You little charmer. What am I going to tell Inessa?"

"Don't make fun. You buy lunch today." Satoru poked her back. "Maybe I tell boyfriend on you."

Alisha rolled her eyes. "Yeah, my man's so threatened by a pair of kids half my age. Close enough," she said before Eric could protest. "I'm treating, so I get to do the most teasing. That's the rules. Eat up!" Satoru grinned and turned back to his salad, as Alisha sat back and sighed. "Too bad Damien didn't come. Snarking is way more fun with a Frenchman on your side."

"Hmph, Damien never wants to do anything," Eric muttered, and he sounded a little bitter. "He's such a snob."

Satoru paused. Everyone always thought that of Damien. Of course, Damien was certainly earning his reputation of late. "Isn't you. Dami just have trouble to be social. Can't handle place like this." He gestured to the sandwich shop they sat in, with myriad sights and odors that couldn't be blocked out. "You ask him do something where no food, he say yes." That left very few options, particularly in Granville. Even a simple movie was marinated in the smell of popcorn. But that didn't make it impossible. "It's like how you no fun when we ask play basketball."

Eric made a face, but nodded into his sandwich. "I guess. But he could try harder. I don't think he has any friends outside of skating." Satoru opened his mouth to argue, then closed it. He didn't have any friends outside of skating, either.

Meanwhile, Eric continued his grumbling. "And why are you defending him, anyway? You should be the last person on his side." That really gave Satoru pause. Eric wasn't actually saying he thought...

But it was Alisha who broke in. "You okay, Eric? Your mood's a little... "

"Sorry," Eric said, though whether he meant it was up for debate. "I guess I've got a lot on my mind."

"We can talk about something else," Satoru offered. "Alisha, do you-"

"Why did you switch coaches?" Eric interrupted, still with his dark frown and glaring at Satoru. "Why come here?"

Satoru blinked. "Huh?"

"Like, why Kara Beth? Why nowhere Ohio? Why put up with stupid Damien?"

"Chill, kid," Alisha said, wrinkling her nose, and Satoru was glad it wasn't just him finding the questions abrasive. "That attitude of yours needs work. You make it sound like you don't like it here or something."

"Maybe I don't," Eric grunted. "It was Mom's idea, not mine. Because..." He cut himself off, then pulled back a little. "Because the great Satoru Miyazawa trains here. So it must be the best."

Satoru felt very uncomfortable. "Not all coach work for everybody," he said, though it sounded like Eric had discovered that for himself. "But I come here because... many reasons. Best option for me."

"Here? Old rink, an outdated gym, you have to drive at least an hour in any direction for any cross-training..." Eric shook his head. "What, there's no coaches in Japan?"

There were, good coaches. And one really terrible one. "I don't know how to say. Is..." He looked to Alisha, though he wasn't sure why he'd find the words he needed in her face.

But Alisha rescued him all the same. "He doesn't have to answer when you're being so rude. What's with the grilling?" Eric muttered something non-committal, and the conversation moved on to more banal topics.

Later, after they'd eaten and parted ways with Eric, Alisha brought it up again. "That kid's been acting really weird."

"Yeah..." Satoru wished he could speak more to that, but he didn't know what was going on in Eric's life.

"Must have lot on mind," he said. "Maybe sad about Nationals?"

"True, it wasn't his best performance," Alisha agreed, wincing a little. Eric placed fifth, better than last year, but had been capable of so much more. "I know what that's like."

"Not this year. You do so well, gold medalist!"

"Ha! Well, thank you," Alisha tried to ruffle his hair, and Satoru ducked out of the way. "But I'm kind of curious too, if you're okay to answer, no pressure. What was the allure coming here? I can't argue Bonogofski's a legend, but there's got to be more to it than that."

Satoru paused. "Why you want to know?"

"Eh, I just wondered. In addition to small town living, there isn't a person for fifty miles who looks like either of us. It's gotta be tough." Satoru could have pointed out that he wasn't the only immigrant of color in Granville, but he saw what she meant. Alisha shoved her hands in her pockets and took on a more serious tone. "You don't have to tell me. I've just been thinking, lately. Was it all worth it? Coming here, all the sacrifice to live the dream?"

Was she talking about Satoru, or herself? "Sometimes I have doubts," he said honestly. It was easier to talk about these things with Alisha, for some reason. Maybe it was because she was going through something similar herself, maybe it was the sisterly way she'd looked out for him at competitions.

His secrets were safe with her. "Doubts, but is just hard time now. I don't think I would change." He took a seat in the lounge area and stretched out his legs, Alisha following suit. "Has all gone good for me, in skating. This place was good choice."

Alisha nodded, but looked a little disappointed. Satoru got the feeling she was looking for a deeper answer than that. She stared off into the distance for a bit, and it reminded Satoru of Inessa ranting about a life filled with cardboard cutouts rather than people.

He understood that a little better now. Good friends shared beyond the surface image. "Is hard for me to talk about, but I feel, like…" he scrunched up his nose as he searched for words to describe feelings he wasn't so sure he could explain in Japanese. "My old coach was awful. Always afraid. Couldn't stay, but scared to leave home. I come here, and make new home. It's safe place." He shrugged. "No one yells at fall. Other rinks don't make that happen. Other coach don't." But Kara Beth, he could trust. This home he'd made in America with Damien and Eric, he could trust that. "Skate better because that."

He didn't know why Alisha was asking, but it seemed to soothe her, too. "I'm glad you have that, then. You've done so much, Satoru. You should be proud of your career."

"I am," he said, realizing it to be true for the first time. He wasn't content, not exactly, that fear kept gnawing at him to get on the ice and train, make apologies to everyone in the vicinity, go out and run laps or something, but he was learning to see things with new eyes.

"But you're still not done, are you?"

"Nope." Satoru shook his head, a little sheepish. "Maybe I never be done."

"Yeah, screw retirement. You'll just hit the 400 point mark and ascend to heaven in a pillar of flames." Alisha laughed and leaned back in her chair, her voice growing quiet. "I'm not done, either. I can't just quit now."

"Then don't," Satoru said, feeling bold. "No quitting. We both fight. Everyone go to Worlds and have best skates ever and be proud."

"Oh, I love having you around." She was about to continue when Eric shuffled over to their party and plunked himself in a chair. "Hey, you."

"We came back too early, rink's still booked for kiddie hockey." It wasn't much to complain about. Kara Beth had to allow others access to the rink in order to keep the business viable, but the small population in Granville still meant her three skaters could monopolize the ice time. In Japan, access to a rink was much more difficult, too many skaters, not enough ice. Even in bigger cities and private skating clubs, Satoru didn't think they'd have as much ice time as they currently enjoyed in "Nowhere, Ohio."

But he didn't get the chance to point that out, since Alisha caught sight of Amina walking by with Kara Beth and squealed. "Oh, sorry, guys," she said immediately after, and ducked down in her chair. "I'm still not over it. That woman's my goddess. I've been looking up to her since I was in my baby skates."

"Didn't you compete against her, though?" Eric frowned, looking back over his shoulder at their coach. She didn't seem aware that she was being fangirled.

Alisha waved her hands. "There was a season where we overlapped, but it doesn't matter. Didn't make her more human. The Triple Axel Queen skated by and I just saw sparkles and descending angels."

"Yeah, me, too," Satoru laughed, only to have Eric's strange frown turned on him next.

"Who's your idol? In skating, who's the one you look up to most?" he asked, and Satoru tilted his head. He was asking so many questions today.

"Easy. Surya Bonaly."

"Who's that?" Who was Surya? Satoru felt wounded, and Alisha giggled at the face he made.

"She's French skater," Satoru explained. "In 90s. And gymnast. She lands backflip in Nagano Olympic free skate! Is disqualifying but does anyway."

Eric looked curious. "I've never heard of her," to which the other two looked scandalized.

"Kid, learn your history! The woman is an icon!"

"Why would anyone do a backflip in their program?" Eric scoffed, trying to deflect embarrassment. "Go all the way to the Olympics just to get disqualified..."

It was hard to explain in words, but Satoru tried. "She doesn't have best skate, falls at Olympics, but still makes impact," Satoru sighed, reflecting on the moment. "No gold then, but I like her. Big talent. And she gives skate that makes her satisfied, does jump no one else can do. I want to be brave like that." He blushed a little and looked down. "Quad Axel is backflip for me, I love jump, I love skating." To tune out the expectations of others and leave the sport with no regrets.

But Surya was denied her gold so often and didn't even podium at the Olympic games. Could Satoru fall short of gold but still feel satisfied with his performance? It was a question he was scared to ask, not when he couldn't live *with* all his accomplishments.

But maybe he could get there. "She is most amazing. Tries to land Quad Toe, but isn't rotated. Lands backflip at Olympics because she wants to. Takes off silver medal during world ceremony, even! I don't like that, but she's not afraid to say she's mad. She's black skater, so some people don't see past face, but Surya's not afraid to say what hurts. Not afraid to do what's important to her."

"I remember when you used to do backflips during practice sessions," Alisha teased. "Along with that Tano Quad Salchow. You were a little firecracker back then."

"I am firecracker now," Satoru sniffed, but he had stopped frivolous backflips. There were better uses of practice time now.

He'd discovered Surya Bonaly as a novice, thanks to the internet. The experience of being looked over and unlucky was one that resonated with him at the time. As he learned more about Bonaly, he got the impression that she never would have stood to be ignored. So he taught himself to backflip even though he could never use it in competition. Tano and Rippon variants were visually impressive, and Satoru added them to every jump. He would make his coach take notice, and the world. If he couldn't win with that strategy, at least he'd go down remembered.

After moving to Ohio, Kara Beth had caught him attempting a shaky one-footed backflip unsupervised and she didn't take it well. But her criticism was tempered with such obvious fear for his safety that it shook Satoru from his withdrawn defiance. He felt furious that someone had noticed him enough to stop his attempts to be noticed. He angrily thought of Bonaly stripping off her own silver world medal despite the boos of the crowd, of her landing that illegal jump just to show the world she could. She would never let someone tell her she couldn't do something, she would never be silent about the injustices done to her, and she would have the courage to stand up for herself.

Satoru opened his mouth to yell at Kara Beth, but the words didn't come. Somewhere between his brain and his tongue, he realized that his idealized Surya Bonaly would never be in this position. Because she had real courage.

With a trembling jaw, he'd told his new coach that his knee hurt. And everything changed.

"Other skaters, I look up to for skating," Satoru said, remembering. "But Bonaly is idol because of person. Want to be like her off ice, have courage to do what's important to me." He looked up to find Eric and Alisha with their eyes locked on him. He felt a bit embarrassed and cleared his throat. "What about you, Eric? Who's your idol?"

Eric started, then looked away. "I dunno. If I ever make it to Worlds, maybe I'll tell you..."

23

––––––––––

AS IF SUMMONED by the memories, Satoru wrenched his knee on the Quad Flip. He really hated that thing. And since thoughts of Surya Bonaly and her courage were fresh in his mind, Satoru had no choice but to come clean to his coach.

The result was as expected. No more jumps today, get off the ice and rest, hope it wasn't serious enough to set them back more than a day or two. Satoru bit back the retort that he needed every day he could get, because at least Kara Beth hadn't said "I told you so." She'd been trying to get him to revisit his Flip technique for years, hating the Quad version more than he did.

They'd fought over it, but it came to nothing in the end. To go all the way back to basics and relearn the jump from square one was more time-consuming than people realized, and all the harder because Satoru had developed habits and muscle memory like the foundation of a skyscraper. And another issue that he still couldn't confess to, a mental place he didn't dare go back to. He knew his Flip was a barely contained disaster, but it worked well enough to keep.

Except for the part where he'd blown out his knee. Satoru trudged to his car and ignored the ache. He didn't think the damage was that bad overall, but it had snowed during his skate session and the piles of snow just added insult to his injury .

Since their last argument, Damien had started finding his own rides to the rink. Satoru thought that was stupid. Carpooling was economical, it just made sense. They lived too close together and shared so much ice time; it was ridiculous not to share a ride.

Satoru grimaced and wrapped his arms tighter around himself. Damien had been getting so testy lately, so maybe it was just as well they weren't sharing a vehicle. France might go to war if Satoru shoved their champion out of a moving car.

As he came around to the driver's side, he noticed other footprints, leading to his car. Satoru stopped and inspected them, crouching down despite his protesting knee. He couldn't make heads or tails of what he saw, but nothing seemed to be amiss. There were tire marks nearby, maybe a little close to his car, but no note tacked to his windshield. No evidence that said car had scraped his bumper, either. As much as it seemed someone had walked directly to his vehicle, there wasn't any reason or result for it. If Henri wasn't currently in custody, Satoru would have been more worried than he was. For all he knew, some poor soul had just been chasing after an object lost to the wind. And then he saw that watch on the ground.

He almost missed it, the gray blending with the dimly lit snow, but when Satoru picked up the atrocity and squinted at it, he realized it was Damien's hideous lucky watch, orange appearing gray to his compromised vision.

"Again?" he mumbled to himself, and shoved it in his pocket. There was no question as to how Damien kept losing that broken thing, just when he'd finally decide to get rid of it. Maybe he'd delay giving it back for a few days, just for a little revenge. Satoru did wonder for a minute what it was doing near his car, but dismissed it when a gust of wind tore through all his winter gear. There were plenty of reasons for Damien to have walked through this area of the parking lot and none of them warranted freezing to death while he considered them.

He slipped inside his car as quickly as he could. It started just fine, confirming Satoru's earlier analysis. The brakes felt fine, not spongy, as if they'd been cut. No mysterious ticking, smoke or smells. Satoru accepted he was being paranoid. No one had messed with his car, and the footprints were just from Damien losing his stupid watch for the millionth time. He pulled out of the stall as soon as his windows defrosted.

The real danger would be from the ice and snow. Satoru crawled through the parking lot, foot hovering over the brake but never going fast enough to do more than tap it, and then applied the gas to get him onto the highway.

From there, the street had been plowed and he dared to go a little faster. If there was one thing Satoru was proud of outside of skating, it was his driver's license. The minimum age for a driver's license back home was eighteen, so his mother had flipped out to hear that her sixteen-year-old son had a learner's permit and was sharing the road with semi-trucks, albeit with supervision. Since that supervision was Kara Beth, his coach hadn't been all that thrilled about it, either.

Passing the written exam had been torture. Understanding the instructor when he finally tested for the real thing was nerve-wracking. But he'd passed, on his first try, something many of his native-born peers hadn't been able to do, and that was an accomplishment to be proud of. People might not hold it in the same esteem as his Olympic gold, but Satoru had worked almost as hard for it.

In front of him, the light changed from green to red, or top to bottom, as it was these days. Satoru gave the note on his dashboard a quick glance before hitting the brakes...

Boom!

At first, Satoru didn't know what happened. He thought he'd been hit, but no, a look out his window debunked that. He might have run over something, blown a tire, but that felt too minor for what felt like an explosion and was that smoke? In his mind, the voice of his mother's past worries started screaming, and maybe Satoru was screaming along with her, as he reached for the emergency brake.

It wasn't enough. Even killing the engine didn't stop the inertia. He was spinning now, straight into the intersection, with horns blaring and flames rising from the front of his car. Images passed in a blur, lights, cars, sky, the median. Satoru was going to die as the first man to perform a Quintuple Lutz in a Honda Civic.

And then there was impact.

SATORU DIDN'T THINK he'd blacked out. If he had, he'd never admit to it, since blacking out probably meant concussion and that meant forced rest and the end of the season, even though a voice from his conscience said that should be the last thing on his mind.

But there was no blackness, no lapse in time, just a strange detachment, like Satoru was watching a movie with no plot and a lot of special effects. Snow falling, blue strobe lights, occasional vehicles passing and people standing on the edge of the highway .

Even the strangers coming over to remove him from his car weren't enough to snap him out of it. Dazed, he watched the dancing flames still peeking out from under the hood. Fire wasn't usually that color. Someone had a small fire extinguisher and was trying to put it out, but Satoru thought the thing too tiny to be that effective. He asked where Jeremy was, because Granville was a small place and if Jeremy wasn't the paramedic carrying him, then it must be Carson or Angela's shift and he didn't see either of them here. It wasn't until Jeremy was actually in front of him and shining a flashlight in his eyes that Satoru snapped out of it, and he was pronounced as being in shock.

That sounded accurate. If it wasn't, shock certainly kicked in once Satoru caught sight of some of the other vehicles on the road. A semi-truck was stuck in the ditch, and a small sedan was a crumpled mess after crashing into the van in front of it. Paramedics were rushing around that car with a stretcher, Carson and Angela among them. The ambulance illuminated the entire scene of destruction, flashing its gray and slightly less gray lights. Satoru decided it was safer to look at the ground.

How Satoru had missed the carnage, he didn't know. "Luck", Sheriff Bennet told him later, and had just smiled when Satoru told him where the universe could shove all of that supposed luck. But while others had crashed trying to avoid the small car reenacting Torville and Dean's "Bolero" routine, Satoru managed to miss everyone and skid to a stop along the median. The side of his car was scraped bare and it blew a good chunk of the front left to bits, but not much else was damaged. Satoru's neck ached a little from whiplash, but even that was minor. It didn't seem quite fair, but as everyone kept pointing out, Satoru was lucky to be alive.

As with the poisoning, luck was relative. No injuries to his person beyond bruising, but further investigation revealed that someone had placed a bomb at the front of his car, connected to Satoru's brakes. Getting out of the parking lot hadn't been enough to set it off, but trying to stop at a higher speed triggered the detonation and he'd lost control of the car. Once again, someone tried to kill him. This time, they'd nearly taken out a family of four in the process.

Not expertly done, the sheriff and his detectives thought, another reason Satoru was supposed to feel lucky. Too small to total everything, it would have taken a more powerful incendiary device to kill the driver of the car. Even the accident that resulted was circumstantial; if Satoru had triggered the bomb earlier, he might have pulled over and escaped the danger without anyone else being affected.

So that made it his fault. Wonderful. But it suggested that the attempted killer wasn't a bomb expert, if they didn't know such a small explosion wouldn't do the necessary damage. Anyone could look up instructions for a bomb on the internet, but that didn't mean they knew how to best employ them. Of course, that clue felt like a huge step backwards. It could be anyone? Nothing they didn't know before.

The police took statements and investigated the area, looking at the footprints Satoru had mentioned, combing his car for trace evidence, and checking security cameras. They spoke to everyone who'd been at the Granville Ice Rink that day, even getting a statement from Amina and Alisha before they both returned home. Both girls rushed straight to Satoru's apartment as soon as they heard the news and Alisha wrapped him in a bear hug.

"I'm so sorry, I'd hoped this was finally over," she wailed, and Satoru hugged back with pretty much the same sentiments. Something in his gut told him not to let his guard down just because Henri was in custody, but he hadn't listened.

First his water bottle, now his car. Was he safe anywhere?

He was a wreck through the next few days of practice, made all the worse by his knee barring him from full athletic endeavors. No triples and quads to burn out his tension, and he was finding it hard to stay calm on the ice. He kept looking over his shoulder and jumping at shadows, but he did the same thing at home, so he might as well practice, right?

And then one day, the police came and dragged Damien off in handcuffs.

24

———————

THERE WERE manuals on how to be a coach. Several, in fact. Good ones. Kara Beth had read most of them, much as people accused her of tossing them in the trash. But Kara Beth never did anything halfway, and if she was going to coach, then she was going to give it her best. That meant knowing the rules and policies, as well as studying up on the best motivational techniques. It also meant a fair bit of gut instinct, since her skaters had passed over the best coaches in the world for what only she could give them. So between her instinct and said manuals, she felt she had a solid grip on how to mentor athletes.

What there wasn't a manual for? "How To Be A Good Coach When One Of Your Skaters May Have Tried To Murder The Other." And as for instinct, well, Kara Beth had doubted that since allowing someone to get close and poison her skater.

So saying she was a bit on edge was an understatement. And it still paled compared to whatever Satoru was feeling. He hadn't been willing to talk about that since the whole debacle went down, but it wasn't a stretch to say he looked wrecked by the news. Like a child being told his puppy was actually a wolf and it had eaten his parents.

Damien hadn't been much better. He'd protested and fought for his innocence, but was forcibly removed from the building. Normally buried under layers of disdain and sarcasm, Damien had actually looked grieved when he'd passed by Satoru. He insisted that none of the accusations were true, but Satoru had only stared back in wide-eyed horror.

Other coaches didn't have to deal with this crap. But Kara Beth had long ago accepted that her job involved so much more than skating, and that meant driving down to the sheriff's office to face Damien properly.

Along the way, her mind swam with the facts, as much as she was permitted to know them. Someone claimed to see a figure walking around Satoru's car, even crouching down by the tires. There were footprints leading to the spot that roughly matched Damien's size and his lucky watch in the snow where the car had been parked. And his fingerprints on pieces of the car.

Pieces. There were pieces of Satoru's car over fifty feet from the crash site, and it was a plain miracle that her boy wasn't blown to pieces as well. Just some bruises and a stiff neck, nothing permanent.

A better outcome than the last time someone tried to murder him. Kara Beth parked the car in front of the sheriff's office, but didn't go inside. She shut off the engine and just breathed for a moment, trying to calm herself with the flow of air, inside and outside. It was the same breathing technique she'd used to calm herself before competing, though this was so much worse. Once again, she'd let someone hurt one of her kids. It had happened right under her nose, at her own rink.

And maybe by her own student? No, that couldn't be true. As suspicious as things looked, she couldn't believe she'd read Damien so wrong, and that defiant hope pushed her to exit the car and walk inside.

It was good she did. Damien was being moody and uncooperative, his usual behavior when he was on the defensive. "I do not care for some stranger's statements, I did no such thing!"

"Then why are your fingerprints on the vehicle?"

"We carpool together! I helped change the oil and winter tires. My fingerprints should be all over that car! It is a horde of Neanderthals I am talking to, you could not find a clue if it bit you on your oversized noses!" Even if he was totally innocent, he'd be locked in a cell before the day was through if he kept insulting the police officers like that, and Kara Beth told him as much. "What does it matter?" he sneered back, "Everyone is already convinced I am guilty!"

"I'm not," Kara Beth said, and Damien stopped. "It'll take a lot more than this to convince me you'd kill the person keeping you alive." Some of that was bravado. There were footprints and fingerprints and a car bomb, after all. But she knew Damien like she knew Satoru, like she knew her family, and her gut told her she wasn't wrong to trust him.

Instinct had to be worth something.

Damien was quiet, looking up at her, and his mask had slipped a bit. Beneath the pride and attitude, he looked like a frighted puppy on an animal abuse commercial. "I've never said that..."

"You never had to," Kara Beth replied, taking a seat beside him. It was a very personal conversation to be having with the Sheriff and his officers less than five feet away. "I'm coach, I see all." She took Damien's handcuffed hand and gave it a squeeze. "I've always been on your side, Damien. We'll get through this, too."

He nodded, squeezing back, and the police interrogations went much smoother after that. Kara Beth listened, much as she wanted to just check out of the whole mess. She wondered if other coaches would have.

But other coaches didn't serve as surrogate parents to a pair of ex-pats trying to navigate a new country. They didn't hover over their skaters in order to catch the exact moment when a self-destructive mindset passed the point of no return because no one else would, or try to memorize the behavior of a young man who never cried or asked for help when he needed it.

And if they did, well, it was about time one of them wrote a manual on the subject. Kara Beth could really use it.

· · ·

THEY RELEASED DAMIEN BEFORE LONG, all charges dropped. The same fingerprints that condemned him also saved him, since there were two sets of hands pawing the underside of Satoru's car. Damien had plausible reasons for his fingerprints to be there, and none of those prints matched the ones on the pieces of bomb strewn all over the road. That gave his alibi a little more weight, that he'd been inside the Granville Ice Rink since before the snow started, and didn't leave until after Satoru's accident.

Probably the one day in history where Satoru wasn't the last one off the ice, but Damien's presence could be confirmed by Kara Beth, Maureen, Rachel and a host of other skaters. Those footprints in the snow couldn't have been made by him. "Convenient, that he always has an alibi," Eric muttered when he'd heard the news, and Satoru should have said something.

But he didn't. He didn't know why.

The lucky orange watch at the crime scene was still a problem. It had always been a problem, the joke came unbidden to Satoru's mind, but Damien claimed it must have gone missing earlier in the day. It fell off or got snagged all the time. That wasn't anything new, but to have fallen off under Satoru's car? Where a bomb had been attached to his brakes?

There was a smudged fingerprint on the watch that couldn't be confirmed as Satoru's or Damien's, and Damien thought that maybe someone had tried to frame him. All Satoru could think of was finding that lucky watch in his private skate bag hours before he'd nearly died.

"You believe me, don't you?" Damien had asked, when he'd finally been released and crossed paths with Satoru again.

"Police say you're innocent," Satoru said with a shrug and all the nonchalance he could muster. But that wasn't a yes, and they both knew it.

Security wasn't a new thing in their lives, ever since Satoru had won the Olympic medal. They had security present at major events, more for the crowd's safety than Satoru's. Sometimes they accompanied him when he travelled, and occasionally guards would stand outside the rink to kindly deter any overzealous fans from intruding on the private skate sessions, though Granville's remote location prevented a fair bit of that, too. And if not for Satoru, occasionally they had to deal with Henri.

Now, security detail picked Satoru up from his apartment and ferried him to and from the rink. They were a common sight around the building, they quietly supervised every task he did, every person he talked to. This should have made him feel safer, but it didn't.

Kara Beth revised the rink schedule, splitting up her three students as much as possible. They rarely did freestyle sessions together anymore; They kept Satoru and Damien separate whenever it could be managed. It was impossible to avoid each other completely, for there was only so much time and so much ice, but the new arrangement came very close. Satoru wasn't sure how he felt about that, either.

But it didn't matter how he felt, because like everything else in his life, he didn't get a choice. Inessa said his confusion and frustration were probably normal. "You did go through something traumatic," she'd reminded him during one of their late-night phone sessions. "Trauma lingers. And with Worlds coming up, you are under more pressure than usual. It might not hurt you to talk to someone." Satoru had dismissed the idea outright. But Inessa kept bringing it up, so he'd finally allowed himself to consider the option.

That didn't mean he was considering it in a positive light. "You think something's wrong with me? Because I don't deal with thing like you want?"

His tone was awful, but thankfully, Inessa hadn't hung up. "I think this is not the first time your life has been hard to deal with." She paused for a moment, to give Satoru's resentment a moment to clear. "Am I wrong?"

"No," Satoru muttered. There was no point in denying it, he wasn't dating an idiot. "But what's point?"

"You don't talk about it. Maybe I can't understand. But if you were injured, you would seek treatment for it, yes?"

Satoru grimaced. "If injured, old coach would say skate anyway, new coach say no more jumping and someone else say it don't matter because I kill you. Who you want me talk to, Inessa?" The conversation didn't last long after that.

Talking wouldn't put whoever was trying to kill him behind bars. It wouldn't get him back on top where he needed to be. The first, he couldn't do anything about, but he could control skating. And if his life was being blown apart, Satoru would make sure he had something worth destroying.

DAMIEN KNEW that hovering around Satoru was a bad idea, with security giving him the side-eye and every other person in the rink giving him less subtle missives. He knew not everyone in Granville hated him, but it felt like it sometimes. Especially with Eric going from rude to volatile. Twice, Kara Beth had dragged the boy into her office to either calm him down or let him burn himself out.

"He doesn't actually think you're guilty," Kara Beth told him, looking more tired than she'd ever seen her. "No one does. Everyone's just looking for a place to direct their frustration, and you're convenient." Damien wasn't sure that made him feel better .

But what was he supposed to do about it? What could he say about any of this? Nothing, he could only go through the motions of practice, eat food with mechanical enthusiasm, try not to throw up. Wonder if there really was such a thing as unconditional or constant love in the world.

Henri was also released from custody in time, but the restraining order ensured he went back to Belgium without further incident. He'd wanted to talk to Damien, but should have known that wasn't going to happen. Though, ironically, Henri might have been the only person unequivocally on Damien's side. His parents sure weren't, not because they actually thought he'd committed a crime but because he'd embarrassed them, and even Kara Beth had to divide her loyalties between him and Satoru.

Speaking of Satoru, he was alone on the rink now, trying to destroy himself on axel jumps. Damien was rather certain he wasn't supposed to be attempting that Quad Axel at all, let alone without someone around to monitor. He'd overheard too many arguments about whether Satoru had regained the strength to be drilling that jump multiple times.

But who was he to say anything about it? Satoru wasn't a child to be baby-sat, and Damien didn't need to tattle on his peers to feel more secure in his position.

Still, he slowed his pace a bit as he walked by, just in case. And it was just as he had that thought that Satoru took off on his next attempt. His rink-mate's axel technique was similar to Kara Beth's, relying on technical mastery and speed to get the height that Damien achieved with muscle. Those two used to chase each other around the rink in speed skates, as Axel Paulsen himself had used, and Damien couldn't say Satoru didn't get close to some of those high track speeds as he entered into that Quad Axel. So fast, so low to the ground, then vaulting up into the air like a madman. Somehow, he controlled the velocity and landed with stunning beauty.

Usually. The amount of time in the air let Damien consider that Satoru had taken off several seconds later than usual and wasn't he a little close to the boards- *no, he's nearly cleared the boards, Dear God, he's-*

And then, disaster. Satoru landed on the ice, but just barely, and the momentum smashed him into the side boards, where he bounced off and spun like a drunken whirlwind until he fell over. Damien thought he heard Satoru moaning, and he sprinted over as fast as he could.

He made it around to the ice in his shoes found Satoru sprawled on the ice. There wasn't any blood and his friend's limbs seemed to bend at all the right angles, so Damien allowed himself a sigh of relief as he dropped to his knees. "Stay still, you crazy duck. What if you've cracked your spine with this nonsense?"

"I'm fine," Satoru protested and demanded a hand up. Coherent and speaking English no less, Damien took that as another good sign. "Just small mistake. Wait way too long, won't happen again."

"I hope not. The game is skating, not pinball." He was rewarded with a laugh, such a beautiful, sincere thing. It chased the shadows away for a few seconds. "What am I going to do with you? Birds must wait for their wings to grow in before they can fly such long distances."

"You are strangest man ever. Just talk words with no sense, blah, blah, blah..." Satoru sat up of his own accord, since Damien wouldn't help him, and while Damien protested, it didn't seem any structural damage had been done. Satoru stretched and rubbed his shoulder. "Ow."

"Serves you right. You're lucky I won't tell Kara Beth of this foolhardy behavior."

"You don't lecture me about that!" Satoru snapped, and just like that, the shadows returned.

Damien hesitated, as if just waiting a few more seconds would prove this to be some horrible dream. The real Satoru would knock on his door and demand to know why he'd slept in so long, say that Damien needed to get up on time if he wanted to get free rides to the rink. Their friendship wasn't something that could disappear in the blink of an eye.

He was about to say that, ask if they couldn't get past the issues between them and prove he hadn't spent the past several years believing in a lie, but was interrupted by a voice on the other end of the building. "It's not my fault everyone's jumping quads like there's no tomorrow! You don't get it 'cause you're a girl!"

"Oh, I can't wait to hear this," came the dry voice of their coach, frostier than the rink itself. Satoru and Damien exchanged glances and decided to stay quiet. Eavesdropping was unkind, but neither of them wanted to end up in the middle of that.

So they sat back and pretended they weren't watching Eric flip out at Kara Beth. "The ladies division doesn't have a crazy arms race like the men do! I thought Satoru was bad, but now I've got to deal with Damien? If they were born three years earlier or later, my scores would be fine!"

"And how do Satoru and Damien disappearing explain how you're not doing a bracket on the right edge?"

"Who cares about dumb footwork? When we're dealing with this explosion of new jumps and better jumps, someone's gonna break their femur jumps!" Eric waved his arms, and Damien couldn't help give a meaningful look to Satoru's surely bruised legs. He got a dirty glare in response, while Eric kept up his rant. "I mean, the ladies have a ceiling! Even if some of them are doing quads now, it's not a requirement, it's not insane! You don't get it!"

Kara Beth pursed her lips. "I can see how, from that extremely limited perspective, it must be frustrating."

"It's not like we knew since we were kids that we'd have to be training quad lutz *combos* just to be in the conversation! Like, isn't that why they changed the rules again? But because Satoru and Damien are crazy, everyone else pushes themselves harder to keep up. How am I supposed to compete?"

"By pushing yourself harder, and developing your own skills," Kara Beth responded. "That's kind of how competitive sports work."

"Yeah, but my body won't do that!" Eric burst out, and he sounded just a little desperate. "And even if I could get to where the rest of the guys are, by the time I did, they'd *all* be doing stupid Quad Axels and probably quints! It's not fair!"

And now he'd hit on something Kara Beth had no patience for. Damien had been on the receiving end of this before, and by the look on Satoru's face, he'd heard a version of it, too. "What's not fair? That other people try their best? That they won't suck on purpose so you can win without showing up for practice on time?"

Eric scowled. "That's not what I meant."

"I don't care what you meant. You need to stop making excuses." Kara Beth ignored what appeared to be another excuse from Eric. "You talk down about the women, but my spin combos are still the best in the world. I can't do Satoru's Quad Axel but my triple could have gone head to head with his. And in Grade of Execution, components? I can still wipe the floor with all of you." When Damien cast a glance at Satoru, his friend looked a little proud, and he knew it wasn't for his own praise. Satoru had come here with stars in his eyes concerning

Kara Beth's Triple Axel technique. He knew full well of his coach's capabilities.

"There's always going to be people doing things better, and you're always going to have things you can do better than others. None of this is what's holding you back from your Olympic dream, and it's not going to stop you from being a great skater."

"Please," Eric huffed, "We all know I'm never going to win the Olympics. And nobody cares about the dude in ninth place. Our own country barely watches Nationals."

"Is that why you train every day? To have a bunch of people watching you? Skating's only important if you win?"

"Well, it doesn't hurt!" Eric shot back. "Aren't you supposed to turn me into a champion?"

"I can coach you there, but I can't just wave a magic wand and make it happen!"

"You can't do anything, can you?" Eric sneered, and both Damien and Satoru went ramrod straight. "You can't even keep a murderer out of your own rink! Maybe I don't want to train under the threat of death every day!"

The real surprise was that Eric was able to quit before Kara Beth kicked him out.

"OKAY, so which one did you like better?" Izumi asked, and Satoru struggled to come up with adjectives. His mind was still back in the rink, where Eric had stormed out on his coach without even a good-bye. All the drama was enough that Kara Beth didn't even notice that Satoru had been practicing the Quad Axel against advisement, let alone that he'd nearly swan dived into the penalty box.

His life was turning into a soap opera. "Well, they sounded about the same to me, if I'm being honest..."

"The same? No, those two tracks were completely different!" Izumi insisted, and then proceeded to explain the different types of reverb and the subtle changes that no one would notice unless they knew about them.

Satoru tried to understand. "I guess I did notice a little difference..." She forced him to listen to both tracks again, and Satoru wondered if he would be an unsupportive brother if he muted his end of the internet call. But Izumi had some sort of DJ event coming up and he wanted to give her whatever confidence he could. And even if he wasn't getting distracted from the second murder attempt in less than a year, it was nice of Izumi to try and be normal. That was a comfort, one he usually found in Damien, but... yeah.

After a while, Izumi gave up and moved on to another one of her projects.

"Okay, you've got to listen this! I remixed your long program music, made it nice and modern!" Satoru clicked on the link she provided and listened through yet another track, while the webcam showed his sister nearly bouncing with impatience. "So, what do you think? Way better, right?"

"It's interesting..." Satoru began, but waited too long, and Izumi groaned.

"Aw, no! What's wrong with it?"

"Well, it's hard to explain. It's like your beats and effects are trying too hard. It's taking over the original music." He saw Izumi frowning, so he tried to elaborate. "Think of it like my skating-"

"Everything isn't about skating," Izumi whined, and dropped her head into her arms.

Satoru ignored her. "This music has some powerful chords and harmonies. If I just put my huge quad jumps wherever I feel like it, the performance falls flat. The movements of my body have to match the movements of the music. It all needs to work together so each side is elevated. You don't want your musicality to be fighting what's already there, you want to be building it up."

Izumi grumbled a bit, enough to make Satoru wonder if she'd been looking for encouragement rather than feedback today, but then she shrugged it off. "I'll give it another shot. Classical music is so boring, I want to add some excitement."

"Hmm, my musical tastes are boring?" Satoru raised an eyebrow.

"Just remember, this music was exciting when it was first performed. Life changing. A lot of people still think so, that's why it's lasted."

"Yeah, yeah." Izumi waved the comments off, then propped her chin up on her fists. "So, how's Inessa? I hope you're not distracting her too much. If she loses Worlds, I'm blaming you."

"You're horrible, and she's doing fine," Satoru rolled his eyes. Distracting her? Ha. "The European Championships are coming up, so she's focused on that. But I'm planning a trip to Israel after World Team Trophy, before all the ice shows start up back home. We'll see if she can stand my company for longer than a weekend." Assuming he lived that long. But it would be nice to get away from all the insanity, be a normal person with a normal life and a normal relationship, if only for a moment.

"The long distance relationship thing sounds hard," Izumi sympathized. "I couldn't do it." But she must have had some more serious conversation on her mind, because her posture slumped and she mumbled out, "Hey, big bro, you love her, don't you?"

Satoru was a little startled, but replied in the affirmative. "Yes." It still felt too bold to say that, too presumptuous, but Inessa liked to hear it, and Satoru was finding he liked having the right to say those thoughts aloud. "Of course I do."

"Would you ever marry her?" If God and his angels held any affection for him, then yes.

But Satoru still coughed on the answer, "I think it's a little early to start thinking about that..."

"Yeah, but it's important, right?" Izumi pressed. "Like, if you guys are dating, you only have time to see each other in the off-season, so who's hanging out in which country? And if you get married, where are you gonna live? Is she gonna move to America, or would you switch coaches and move to Israel, or are both of you gonna come here?"

"We've been dating for less than a month. You're moving too fast," Satoru protested, though similar thoughts crossed his mind from time to time. "Even if we did start talking marriage, we wouldn't make any of those decisions until our competitive careers were over. It's too hard to know where we'll be and what we'll be doing until then."

"And what will you be doing then?" Izumi's question stopped Satoru short. "And when is then? Are you retiring after the next Olympics or the cycle after that or after your landing knee finally falls off? You gonna stay in America that whole time?"

"Is this an interview? Why so many questions?" Satoru asked. He ran a hand through his hair, frustrated that he couldn't escape that looming future anywhere he went. All he wanted to do was get through this season without drinking poison or getting blown up. "I honestly don't know, Izumi. There's kind of a lot going on now." And while he didn't like it that way, it did give him an excuse not to look at himself too closely. "Why? You have opinions?"

"Well, not really," his sister muttered. "Just forget about it."

But her face looked like she couldn't forget about it, and neither could Satoru. "What's going on? Why's this so important to you?"

"It's just... you're going to come home eventually, right?" And that plea in her voice stabbed Satoru right in the chest.

"Izumi..."

"I mean, I barely remember what it was like to have you living here," she complained. "Mana was crying last week because her sister's moving to Hokkaido, and I was trying to be a good friend, but inside I was thinking, 'You're such a baby!' Hokkaido? My brother's been on the other side of the world for forever. I have to plan and save up for a year if I want to visit him! And even when he's here, he only cares about skating!"

"I'm sorry..." Satoru wasn't sure what to say. "You know I'll be home during the summer."

"In the country, not home. You'll be doing ice shows the whole time."

"Not the whole time. And I can still take some time off before I go back to Ohio. I could even..." It was a bad idea, even as he thought it, but she looked so miserable. "Four Continents is in Beijing, that's not far. I could come home for a couple of days." Even though he was supposed to be building himself back up to his old fitness level, and losing entire days was going to kill his exercise regime. Let alone the stress, but if it would make his sister happy...

"A couple days? You might as well not come home at all." Izumi's words struck Satoru like a cold sheet of ice after a fall. "That's nothing! You're still living out of a suitcase. It's not like you really belong!" She must have seen the look on her brother's face, because her tone dropped to a soft mumble. "I liked it when you were sick. You stayed here long enough I could pretend you lived with us."

"I wasn't sick, I was nearly murdered," Satoru reminded, a little harsh. "Would you rather I was cremated so I could stay on a shelf in the house forever?"

"No!" Izumi pushed back from the desk, giving herself a little distance. "I just miss having a brother around."

"You have Wataru."

"That's not the same." Well, Satoru couldn't argue there. He saw her whip her head around, just to check if Wataru had been nearby to overhear.

Satoru grimaced. "If you gave him a chance, he might surprise you. He's... different lately." His behavior since the Grand Prix finals was almost supportive. Satoru had spent weeks waiting for the other foot to drop, but finally had to accept Wataru was sincere. "Even if he's hard to relate to, he is your brother and he cares about you just as much as I do."

"I know, but he's not you," Izumi sighed. "And I hate that there's always someone missing, like sometimes I forget I even have another brother. And other times I miss you so much it hurts. But you don't even care, you're too busy skating and hanging out in your other home. Like a cheating husband or something. The media talks to you more than I do."

"That's not true. And it's not that I don't want to be home," Satoru tried. "I miss you, too, you know."

"Yeah, but..." Izumi tapped her fingers against the desk and looked so despondent that Satoru's heart broke. "I just want to know what it's like to be a normal family..."

25

SATORU WARNED Inessa to give up investigating his poisoning at the Grand Prix, but warnings could be ignored, and so she did. Satoru wasn't happy to hear it. "I'm boyfriend now, please listen to me!" he whined across the internet connection, and he both looked and sounded like a petulant child.

"Spare me, I'm a woman who knows my own mind." But Inessa did take some pity on him. To say he was stressed out was an understatement, and maybe he just wanted to know there was one certainty he could count on. "I'll be careful, I promise. I don't want you to worry."

"You don't know careful. Stop looking for video, then I stop worry!" Satoru shot, then leaned his head on his arms. He poked a bit at the webcam and sighed. "I miss you."

"I miss you more." She gazed at his face for a moment and just smiled to herself. Not much had changed, really, between dating Satoru and not dating Satoru. The distance saw to that. They spoke more on the phone or via webcam, but there was no opportunity to act on this new relationship while in the middle of the skating season.

Perhaps that was why Inessa's parents didn't seem to take the news seriously. "That's nice, dear," her mother said, when Inessa finally returned to her hotel after her night in Osaka and announced that she was dating Satoru Miyazawa. The faces of her parents had been indulgent, as if she was a little girl with a fantasy crush. Even after insisting she was serious, there wasn't much change. Inessa wasn't expecting her parents to throw a party or a fit, but Satoru was both older and a Gentile. She thought there might be some commentary.

But if they joined the rest of the world in seeing her as a child, Inessa would have to accept it. She had enough on her mind as it was. "I worry for you just as much, you know. And the rest of us. What if this killer strikes again and I do nothing to help?"

"If it's about skating, then maybe no one bother," Satoru grumbled, then forced a smile to his face. "Quads are not so good right now. But you're right, maybe killer hurt someone else next." He straightened up with reluctance. "But no new clues, right?"

"Well, there is something that has been bothering me," Inessa began, tapping her finger against the table, "But I cannot explain what it is." She pulled up a video clip again, muting the sound and playing it one more time. It was a typical backstage activity, just people coming and going, stopping to chat and then carrying on through the hallway. "There's nothing I can identify as suspicious, but something in this video feels wrong."

"Like, person who shouldn't be there?"

"I don't think so. I see your coach, other skaters, the press and staff, Damien's stalker..." A security official passed in the hall, casting his eyes over the area. Coach Bonogofski discussed something inaudible with Maureen Shibutani. Derek Donner came through the area and shot Satoru a glare as he refilled his water bottle, but passed on by. Alisha Brian dashed from Satoru over to Marco Velázquez and handed him a small package.

"No one is behaving out of the ordinary, and yet, something is wrong." Yukiya Minami spoke to the man identified as Damien's stalker, who pointed out a direction and Yukiya scampered off. Maureen Shibutani left and Kara Beth approached Satoru. Eric

Blaine entered the frame and was stopped by a journalist for a comment. Alisha took a drink from a nearby water fountain before leaving the area, while Marco headed off to the locker rooms, Yukiya reappeared alongside Alexi Buryakov. Eric went over to Kara Beth and Satoru, then left again...

Nothing of consequence in any of these actions, and yet... Inessa shifted on the bed and readjusted the laptop in front of her to get a better view. The plush rabbit Satoru gave her during Skate America tipped over with the movement, and Inessa sat it back up and smoothed out its little skating dress. "You were feeling fine when you talked to me, right? When Derek arrived? If you had been poisoned before then, you'd have been showing signs earlier."

It gave Satoru something to think about. "I do feel fine, then," he agreed. "Was after, like, before warm up that I start to get..." He trailed off and said something in Japanese, but though Inessa didn't understand, she nodded.

"So perhaps this feeling of mine is nothing..." Inessa wanted to make sense of it so badly. But for all her efforts, no solution was rising to the surface. Even the trail of Damien's stalker had gone cold, with no arrest being made and no news released. The car bombing hadn't brought them any closer to the culprit, just closer to losing Satoru forever, while adding new people to the suspect list. And while they had video and eyewitness accounts of everyone's interactions at Skate America, it didn't reveal the moment of truth.

Inessa twirled a lock of blonde hair around her fingers, lost in thought until Satoru spoke, "I don't see you like this before."

"Hmm?"

"Messy hair, no makeup, clothes with hole." Inessa blushed and fingered at the sleeves of her oversized and faded blue sweatshirt, which was wearing holes in the cuffs and around the collar. It had a small stain, too.

But it was warm, and sentimental. "I promise, I am not always a slob!"

"Don't mind, Inessa," Satoru laughed, and his expression was so sweet that Inessa forgot her embarrassment. "Always see you with sparkles before. Glad you let me see this, too." He grew wistful. "Wish we'd train together."

"I doubt we'd get any training done," Inessa teased, but she wished for the same thing. She wasn't about to give up her coach, any more than Satoru could give up his, but it was nice to think about. "Maybe we can work something out in the future. When things aren't so crazy."

"Yeah." Satoru gazed at her through the screen, and the expression was so fond, Inessa wanted to touch it. But he wasn't looking directly at her, as the angle of the camera meant they were always looking slightly up or down, never making eye contact. It was a downside to communicating over the internet, so small when one realized what a marvel it was to talk across continents, but it made Inessa's heart ache sometimes.

"We'll see each other at the World Championships. Then we can go on a proper date."

"Yes!" Satoru grinned. He'd told her he was planning the perfect "first" date, and while Inessa hoped he didn't trouble himself too much during such an important time, the relish he took in the activity was getting her excited. "But is secret, we don't talk about that now. Or ugly things like murder. How is school? Or skate, you go to Europeans soon?"

"Both are going well, thank you," Inessa smiled. They chatted a bit about more pleasant topics, but despite Satoru's admonition to not think of ugly things, Inessa couldn't help herself. It bothered her for the rest of the night, and for many days after.

She'd never been one to accept being helpless.

* * *

THE EUROPEAN CHAMPIONSHIPS stole the majority of Inessa's focus, and it forced her to put aside any other pursuits when the time came for competition. But as soon as she had finished her short program, the nagging feeling that she was overlooking some important detail returned.

By now, Inessa had seen the confusing video so many times she had it memorized, and so cast her mind over it while she waited for journalists to take their seats for the Short Program's press conference. What about any of the images she'd seen were unusual?

Talking with his own coach was not out of place for Satoru, nor was trading verbal barbs with Derek, and they had only done the latter from a distance. Jogging in the halls, walking through his program layout, stretching with Alisha, all of it seemed benign. She thought of Eric and Yukiya, wondered if their eyes had lingered on Satoru a little too long or if they'd spent too much time near someone unusual. Was there a handoff gesture she missed? It was enough to make her pull out her hair.

But before long, the media had assembled and the lights were flashing. Time to put on a smile. She was leading after the short program, so despite all of Inessa's outside cares, her happiness wasn't fake.

Unlike poor Ekaterina next to her, sitting in second place. Someone was always upset on the podium, no matter what the results, and that had been true of Inessa once or twice. Bronze and silver were wonderful honors, but not when one thought they deserved gold and oh, Ekaterina had been so close.

Ekaterina had worn a smile when she received her scores, but that smile dropped the second the cameras pulled away. She thought they should have scored her higher, thought some of Inessa's components and GOE scores should have been lower .

Whether that was true was irrelevant. Inessa and Ekaterina didn't score themselves. The results were the results, and they would just have to keep doing their best. Inessa knew she had earned her first place, and the lead she currently had didn't mean she could let her guard down in the free skate. There was still room for Ekaterina to overtake her.

Which is what Ekaterina said when asked if the scores they'd both earned tonight were fair. "As if either of us need help to earn high scores," she'd whispered to Inessa after the reporter moved on to the next question. Inessa had felt confident enough to grin back.

The press conference continued on without much incident until a Japanese reporter stood up. Wataru Miyazawa, Satoru's older brother.

It startled Inessa, but not so much that it stopped her from waving. It seemed to throw Wataru off his game a little, but he asked a question on behalf of the colleague next to him, stoic and professional. His accent was different from Satoru's, closer to fluent, but stilted. Satoru, for all his incorrect grammar, spoke with the musicality of a native speaker, while Wataru had the rhythm of a computer program.

When he spoke Japanese, Inessa heard the familial resemblance to Satoru, but when they spoke English, they were completely removed. Inessa found that very interesting. After Wataru finished translating for his media team, the press conference was over. Inessa ran up to him as soon as they released her. "Hello! I didn't expect to see you here!"

There was an awkward moment, and Inessa would have thought Wataru didn't recognize her. But he soon gave a small smile. "I didn't realize you knew who I was."

"It's been a while, but I remember you," Inessa reassured. "You used to come to competitions with Satoru."

"Sometimes. That was a long time ago." Wataru looked her over, then asked. "You're dating my brother, aren't you?"

His tone was abrasive, but not because of anger or anything Inessa could place. She'd felt the same when she'd met him all those years ago. Satoru said that was just his way. The disappointment of what he said was more off-putting. "Yes. Did he not say anything?"

"He did. I just... thought he was delusional." He shrugged, and Inessa wasn't sure how to respond. But then, he added, "I'm glad. He really likes you, so... congratulations."

Inessa thanked him, but still felt adrift in the conversation. Another disadvantage to the long-distance relationship, few opportunities to ingratiate themselves to their significant other's family. "He talks about you all the time."

"Hmm. Nothing good, probably."

"He has told me you don't get along well..." she hedged. "But

Satoru is very complimentary of you. More than himself," she added, and Wataru looked up in surprise.

Then, for the first time in the conversation, his features softened. "Yes, he's like that, isn't he?"

And with that, they had nothing left to say to each other. Inessa fidgeted, not knowing if Wataru even wanted to continue a conversation with her, but feeling she should make some sort of effort. She was dating this man's brother after all, she couldn't see him and not stop to talk. That was polite, right? "I am surprised to see you. I didn't think Japan would send a media team with none of their athletes here."

"We love our figure skating," Wataru replied, with a tone that suggested he might not be included in that 'we'. Inessa wasn't sure what to make of that either, but since Wataru was gathering up his things and shifting towards the door, she ended the conversation with a few pleasantries and left him alone.

But she found herself next to him a few minutes later, when a gaggle of people jammed up in the hallway. Standing on her tiptoes, Inessa could make out the tall, willowy frame of Anna Stein, a German skater currently in fourth place who had accepted a small role in a popular film franchise and thus gained a new legion of fans. She'd been accosted in the hallway for photos and interviews, and looked aware that this was holding up traffic and embarrassed that she couldn't deter the mob.

Inessa looked behind her, where the flow of the crowd was redirecting down another hallway. She wasn't familiar with this building and wasn't sure if she'd be able to find her direction if she took another route.

"What's the commotion about?" She jumped when she realized Wataru was beside her.

"Anna was in a movie over the summer," she explained. "A small part, but it's a very popular franchise in Europe. She's a bit of a celebrity now." Inessa wondered if that would give a boost to the popularity of their sport in Germany. The way Anna talked, the average person there only cared about football.

"You're all celebrities," Wataru said with a dry smile, then gave her a confused look. "Don't you need to catch the shuttle?"

"Well, this is the only way I know," Inessa blushed. "I'm afraid that if I take another hall, I will get lost. It is better to wait until the path clears."

"Ah." And Wataru laughed, suddenly sincere. "Me, too. I just didn't want to admit it."

He really was a hard person to read, Inessa thought. She could see why it might be difficult to get along with Wataru, or misinterpret his words. But she could also see why Satoru defended him. The reflection on the surface wasn't necessarily what was underneath the water.

"So, what made you want to be a journalist?" Inessa asked, since they were stuck in a hallway together. Might as well make small talk. "Has it always been your dream?"

Wataru scratched at the back of his neck. "Not really. I used to want to study science. But then skating happened and..." He trailed off with a hal-shrug. "But it worked out. I'm fluent enough to translate, and all those years of following Satoru got me personal connections to athletes like Damien Saint-Michel and Alisha Brian. Contacts like that help a lot in securing interviews, so I ended up getting a pretty good job, considering I didn't go to university."

For Inessa, whose job, dream and passion were all the same, it was hard to understand. "Would you ever go back to school? Surely it is not too late."

"It's not so easy," Wataru said, a little sharp. It startled her, but they didn't know each other, not really. Perhaps she was being nosy. So Inessa turned and looked over at the crowd. The reporters were slowly making way so a few people could trickle through the hallway, though some were obstinately holding their ground and blocking Anna in. The poor girl looked like a trapped bird.

Across the hall, his height looming over some of the crowd, Inessa saw Damien staring back at them. His gaze was positively murderous, and it took her by surprise. "What?" she mouthed at him, and after a startled moment, he shook his head. But his gaze was still in her direction, and still perturbed about something.

"What does he want?" she murmured aloud, and felt Wataru's posture change.

"I can't believe they let him go."

"You suspect him?"

"You don't?"

The voice of Satoru came to her mind, screaming that she shouldn't be discussing such things in an open hallway, but Inessa couldn't help herself. And no one seemed to care about the conversation of a little girl and a nameless reporter, thanks to Anna. The only person paying them any attention was Ekaterina, also trapped in the hallway. She leaned on the wall next to the water fountain and waved while taking a languid sip from her water bottle.

Inessa couldn't say why the sight filled her with murky unease. The same unease as when she watched that video clip with some unidentifiable wrong. She turned her attention back to Wataru, who was shaking his head. "I know he was released, but I still think he's behind this. Even if he didn't do the deed himself. I always thought he was strange, and I'll bet that's why."

"Damien and Satoru are best of friends," Inessa said, somewhat reluctant to blame Damien, despite all the suspicion. But maybe she was thinking with her heart, and not her head.

Which is what Wataru told her. "Anyway, just because people like each other doesn't stop murder from happening. When a gold medal's on the line, I bet some people would give up everything." Though it had been on Inessa's mind for weeks, her heart still dropped down to her stomach to hear it aloud.

She couldn't stop herself from turning to Ekaterina. Still standing by the water fountain, still a quiet smile on her face, an easy wave for any acquaintance that passed by. She took another drink from her water bottle, and Inessa couldn't explain for the life of her why that bothered her so much.

But the crowd around Anna was finally parting. The girl dashed down the hallway to escape the press hounds, and the flow of human traffic soon resumed. Wataru slipped into the space in the crowd, hurrying on his way, and someone else squeezed through to get at the water fountain. Ekaterina moved to the side to allow access, and that's when it clicked in Inessa's head.

She stood stock still for a moment, eyes darting from that water fountain to Ekaterina, considering each factor. But each question and thought now connected like a jigsaw puzzle, finally forming the picture she'd been looking for.

She knew who had tried to murder Satoru. Now she had to prove why.

26

———————

AS MUCH ENERGY as Amina Massot of Belgium poured into her skating, she gave an equal amount to her social media presence. A running joke in competitions was that you hadn't "made it" as a figure skater until you appeared in Amina's vlog. For Amina, sharing the world of skating with the masses was a calling. She knew she'd never make the world podium, would be lucky to get to represent her country at the Olympics, but her experiences were just as life changing and valuable as those of the champions, and she was privy to stories and lessons that could change the world.

On and off the ice, she was an exceptional storyteller. She thought Planet Earth could use some positive stories, ones that transcended countries and even languages. To this end, she went hunting down Inessa Levi, who'd promised to record a brief segment with her once the Women's Short Program had finished.

She finally spotted Inessa in the arena's hallway, eyes only for her phone. She was frantically tapping out a message when Amina touched her arm. "Where have you been? I've been looking everywhere. We were supposed to meet at the shuttle stop!"

"Excuse me?"

"Remember? The video?" Amina sighed, since Inessa was looking so distracted. "You seem busy. I'm sorry, we can do this another time..."

"No, forgive me. I am distracted." Inessa pressed her lips together and had a quiet, seething moment. "I don't suppose you speak any Spanish?"

Amina shook her head. She cast her eyes around for some members of Team Spain. "Or I think Anna Stein speaks Spanish! She learned in school, and she's just down the hall. Perhaps she could help?" But even as she said it, her lips curled into a rueful smile and Inessa's followed suit.

"I think poor Anna will be busy for quite some time," she said, and resigned herself. She looked at her phone again, that furrowed brow returning, and Amina felt the concern rubbing off on her.

"What's wrong? Is there something I can help with?"

Inessa looked up, almost as if she'd forgotten Amina was there. "Oh, um, thank you, no..." But she looked torn between silence and full disclosure. "I am having trouble reaching people today. My parents will not pick up their phones, my boyfriend's phone keeps dropping the call, and my coach is busy with the ice dancers he also trains. It is very frustrating when one has something to tell."

And not happy news, by the looks of it. In fact, Inessa looked nervous. "Are you in trouble?" Amina asked, and again saw that skittish, startled tension.

It looked out of place on Inessa Levi. "Probably not..." she said, eyes darting around, though who knew what she was looking for? "Still, I don't know what to do..."

Though Amina wasn't sure how she could help, she was about to offer anything she could. But she was interrupted when she saw Damien Saint-Michel stalking towards them.

He looked quite cross. "I need to talk to you. Alone," he directed at Inessa. She drew herself up straight and shook her head.

"It will have to wait. I am busy."

"This is important."

"So is my time." Inessa frowned at him. "Why are you so rude today? Who would want to talk to such an angry man?"

The comment didn't seem to help Damien's mood much, but he took a deep breath and apologized. "I beg your pardon. But there is something on my mind and I think you may have an answer."

"It cannot wait?"

"It concerns Satoru," Damien said, and that got Inessa's attention. "I hear you may know of a video I should see."

"Is this about that sleuthing project you guys are doing for Miyazawa?" Amina couldn't help but ask, then clapped her hands over her mouth when Inessa looked petrified. "I'm sorry! I didn't know it was a secret!"

"Does everyone know about this?" Inessa asked, but mostly to herself. She looked over at Damien. "I didn't realize you were in the confidence, either."

"Your group is not as stealthy as you'd like to believe."

"It seems we're not," she sighed, giving one last look at her phone and growling. "Fine, Damien. I have questions for you as well. Meet me by the east entrance? I want to make a call first." He seemed satisfied with that and left with a curt thanking. Inessa looked apologetically at Amina. "I'm sorry, could we do the video later tonight? I can meet you at the hotel..."

"Sure, whatever you want. It's not that important," Amina said, and certainly it didn't seem to compare with whatever these two had going on. She left Inessa, still distracted by her phone, with a wave and a promise to pick up their little project later.

Later never came.

* * *

"SATORU... *important... call me back... as possible...*"

Damien Saint-Michel found Inessa Levi unconscious at the bottom of the east stairwell in the sporting complex she'd been competing in that evening. Her landing knee was a shattered mess, and her head struck twice between hitting the seventh step and

Damien's alleged arrival. He claimed to see a masked man fleeing the scene when he opened the door but was unable to stop him. The paramedics were called soon after.

Before that occurred, she'd made a few phone calls. The first one was to the Spanish police; they could not understand the young girl who had called in, and it didn't appear she knew any Spanish. When translators later transcribed the call, Inessa had told them she had information on a murder and needed to speak with someone. Because of the inability to communicate, she'd ended the call ended shortly afterwards.

"I don't want... over the phone, but... think I know who... be careful..."

She placed the second call to her coach, who had not answered due to the ice dance competition taking place at the time. His phone was buzzing at the same time his two students were flying through their twizzle sequence. The message she left carried much the same information; she thought she knew something about Satoru's murder, she needed advice on what to do.

"... why else would... no motive unless... I wouldn't suspect except the water... I don't know who else... you can't trust anyone... tried to contact police... they'll know what to do..."

Several calls were for Satoru himself. He'd picked up some of them between training sessions, but the connection hadn't lasted long, and the final call had gone to voicemail. Due to distance and bad connections, the message had been garbled. Even after sound technicians went over it with every filter imaginable, the full content was unknown. But it was enough.

"Please call back... I'm scared."

As soon as the news reached him, Satoru was out of his skates and looking up flights. "I have to go," he told Lisa at the front desk in a state of panic. Not that the teenaged rink employee had anything to do with his training. But much as Satoru wanted to just run out the door, he thought he should let someone in the country know where he was going. "I don't know how long, but I can't just sit here!"

"You don't need my permission, dude!" she'd told him with a

bracing hug. "Just go!" And packing nothing but a passport, he was on his way to Barcelona.

During the flight, he listened to Inessa's message on repeat, trying to catch an extra syllable or two. Maybe she'd left a name and an explanation buried in all the static and clipping, maybe she'd thought the information was too important to leave unattended. They wouldn't know unless someone finally unscrambled the distorted message. "And I don't think they can," Izumi told her brother when he'd finally gotten to ask her about it, explaining analog sound and sample rates and converting to digital for satellite transmission. "As far as I know. You can't clean up the sound if pieces of it just aren't there. But don't give up hope!" she hurried to add, sensing Satoru's mood. "What do I know? Maybe there's a way."

Hope was a concept Satoru was finding hard to grasp. Whatever information Inessa left in her last message, even if they managed to decode it, wouldn't change the present. Satoru replayed the fragmented mail to himself over and over. "*I'm scared...*"

"*You can't trust anyone...*"

When he arrived at the airport, the figure skating competition had not yet finished, though it was in a state of disarray. Events carried on as usual, but the added presence of the police and the questioning of athletes and staff added a new level of tension. Most of it seemed to be centered around Ekaterina Raskolnikova of Russia, one of Inessa's biggest rivals. The teenaged girl claimed innocence, and had no real evidence against her besides obvious motive, but was falling apart under the attention and pressure. As Satoru heard from Wataru, she'd bombed her free skate and ended up in twelfth place.

"If she had anything to do with it, it doesn't seem to have helped her much," his brother commented when he picked Satoru up from the airport.

Satoru just glowered at their taxi. "I don't care about any of that. I just want to see Inessa."

"Right." Even so, Wataru filled him in on the relevant information, and Satoru was grateful despite all his attitude. Wataru wasn't good at giving comfort, but at least he tried. He reported that Inessa had finally woken up from her emergency craniotomy and seemed to be doing well, all things considered. She spoke coherently when she could stay awake long enough to hold a conversation, which was more than most had hoped for when she'd been found. Inessa also seemed mostly aware of her surroundings, though she did show a confusion from time to time that was a bit troubling. She remembered little about the attack, but the doctors thought that could change with both time and the absence of high-level painkillers coursing through her system.

Her knee, though, was another story entirely.

Inessa was a fighter, a champion, and Satoru believed she'd pull through, if only because his mind wasn't ready to accept anything else.

Seeing Inessa's parents was awkward. He'd met them formally before, back when they were Juniors and running around foreign hotels together. Inevitably, skating friends would introduce each other to the family members hovering just out of reach. But they weren't close, and with their daughter lying ill in a hospital bed, Satoru felt like he was intruding on something. The Levi family didn't seem sure just what their relationship to Satoru was, either. And that was frustrating; he'd been dating Inessa since December, nearly two months. But to them, Satoru was just a boy their daughter once kissed at the Grand Prix.

If Inessa were awake, she'd have thrown a fit about how no one took her seriously. And Satoru would have let her. He'd have raged alongside her, because if there was one moment above all others where Inessa Levi needed to be seen and acknowledged, it was the day she uncovered a murder plot.

But Inessa wasn't awake. She'd been attacked in the back of a stairwell, alone and scared, and now barely fluttering an eyelash. As before, there was nowhere to direct the anger and blame.

Satoru sat by his girlfriend's bedside and took her hand, waiting for some return of pressure that never came.

"You can't trust anyone..."

· · ·

FAITH WAS A HARD CONCEPT. Inessa had a quote she was fond of, one that she wrote on a piece of paper and sewed into a fold of her costume for each competition. *"Now faith is the substance of things for which we have hope. Faith is the conviction of things not seen."* So she'd said, since Satoru couldn't read the Hebrew script for himself. She told Satoru it was from her Bible.

"It's not a superstitious ritual," she'd insisted. "It's a reminder. If I were to lose perspective on this with all the pressures of competition, I would surely lose my mind, too!"

Satoru had just nodded and moved the conversation along. Despite all her attempts to explain it, he'd never understood the quote, or how it helped Inessa come to peace with wins, losses and the expectations of others. But the understanding they'd come to was that faith was more than hope. "I hope for many things, but they are wishful thinking," Inessa tried to explain. "Faith is evidence. If I have faith in something, that faith is proof that what I hope for is real, even if it cannot be seen now ."

"But isn't that same thing?" Satoru had been so exasperated. "You want something, you convince yourself it's real. How can you tell difference between faith and wish?"

"You don't get faith by simply wanting something." It was a discussion that Satoru resigned himself to ignorance on. Perhaps he would never understand Inessa on that subject, when he wasn't secure in anything he believed.

But now, with Inessa in a hospital bed and Damien being one of the last people to see her before the attack, Satoru was looking for a little faith in the unseen. "It's just big coincidence."

"And that's all it is," Damien insisted, nostrils flaring a little. "What do I have to do to make you believe me?"

"I don't not believe you," Satoru said, and he didn't. If he was being honest, he didn't really think Damien did or could commit such crimes, for any reason. Was that conviction, evidence of unseen truths? Or desperate delusion? What even was the difference? "Glad you there and find her. It's just strange. What you even meet her for?"

"To talk! We're friends! Do you think I go around whacking other skaters for fun?" Damien sneered, but all his anger was turning inwards. Pain, worry and fear were the stronger emotions. The police had questioned him enough, thoroughly examined the evidence around him, but Satoru could see his friend was more concerned with Inessa than himself. "I could no more hurt Inessa than I could hurt you. I do not have so many friends that I can afford to be killing them off."

Satoru released a breath of tension, still frustrated. It made no sense for Damien to attack Inessa. There was no benefit. Unless...

He heard Wataru's voice in his mind, and hated himself for going down that road of thought. Still, Inessa was hurt, the stakes were high, and if there was even the slightest chance that his brother was brushing against a clue... "Can I ask you something?"

"Why not? I've had no shortage of questions today." Well, if Damien was innocent, the world owed him one massive apology. Until then, Satoru pressed forward.

"Are you... jealous of Inessa?"

"Why?" The understanding dawned on his face before Satoru could abort the whole conversation. "You think I would attack your girlfriend to have your attention all to myself?"

Giving it actual thought, it did sound out of character. "No..." But things with Damien were weird lately, and he'd already said it. The damage was done.

And what heavy damage it was. "You actually think this of me?" Damien asked, some combination of anger and deep hurt. "Why? What have I done to make this impression?"

Satoru could have replied with the mounting evidence of stalkers, car bombs, broken watches and the fact that he found Inessa's unconscious body in the exact place they'd decided to meet alone, but he knew that wasn't what Damien was asking. At face value, Damien had interrupted a murder attempt. He might have saved Inessa's life, Satoru should be thanking him.

"You didn't get this thought on your own," Damien declared, and his lip curled with the realization. "Goodness, but wouldn't it be refreshing to decide my own love life? Who tells you I would hurt others? That you trust over me?"

"I'm not stupid! Can think for myself!" He faced Damien with a glower of his own. "I'm not tiny duck for you protect."

"I swear, if that awful brother of yours said-"

Satoru threw up his hands. "What is your problem with brother?"

Whatever Damien was going to say was put on hold when Inessa's mother appeared around the corner of the hallway, and Satoru couldn't care about anything else.

"Inessa is awake now. I told her you were here, and she asked to see you."

"I've got to go," Satoru said, and Damien made no obstacles.

"Of course. Go."

Satoru fled into Inessa's room, as if waiting too long would make Mrs. Levi's statement untrue, somehow. But Inessa was awake when he arrived, if barely so, and Satoru slid into the chair by her bedside and took her hand. "How do you feel?"

"I don't know. *Ayefa...*" Inessa gave a grand exhale that appeared to put her to sleep again for a minute, before her eyes blinked open again. "You came?"

"Always, Inessa," Satoru said, squeezing her hand. He shifted closer as Inessa's parents left the room. He still wasn't sure if they were grateful for a break or resentful of the intrusion. The two kept their emotions quite close, and Satoru couldn't read their expressions. How he still had the energy to worry about outside opinions was a mystery, though. Satoru moved his chair close to the bed and gave Inessa the most optimistic smile he could manage. "I'm glad to see you."

"Hmm..." Inessa smiled, sleepy, and then furrowed her brows. "I was going to tell you something..."

Satoru swallowed. "You remember?" he asked, afraid that this was what got Inessa in trouble. He'd told her to stop investigating, and the timing seemed too much of a coincidence. "You know who hurt you?"

"I..." Inessa sighed again, broken by a small yawn. "I'm so tired..."

"Then sleep, don't worry more than that." Satoru reached around and squeezed her shoulder, holding her in a stilted embrace. He had to be careful about the needle in her other arm, after all. There was nothing holding those down but tape, it was like nurses didn't even care what happened once they'd skewered the arteries. "Can wait until better, just be safe." That was all he could hope for right now. "Just be safe..."

There was security outside Inessa's room, and she was alive. The attacker had all the opportunities in the world to destroy more than just her landing knee, but Damien had found Inessa alive. That had to mean something. Surely the danger was over.

Or maybe it was a threat? Maybe the attacker was as incompetent as the person trying to kill Satoru? They could be the same person, always coming close to the goal but never quite succeeding. Leaving behind meaningless clues and less motive, just enough for the victims to live the rest of their lives in fear.

"I'm scared," he thought he heard Inessa say, or maybe it was Satoru who'd said that. Either way, he agreed.

27

———

Kara Beth winced when Satoru picked himself up off the ice and flew into another triple axel without even a second to refocus.

At some point, everyone had to come home from Barcelona. Damien and Kara Beth left before Satoru, who followed a day later. Inessa was fortunate enough to return to her home country soon after that. Not under her own power, of course. That knee wouldn't be taking weight anytime soon.

Kara Beth felt nothing but sympathy for Inessa's situation. There would be no competing at World's in a month, and that meant no one could qualify a place for Israel at the Olympics. Perhaps Inessa could be well enough to skate at one of the other qualifying events in the early fall, but it would be an uphill battle, and the Quadruple Salchow was out of the question.

It was enough to break a lesser person. Inessa was managing to stay positive, at least in front of the media and mutual friends. She handled the situation better than most would.

Her boyfriend, however...

Kara Beth watched Satoru botch yet another triple axel and try again. And again. Axels. Salchows. Toe Loops. That evil Flip. All crashed into the ground.

"I think you're trying too hard," Kara Beth tried to advise. "That, and I see you wincing on the landing. Your knee's still sore?"

"It's fine," Satoru muttered, and threw himself back into the destructive pattern. Kara Beth pinched the bridge of her nose to stave off a headache. It had been like this ever since he'd gotten back. Satoru had always used skating to deal with or hide from his feelings, and the attack on Inessa Levi had thrown him into a tailspin.

Meanwhile, Eric had quit the club with a door slam so loud Kara Beth was still hearing echoes, and Damien only left his apartment to train. Her happy little rink family was turning into a dysfunctional nightmare.

To say nothing of her own feelings. She'd been at the European championships with Damien when the attack happened, but not with him when he found Inessa. When all the accusations flew at her top skater yet again, it was like being stabbed in the heart. She felt for Inessa, both as a friend and a former skater, and then seeing Satoru arrive on the scene in a state of panic would have moved anybody. But she was the authority figure now, the person everyone turned to, even if her boys were now adults in their own right.

So she waited for Satoru to finish his next disastrous quad, then skated over to him. "I know it's hard to stay focused right now," she began, but swallowed the words when Satoru shot her a look that said he didn't think she knew anything. Normally, she would face his attitude with some of her own. She was the coach, she saw things from an outside perspective, and she could see when things were and weren't working.

But if that was the case, then why did Eric leave? "We leave for Four Continents in two days," she tried again. "Do you want to downgrade the technical content? I think some of your quads need a bit more time."

Satoru looked up in furious disbelief. "You're the one who says wait for quad! 'We have time, we have time!' Now, no time?"

"I'm trying to keep you from hurting yourself," Kara Beth replied through clenched teeth. "We can plan your full layout for Worlds, but you're stressed out and distracted." The Four Continents Championships involved skaters from non-European countries, so Satoru would only face half of his main competitors there, and it wouldn't affect his qualification to the World Championships. "There's no need to risk an injury right now. Let's use it to just get used to competing again."

"No competition is just anything," Satoru scowled. He turned in a slow circle, stewing. "And can't go easy. Not with Sione and Aaron and Yukiya all making changes. And Derek. Dami. New jumps, new layouts, everyone decides now is time for risk." He stopped in front of her, dead serious. "I need to learn Quad Lutz."

Kara Beth gave him a strange look, but nodded. "Okay. If that's what you want. It'll be difficult for you, but a good goal for next season."

Somehow, she knew that wasn't what he meant, even before he started shaking his head. "No, not next season. Now."

"Now?" It was going to be one of those kinds of days. Kara Beth made a mental note to stop by the liquor store later for a bottle of wine. "Kid, you haven't done a Triple Lutz since you were fourteen. And now you want to learn a quad version in time for Four Continents?"

"Everyone's changing layout. Going bigger. More quads, good components and GOE. I have to keep up."

"And if everyone lutz-ed off a bridge, would you follow them?"

"This is different!"

Kara Beth took a deep breath and exhaled through her nose, causing her nostrils to flare in a warning. Make that two bottles of wine. Or five. "Fine, if you're so sure..." Her voice was dangerous, more so when she dropped the volume so the other skaters couldn't hear. "Show me your *Double* Lutz. Let's see what state that's in first."

"Just double?" Satoru sneered, and Kara Beth cast her eyes to the heavens. But if he thought she'd let him face plant on a triple or worse... "Double is easy."

"Then do it."

With great care, Satoru carved a large circle, slow and deliberate. Maybe too slow, for him. He made a great show of making sure none of the other club skaters were in his way, then picked the ice with his foot and rotated a satisfactory 180 degrees. Kara Beth could critique it, but he'd held the edge and rotated, which was more than she expected considering the last time they'd tried training the lutz.

"Nice single. But I asked for a double."

"It's fine. I proved I know!" Satoru brushed hair out of his eyes, revealing a face that was significantly paler than it had been a minute ago. "Now help me. Need better than basics to do quad."

"Do you want to talk about this in my office?" The ice wasn't crowded, just a few novice members running through exercises, and then Damien hanging just off the main entrance. Not a huge audience, but more than Satoru would want when this hit its breaking point.

"I don't want talk about lutz. I want to do lutz!"

"Then do a double like I asked." He was shaking. Kara Beth saw his knees and his hands quivering in front of her, those childhood demons screaming so loudly that they were echoing inside her own head. But he went for it anyway, building up speed and leaping into the air.

His knee buckled on the takeoff, and he ended up popping it into a single. He landed with a bit of a skid, shoulders heaving.

Kara Beth was cautious when she approached him. It killed her to see him like this, knowing how hard he'd worked to get this far. And there was too much on his shoulders already without trying to add the baggage associated with the Quad Lutz. Kara Beth let a hand trail soothingly against Satoru's arm, trying to guide his thoughts back out of whatever hell they'd fallen into. "It's okay. I know this is hard for you."

"Nothing's wrong."

"Except you have some kind of PTSD episode every time you try your lutz. It's the same problem we have when we try to revisit your flip technique."

"This new coach strategy, tell me I suck at things?" Satoru seethed at the ice below his feet, and Kara Beth tried to keep her tone gentle. Tears of frustration were pricking at his eyes, and a full meltdown in front of the other club members wouldn't help anyone.

Not that it hadn't happened before, but still... "Sato, I would love to see you finally get quad bingo, but you need to face reality. Pretending you don't have a problem isn't the answer." His ordeal had thrown him. They'd all been thrown. "I'm glad you want to try again, but it's not happening like this and it's definitely not happening today."

"What problem? Injury is healed."

"Your body healed, but your head sure isn't."

"Shut up," he grimaced, and gripped his elbows. He was still trembling a little, but tried to pass it off as being cold. "... I don't need sports psychologist."

"Kid, after everything you've been through, you need to talk to someone. This season alone put you through the wringer ."

"Don't call me kid!" Satoru snapped his head up, full of humiliated anger and now having a place to put it. "Always call me kid! I'm not child!"

"Okay, okay. Satoru," Kara Beth placated, both her hands out in front of her. Usually the familiar, motherly technique calmed him down, he clung to comfort and affection like it was his life preserver, but she wasn't sure how to deal with this new mood of his. She'd fought with him before, sometimes quite heatedly, but never with sneers and disdain in his voice. Her boy got angry and teased, but he didn't hate, and he didn't strike to hurt.

Until now. "Not your kid, so don't tell me what to do!" Satoru snapped again, and this time he was loud enough to get the attention of the other skaters. "You're coach, not mom!"

After a speechless moment, he sped away from her, and Kara Beth stroked listlessly back to the boards. Maybe she needed to call Vinny's Liquor Store and see if they did deliveries. In bulk.

· · ·

BACKFLIPS WERE an illegal element in competition. That didn't stop ambitious souls from trying to learn how, and back- flipping was always a crowd pleaser in show skating. Satoru could understand why it wasn't allowed in competitions, but he didn't think the danger as great as everyone made it out to be, and there was the wow factor.

So, of course he was going to learn it. He didn't get that reputation as an insane jumper for nothing.

His backflip was useless in competition, but as valuable to Satoru in his younger days as his Tano Quad Salchow. In fact, once he'd blown out his knee, the backflip ended up being easier. Fueled by images of Surya Bonaly, he'd thrown himself into a jump that could make people turn their heads and think there was still some potential in that odd little boy from Tokyo. Satoru was older now, a little less desperate and more safety conscious, but he still loved to throw out the occasional backflip in shows. It was his tradition to close out the season with a backflip in his final exhibition program. It was just for fun, now. He'd come a long way from the days where he was throwing out backflips in a desperate attempt to be noticed and valued.

Or he thought he had. "Don't even think about it."

Satoru paused, straightening his legs as he glided backwards, and tried to look innocent in front of Damien. "What?"

Damien wasn't fooled. "I see the look in your eyes. You smell of crazy." He crossed his arms over his chest and followed Satoru around the curve of the rink. "Don't do it."

"I don't know what you're talking about."

"You were two strokes from a poorly positioned backflip, Satoru, don't play dumb." Damien shook his head, and Satoru felt the beginning of a lecture coming. He turned around and skated to the boards, but Damien still followed. He got close and continued in a softer voice, "I know you feel frustrated. You want everyone to know what you are capable of. But you will show them in competition, yes? Be patient."

"You don't know what I feel," Satoru muttered as he stumbled into his skate guards. Graceless, he made his way to the bench and made a show of taking off his skates, but Damien didn't take that as a sign their conversation was over. He mimicked all of Satoru's actions, and once both of them were side by side on the bench with their skates unlaced, it felt stupid to tie them up again. Satoru accepted the unwanted break, and the lecture.

"I am worried for you, Satoru. You're not yourself. Perhaps it is not my place, but as a friend, I must say something..."

"Why? Because I do something I do always? You don't stop before."

"You've not done backflips in the middle of a competitive practice before. Certainly not with such agitation." There might have been something to that. Satoru felt so restless and frustrated that he almost vibrated. "To take such a dangerous risk so close to an event is foolish. And for what? A few minutes of petty ego? What if you twist an ankle or dislocate your shoulder?"

"Stop talking to me like I am child," Satoru growled, and received a frown in return. "This none of your business."

"Incorrect," Damien snapped back. "There are many skaters on the ice today and your backflip is startling. You had no care for your surroundings, and could have easily caused an injury. Anything you do on group ice is my business." When Satoru didn't answer, he huffed. "If you want to break your neck, do it someplace where I won't have to trip over you."

He began lacing his street shoes, and Satoru gave in. "You're right. Sorry."

"Of course I am. Now, tell me why this sudden need to prove your masculinity."

Satoru wrinkled his nose. "Not about..." Well, maybe it was. "You know me. When I skate, everything is okay. Now I can't skate."

"How do you mean? I see you doing run-throughs out there." Yes, to the outside viewer, it would seem as if the only obstacle Satoru faced was building stamina and strength to get through his programs.

"But Kara Beth still say hold back on quads. No new jumps. I planned six in program, need to practice, I don't know why she says no." He tapped the heel of his guarded blade against the ground and deflated a little bit. "Skate used to calm me down. Now I feel like other person. Need to get back to normal."

"Maybe that's why she holds you back?" Damien posed. "If you skate angry, you might get sloppy and hurt yourself on the bigger jumps."

"What I do about that, huh?" Satoru groaned, and leaned back on the bench. Fury boiled inside him, but it wasn't directed at Damien. It had nowhere to go, and that was the problem. The only direction pointed towards friends, who still couldn't explain why they kept showing up whenever someone had an attempt on their life. "Inessa is hurt! Someone tried to kill me, I lose everything I work for! Of course I skate angry! But have to skate!"

"What have you lost? That silly little plaque on the wall?" Damien gestured to the aforementioned herald of his new superiority at the Grand Prix. "You have so many medals to say you are an exceptional skater. Your victory banners still hang over the rink. These did not disappear because you withdrew from a competition. And the color of your medals will not affect Inessa's condition." He inched a little closer, enough to put a hand on Satoru's shoulder. "Pushing yourself too hard won't solve the problem, even if you win. Has it ever worked before?"

Satoru's head snapped up, and he glared at Damien with an intensity he usually saved for his Quad Axel. "What you know about that? About anything?" Someone was out in the world attacking skaters, Satoru was losing every title he'd ever fought for, and Damien wanted him to relax about the one thing still in his control? "You win one big skate and think you know what it means to be champion? You're still nobody."

He felt the shift in tension the second the words were out of his mouth, but didn't take them back. Damien's returning salvo was scathing. "I am the nobody who sat up with you as you vomited up your weight in vodka, because even winning the Olympics wasn't enough to make people love you!"

"If I know you hold that over me, I maybe don't call you!" Satoru chucked off his skates and shoved his feet in his shoes, trying to make a break for the locker room.

Damien followed. "And maybe I should not have answered!" That almost made Satoru stop, but he pushed on, palms sweating and breath hitching as he left the rink. "Let you grind yourself to pieces right then, instead of dragging it out for three more years! Why anyone tries to kill you now is a mystery when they can wait for you to do the job for them!"

The door to the locker room flew open with a crash, echoing off the empty walls. "I'm fine! You're one always in hospital. You eat maybe cracker, and think that's good?" He wouldn't say whether Damien's words had hit close to the mark, but by the look on his friend's face, he didn't need to.

"You are a stubborn little duck. We already like you, can't you see? You do not need to win to maintain this."

"I don't want you call me duck!"

"Yes, I should call you brat!" Damien was losing patience. Good, because Satoru's was so dead and buried that they'd need to hold a séance to find it again. "I know you will skate on an injured knee for a year, I know you will try insane jumps you know you cannot land and push yourself until the thing you love becomes the thing you hate! And anyone who tries to talk sense into you is pushed aside! This is not what you are, Satoru! You are a majestic swan, so stop looking for answers among the muddy ducks."

"What you talk about? You never make sense!" How did he ever find those words endearing, and why was he fighting the urge to run into Damien's arms and sob it all out? Why did he wish he could run across town and bang on Kara Beth's door until she let him back into the safest home this side of the Pacific Ocean? Satoru was an adult, his friends were opponents, and his family was at a distance.

He was alone in this, and he had to be stronger. "You think it's fun to make me cry? Watch me fall and tell me I'm awful?"

"You know that's not what I'm doing."

"I don't know what you're doing! Trying to play mind game with me? You so desperate to win?" He was wearing Damien down, he could see.

Good. Someone should hurt as much as he was. "Do not accuse me of that. I am trying to talk some sense into you."

"Didn't ask for that, did I?" Satoru sneered, then flung open his locker. "I'm busy. Don't you have toilet to throw up in?"

That second of silence was the most frightening moment of Satoru's life. He knew he'd said something horrible, knew he'd gone way too far, and some part of him recoiled at the thought that he could ever say something like that to Damien.

But the other part of him relished in the force that now torpedoed at him. As long as he kept finding new targets for the pain, it couldn't hurt him.

Damien did hurt, though, when he crashed into Satoru with every ounce of weight he had. It felt like they may have dented the lockers, or perhaps that was Satoru's head, but it didn't matter. That kind of bruising went away with ice and some rest, could be endured and managed. So when he felt Damien's hand twisted in his shirt collar, breath hot, fierce and demanding how anyone could say that to a friend, he cackled.

"We're not friends." He twisted his neck to fix Damien with the darkest, most mirthless face he could manage. "We just train in same building."

The next thing Satoru knew, he was on the floor. "I always wondered how you and your brother could possibly be related," Damien panted between attempted punches, while Satoru squirmed and blocked his arms. He eventually got enough leverage to flip their positions, and the two of them went rolling into the nearest bench. "I see the resemblance now. He must be so proud!"

"You keep saying trouble about brother," Satoru challenged, and managed to land a good punch to Damien's shoulder. He soon found his arm twisted behind his back for those efforts. "You jealous nobody like you?"

"God above, and you wonder why people are trying to kill you?" Damien grunted and kicked Satoru's legs out from where he was trying to get some traction. "I should have known better! People are always like this! Even you had to be disgusting and ugly inside!"

"Least not ugly outside." Not his best comeback, but it would do. Satoru was above biting, but only just. He swung his head back and managed a satisfying smack against Damien's face, enough that the other man loosened his grip. "I hate so much when you come here! Wished every day that you'd go back to France!"

"And I wished you'd-" the sound of the door opening cut Damien's words off, followed by a terrified squeak. One of the youth hockey players had arrived, but at the sight of two figure skaters with murder in their eyes, skittered back out the door.

It was enough of a break that it killed some of the tension. Both Satoru and Damien stumbled to their feet, fight over for the day.

But the anger remained. "Perhaps we will get our wishes after all," Damien hissed, and gripping his bruised shoulder, he stalked out of the locker room.

28

———

S ATORU WASN'T PREPARED for Four Continents. He thought he was, aside from some of his jumps, but he'd been so eager to get back to competition, any competition. The Four Continents Championships were by no means small, but with all the Europeans competing at their own event, it was slightly less stressful than Worlds. Satoru thought he was ready.

He hadn't expected the panic attack. If anyone asked, he was fine. That was what he told his family, the media, even Kara Beth, but the trouble started the minute his plane touched down in Beijing to crowds of fans and press. He hadn't seen that many people since he'd returned to Japan with Olympic Gold. And it only got worse when he took to the rink. Hundreds of cameras trained on his practice, trying to determine his exact level of physical fitness, fans in all the seats trying to do the exact same thing. Media everywhere he turned and competitors mixed in like spies. These people used to be his friends, his source of energy. Now, all he could think of were Inessa's half-obscured words. *"You can't trust anyone."*

Even security? Because they were all over everyone at this competition, and no one could say they felt safer for it. There were a few skaters who opted to withdraw from competition until the culprit was caught, and some of those who stayed showed a little resentment at all the extra security measures. Satoru wondered how much of that was being heaped on him. *'If only Miyazawa hadn't gotten himself in trouble...'* It wasn't like they had anyone else to blame.

As suspicious as he was of the other skaters, some tried to be friendly. The Bertinelli triplets and Hser Nay all approached him to welcome him back to competition, though Satoru hadn't felt like talking. Alisha passed him in the hallway and gave him an energetic clap on the shoulder. Aaron Leval did a full pirouette in joy when they crossed paths. "Satoru! You're back! We've missed you!"

The attention was all too much. "That's not my name," Satoru snapped, and Aaron withdrew the hand he'd been extending.

"Huh?"

"My name, that's not right, you always pronounce it wrong."

After a mystified beat, Aaron dropped his hand and stepped back. "Well, good talk, man." He left, and as he passed Sione, gave a dramatic shake of his head. Sione gave Satoru a warm nod of acknowledgement in lieu of coming over, which Satoru did not return. There were too many people here, he wanted to get away. Or at least get on the ice, where he'd only have to deal with six people at a time and none of them would speak a word to him.

Next to him, Kara Beth was trying to disguise a chuckle as a cough. "What?" Satoru asked, impatient.

"Nothing," she said, mouth quirked in a suppressed smile. "Just marveling at the miraculous disappearance of your own accent, that's all. *Satoru.*" She knew how to pronounce his name, where to place the emphasis. Satoru couldn't weave his tongue around some syllables in hers, or Aaron's family name, for that matter.

He'd been very kind, not to call Satoru out on that hypocrisy. But Satoru couldn't appreciate it, not with crowds pressing in on him and the knowledge that anything could happen, death could come from any angle. Israeli reporters squeezing through and reminding him that his girlfriend was in a hospital and might never skate with him again and it was probably all his fault.

Among his other personal problems. He hadn't spoken to his

family in days, though not for lack of trying on their part. When Kara Beth told him she was sick of playing liaison, he told her that everyone should know how busy he was and leave him alone.

Some people had taken that advice literally. "Damien went back to Paris!" Kara Beth had told him then, and the snap in her tone had brought Satoru to heel for a brief second.

"When?"

"Sometime after you blacked out his eye. He settled some things with me, then caught the next flight to France. He'll be staying with his parents until Worlds." And that was sobering, to realize Damien would rather prepare for competition surrounded by his toxic family than his friends. Kara Beth could watch videos of his practices and monitor his training from afar, but Satoru knew their coach was more than that to Damien, as she was to him.

"After Worlds," Kara Beth had told him in a soft voice, but no less stern, "The three of us need a meeting. We'll decide if this coaching arrangement can still work." What would happen if it couldn't was left unsaid, but Satoru thought he had a pretty good idea.

The practices and six-minute warm-up came and went, and suddenly it was Satoru's turn to skate. It came up as suddenly as a train. He wasn't sure how a routine he'd been through hundreds of times could sneak up on him like that.

He saw Kara Beth reaching into her bag for the pom-poms. "Don't!" he hissed, suddenly mortified. Even though it was their tradition, part of the competition routine, even though it had been half his idea to start bringing them in the first place. After all, the entire world's eyes were on him. Not since his abysmal Junior days had the entirety of Planet Earth held their breath for him to fail. "You're embarrassing me!"

Kara Beth put them away, now as off her game as Satoru. All their rituals were getting abandoned and thrown out the window, he couldn't look to her to be an act of constancy. But still, she tried. "You can do this, Satoru. You know this program, you've trained it a million times. Take a deep breath and focus on your job."

The scores for Lin Cong of China were announced, and Satoru

felt his breath catch in his throat. So high, way too high, he was only gone for a few months, why were everyone's scores so high? His hands were sweating so much that his gloves were sopping, his skates felt three sizes too small.

"Satoru." Kara Beth's hands smacked lightly next to his, her voice urgent. "Satoru! Let go of the boards!"

That's right, he had to start, didn't he? There was a time limit, he'd lose a point if he didn't start before then. He pushed back, like falling off a cliff, and raced into the center. After taking his place, he froze for a second, almost forgetting his opening pose. And then, after a sentence pregnant with a million camera shutters clicking, the music started.

Giselle. He was supposed to focus on the story; he was supposed to build up speed for the upcoming 4F. He was supposed to use transitions and edges, he had choreography, he had inhuman jumps to do and amidst all that, he was supposed to be acting? Impossible. Meanwhile, he could feel the killer's eyes on him, even without knowing who the person was, and Wataru beyond that, watching from some media box and hoping his little brother didn't embarrass him in front of his coworkers.

Satoru couldn't mess up that Flip now. He wouldn't. The time came, he stretched back his leg, found the edge, picked, turned-

-You can't trust anyone-

And he fell, straight onto his hip bone and all but bounced across the ice. Satoru pled within himself, but there was no rewind feature, no chance to wipe the mistake clean and try again. He scrambled to his feet and tried to get back into the routine.

A fall. He could count on one hand how many times he'd fallen in competition over the last three years, and two of them involved battling arsenic poisoning. Why now? Why, when he needed to prove himself more than ever?

-Your foot is splayed again. And you only did 3.5 rotations. Wasn't the plan to do four? Come on, Satoru, I followed you out to Ohio so you could get better at skating, not worse.-

Wataru was watching this, somewhere. Satoru pulled out of his spin sequence, shaky and disoriented. That wasn't the right number of rotations, he knew it wasn't. There would be no positive GOE on that element, he wouldn't hang on to his level. And wasn't there supposed to be some artistry or storytelling going on, too? Maybe this was what it felt like to dance until you died, maybe this sham of a program was the ultimate interpretation of the Giselle story.

He felt sick to his stomach. The ads printed on the walls of the rink all blurred together in a mess of grayish-green, and he thought he might throw up. He tasted metal in his mouth.

The combination was next. Satoru cast his eyes to the boards, to Kara Beth. He couldn't find her, no colorful pom-poms to help her stand out. Even if there were, he wouldn't have seen them. Red meant nothing to him anymore.

Kara Beth advised him to do a 3S+3Lo, to not go for his full difficulty today. But after messing up so much, he didn't have a choice. Satoru had to make up the points somehow, and he'd done the 4S+3Lo so many times, it would be easy enough, he had to go for it. That meant changing a few things in his entrance, in his timing, but he could do it, he could-

-Why anyone is trying to kill you is a mystery, when they can just wait for you to do the job for them!-

He didn't even make it through the first jump. He landed on two feet, then tripped onto his knees. A quick push and he was upright again, but his chest had constricted in horror.

No second jump, just a single. The rules of the short program demanded a combination pass, he'd just invalidated an entire element. Zero points.

Zero.

It was like a nightmare. But he couldn't stop and assess, not when the clock was still ticking, not when Giselle was dead and a bunch of vengeful spirits wanted to drag him down, too. There was only one more jump left, his triple axel, the most reliable jump in his arsenal. At least he would end on a positive note.

If his legs weren't shaking. If he couldn't feel every bruise throbbing, cold ice under his arms instead of his skates.

-Sometimes I forget I even have another brother.-

But first, the spin sequence. He could build some momentum with that, remind everyone that he still knew how to skate. A little speed, a quick leap, and he was flying into his camel spin.

He slipped off the edge, and landed on his back. For a second, he couldn't get back up. He'd just fallen on a spin! Another element, tossed out the window, when he couldn't afford to lose any more points. And to mess up his camel like a slapstick comedian slipping on a banana peel was too humiliating for words.

-Blame it on the ice if you want, Miyazawa, but the rest of us skated just fine.-

But the program wasn't over. The conga line of shame still marched on, and Satoru had to keep going. Even if he couldn't see for tears, couldn't feel for bruising, couldn't think for pressure. This train wreck of a performance was going out to the world. Cameras lined the rink and all of them were trained on him in order to capture his mortification in perfect, 4k detail. Each stroke commentated on in a hundred different languages and then translated by the fans into a hundred more so that no person on earth would miss a single word of criticism.

How was he supposed to go home after this? How could he face everyone? Satoru tried to pump some energy into the footwork section, one of his last chances for redeeming points, but his heart wasn't there. He was doing math in his head, trying to calculate up the missed points and determine if his technical score was even going to break into double digits.

-This part of you is ugly. I feel like I have offended you somehow.-

Because it didn't matter what he did, at this point. He could fight for every step, but this program was lost. He could hear the voice of his former coach as if he were skating next to him.

-Is there anything inside that head? Can't speak, now? What's the point in training you, then?-

The Triple Axel was next. The last chance to get something positive out of the whole experience. He threw his head down and went into his backward crossovers, not caring if he was telegraphing the jump. As long as he could land one thing, prove he could do at least one thing right. Satoru flipped around to face forward-

-*My best isn't good enough.*-

Down on the axel. And that was the final straw. The last notes of "Giselle" echoed in the arena to complete silence as Satoru pulled himself to his knees.

And he stayed there.

With a trickle, the tepid applause started up, sympathy clapping, and Satoru knew he needed to move. He needed to stand, bow to the judges, thank the audience for staying with him and enduring that horrible display, but he couldn't move. He heard the legendary Scott Hamilton in his head, resurrecting a past workshop where he'd gotten to meet the man, and was ordered not to admit to his mistakes after ending the program. "*If you're not selling, the judges won't buy. I can't repeat that enough! No one can buy what you're not selling!*"

But who would he be kidding? Everyone saw him fall, again and again and *again*. And they saw him now, the Olympic Champion, defending World Champion, on his knees in defeat. And thanks to those cameras, they would see him when he bowed, they would see him when he left the ice, in the Kiss and Cry, backstage, leaving the venue...

Satoru let them all down. His coach, both of them, and his family. Wataru. All the friends who'd hoped and prayed for him to get better, and Inessa. Damien. His sponsors, his Federation, Japan, all the little kids in Granville who'd ever taken a Learn to Skate class. He'd let down so many people, and there was nowhere to hide.

So there was no point in trying. Satoru touched his forehead to the ice, put his hands over his head and sobbed.

HE WASN'T sure when or how he got off the ice, but came to his senses as he was gliding back to the exit, Kara Beth there to meet him. His vision blurred, and he wasn't sure if that was the tears or if he'd lost a contact lens.

As he got closer, Kara Beth extended her arms, and the sight flipped something in Satoru. "Don't touch me!" he growled. He wasn't sure if he'd said it in English or not, but it worked, and Kara Beth sprang back.

"It's not the end of the world," she said, in her calm, soothing tones. She handed over his guards, and Satoru fought the urge to stab something with them.

But he said nothing and stalked to the Kiss and Cry. There were cameras everywhere, already seeing more of his heart than he felt like sharing at the moment. He had to keep something in reserve. And anger was a beautiful shield.

The two of them waited for the scores to be posted in stoney silence. It was quite the wait, and Satoru wondered what could be taking the judges so long. He'd made his falls pretty obvious, did they need to make up brand new deductions to address the atrocity they'd just been handed?

Over the intercom, a pop song was playing, English lyrics mixed with Chinese. Something about persevering through trials, getting up after falling. Satoru decided he hated it. "What's taking forever?" he muttered, and Kara Beth just shrugged.

"Don't know. Look, the score today doesn't matter, all right? We can talk about what happened and-"

"Don't need to talk," Satoru replied, moving his lips as little as possible. He could see the fans and their telescopic lenses across the arena, even if the official channels didn't currently have fifteen cameras all up in his face. He kept his voice down, too, just in case the microphones were hot. "I sucked, end of story. Nothing to say." He paused for a minute, trying to stop his eyes from burning at the memory of all those failed jumps. "Told you we should practice quads more."

"I told you we should have gone with the downgraded layout." Kara Beth's voice was light, reluctant to get dirty in the fishbowl that was the Kiss and Cry, but not backing down, either. "Guess we were both wrong."

No, Satoru wouldn't accept that. His life had been out of control since the Grand Prix, not a single choice he made came without shackles on his wrists, and there was no way he was going to sit politely and nod while everyone judged him for it.

Not when no choice was the right one, not when he'd turned himself inside out just to even be here. If the world wanted to drag him off his pedestal, well, he'd pick the thing up and throw it at them first.

And that attitude gave him energy enough to last until the scores appeared on the screen. Even the stoic announcer sounded disappointed. "Satoru Miyazawa has earned in the short program... 54.80 points. He is currently in fifteenth place."

Fifteenth? There were still three skaters left to go, three world class skaters, unless one of them accidentally sliced off their own leg in their program, he'd be eighteenth! Four fall deductions, in a program with only three jumps?

"Well," Kara Beth said with a faint laugh, as if she wasn't sure what she was looking at. "At least you still qualified for the free skate..."

He'd be in the first flight. He'd entered into some sort of mirror universe where up was down and the World Champion skated in the first group. He was going to have an aneurysm right there in the Kiss and Cry. They could bury him in the metaphorical pit he'd dug for himself, Hanyu Yuzuru and Surya Bonaly could give speeches at his funeral about how disgusted they were to be his idols and then he could be reincarnated as a bit of fungus on the bottom of Axel Paulsen's speed skates.

"Satoru?"

Satoru whirled on Kara Beth, cold fury in his eyes. "I don't score so low since Juniors."

The accusation struck. She didn't challenge it.

29

INESSA WAS the first caller to get through. She seemed much more alert since Satoru had seen her in Barcelona, and that was something to be grateful for at least. But while taking time for him when she herself needed cheering up should have made Satoru feel loved, it didn't. "I'm fine!"

"I'm sorry. I meant to call my boyfriend, not some child in a tantrum. My mistake."

Satoru grimaced, but felt his blood boiling. "I don't want cheering up. I want to work. Want to erase bad skate."

"Understandable. But please do not be so hard on yourself. Or us. You're the best skater in the world, after all. This is only one day."

One awful day, the worst day of his life. "I need to go over protocol. Find mistakes."

"Forgive me, but what you're looking for is not on the protocol sheet." Her voice was gentle, but Satoru wanted to scream at her. "You are not yourself right now, and have more outside stress than most. There is no shame in this."

"You don't understand anything."

"Then explain to me." But Satoru couldn't. He could barely explain it to himself. Things that hadn't been a part of his life for years suddenly came back to destroy him. He was going to lose yet another title.

And who was supposed to help, when Inessa herself had told him not to trust anyone? "Please, I need to work."

It was rude, and he felt a twinge of regret when he heard the change in Inessa's tone. "If you're sure... But if I can do anything for you..."

"I don't need anything. You just focus on get better, I focus on me, everything will be fine." Except that the walls around them were on fire and neither of them could help themselves. But they couldn't do anything for each other, either, so what did Inessa want from him? He rubbed at his forehead and sighed. "I just want to be alone now. You're very nice, but I need everyone give me space, please?" Being polite was so much effort. It meant putting oneself in a position of vulnerability and he'd had far too much of that for one evening.

But telling Inessa to back off was a little rude, and maybe he'd had a little too much of that, too. "Inessa? Sorry, I don't mean that you-"

"Satoru, they're going to put metal in my knee." Her response came in a broken voice, wet through the speakers.

"Huh?"

"The injury, they must insert pins to hold my knee together. It will be very difficult to jump, when I am healed..."

Satoru felt his mouth go dry, but the dread had yet to catch up with the confusion. "Inessa..."

"I want to research this more, but I can't do it. And I am behind in school..." He heard a whimper. "The homework is impossible, I can't read anything."

"Because the medicine? Makes you sleepy and distracting?"

"No, because I have a concussion and now I can't read!" Inessa snapped, and a leashed frustration lunged against its fetters. "It gives me a headache to focus on my homework! I solved a mystery I can't remember, I forget and stare into space, I can't skate and now I can't read about my own condition!"

In his hotel room, alone, Satoru sat on the edge of the bed. He didn't trust his legs to bear weight right now. "It will change. Doctors say. Getting better takes time-"

"If it does not?" Inessa asked, and her anger was palpable. "In the meantime, I must be helped like a child, and I cannot finish assignments for a teacher that already thinks I'm incapable! With no skates and no brain, I am running out of reasons for you to love me!" Her voice hiccuped, and it seemed to fuel the rage. "So if you can find one small thing for me to do for you, I am grateful! That is, if you can stand to be bothered!"

She hung up, and though Satoru kept the phone pressed to his ears for several minutes, their connection was nothing but dead air.

LOOKING up Inessa's symptoms on the internet was probably the worst thing Satoru could have done with his evening. He didn't sleep all night, convinced his girlfriend had somehow gotten hit so hard she'd instantly developed a tumor the size of his fist and was going to die of Alzheimers. It took most of the morning to talk himself down from that ledge and remember that Inessa was only a week into her recovery. It was a bit early to give up completely.

The metal pins that would be reshaping her knee, however, presented a more grim prognosis. Ironically, the awful news helped him break the ice with Kara Beth, after the frosty way they'd left things after the short program. He'd told her over breakfast, and she'd immediately wrapped him up in her arms. "Oh, honey, that's terrible!" Satoru decided not to mention the current ban on childish endearments. It felt too good to pretend he was home again.

The sympathy helped, though he didn't want to discuss it much further. Satoru couldn't help but fixate on the quaver in Inessa's voice over the phone. He thought of how long it would take her to even walk again, let alone skate, of her needing to be coddled and assisted in everything. Unable to assert herself physically, unable to escape into a book or read simple instructions, for however long recovery took.

Satoru could think of no greater nightmare for Inessa than to spend days upon days viewed as helpless. But he couldn't think of a single intelligent thing to say.

The unease followed him onto the ice, when the next practice session came. The media, not content with the tense interviews they had forced Satoru to give last night, would watch him like hawks after prey.

Satoru wondered if it was too late to withdraw. But no, that meant quitting, and that was worse than failing. So he grit his teeth and took the ice alongside the others.

He and Kara Beth had a plan for the practice, though they hadn't talked much about it since last night's debacle. Kara Beth had wanted to, but Satoru hadn't wanted to do anything but hang himself from the lighting grid above the rink, so the business talk didn't last long. They'd got a few things ironed out over breakfast, though.

"I want to go hard, make up for bad score."

"You've had a rough week. I still think scrapping the Quad-Quad and Axel are the way to go. And maybe downgrading the Flip as well, it's... not reliable for you right now."

"Well, that's not what I want." And for all Kara Beth's authority, she wasn't the one in charge. It was Satoru's skate, Satoru's career and Satoru's right to commit seppuku via quad rotation if he good and wanted to. She could motivate and advise, but she couldn't order him around.

A fact he wanted to make sure everyone knew. Satoru was not a puppet to be manipulated, or a broken object to be cast aside. Even murder attempts couldn't stop him. Satoru was going to carry himself with confidence and self-assurance, letting everyone know who had the power now.

It made the official practice a bit strained. All of Kara Beth's earlier sympathy evaporated in minutes. "I don't know what your deal is, but if you're that against working with me, then you can practice on your own."

Satoru grimaced and apologized, more out of ritual than sincerity. He was still mad about the short program, and blaming her meant at least some of the weight wasn't crushing him to death. But he just needed to get through the free skate, prove his worth again, and everything would be normal. Maybe he could skate well enough in the free to even get back on the podium?

Yeah, and maybe everyone else in the competition would get measles. Overhead, Satoru heard the music for Micah Edwards of Canada coming to an end, and knew he would be up next. "Take it nice and easy, okay? We both know you can do the jumps, so if you relax, you'll be fine." She gave him pointers for the Quad-Quad combo and then asked him one last time if he really wanted to be doing that alongside his 4A and Tano Salchow today.

"I have to," Satoru replied, feeling a little helpless, then shaking it off. "What happen to 'I know you can do it, Satoru'?"

"I do know you can do it," Kara Beth replied, suddenly grave. "But is it going to help?" That was a strange question to ask, but Satoru didn't get his clarification because he had to take center ice. "All right, Sato, you got this. Shake it out and go get those jumps of yours." She grabbed his shoulders and squeezed. "Try to relax out there!"

Satoru yanked himself backward, away from her hands, even though his shoulders ached from the loss of warmth.

"Practice isn't relax. Is work." Kara Beth looked back in disbelief, like maybe he'd been breathing in too many Zamboni fumes. Satoru skated off before she could ask just who she was training.

Relaxing wasn't an option, but Satoru did get a sort of glee from anticipating his jumps. These were his favorites after all, his dream program, he couldn't help but enjoy himself a little. Still, he tried to clamp all that down. He'd spent too many years treating competition like a game, when he should have been serious. Now it was catching up to him, his rivals were catching up to him, and Satoru couldn't be jumping his Tano Sal for fun.

He needed to win. That was the only thing that mattered.

To his satisfaction, the 4A went off without a hitch, and Satoru glided out of the landing with a smirk on his face, taking in the applause from the stands. He knew Wataru and the media team would be somewhere in the arena, and that was sweeter than any victory. Maybe the attempted killer was watching, too? Maybe they'd be intimidated enough to give it up?

The next jump was the Tano Sal. It felt like poetic justice now, to do the jump everyone once mocked him for. He'd land this next one like a slap in the face, proof that he wasn't worthless, that his new coach had found what the old one could never see, Satoru was still the World Champion and nothing would change that.

He was about to leap, when a black blur came charging at him. Satoru aborted the action and went spinning into the boards, though he stayed on his feet, and gripped the side as he caught his breath. His heart took a minute to realize it wasn't under attack, and Satoru's brain wasn't much better.

"I'm so sorry! Are you all right? I'm so sorry!" Julian Saunders, an Australian skater, new on the scene. Satoru had only met him once or twice before. "Really, I'm so sorry, you're okay? Ugh, it was my fault!"

"Watch out!" Satoru snapped, heart still racing. It was his music playing, he had the right of way, and collisions were a serious matter. People had gotten concussions and broken bones from smashing into each other during the warm up, Satoru could have found himself in another ambulance ride on his first competition back.

"Sorry! I swear, it was an accident!" Was it? Could Satoru trust anyone in this place? Satoru pried his eyes away from his shaking hands and looked up. Kara Beth was on her way over, as was Julian's coach, both with concern on their faces. Julian continued to babble, openly distraught. "Really, I'm sorry! I didn't mean it!"

How old was he, seventeen? Had to be at least that, but he looked younger. These kids got tinier every season. Satoru exhaled, trying to get some feeling back in his limbs. "It's fine. Just be more careful." And he sped back into the routine, cheeks flushed and burning. So much for Tano Sal. But there wasn't time to waste.

He made it through the rest of the program, somehow. There wasn't enough time to build up speed for the 4S+4T, so he popped that into a pair of doubles. He went for the Flip, but it was under-rotated. As far as a practice run went, it actually wasn't horrible, but as a redemptive statement... "I see that look in your eyes, but there was a lot of good things going on there. Even with the interruption." Kara Beth tried to bring his attention to his Axel entrance. "I know you don't have much choice about telegraphing the 4A, since you need the speed," she told him, "But remember to keep your posture and let the music breathe while you're coming around for it, it'll make the buildup feel more like a choreographic choice than just a series of crossovers-"

"I go run Flip again," Satoru interrupted, only half-listening anyway. His eyes were in the stands, where all the spectators were taking videos and blogging about his latest falls, his popped jumps, his failed moments in practice. As if any of them knew what kind of work went on behind the scenes and what all of this meant. He wasn't a person to them, just an object who existed to win things, and to criticize when he didn't.

Then there were the representatives from his Federation, who hovered around and shared in his successes but none of his failures. Some were more guilty of that mindset than others, but not one of them had heard his cries for help when he was a twelve-year-old with an abusive coach and a busted knee. And if that killer out there succeeded, they'd just turn to Yukiya or whatever new talent was coming up the pipeline. Satoru waited until he had an open corner of the rink, then jumped the Quad Flip.

It went up kind of sidewise, and came down much the same. It wasn't a total fall, but Satoru felt humiliated all the same. What was with him this week, that he couldn't manage his usual jumps, couldn't manage a clean program? A cold fear gripped him, when he pictured his free program going the same way as the short. Two disasters in a row, he wasn't sure he could survive that.

"Talk to me, Satoru," Kara Beth said when he returned to her. "I can't help you if you don't. You're all over the place this week."

"I'm fine." He blew his nose and tossed the tissue down in their little plastic bag for refuse, feeling detached from himself. "You make too big a deal."

"Unbelievable." He'd made her mad. Well, she could get in line, and Satoru dared her to be more mad with him than he was with himself. It wasn't like he planned to screw up all his practices. Kara Bath turned away for a moment, teeth grit in consternation, and it was like being a Junior again. He was twelve, adding Tano variations to all his jumps in a desperate attempt to set himself apart from the crowd. He was thirteen, surrounded by so many other students who were better, always better, his coach told him so every day. Fourteen, trying to convince his parents and the world in general that he needed to stay in Ohio with Kara Beth, even as Wataru ditched him and that French skater was encroaching on spin lessons.

Frustrated, he pushed back from the boards and stroked aggressively around the rink. Everything was falling apart, both on and off the ice. Satoru saw the security stationed around the rink with their fluorescent vests, as if reminding him that there was no guarantee he'd even live through this event. An attack could come from anywhere, at any time, and if this might be his last competition, is that how Satoru wanted to be remembered? Falling all over the ice, crying in humiliation?

No, never. But for all he wanted it, winning wasn't going to happen today. Not with him sitting in eighteenth place. He wouldn't make the podium, but he might just win the free skate. That was a small something. In the meantime, Satoru could work with this practice, he had eyes on him, he had legs to move. He just needed to prove that he could still use them.

And seeing a bit of an opening, Satoru decided to go for a jump that was guaranteed to turn heads. Even if backflips weren't allowed in a program.

Maybe it was crazy, but Satoru didn't care. It would make him feel better. No point value, but not everything had to have a point. Poisoning didn't have a point, color blindness didn't have a point. No purpose, no accumulation of value, just random events that smashed through whatever expectations humanity had.

And if the world was surrendering its order, then Satoru wouldn't fight it. He jumped, and felt the rush of wind as he rotated backwards, feet up and over his head.

That one, he landed. Couldn't be counted on to land anything in his competitive program, but that backflip had been beautiful. And it got the results he wanted, people were astounded, whispering and chatting about him, his opponents were taking notice, Fujiwara Ainosuke had actually come to a dead stop as Satoru glided out.

Kara Beth was not impressed. Nor was the referee. Apparently, he'd come close to hitting Julian. The two flanked Satoru with only the sideboards separating them from their quarry, and Kara Beth spoke first. "Why?"

That should have been obvious. "You said relax. Felt good, so I do."

"This is a competitive practice! You almost sliced that poor Australian kid!"

"He almost hit me first!" Satoru snorted. "Not like I do on purpose. Is crowded ice."

"Which is why you shouldn't be doing backflips out of nowhere! Have you gone insane?"

The referee was calmer when he said his piece, but clarified that any more reckless behavior and they would ask Satoru to leave. For all the time there was to go. Satoru nodded and promised to behave, but while that was enough for the referee, it wasn't enough for Kara Beth. "I don't know what's gotten into you, but it's got to stop."

"I have practice."

"This isn't practice." Satoru huffed and was about to skate away, but Kara Beth lunged over the boards and grabbed his arms. "I'm serious! Tell me what your deal is, or this session is over."

"Session is over anyway," Satoru nodded up to the clock, once he'd wrenched his arm away. Just about a minute left, the announcer was already giving the notice. "Stop bothering me."

"Stop bothering you?" There was a moment, a brief moment, where Kara Beth looked like she might perform physical violence. "Kid, you need a reality check, and you need it right now."

"I said don't call me kid!"

"I'll call you whatever I want if you keep acting like a spoiled toddler!" She moved a bit down the boards to gather up their things. "We're done here. Let's go."

"Still thirty seconds," Satoru challenged, and Kara Beth scoffed.

"Trust me, you've done way more than enough."

And even though they wouldn't lose more than twenty seconds, even though things hadn't been so productive anyway, the thought of cutting practice made Satoru's blood boil. "What? You bored with me already? Rather be with your new champion?"

He thought he'd make Kara Beth angry, but the look on her face was something else. "Is that what all this is about?"

Was it? Who knew, anymore? "I know that all season you help Dami be champion and I get yelled and poisoned and told no! Because I can't jump and you have new favorite now, even Eric sees!" Everything was wrong and people were too close, whispering and judging and deciding his worth as a human being based off a few rotations in the air, while any of these people could fill his water bottle with poison or blow up his car, smash in the heads of girls who'd never done a thing to hurt anybody .

He felt the tears on his face and wondered how long those had been there, wondered if ripping out every seat in the arena with his bare hands would be enough to siphon out the energy coursing through him.

Kara Beth leaned forward, gripping his elbows with her gentle strength. Satoru would have hugged her back if he weren't so furious. "Honey, no, that's not what's happening-"

"Call me dumb name again and I shove skate through your face!"

And that brought silence to the rink. Shouting such violent rhetoric at the top of his lungs was out of line.

"I'm sorry," he quickly stuttered out, as startled as anyone to hear those words coming out of his mouth. That wasn't the person he thought he was, and yet, Satoru had wanted to see someone hurting as much as he was. Kara Beth didn't give him the satisfaction, but the words produced an effect.

"If that's how you feel, Mr. Miyazawa," she said, colder than the rink itself, "You can find yourself a new coach."

30

IN HINDSIGHT, having an extremely public meltdown and breaking with his coach the day before the free skate event was a poor move. The myriad consequences hit Satoru once he'd arrived at his hotel room and slammed the door. From there, he just slid down to the floor and hugged his knees, realizing he was in the absolute deepest pit of trouble he could have possibly dug for himself.

His phone rang non-stop. Satoru didn't turn it off, but didn't answer it, either. He just let each tinny siren damn him a little further, oscillating between despair and rage with every space between.

And that was all he did for several hours until a knock came that he couldn't ignore. "Satoru! Open up this door!"

The tone was commanding, the words unmistakable. There was no telling what Wataru might do if Satoru didn't obey.

But that didn't mean he had to be reasonable about it. Satoru flung open the hotel room door with a scowl. "What do you want?"

A raised eyebrow met him, though the placid mask was such a lie. "We had plans to meet."

Hours ago. Satoru had blown that off, along with most of his dignity. "I don't feel like going out."

"Good, because I don't want to be seen with you in public." The door closed behind Wataru and he crossed his arms, heralding the inevitable lecture. "Do you have any idea how upset people are with you?"

Satoru flopped down on the bed. "I don't care."

"Do you care about Mom? Because she thinks it's her fault that she raised such a disrespectful son." That stung a little. Of all the people Satoru wished he could blame, his mother wasn't one of them. "Izumi's straight up scared to talk to you. If there's any explanation for your behavior, we'd love to hear it."

"I can't." Satoru rolled over and buried his face in the mattress, feeling despondent and listless, but also like he could spring up at any moment and throw Wataru out a window. It was an exhausting state of mind. "Leave me alone."

Wataru came over and stood by the bed, and Satoru felt the disgust radiating off him. "Look at you. You're rude and miserable all the time." Wataru gave the edge of the bed a kick when it looked like Satoru was drifting off. "Why are you even here? You've already won every title there is to win. Why keep suffering like this?"

"It's not suffering. I love skating," Satoru began, but Wataru just snorted.

"After today? No one believes that."

Satoru dropped his head back to the bed. He had to admit, he was having a hard time believing it, too. "You wouldn't understand. Just leave me alone." A fist seized around his shirt collar, and Satoru's heart stopped at the sudden movement. And then it revved into gear with the power of a jet engine. He looked up into Wataru's snarling face with fear, adrenaline pumping in his ears as his heart muscles switched back on and sent the fight-or-flight chemicals straight to his brain.

Wataru tightened his grip and leaned in. "The *entire world* is being patient with you, Satoru," he said, then released his brother with a small shove. "Stop screwing around."

Satoru couldn't say anything in his defense. His brother could be downright terrifying sometimes.

But he wasn't wrong. And that put a chink in the armor Satoru had been trying to forge around himself. He couldn't hide from his anguish by hating the world because, as Wataru said, the world loved him. They weren't to blame for this and were just waiting for Satoru to rise above it all.

At what point were they going to realize he wasn't worth that? Slowly, Satoru curled into the fetal position. He told himself he wouldn't cry in front of Wataru, but even thinking that caused the heat and pressure to build inside his sinuses, and it was only a matter of time.

Wataru noticed, and turned away. "It won't be like this forever," he said, soft and quiet. One might almost think he cared.

"Why? Because I'll get better or because I just ended my amateur career?" Satoru muttered back, voice thick with the impending system failure. "Everything's a mess."

"Yes, well..." Wataru didn't deny it. He couldn't even lie to cheer his brother up. Satoru remembered all the times he'd wanted to follow his big brother around, do what Wataru did, be exactly like Wataru.

Wataru sucked. Then again, he hadn't burned absolutely every single bridge between him and the people he cared about, so maybe he deserved some credit.

While Satoru wallowed, Wataru leaned against the window frame. "I used to think that once you were done skating, things would all go back to normal," he said. Satoru shut his eyes and tried to sink into the mattress while the spiral started up again.

Skating was a burden to others, but if he couldn't skate well, everyone was mad. And them being mad made it hard to enjoy skating, which meant he did even more poorly. But quitting meant all the sacrifices were a waste, so he had to keep skating, which put more strain on everyone, and so on until the end of the world, where Satoru would probably then be forced into some hell where the ISU got rid of the free skate and reintroduced compulsory figures.

"But everything's skating to you, isn't it?" Wataru carried on, ignorant of Satoru's internal crisis. "It's your whole life. You could retire right now and you'd still be you and it would still drive you nuts. You'd always be like this."

That... made sense. Satoru sat up in a bit of a daze. Everything he did and everyone he knew were related to skating. He found them because of it, and they fed his training in return. The friends he'd made across the world, the immigrant experience, learning new languages, sewing and drawing, all happened because of skating. His love of buildings came from that same global awareness and opportunity to travel, from meeting Damien and getting a sense of how French culture related to the designs he saw in photos, from seeing the changes over the history of his sport and finding metaphors and parallels in the history of architecture

Skating helped him find common ground with Old Mrs. Grinkova when she immigrated to Granville and led to him learning a passable amount of Russian phrases to communicate with. He'd seen every single one of the Alvarez children in a skating class at least once, and saw them finding friends and confidence that they weren't getting from school, saw their mother Carlotta bonding with the Ditta family despite both mothers' broken English. Satoru took those lessons home to Tokyo whenever he ran workshops there, because the ice was an equal amount of slippery for those of Japanese descent as it was for those of Korean, Chinese or Filipino. Kara Beth's house was tied to skating, as was bringing home stuffed animals for Izumi.

Everything was skating, and skating was everything. It didn't matter if Satoru was on the ice or not.

So why did he feel lost?

"You're right." He sat cross-legged and clutched at his feet. "It's not always crazy, though. Usually I love competition and everything else."

"What makes this one different?"

"You mean besides almost dying?" Satoru shrugged. "I don't know. I've been so scared of disappointing everyone with a bad skate, but turns out you're all disappointed in me for a completely different reason."

"We sure are," Wataru replied, and Satoru winced. The depression came back in full force as he thought of Inessa, Damien and

Kara Beth. Of the videos that were now circulating in the press and internet, bringing shame to the parents who'd worked so hard for him. Julian in his first senior seasons, having such a poor example of sportsmanship to look up to. Even if everyone forgave him, there were things out in the world that he could never take back.

If everyone forgave him. He fell back on the bed and realized that none of this changed the fact that someone still wanted to kill him. Inessa was still injured, he was still color-blind, Damien and Yukiya had still broken his streaks for consecutive wins at the Grand Prix and Nationals. None of that was coming back, either.

"I don't know what to do," he mumbled out. It sounded whiny and childish, but possibly less so than most of the other nonsense he'd uttered that day. He didn't know how to fix things, though copious apologies seemed an obvious place to start, and he didn't know how to stop it all from happening again. Satoru wanted to run home to safety, to either of his homes, wanted to be his parent's pride and Kara Beth's kid, Inessa's ideal boyfriend and Damien's *cygneau* again.

But as much as he'd said the words out of anger, it was true that Satoru wasn't a child anymore. He couldn't demand that other people take care of his messes anymore, or shield him from actual consequence and responsibility. Satoru pictured the feel of his foot during a series of twizzles, trying to balance on that perfect spot where the blade curved, because a mere centimeter forward or backward would cause an uncontrollable rocking and eventual fall. Where was his balance now?

Wataru sat on the bed, but kept his back to Satoru. He cleared his throat. "So, I once had this dream of getting into Tokyo University. I was going to go to the best school in the country, get my PhD and then cure cancer or send stuff into space, solve the mystery of God or something." It seemed like a non sequitur, but Wataru never talked to him just for the company, so Satoru waited to see if this story had a point. "I put everything I had into studying and graduated at the top of my class. But my little brother had a dream, and there was only so much strain the family could take..."

Oh. One of those stories. Satoru clenched his eyes shut and curled in further on himself, but said nothing. He probably deserved the guilt trip, after all.

Wataru continued, "So I gave up my dream school, even though none of my friends understood why, even though it disappointed all my teachers. But I went with my brother to America anyway, thinking I'd prove myself. I'd perfect my English, work my way up the company and do something that none of the friends back home had the guts to do. I was so eager for that chance, and so desperate."

Satoru had never heard Wataru talk that honestly about it. "I didn't know you felt like that."

"Why would I tell you? You were a kid. I was supposed to be taking care of you." He shrugged. "But I botched it. I failed about as hard as I possibly could have, and it was humiliating. And no matter what I do going forward, no one's ever going to forget that one time in Ohio where I completely fell to pieces."

He stopped talking, and Satoru felt confused as the silence wore on. "Was that supposed to cheer me up?"

"I don't know. Maybe not. But congratulations." Wataru leaned back, far enough that Satoru could see his face. The smirk was soft around the edges, the eyes warm enough to put some life in his next words. "You finally found something we can relate over..."

31

KARA BETH HAD DISAPPEARED into the streets of Beijing after spending several hours trying to tactfully get reporters out of her face. If she couldn't put words to what was going on between her and Satoru within her own mind, then she didn't want to risk saying anything out loud. And when the reporters weren't dogging her, the representatives from the Japanese Skating Federation were, and she definitely wasn't ready for that conversation.

She liked China. The city streets were loud and chaotic, but not in a way that felt aggressive to her. They just felt alive, teeming with a million different lives and secret stories that she might never have the chance to know. And no one cared to know hers, which made it a wonderful place to lose herself in for a few hours.

But she had to go back eventually, and whatever peace she'd managed to scrape together disappeared as she walked through the hotel doors. The events of the day regained their weight like a bunch of chains she now had to drag across the lobby. She buried her face in her scarf and trudged onward, trying not to think about it, hoping she could just make it back to her room in peace.

It was not to be. Satoru materialized in front of her, and a hush went over the lobby. She tried to go around him, but that plaintive voice stopped her before she could get too far.

"Please."

It was that same voice that begged her to take him on as a student. She was weak to that. Kara Beth turned around, and tried to keep her face neutral, but it must have betrayed how badly she did not want to be there, because Satoru flinched.

"I'm sorry for yelling. And being selfish. It was wrong to break trust and say those things. I hurt you."

"You did." Her hands twisted in the linings of her black wool coat, but the rest of her was still as a rock. The apology was something, a sign that Satoru hadn't gone so far off the deep end that he couldn't be dragged back to shore, but it wasn't enough to settle things. Not until she got over the feeling of being stabbed in the heart. Maybe then, they could have this talk, but for now, Kara Beth just wanted to go upstairs and forget she'd ever decided to coach.

"I'm sorry," Satoru swallowed. "I'm the one who is doing wrong. My fault, but I yell and blame you. I'm sorry." He looked serious.

"Thank you, but I'd like to go. Since I have this new, clear schedule and all."

"Wait! Please? We can't... leave like that."

Kara Beth was reluctant to give any ground, but compromised. As long as she didn't have to deal with it in the lobby, of all places. She wasn't in the mood.

"You want to continue this conversation tomorrow? In private?"

No," Satoru insisted, but though he sounded determined, his breath was shaky. "I yell at you in public. I should apologize in public." And before Kara Beth could make sense of that, he was on his knees.

Anything that hadn't already stopped to eavesdrop went deathly silent, then broke into heated whispers. Amazement and confusion at the sight of Satoru Miyazawa completely prostrate on the floor, head touching the dirty carpet. Making a public scene.

"Please forgive me. Please be my coach."

When the cell phones and cameras came out, Kara Beth began to wonder if Japanese *dogeza* was less about humility and more of a power play. How could she not forgive him after this display without looking heartless? But when she looked at her student's face, she had to admit the position of shame was sincere, even if the greater cultural nuances were lost on her. She wasn't sure if that took away from the gesture or strengthened it, since Americans didn't get on their knees for anybody.

But there was something universal about a position of submission, forcing oneself to breathe in the dirt and grime from everyone else's feet. When Kara Beth's eyes flicked over the assembling crowd and found some of the Japanese athletes, they were part of the staring contingent, showing this was unusual for them as well. "I'll forgive you if you get up off the floor ."

Satoru did and faced his coach, though he didn't meet her eyes. Kara Beth sighed and glanced around at the growing number of onlookers again. No way was she continuing this awkward conversation with an audience.

"Follow me," she ordered Satoru, and marched out of the lobby.

"I'VE BEEN DODGING the JSF all day," Kara Beth said as she slid her keycard into the door reader. She had to jam it in there twice before the little light turned green and allowed her into her hotel room. She held the door open and gestured for Satoru to enter. "They've got some pretty strong opinions about this training arrangement."

"Skating Federation can shut up," Satoru said as he passed, and Kara Beth released the door with incredulity

"You are firing on all guns today."

"Sorry," Satoru grimaced, and while he didn't say that casually, the result was complicated. "I shouldn't be rude. But I'm still mad."

"Okay." She could work with mad, she could work with honesty.

Kara Beth sat on one of the beds and gestured for Satoru to take the opposite. It wasn't the most austere setting for such an important meeting, one that could define their future together. Assuming there was much left to say on that front. But the surroundings felt less like they were going to discuss their coaching arrangement and more like they might start braiding each other's hair.

After a few minutes of solemnity, Kara Beth spoke. "We can call a translator in here if we need it. We can whip out our phones and some dictionaries and figure it out. But I can't speak silence. You have to talk to me."

"Don't know what to say." Satoru's fists were clenched over each knee, agitated. "It's not my bad words, feelings are too complicated to explain."

Kara Beth wanted to retort that maybe he should have gotten himself figured out before starting this conversation, but held it back. After all, he was trying, and that was a lot better than she'd gotten out of him all week. "Fine, I'll start. Your behavior lately has been unacceptable. It's hurtful and reflects badly on your training. I don't like the idea of kicking you to the curb, but I'm not going to put up with this and... and..." She couldn't help but throw her hands up, "And you're *better* than that, Satoru. You know you are!"

She watched Satoru wilt before her. There was once a time when they were in perfect sync, able to understand each other without words, knowing where the other's head was like a seasoned pairs team. When had that changed? The Grand Prix? The day Satoru moved out?

"How do I make up to you?" the dark-haired boy asked, voice barely above a whisper. He sounded like he did seven years ago, confessing that he'd been skating on a knee so busted that he sometimes blacked out when his toe pick hit the ice. Or six years ago, no longer able to hide the fact that his brother had left the country with little more than harsh words and an unpaid electric bill. Or three years ago, when he'd convinced himself that Kara Beth would stop training him if he didn't win the Olympics.

It had been a long road with Satoru. "Be honest. Give me some kind of explanation, even if it's a bad one. As long as it's real."

Satoru nodded and bit his lip. "I... don't like that you tell me hold back program. It's frustrating," he added with an absent jab at his thigh. His foot bounced up and down, a barometer of his restless energy. "Is only thing I control, my program, so tell me less jumps makes me... like, helpless."

"Okay." That was a start, though nothing new. "But I've told you my reasoning behind that. These are high-risk elements, and you have the focus of a gnat this weekend."

"Is that only reason?" Satoru pressed his lips together when he didn't get a reply, so hard they started turning white.

"What other reason would there be?" Kara Beth mulled it over, but still drew a blank. "Look, I get that you're tough and fearless and want to take on the impossible, but-"

"No," Satoru interrupted, a wet, guttural sound. A wounded animal, on its last legs. "Not fearless. My whole life, I'm afraid to fall." His hands struggled to grip at his jeans, trying to find security, and failed. "Because I land worse place than ice."

Well, she'd wanted honesty. "I know."

"I fall so much when we first train. You don't say stop, then. You say it's safe to fall, not end of the world, helps me grow. Don't be ashamed." A whimper escaped his throat. "And I believe you. Now you say don't jump, you might fall."

Kara Beth thought she understood, or at least was on the cusp of it. "That's different."

"Why?" Satoru challenged. "Makes no sense! Why don't you say in Juniors, when I fall in competition all the time? Why is it bad now?"

"I told you, you're not-"

"Old coach awful at me for fall," Satoru spat back. "Once, he throws skates in trash and I have to dig out of *dumpster!*" Kara Beth hadn't heard that anecdote, but it tracked. She wondered if he'd told Aoi and Shinji. "But I can't do anything because he's elder and I must respect. Wataru is same. No one listens because I'm nobody, be humble and polite, don't cry and speak mind."

"Satoru..."

"I didn't care if you aren't different," he said in the floor's direction, harsh and not attentive to her sympathy. Not wanting it. "But you are. You make safe place for mistakes, so many years. It's not disrespect to say I'm angry, I don't want, I *hurt*." He raised his head, eyes fierce with challenge. "I don't know why you won't let me fall now."

Kara Beth clasped her hands in front of her, trying to squeeze extra strength out from between her palms. It didn't work. "You want to fall? Then *fall*," she said, stressing the last word. "Stop being that perfect champion who has to die for his medals and be my kid who tells me when he's hurt and angry and rattled by a murder attempt" She grimaced. "There's more to you than being a gold medalist. If falling off the podium helps drive that point home, then let it happen."

"But what happens to me after?" Satoru had been wringing his hands, then noticed, and stopped himself. "I don't, um, before..." he stopped himself abruptly, a strange hitch in his chest. Kara Beth swallowed, somehow afraid even though she knew what he was going to say. In the back of her mind, she wondered if he'd been waiting his whole life to finally have this conversation. Satoru clenched his eyes shut, and pushed forward with the words that hurt Kara Beth as much as they hurt him.

"Before I start winning, I am waste." The effort to say so was hard to watch. "Waste of person. Old coach tell me. Wataru tell me. I feel from everywhere. So I can't fall off podium now. Even if it's risk, because I'm..." He trailed off, the words losing their air.

Kara Beth leaned in. "Satoru," she said, and it was a trial to leave off the loving endearments. "That is not true." She paused for a moment, letting the weight sink in. "I know how deeply you believe it, but it's a lie. Your old coach is a piece of garbage." The twitch of Satoru's mouth was a promising sign. "And I know you love your brother, but he was going *through it* when you were a kid, and the stuff he said to you wasn't okay. It definitely wasn't true. You are worth more than anything you'll ever achieve in skating." Some things, no matter how often you said them, couldn't break through the walls that insecurity built up. But Kara Beth knew from her own experience that if you kept saying them, kept up that gentle force, those same words that did nothing would find the weak points and stick.

She saw the little crack in Satoru. "You say more than win, but I don't feel. Here," he pointed to his heart, and then to his head. "And here. I want to believe you." He rubbed his knees a little, words failing him. "I want to... I can't even say. It's scary to fall."

Kara Beth pursed her lips, but then she nodded. That he still didn't know this after so much time was incredible. "I get it, you know. We give up our lives to compete at this level, and everything else feels like a void. But you've got the whole world in front of you. You don't even realize how talented you are."

"Only with skate," he said with deep bitterness, and Kara Beth stopped him.

"No, with everything," she insisted. "Satoru, you're one of the smartest people I know." He raised his eyebrow then, slow and disbelieving. Kara Beth smirked a little. "How do you say 'Thank you' in Slovenian?"

"*Hvala,*" Satoru replied without a thought.

"And why do you know that?"

"Worlds is in Slovenia this year," he said, confused. "Haveto talk. But, I only know some words! Anyone can look up."

Kara Beth laughed. "There are people that don't know Slovenia is a country, but you're learning how to talk to its people. Don't you think that's impressive?"

"But, I'm not good..." Satoru looked deeply confused. "Only some words, and always make mistakes."

"When old Mrs. Grinkova is homesick and needs to talk to someone, do you think she cares your Russian is only basic?"

"Other people do better."

"Yeah, and my Triple Flip can eat yours for breakfast," Kara Beth said with a shake of her head. "Doesn't mean you stopped doing it."

She saw Satoru contemplating that, but knew something so simple would never solve the issue. So she leaned in, trying to be gentle. "It's less what you can do, but how and why you do it that make us all admire you. I didn't agree to train you because I saw a champion."

Satoru snapped his head up at the blasphemy. "What?"

"And your parents didn't let you move to Ohio because they thought you'd win Worlds." Her smile was fond, eyes twinkling to think it. "I trained you because you had passion. Because you wanted to build something bigger than yourself. Your parents and I agreed to this unconventional arrangement because you only needed a sewing needle, an architecture book, or a handful of words to connect a whole room. The winning was never for you. You were in it to connect with the world."

Satoru blushed. "It's a little for me. Winning is nice."

"Well, you wouldn't be human otherwise," Kara Beth teased, then grew serious again. "But now, you're obsessed with winning, and you're hurting everyone you're connected to. If you feel you're only good for skating, it might be because you've thrown out all the other things that made you Satoru. It's hard to recognize you, some days."

She could see that she was getting through, but then saw a little furrow between his brows. He grimaced as he floundered for the right words. "This is why I feel not smart. I can't say when important."

"Take your time," Kara Beth said. He'd find the right words, he always did. And even if he didn't, Satoru had always made his most important feelings known without them. As long as Kara Beth could listen, they would be just fine.

Satoru braced his hands against his knees. "Everything changed," he said, and Kara Beth tilted her head in confusion. "Even before poison, but really then..." His lips twisted in a painful smirk. "I change, too. Want to make everyone happy, but can't and... you make safe place to say anger. I don't use right. To you, and Dami and Inessa. I'm sorry. But..." he exhaled, then said clearly, "Situation is not okay. Training, and family... everything. I act bad, don't communicate. But I can't stay like this..." He looked about to cry, and the sight never failed to pierce Kara Beth's heart. "I can't stay like this."

"Neither of us can. But it's your life, Satoru. You're the one who has to decide." Kara Beth held her breath for the question, even though she was already resolved to ask. "So? What are you going to do to fix it?"

32

SATORU DIDN'T REALLY HAVE a plan for how the conversation with Kara Beth was supposed to go. Much as he'd tried to overthink it, he couldn't predict how she'd react, or if she'd forgive him. As long as he could grovel well enough to open the doors of communication again, he thought they'd be all right. Teamwork like theirs didn't disappear after one bad day, did it?

Except, it had been a little longer than a day. Satoru had been pushing people away for months. Now, it was like that first day he'd moved into Kara Beth's house, full of awkward silences and unsaid apprehension.

But back then, Kara Beth had opened her phone to a translation app and made the effort. If she'd been afraid to step into the unknown, she'd moved past it for him. He could only hope she'd be willing to do so now.

His life was out of balance and he wanted it back. He wanted to be the Satoru that Kara Beth described, the one who was happy and connected with the world, flew as high as he wanted with nothing to fear from the ground. But he also wanted his family back, his friends, his ability to trust that people meant it when they said they cared. He wanted to look at the world and not wonder where a killer might be hiding.

And to be happy with himself? If he asked for that, would he be able to hang on to everything else? "Everything changed. Even before, way I see world is not always right." He looked away from Kara Beth's dark hair, remembering the way the red strands fanned out around her in spins, the way he used to chase that ponytail around the rink.

When he looked back, her hair was still brown. His way of viewing the world was flawed. He had to learn to see it with new eyes, and that meant changes. "To fix things... I want to skate tomorrow. But I trust what you say." The words themselves didn't seem like enough, but it clenched something in his stomach to mean them. If she told him no... "I mean it. Your advice... I'll take it."

Kara Beth hummed. "That's not a bad start. And the day after tomorrow? The next competition? Next season?" She stopped there, and Satoru was able to catch his breath while the future loomed over him.

He blushed a little. "Still working on that. But everyone wants to help, so..." he gulped, again feeling control slipping from his fingers. Falling. "I'll listen."

"You know it's not about just doing what other people say, right? It's what you need."

"Yes. But I need you." Satoru gave a shaky smile. "I don't tell you when I move out, but you're not just coach. There isn't word for you, but it's important, and I'm sorry I don't appreciate." His throat was dry, oddly. Usually, he'd be sobbing by this point in the conversation. "You do so much good this season. Every season. I'm wrong to say different."

"It's all right, kid. I forgive you." Then she shook her head. "Sorry. Satoru. Old habits..."

"It's fine, I like you call me that..."

"Really? I thought you changed your mind."

"Sorry." He blushed, remembering what a fit he'd thrown over it earlier. "But it's good. Because you don't mean kid like child, right?

You mean kid like... yours." And that got a reaction. Kara Beth sat up straight as Satoru finished in a rush. "I want to be your kid forever."

Crying was his thing, not Kara Beth's. But his coach turned her head up to the ceiling and rapidly blinked. "Oh, boy," she said with a bit of a laugh, and Satoru wondered for a brief second if he'd said something wrong, but only for a second. "You'll always be mine, Sato. Don't you ever worry about that."

"Even if I... stop? Because I don't skate forever, and..." he gulped, and tried to channel some of the courage he associated with Surya Bonaly, to stop accepting what everyone else decided and focus on what needed to be said. "I want to go home. Live with family, like, for real." He gulped. "I don't know... I mean... maybe I don't skate, or... need train with someone else, for a bit," he said, feeling the quiver in his voice. "I know next season is Olympic year, so much to do, but I want..." he sighed, and tried not to wince. It felt like ripping off a medal in front of everyone. "I want. That's all."

"Okay." He blinked, and Kara Beth looked exasperated. "What, you think I'm going to tell you no? If that's what you want-"

"No!" he was quick to say, afraid and sick to his stomach. "I don't! But there is distance and finally friends with brother, so..." He trailed off when Kara Beth chuckled a little. "I need to make change. But I want everything."

Kara Beth leaned in with an evil grin, but the sight filled Satoru with relief before the words were out of your mouth. "I told you, didn't I? You want to fall, then fall. But you won't lose me because of it."

"Really?" Satoru's head spun, dizzy with the mere thought of it. "Don't really want to stop skating. And coach is always you. But you can't come to Tokyo with me, so..."

"Can't I?" she murmured, then tilted her head back. "It's a lot to think about right now. I don't expect you to work your whole life out tonight. But it's good you're finally giving it some thought. I'll support you in what you want." She winked at him, finally breaking through the reserve. "You know, provided what you want is healthy and doesn't involve driving yourself into the ground. I'm always going to call you out on that. But my door's still open for you, regardless."

He'd been forgiven. Satoru could have cried with relief. "Forever?"

"Kid, we've been through too much to just forget about each other. We're skate family."

She extended her hand to shake. "We can work some changes out when we get out of Four Continents. Plenty of time to decide what the future looks like then. For now, my kid's got a free skate to worry about. Let's see if the two of us can't find a little redemption this weekend."

Redemption didn't even begin to cover it. Satoru bypassed the handshake for an embrace. He tightened his arms around Kara Beth like a pair of iron girders and vowed to get revenge on gravity and all other forces before the weekend was out.

33

———

I NESSA WAS Satoru's second item of business. He'd been afraid she wouldn't pick up, the ringing in his ears went on for so long. As he waited, he cast his eyes out of his hotel room window at the skyline. In the distance, he could see the financial district and the results of China's skyscraper building boom. He'd had the curtains drawn since he'd arrived in Beijing, never looking outside. What a waste.

His patience was rewarded after the seventh ring. "Yes?"

"It's me," Satoru said, nervous. He fiddled with the curtain before sitting down on the bed. "You asked if you can do something to help? I need two things you can do..."

"Oh?" Her voice was reserved, but Satoru sensed a bit of curiosity, something eager to be of use. "And what would that be?"

"Well, first, I need you listen to apology..." He held up the small note in front of him, where he'd scribbled out the message with the help of a translation app. "*Ani meod mitzta'er. Hayah lo menu-* um, *lo menumas...*" He stopped his stuttering attempts at Hebrew when he heard Inessa snickering in the background. "I'm trying to apologize."

"Yes, and I accept, but please!" she shrieked, taken with hysteric giggling. "I am worried you will swallow your tongue if you continue!" Satoru felt his cheeks turning red, but couldn't say Inessa was wrong. Her voice was much kinder when she finally took control of her laughter. "Oh, Satoru, you were forgiven already. It is over."

It felt like he was getting off the hook a little too easily. "I don't think how you feel, only of myself."

"Well, I am guilty of this as well," she said, though the words were broken by a sleepy sigh. "I have much to be grateful for, yet I am scared like a little girl? Afraid of things I don't know will happen? This is not me."

"You shouldn't be scared of anything," Satoru agreed, cradling the phone closer to him as if it would shorten the distance between himself and Inessa. The world was not so far apart. The hotels and towers outside his window touched the same winds that touched Israel, after all. "Because if concussion doesn't get better, I'll read for you. And if you don't skate, I push wheelchair on ice and we make new pairs discipline. All will be okay."

"You are too much," Inessa snickered, then grew sober. Satoru heard her quiet breathing growing thick. "I wanted to go to the Olympics so badly…"

There was only the slimmest hope. "Maybe not next year, but if you want, you will do. I believe in you."

"Hmm, but what if reality says no?" Inessa sighed, one that seemed to require her whole body's effort to accomplish. "And even if I heal well, there is still damage to Damien and Ekaterina from this, even though they are innocent."

Satoru sat up. "You remember?"

"No," Inessa replied, and Satoru heard the tired scowl. "But my heart says so. I have faith in them." Faith. When Inessa used it, she meant more than hoping, more than thinking or believing. She had evidence, proof of something unseen. But how could she? "Ugh, I'm so sorry to forget that whole day! I don't even remember all the phone calls I made. If the memory would come back, your troubles would be over!"

Satoru made a face, but couldn't do anything about that frustration. "Well, I make plenty of own trouble in meantime, so maybe don't feel too bad."

"Yes, I heard things were not well for you." Hopefully Inessa hadn't watched that monstrosity of a practice on the internet. "But you sound more like yourself. You feel better now?"

"Yes." The drive inside him had changed, even if most of his surroundings hadn't. Maybe it took destroying a building down to rubble in order to address the cracks in the foundation. "Kinda. See if Damien forgive me first, then ask."

"He will." Inessa seemed so confident about that. Satoru decided he could bask in it for a while. He didn't have Inessa's concrete hope in the unseen, but he had some faith, and could hold on to that.

"And you'll skate again. So whole world sees you serious and hears what you want to say. Even if it's not Olympics," Satoru said. Of that, he was certain. "I know this about you. This is bad time, but it's not ending."

Inessa was quiet, enough that Satoru wondered if she'd drifted off again. But then, her sweet, exhausted voice whispered through his ears like a treasured song. "Thank you." There was some rustling, as if the bedclothes had moved. "You said there was a second task for me?"

"Yes. I need distraction, and you need pretty Juliet costume for return. Talk to me about program, I draw."

"That may be a bit far off..."

"It will wait for when you can do," Satoru said with a bit of a grin. "And maybe dress is so awesome you'll have to get better faster."

Inessa's laughter was the best sound in the world. "Yes, this is good motivation!" Her chuckling continued as Satoru positioned a pencil and paper, phone balanced in the crook of his shoulder .

He had some ideas for colors, but not much beyond that. "So, what kind of Juliet is Inessa? Tell me story."

"To be honest..." Inessa hummed a bit, and Satoru would have thought she sounded embarrassed if it were anyone else. "I'm not sure I am a Juliet after all..."

"What?" But this was her dream program! "Why not?"

"It seemed natural, as a girl," she said with consideration, "But it is Romeo who climbs up the balcony and confesses first. Romeo who fights with passion. It is Romeo who is exiled from the place he loves, and sustained by the person he loves..."

Satoru listened to that analysis. "So... does that make me Juliet?"

"Well, you did drink poison," Inessa said, and Satoru almost fell off his hotel bed, realizing that Inessa was the first person to bring up that event in a way he could laugh about.

"Okay, okay," he said, a smile stretching his face. He'd missed that feeling. "Inessa wins. I will make you Romeo." He took some notes and chatted for a bit with Inessa, his looming free program a distant concern, even with skating at the front of his mind. He couldn't control everything, but he could make some choices for himself. He could treasure his family and friends, find purpose without winning, and even begin to think about the future. For the first time, he was able to seriously consider dreams and goals beyond another gold medal. It was all part of the same tapestry, he now knew, and Satoru didn't need to fear the part of his life waiting beyond the rink.

Outside, a bit of sun was poking through the clouds, and he could see the CCTV headquarters on the horizon, though not in as much detail as he'd like due to the angle. The building's design was rather unusual, and Satoru had always wanted to see it up close. Maybe he'd have time to take a trip into the city before the competition was over.

He'd heard a building in the complex had caught fire, a decade or so ago, before the building was even fully completed. Yet it was still standing, still functional. Still impressive.

THE NEXT THING TO do was call home. He was expecting something in the way of punishment, some expressed disappointment, after the way he'd disgraced the Miyazawa name in front of the entire world. He'd been rude on the individual level, too, ignoring phone calls and being short with those just trying to help. Even if he was dealing with an understandable level of stress, his behavior was worthy of being reprimanded. But when his parents picked up the phone, they met him with warm words and concern.

It wasn't until half an hour or so into the call when Satoru's father seized the moment and delivered an entire speech about duty, gratitude and respectful behavior, all of which his son seemed to have discarded in the past few months. The words were harsh, but Satoru was so relieved to have his world spinning back on its normal axis that he listened to every word, nodded and bowed in the appropriate places and then thanked his father for the correction.

The lack of excuses and sincere joy Satoru took in being reprimanded seemed to throw Shinji off his game a little. But he finished his lecture with a kind tone. "You're a good son, Satoru," he'd said. "Just tell us when things are too much. Not one of us wants to see you suffer."

Of course, the new, content attitude of Satoru's didn't negate the unease and anxiety bubbling just under the surface. If he thought about his circumstances too long, he could easily find himself in a downward spiral again, and unfortunately, he needed to think about them. He had a job to do, after all, and he couldn't show up to do it tomorrow night without some thought.

With all the drama of the season, he hadn't put many competitive miles on his programs, and was feeling a little disconnected from them, and from skating in general. Satoru had no doubts of his ability to do his free program as originally intended, if not here at the Four Continents, then at Worlds a few weeks later, but he wasn't sure he wanted to, anymore. He missed his wild and crazy jumps, but it was no good to go back to them if he ended up as tense and insecure as he had in the short program.

But more troubling than that was the general sense of the free program itself. He'd built it, the jumps, choreography, costume and music, around a sense of himself that didn't really exist anymore. His costume didn't fit his current mindset, though he couldn't say why, and though he loved the choreography, it didn't seem to excite him alongside the music in the same way it once had, as if one of those elements was slightly out of sync. Satoru no longer sat on the lofty mountain peak, looking down over anyone who dared to challenge him, nor was he the confident warrior ready to challenge obstacles more grandiose than myth. There were different things he wanted to prove with his skating now, to the world and to himself.

After a season where he'd lost control over so much, he wanted to own his skating again. It was too late to just make a new free program, and going back to one from a previous season wouldn't solve his problem. There was no way to fix this by competition tomorrow, but Satoru had time before Worlds, and he intended to use it. He felt confident that once the right artistic inspiration hit, everything would fall into place. He just needed to find it.

In the meantime, he still had to make up with Damien, and that filled him with less confidence. He'd tried calling, texting and leaving apologetic messages, but had yet to get a single response. There was no sign if Damien was just that upset with him, or so focused on his training that he couldn't be bothered. He had Kara Beth's assurance that she was still in contact with Damien and his training was going well, so that was some comfort. Maybe Damien wouldn't forgive him, but if he wasn't too broken up by Satoru's words, that was a silver lining, right?

He felt guilty that didn't help his mood more than it did. It weighed on his mind all day, even in the middle of conversations. "You okay, big bro? You're spacing out on me."

He snapped his head up at Izumi's voice and nodded before remembering she couldn't see him over the phone. "I'm fine. Just thinking about Damien. We had a bit of a fight earlier."

"Wow, is there anyone you didn't fight with this week?" If Izumi had been present, Satoru might have pinched her. "Okay, okay, but did you get the file I sent? I thought about what you said and tweaked your free skate music again. Tell me what you think?"

"Sure, hang on."

Satoru opened his email and clicked on the file, while Izumi kept talking. "By the way, I don't know if Mom's told you yet, but we're all coming to the World Championships. The whole competition."

"What?" Satoru paused the music so he could hear better.

"Really? But what about school and work?" And the effort and expense? Wasn't life busy enough without the family taking a sudden vacation to Europe?

But Izumi didn't seem concerned. "Eh, Mom said it would all work out. I think she's been wanting to do more family stuff lately. She even dragged me out of cram school once or twice for some bonding time. We've been picnicking under the cherry trees since before they were blooming. I'm trying to enjoy it, 'cause next year I graduate and I'll bet the laid-back attitude ends."

Satoru couldn't help but laugh, even with the morbid thought that his mother's new appreciation for fleeting moments probably stemmed from how close he kept coming to death. But they'd turned from that death and into life, and there were still wonderful things in the world to appreciate. Each blossom of a moment was precious, and when they inevitably fell, Satoru knew the tree would bloom again the following spring.

"We'll have a great time. There's so many old castles and museums in Slovenia..."

"You're such an old man." He could almost hear the eyes rolling. Satoru shook his head and double clicked on her music file. As the deep bass of the remixed version hit Satoru's ears, he heard Izumi fidgeting. "Well? Is it better?"

Better? Definitely. In fact, Satoru's heart nearly stopped at the familiar chords and movements made fresh and unique with modern drums and record scratches, building up tension to moments that made Satoru visualize his jumps as if they had enough height to clear the moon. Izumi had made the piece so aggressive with her glitching electronica, the synthesizer adding new depths and layers to the themes established by the original composer. And yet, Satoru could see where she'd taken his earlier advice, allowing the original melodies and harmonies to breathe, and sections of the song took on a new vulnerability. This music had always been bursting with life, but just as Satoru was feeling dead to it, Izumi had made something new to rise in its wake.

And with that, an idea started taking place in his head. He knew just what direction his program needed to take in order to regain control over his story...

"I'll interpret that silence as a good sign."

Satoru felt as if his face was splitting in two with the excitement. "Get to your keyboard, Izumi. We've got work to do."

34

SATORU MISSED most of the practices leading up to the free skate. He and Kara Beth were too busy figuring out what that skate was going to look like. Winning wasn't an option anymore, or even medalling, but Satoru thought he could torpedo back into the top ten if he applied himself.

But they still had some issues with the jumping passes to work out. "Body is capable to try, but we hold back because I'm scared. Not a good way to live."

"Fair enough." He was convincing Kara Beth, but she wouldn't admit it just yet. "But doing a Quad Flip that's giving you trauma flashbacks is also not a good way to live."

Touché. "So, if I surrender Flip, you give me Quad-Quad?"

"It's not a hostage negotiation! What do you actually want out of this program today?" That had been tougher to answer, and Kara Beth had sighed at him. "There's no pressure. You've officially killed any and all expectations. And if you're not mentally there, I'd hate to see you give yourself an injury and not get to go to Worlds. Or worse, take yourself out of next season and miss the Olympics."

"I think Olympics is not important to me now."

Kara Beth smirked. "Sorry, I didn't hear you over the sound of the Japanese Skating Federation's collective heart attack."

Satoru had the decency to wince. But his voice was firm. "I'm a person. Not investment. Need to decide my career, my style, my coach. Winning medals makes me tired." When Kara Beth didn't understand, he bit his lip and tried another angle. "I say medal is real? So I feel good about me? But for other people. To me medal means different thing. More than first place. For everyone else, I win gold. But for me, I want skating like lighting bottle."

Kara Beth tilted her head. "Lighting bottle?"

That stupid word! "Lightening?" Satoru shrugged. Everyone used this phrase about him, now he couldn't explain it? "It's like, thunder and electricity, trapped in glass? Not like lightbulb, more special. Power of storms caught in a bottle."

"Catching lightning in a bottle?"

Satoru gave an emphatic nod. "Like double axel sit spin. No good points for jump pass, but, like, awesome! And Tano Sal, looks so cool, Quad Axel... I feel like lightening, uh, lightning. And competition is one moment to catch and hold in glass forever. Want that skate."

"And what's it going to take to make that happen?" They talked for hours about jumping passes, spin levels and security guards. About footwork and edges and the meaning behind the program music. What it would take to stay focused, and what he wanted to focus on.

Now, Satoru stood waiting for his six minute warm up, feeling slightly out of place. The atmosphere in the rink was different in the first stage of the competition, some of the audience hadn't even made it to their seats yet. And all the people he'd be skating with were different, none of the familiar faces in the final group, though he'd seen all of them before. They were giving him sideways looks, some intimidated, some judgmental, some just trying to ignore him and failing. It was similar to the atmosphere when they'd drawn for skate order, the general disbelief that *Miyazawa* was going to be skating in the first group.

Bui Xuan Son was happy to see him. "Welcome, welcome! It's

been long! I'm glad to share warm-up with you!" If it were a day ago, Satoru might have taken that comment as rude, an attempt to rub his face in the fact that his short program had been so miserable.

But now, he could see Son's exuberance for what it was, a genuine glee for the positives in life. "Please take care of me!" Satoru said with a bow and a big grin of his own. It had been a long time since he and Son had been in a warm-up group together, not since they were both at the junior level. Satoru had since shot to prominence, and though Son tenaciously kept qualifying for Worlds and 4CC, he struggled to qualify for the free skate and so rarely crossed Satoru's path. The distance was such that Son could be back at the hotel and into some comfortable pajamas by the time Satoru's group began to skate, if he wanted.

But despite lower scores, Son was beloved for his cheerful attitude, and Satoru took advantage of it now. Why wallow in misery over his situation, as he'd done yesterday, when he could enjoy the company of an old friend? Winning was a good feeling, but all the things he most loved about competition were right in front of him.

He bounced a little, waiting for the rink door to open. In front of him, Son clapped his hands together and said, sotto voce, "All right! Today, I will not be the last!"

"You can do it!" Satoru whispered back, and added a silent declaration to the heavens that he had no intentions of coming in last either.

The six skaters burst forth onto the ice like horses out of the gate, eager to maximize every second they could. The six minute warm up was a strange beast, one that was shrouded in paradox. A skater could have a disastrous warm up and then skate the program of their lives, or have an excellent warm up and then completely implode once their music turned on. In the past, Satoru had survived by treating the warm-up with levity, smiling and joking as he did with all aspects of competition. Outside interaction didn't take away from his focus when the time came, just kept him from turning so far inward that he became lost in his own self-destructive thoughts.

Today's competition was a little different. His killer was still out there, perhaps watching Satoru, perhaps not. It would be impossible not to think about. And equally impossible to toss up concrete walls and spend the competition in his own headspace. It wasn't how Satoru trained, wasn't how he competed, and it wasn't how he lived.

They'd have to find a balance somewhere. Satoru went through his warm-up routine, deliberately avoiding jumps for the moment. He focused more on his steps, trying to cut deeper and deeper edges. "You've been so focused on those jumps lately, it's like you've forgotten everything else," Kara Beth had said. "Show me what you can do when your blades are actually touching the ice."

And that was the right move, Satoru found. Carving shapes into the ice with greater and greater fluidity was the ultimate relaxant, it reminded him why he loved skating in the first place. Feeling himself turn and glide and shift edges brought back a control that he'd tried to find by jumping higher, but it had been here the whole time. People could take away a lot of things from him, including the Four Continents title, but the years upon years of training would always belong to him. He didn't have to jump the highest or have the greatest score to achieve excellence, to touch somebody's soul.

Perhaps this was what people meant when they said his best skating came on days he didn't win. He pondered that while he stroked around the rink, casting a small look up at the announcer's booth when she announced him as Satori Miyazawa from Vietnam. Mix-ups happened sometimes, and some skaters had their names completely butchered by announcers in competition, so Satoru had grown used to it. He couldn't promise his own accent could have handled all the foreign pronunciations, though he did think himself capable of reading notes off a page.

A bit later, the announcer listed Son as being from Japan and again, Satoru wondered why people couldn't just stick to their notes. He saw Son approaching and couldn't help but give an exasperated shrug, Competitive Cone of Silence or no.

Son had a twinkle in his eyes, and then unzipped his Vietnamese team jacket. It took a beat for Satoru to catch on, but then he grinned and eagerly swapped out his own jacket from Team Japan. Giggling like children, the two returned to their practice in the apparel of the opposite country, and Satoru heard the crowd laughing along with them.

It was a silver lining, Satoru thought, to having placed so poorly in the short program. He'd been put in a warm up with the one person in the whole competition willing to goof off and interact with him, and that was doing wonders for Satoru's mood. The shadows of his attempted murders could try to put a shade over the competition, but the light of others could drown them out.

Over the intercom, a pop song was playing, a hybrid of English and Chinese lyrics. Satoru only understood some words, but it sounded familiar. Perhaps he'd heard it at one of the practices, or maybe the chorus was just that catchy, but he found himself mouthing along to the foreign syllables as he went through parts of his choreography.

"I missed you," Son laughed after they were off the ice and had returned their jackets. "You're so happy at competition! Everyone else, they're too serious! Sports is game, we should make good memories no matter what the score!"

Satoru accepted the praise, but felt a little guilty. He hadn't been living up to those ideals just a day or two ago. But he could wallow, or he could learn and be better, just like when he stumbled in practice. He wished Son luck and rejoined Kara Beth backstage.

It would be some time before his turn to skate came. Plenty of time to get all turned around again, especially when he couldn't escape the constant sight of security and the media. The anxious feelings crept back with each minute, and Satoru struggled to dispel them by running through his exercises. He tried to think of Inessa, cheering him on from afar, Damien's persistence to try and help in his own abrasive way, and of Wataru up in the stands somewhere, watching him and being miraculously not awful when it counted. But it wasn't long before simple distraction wasn't enough, conversations and exercises with his coaching team weren't enough.

And before he knew it, he was back at the boards, familiar sweat in his palms and bile in his stomach. "Deep breaths," Kara Beth said, and Satoru tried, more afraid of the inability to harness his own thoughts than any result he thought could happen because of it. And that was an interesting realization, that his issues might not even be related to his attacker anymore. Could this all be about control, and the lack of it he'd felt ever since the season started? After all, he had so many people keeping vigilant watch over his safety, and whether people besides his coaching team had opinions on his skating didn't truly matter.

Still, just acknowledging that didn't make his pulse stop racing. "I know, trying to be calm..."

There was still a little time before the last skater's scores were announced. Satoru made a quick loop around the rink, dodging flower kids as they swept up gifts from the audience. He took comfort in the familiar sights, the routine of it all, but still felt a little skittish when he stopped in front of Kara Beth.

"It's okay," she told him, and clapped her hands on his shoulders with a comforting weight. "Last time you competed this free skate, things went sideways. It's natural that you'd be a little nervous." As much as Satoru tried to pretend it wasn't true, that memory of throwing up all over the ice was fresh in his mind. "That's why we're not doing all your crazy quads today. I know you're capable, but you don't need that stress right now."

"Right..." He agreed, he did, but that didn't stop him from feeling scared, frustrated and all the unproductive emotions. Just a minute ago, it was skating that filled him with positivity, that and Son being friendly. But that was part of skating too, wasn't it? The camaraderie, the crowds, the announcers that couldn't get their facts straight, the miracle that two people from different backgrounds could connect via a common language that neither of them had mastered. That there were Vietnamese flags held by the Chinese and Chinese flags held by the Japanese and American flags held by the Australians, it was all skating.

Did Satoru think he was going to ruin it, or something? "Talk to me," Kara Beth said, and Satoru envied her ability to stay so calm. There was a ticking clock over their heads, they would announce the scores any second now, and force Satoru to take the ice whether or not he was ready. "Tell me what you're feeling."

Maureen handed him a bottle of water, prepackaged, because they weren't taking any chances this time. Satoru fumbled with it, but got it open. "I'm scared to skate and be what past says I am," he said, quiet enough that no one outside of their circle would overhear. It was easier to wind his heart and mouth around the admission if he didn't take his eyes off the bottle. He watched the water sloshing around inside the cheap plastic and added, "I'm scared to be someone good to kill. Like, fight back, but then learn I don't deserve it."

Kara Beth squeezed his shoulders all the tighter. He didn't dare look up in case one of his typical crying fits started, but the weight was comforting. "Honey, you are none of those things. I promise." She waited for him to nod in acknowledgement. It was one thing to believe her now, another to still believe it when he was alone on the ice and could only hear her voice from a distance. "And today is not a big deal. Just another competition. Remind me why you love competing?"

Satoru couldn't help but smile, even if it felt weak. "To be with everyone. Try hard and show best. Share with audience."

"Right. And will any of those things go away if you take a little splat on the ice?" Satoru shook his head no, and Kara Beth smirked. "Exactly. You take a fall, you play that thing up like a Marx Brother until the audience is in stitches, do you understand? No gloomy faces."

"Understand," Satoru replied, but then felt a little bit of that brazen audacity he was known for flare to light, like a small candle in a dark room. "But I won't fall."

"In that case, there's no excuse for not delivering the highest components score this rink has ever seen," his coach came back, her intensity mounting as well. "Don't give those judges a reason to give you less than ten in every category."

Ten was perfection. When his old coach demanded perfection, Satoru felt anxious and guilty that he couldn't deliver. With Kara

Beth, he felt empowered. "When I'm done, they have to make new category for more points."

"That's the spirit." Overhead, the score was finally announced. "All right, champ. This is it. Forget the short program, show them the skater I see every day."

Satoru felt like little soap bubbles were growing in his chest, swelling just enough to create a tension, then popping into a pleasing mist. He felt lighter, yet also more grounded.

Above all, excited. "You bring pom-poms?"

Kara Beth rewarded him with a delicious grin. "You know I did."

THE MUSIC STARTED, and Satoru began to move. His first stroke was so powerful that one push was enough to get him halfway across the rink. Each edge was precise, and he was paying extra attention to the ease and flow of his footwork. "Remember, I want blackout tens across the board," Kara Beth told him, and Satoru intended to deliver.

He wasn't only known for his jumps, after all. He could cut a bracket so pretty it would make a grown man cry, and if he was going to downgrade some of his jumping layout, then all the more energy to pour into the presentation. Not a second of posture wouldn't be attended to, not a note of music uninterpreted.

Satoru came down the rink, building up speed with each cross-over, each 3-turn, each rocker and counter. He had downgraded many of his quadruple jumps to triples, but not all of them. Kara Beth had been right about some of his jumps placing undue stress on him today, but one jump was too important to drop, even for one competition.

-Have to do Tano Sal. It's important to story.-

This free skate put him in the role of a warrior. A triumphant one, Satoru had always felt, one who stormed the castle and vanquished the demon. But today, the narrative had changed. He was not the one attacking the castle, but defending it. His soul was a stronghold, like Kumamoto Castle during the Satsuma Rebellion, and it was under siege. One of the strongest fortresses in the land, and a strategic battle point, but Satoru would not let the walls fall.

What upstart rebellion thought they could reduce him to rubble? Satoru had built himself a castle, each stone carved from years of training and proved in competition. He was utter resplendence: enemies could fall on him from all angles, but they would break.

-I agree, Sato. Land that Tano Sal right in front of their arrogant faces.-

Who could say whether his unknown antagonist was watching, but Satoru flew up into the air with his arm over his head, holding that oddly balanced body position for an impossible four rotations. No one else could do such a jump, few had dared to try it before. His castle was too magnificent to break, it couldn't be defeated from the outside.

And so the enemy changed tactics.

-You agree with me, right? That 4F is not your friend right now. I vote we make it a triple.-

Arrows couldn't breach the walls, but doubt and demoralization could. If the enemy waited long enough, Satoru's defending army would run out of food, they'd be forced to surrender or cave to starvation and disease. Every day, the soldiers lost a little more hope, saw the troops outside their walls and felt their own strength depleting.

Satoru could admit to a little desperation himself, but he wouldn't let them give up. He slid across his backward inside edge and slammed his toe pick down in an act of defiance. He'd worked too hard to get this jump back, after everything that happened. Yes, it tended to career through the air like a drunken bird but for now, Satoru could work with that.

-Your knee healed, it's strong. It's not going to break on impact.-

-You're right. I can do triple today.-

Unpredictable as it was, the Flip was still his jump and as a triple, it would obey orders. The flawed technique was evidence of the battles he'd already survived, and the two of them would survive one more. His body was healthy, his heart was courageous, and outsiders had no place in his head.

-If you believe in me, I can land anything.-

Three rotations, straight and tight in the air. And by luck or poetic justice, a flawless landing. Satoru spread his arms out and fixed the judges with a fiery glare. Daring them to give that a negative GOE.

The 4A was another sacrifice, another magnificent jump that had no place in this battle. It would be a long war and that Quadruple Axel would lead the charge when they got to Slovenia for Worlds, but here, it needed to stay in the keep.

Satoru spun into a triple loop and tried not to grimace at the loss. The point value between axels and loops was already significant, let alone going from a quad to a triple. But sometimes one had to give up ground in order to gain it, sacrifice a pawn in order to take the queen. This was war, after all, and the castle was home to thousands. They couldn't risk its defense on one jump.

Kara Beth was right that they should have practiced the lower difficulty layout more before leaving Ohio, just to give him the option. He'd been too stubborn to admit he needed it, but the joke was on him now. Still, lower difficulty it was, he relished in being able to assert his mastery instead of clawing for every inch of height. Maybe some of the new combinations weren't as familiar as they could be, but the triples came to him like old friends, the new layout a fresh army to replace the battered regiment.

And then there was the choreography. The transitions and skills, flow and music interpretation rushing like triumphant cavalry. Satoru was furious in his pursuit of spins and the 4T that followed, braving to leave the castle and attack the enemy forces. He'd been weakened, but so had they. Satoru had support from his friends and family to help him break through their foes.

And in doing so, allow a path for supplies to return to the castle. Satoru now had a perfect opening to land a combination pass, and no obstacles to his solo triple axel. All of his jumping passes were now completed, and while he couldn't do the math in his head right then, he knew he'd done them well. And all without sacrificing his components, or his composure.

Nothing left to do but sell that last footwork sequence like it had never been sold before. The Imperial Army rushed to his aid from without, and Satoru had held the castle from within. There was no quarter left for the Satsuma forces. Kumamoto Castle screamed out its upcoming liberation with brackets and mazurkas, rockers and bauers, a cantilever that streaked down the ice like a flag-bearing steed. One final spin, faster and faster, until Satoru lost track of his rotations and decided he didn't even care. He hit his final pose, fist raised to the sky in victory, gratitude and relief.

The celebrations continued when he took his bow to a crowd that could not have been more astounded or appreciative. And still going when he met Kara Beth at the gate, pom-poms waving like a windmill until she could swing him into her arms.

"That!" she said, when they were finally settled in the Kiss and Cry. "That is what I've been waiting to see! You're back, kid!" The words lit something in Satoru, like a small firework finally reaching the end of its fuse and achieving its purpose. It didn't matter how the points shook out, because he was skating again. Skating with the same purpose and ability as before the accident.

Of course, as much as he said the points didn't matter, he still wanted to see what they were... "Well," Kara Beth whistled, "Components weren't *all* tens..."

Satoru tossed his head. "Judges are blind. I deserve eleven."

"That's my boy," she replied with a laugh and a pat on his knee, and Satoru almost broke into happy tears right there.

He'd survived the siege. On to win the war.

35

SLOVENIA, host of the Figure Skating World Championships, was a small country. But what it lacked in sprawling urban development, it made up for in scenery. Inessa could appreciate the greenery and history on its own, but listening to Satoru babble on about old churches, museums and preservation efforts was too adorable for words.

Of course, even she could only take so much. "Forgive me, but there is a figure skating competition this weekend? Do you intend to do some of that as well?"

She didn't have to see Satoru to know he was making a face. "Maybe I drop out and just be tourist," he joked through the phone, and Inessa rolled her eyes. Much as Satoru might have mellowed out since the Four Continents, the day he willingly dropped out of a skating tournament was a day the world ended.

She heard some buzzing through the phone, and Satoru sighed. "Sorry, Inessa, is hard to hear. Near lobby, there's huge crowd." He paused for a second, and Inessa could hear the many voices echoing. "Maybe someone famous arrive?"

"Or it is just me." She waited a moment for Satoru to realize, searching the crowd. Goodness, but there were so many reporters crammed into the small lobby! Had word gotten out that she was coming to Slovenia? And yet, it was only a few seconds before Satoru was shoving and wiggling his way through the crowds, and pleading with the security guards that now surrounded Inessa like a barrier.

"What you do here?" he demanded as soon as he got through, and Inessa snickered.

"This is how your greet your girlfriend? I would start with 'Hello'."

"Sorry," Satoru huffed, then bent down and enveloped her in a hug. "Hello, Inessa. So happy to see you. What you do here?"

"I'm surprising you!" she replied, and hugged him back with everything she could. She thought of kissing him, but with all the paparazzi cameras flashing, he might not appreciate the action. Besides, her parents were hovering just behind her, and that made the atmosphere awkward. It would have to wait.

There was time for that. Inessa would be in Slovenia all weekend. It had taken some negotiation to get her parents to agree to the trip, and they insisted on flanking her every minute they could. But Inessa had argued that she could be beset by fears and doubts in her lonely room, or surrounded by friends in a place she felt empowered and productive. That hadn't won her the argument; her parents had only caved when she'd pointed out she was old enough to make the trip without their permission and intended to do so. All of that aside, she was here.

And while cheering on her friends was on the itinerary, it wasn't her only purpose. But that, too, could wait.

How she had missed Satoru! That had always been true, but now that they were dating, Inessa found herself missing more than just his person. She'd missed strange details, like his smell, his eyelashes and the glimpse of biceps underneath his t-shirt. It was good that she'd been able to make the trip before long distance dating stole all of her rationality.

"I may not be competing, but how could I miss the World Championships?"

Satoru was pleased to see her, she could see it in his eyes. Even so, his words were hesitant. "I'm glad you come, Inessa, really. But don't you think dangerous right now?"

"For me? You don't think my conquest of the World title has been stopped?"

"We don't know that's reason," he said, and sounded so much like her parents that Inessa wanted to pout. "Uzbekistan pulled whole team, you know. Don't want to put athletes in danger. Even risk not qualify for Olympics to be safe. And you fly in with broken knee."

"You're here," Inessa pointed out, and Satoru winced, but still chuckled.

"That's different, I'm Team Japan. We ride or die for skating," he said, and crouched down to better meet Inessa's eye level. "You even healthy to fly? How is knee? How is headaches?"

"I am cleared by doctors, do not fuss," Inessa said, and she did pout this time. "It feels like a few pieces of my knee were left behind in Barcelona, but this contraption," she gestured to the boot on her leg, currently tighter than a vice, "will keep all remaining splinters together. It is fine."

"Okay," Satoru shook his head. "I just want you safe."

"And I want you safe," Inessa said. "That's why I'm here. I may not remember, but I did solve this mystery once. I can do so again." She cut him off before he could form any protests. "I will find the clues again. And when I do, I do not want to be miles away and helpless."

Satoru looked like he wanted to argue, but dropped his head instead. "What I do with you?" he sighed as he took her hands. "Police tell me Dami's stalker in Slovenia somewhere," he said in a quieter voice. "He keeps call Dami, wants to meet. They try to find him, but..." he looked up again, worry in his eyes. "Maybe is not killer, but is dangerous person. Maybe other dangerous person here, too. You're easy target now, Inessa, don't run so fast anymore."

"That is what they are for," Inessa waved her hand at the security guards orbiting nearby, a group of several patrolling the hotel and the arena. The intimidating men and women should have been enough to deter such talk, but Satoru only narrowed his eyes.

"They let us get close," he pointed out. "What if friend is killer? Or works with them? Can't stop everything." He had a point.

But Inessa didn't care. "And I cannot sit by and wait for more bad things to happen. I cannot drift off while someone hurts you, and I slowly turn into nobody..." Her parents were always telling her to stay hopeful, that even if her competitive skating career was over, she had her whole life ahead of her. But with her schoolwork piling up and her muscles feeling so heavy, it was hard for Inessa to think positively about that future life.

This wasn't how she'd planned for the World Championships to go. She was going to win gold alongside Satoru. She'd stand on a podium in a beautiful dress and be the pride of her country and kiss her boyfriend under sparkling lights at the gala. It seemed neither of them were having the season they'd hoped for.

But Satoru leaned close to her and smiled. Then, regardless of customs and propriety, he pecked her on the nose. "Inessa Levi is not nobody," he said, and those words did more for her than her parents and the doctors combined. "If you think you can do something, I'll help you do. Let's end this."

36

———————

FTER WHAT HAD HAPPENED to Inessa, Hser Nay was more motivated than ever to solve the mystery. Issac thought that should have motivated her to drop everything, and some of the other skaters shared that opinion, but when Inessa Levi said she was coming to Slovenia and was organizing a meet up at her hotel, Hser Nay jumped at the chance. And while some familiar faces didn't show, it was still a sizable gaggle of skaters who arrived and set up camp.

Including Satoru Miyazawa. "What, I don't get to know?" he said when everyone kept staring at him. It was a reminder that there was a real person they were doing this for, and yet they knew so little of value. Satoru plunked himself down next to Inessa, and the two fiddled with a laptop while the others filtered in past the security guards at the door.

The burly men were here for Inessa's sake. "My parents insisted," she said with a sigh. "Though I don't know it is always effective." Hser Nay had similar thoughts, as they had searched her bag for weapons at the arena while armed guards patrolled. Satoru had escorts surrounding him whenever he was at the rink. Maybe it provided some safety, but there was no way to screen people's intentions, and even conventional objects could do damage.

But Hser Nay could appreciate the concern. "I guess it's a parent's job to be a bit overprotective."

"Perhaps." Inessa only seemed half convinced. "It was a chore to get them to leave me for the evening. They think I am hosting a party to watch the short programs tonight." And speaking of that, the men were scheduled to skate, so they'd lose Satoru before too long.

"Let's buckle down, then." She plunked herself down on a spare piece of hotel bed. Alisha followed her lead and began scrolling through a document on her laptop. Hser Nay looked over her shoulder. "Okay, we've time-logged almost everything, identified just about everyone who got within five feet of Satoru and stalked them on the internet. Let's run through our leads."

"Damien's stalker dude," Mark Bertinelli brought up, but Clara shook her head.

"That guy got released. And remember, he was in prison during the car bombing, so it couldn't have been him."

"What about Yukiya? Derek?"

"Weren't in Ohio during the car thing."

"See, that's our problem," Hser Nay moaned and put her head in her hands. "The people with obvious motive weren't around, and the ones that were don't have obvious motive. I don't know what we're looking for anymore."

"Then let's focus on this," Inessa said, highlighting a particular video she'd been obsessing over the last two months. "We know I figured something out before I was attacked, and the answer was here. If it was discovered once, we can do again it."

The group all nodded and peered into their computers, Inessa keeping up a commentary. "There is something unusual here, but I can't say what. Something about the water fountain..." She pursed her lips and thought. "I do remember this... I saw Ekaterina by one at Europeans and thought the same thing..."

"I thought you said it wasn't Ekaterina?"

"Not her, but something in the situation..." Inessa brushed some curls back from her face. "Why can't I remember?"

"Relax," Satoru said, and his arm snaked around her shoulders to squeeze out some tension. "Get frustrated just makes you forget more." He scrolled through the list of names Hser Nay had compiled, detailing every person in the video and their affiliations. "Water fountain can't be poison, everyone would get sick. So what makes it wrong? I don't remember anything weird happening."

"I don't know, but there's not a lot of people using it. Mostly the coaches or volunteers, all the athletes have their own water bottles." Clara rested her chin on her fist and watched the images go by.

Alisha mimicked her posture. "What if everything that happened has nothing to do with skating? What if we're looking for something completely different?"

"Like what? The reigning world everything gets poisoned, has his car bombed, and then someone tries to take out the women's champion and it has nothing to do with skating?"

"We don't know those events are related," Alisha pointed out, and Hser Nay gave her a skeptical look back.

"How could they not be?" Hser Nay was still trying to find some sort of common through line through all of this, some motive that would make everything obvious. Otherwise, they just had a bunch of dots with no connections.

"Well, if someone has some cause and wants to make a statement..."

"They've had half a year to make a statement," Hser Nay challenged. She'd had the same thought too, but abandoned it months ago. "Nothings come up. Activism or terrorist acts only work if someone says what the point is. The sport just gets new champions, staying silent accomplishes nothing." She winced when she remembered that Satoru and Inessa were in the room, and Satoru in particular didn't look thrilled at the prospect of a new men's champion taking his place.

But he kept those thoughts to himself. "Is too big coincidence to not be related," he agreed. "If not competition, you think it's fan, maybe?"

"It's basically what we thought about Damien's stalker."

"Okay," Inessa said, and seemed too calm for a discussion involving her own safety and world ranking. "But we're back to opportunity. No fan has the access."

"Again, Damien's stalker figured it out. It doesn't have to be a spectator, even the venue staff can still be fans," Mark offered, and his brother nodded.

"And another skater could easily have an obsessive one sided love affair with Inessa or Satoru."

Hser Nay fixed Issac with a look. "Easily? How easily?"

"It could be the other way around. Maybe someone wants to keep them apart," he laughed with his arms raised in protest. The idea wasn't rejected out of hand, but it drew a lot of frowns as people considered it.

Hser Nay found herself nodding along, but wasn't sure. "Still, to know Satoru still uses one of those leaky swag bottles is a pretty intimate detail. And when and how to make the switch? No fan knows that."

Issac burst into laughter. "Have you ever been on a skating forum? Those people know things. I took off my wristbands before getting off the plane and someone wrote a fanfic to explain where they'd gone!"

"Where did they go?" Clara asked, and Issac turned to face her and Mark, hands clasped over his heart in mock sincerity.

"I gave one to each of you in the hopes that it would cheer you up after Four Continents and forever bind us as siblings."

"Aw, that's so sweet."

"It actually was, but creepy detail," Issac said with a chuckle, ignoring Mark's question about why he was reading fanfiction about himself. "Like, they knew who had the window-seat on the plane."

"Oh, yikes." And like that, Clara was no longer laughing. "If they've got that kind of focus, it's probably not hard to learn what kind of bottle you're using, or where you park your car, huh?" she said to Satoru, who seemed unsettled by the thought.

What was worse, Hser Nay thought, to have strangers know so much about you or to have a friend betray you? "But again, no one's said anything. Have either of you gotten death threats or weird contacts from a fan?"

"Just Henri," Satoru shrugged, and Inessa also gave a negative. Hser Nay groaned aloud.

"So we're back to looking at skaters. Or their teams." That made sense to Hser Nay; there was a big difference between knowing how to do something and being able to. "And that's nothing we didn't know already."

"We can find the who and the how with that one video Inessa found," Clara said, gesturing to the girl. "We just have to keep watching. What we still need to figure out is why, and why both you and Satoru? Someone killing Sato to take his title doesn't benefit from killing Inessa!"

"Unless she knows something," Satoru pointed out, with a bit of a look at his girlfriend. "She finds answer once. Kill witness?"

"But they left me alive," Inessa reminded them all, until Satoru pointed out that was only because Damien arrived to meet her.

"Which is suspicious on its own," Alisha said, but the thought gave everyone a collective shudder.

"Look, maybe no one meant to murder anybody," Mark tried, and everyone was relieved to not have to argue Damien's involvement. "What if the poison was only supposed to make Satoru sick, just for the one competition? Even the car bomb was minor. It could be someone wants to just injure him."

That was an interesting thought and seemed to cheer Satoru. Until Clara broke in. "Guys, if that's the goal, there's way better things to poison Satoru with than arsenic." She crossed her arms and turned to Alisha, who looked startled at the attention. "Right? I mean, it's not like an obvious option."

Alisha nodded, hesitant. "Yeah, I've used arsenic in some of my school studies, on plants. It's so dangerous to ingest. You could use a million household items to make someone sick." Put like that, it did seem unlikely. "It's a miracle Satoru's alive. No one would have gone through that much trouble just to inconvenience him."

"Okay, so let's look at it from the opposite angle," Mark said. "Let's work backwards from Inessa. Everyone's quick to pin that on Ekaterina, but there's no reason for her to take out Satoru too, she can't compete in the men's division."

"There's no reason for Ekaterina to take out Inessa," Hser Nay added. "The fact that her motive is so obvious makes it the dumbest move in the world. Even if you didn't get convicted, the whole world would think you did it and flay you for it."

"Well, if you only care about winning, who cares what people think?"

"I think she cares," Clara said, thoughtful. "She might not even podium at Worlds, the way she's been skating, and it's all because of the scandal. I wouldn't say Ekaterina benefits from it."

"What about Eric Blaine?" Everyone turned to Alisha, who bit her lip in uncertainty. "I've been watching your video, Inessa, and... well, he'd have been at both Skate America and Ohio for the car bombing. I can't connect him to you, but if the two attacks aren't related, then... we might have a suspect." She turned to Satoru. "He was acting really weird that week I visited."

"All weeks," Satoru agreed, but looked troubled. "I think he's jealous, but to kill is..." He didn't finish, and Issac took over.

"Okay, it's a possibility. One of the only ones we've got. We already know it can't be a stranger who did the actual switch, so even if he's not behind everything, he could be bribed or tricked into doing it."

"Maybe..." A sudden beeping sounded, and Satoru looked down at his phone. "Okay, I have to go. Good luck."

"And to you." Inessa kissed him on the cheek as he left, and Satoru flushed. Those two were too adorable for words. "I promise we'll figure this out."

But despite her promise, the status quo continued for another twenty minutes. "We're talking in circles!" Hser Nay moaned, and the video wasn't yielding any new insights. She could see Inessa was just as frustrated as she was. "You're sure this is where you found the clue?"

"Yes!" Inessa looked ready to throw her laptop out the window. "I was watching that for weeks, and then I saw Ekaterina, I think I called someone... and then my mind is blank! I can't remember what connection I made or what happened after!" She grumbled a little as she rattled off the precious few fragments of memory she had. "There was the press conference, then Damien was upset about something, and Amina..." And somewhere in that period, Inessa had made phone calls to Satoru and the police. "It is connected to that water fountain, I know that! Something about it holds the key!"

"We'll keep looking," Hser Nay sighed, then looked over at Mark and Clara. "What about the motive angle? Anything new come up?"

"I hate to say it, but Ekaterina does have the best motive to hurt Inessa. Well, her and the entire women's division."

"The two events can't be related, then," Alisha concluded. "We're trying to solve two separate mysteries, because no one benefits from taking down both Inessa and Satoru. We'll just confuse ourselves if we keep thinking that way."

"But I am sure!" Inessa protested. "They are connected, I'm sure of it!"

"How are you sure?" Alisha asked, eyebrow quirking up in a show of extreme skepticism. "When you called the police, nothing had happened to you yet, there wasn't any second event to connect." Inessa looked flabbergasted but couldn't deny the logic. She puzzled over that, and Alisha said, "Look, you're one of the sharpest skates on the shelf, Bunny Hop. But you did get a real bad knock on the head. Is it possible some of your memories are a little scrambled?"

"I..." There were few forces on earth more powerful than the sight of Inessa Levi blinking back tears. Hser Nay had to look away, in case she jumped to Inessa's defense despite all logic being on Alisha's side. "It is possible," Inessa had to concede, but didn't seem to believe it.

The connection was out there. It had to be. But time wore on, and it remained elusive. Alisha eventually had to leave, she had plans to meet friends.

Soon, they were down to just Hser Nay, Inessa, Chen/Song and the Bertinelli triplets.

They took a break to watch the men's short program broadcast on the television, but everyone still had their computers open, just in case an idea occurred to them. The skating was a nice distraction, even if they held their collective breaths when Satoru took his turn. But he survived it, and that was just as important as his results. "I don't want to give up," Hser Nay said after the competition had finished and the cheering had died down. She leaned into Issac's shoulder. "But we're not much further than where we started." The internet video had been playing on silent the entire time, she'd questioned every person she saw on the television in her mind, but nothing seemed to connect.

"It is a small thing we're overlooking," Inessa insisted, resolute. "I know we can solve this. We have already done it!"

"Then why can't we now-?" Hser Nay began, but was interrupted when Song Min jumped back from his computer, then started waving at her. "What's up?"

Min conversed a bit with Huan in Chinese, then spoke up. "Both isn't one person. Two people together."

"Huh?"

"Um, like..." He whispered something to Huan again, then tried, "Two people work together, hurt Satoru and Inessa." He stared at Inessa and shrugged, as if that would help the English along. Beside him, Huan was using hand motions to try to convey her meaning.

But after an awkward minute, something clicked in Hser Nay's head. "Oh, I get it! Two people, two different motives, but working together? That's brilliant, Min! Remember that old judging scandal?" she said to the others, who still looked a little confused.

"Which one? There's only been, like, a hundred."

"Ha ha," Hser Nay glared at Issac. "The Salt Lake Olympic one, where the French judge over-scored the Russian pairs in return for the Russian judge over-scoring the French in ice dance."

"I thought it was the other way around?"

"Maybe? Not the point. Maybe two people are working together? You scratch my back, I scratch yours?"

"Oh! That is brilliant!" Inessa turned to the side and thanked Min. "When Satoru was poisoned, everyone looked to Damien or Derek. Someone even tried to plant Damien's watch at the scene. And after my attack, everyone looked to Ekaterina. But the true suspects could be connected to the opposite victim, yes?"

"If two people worked together, it obscures the clues. The person who committed the crime doesn't have motive, the person with motive is nowhere near the crime. The exact situation we find ourselves in now."

"Okay, that's a start, but it doesn't narrow anything down," Clara said, but was interrupted by Inessa.

"It does," she said, and her eyes were wide as she stared at her computer screen. Hser Nay tried to ask what she meant, but Inessa shushed her. "I am thinking! I am..." she trailed off, then paused the video that had been playing on loop. "That water fountain. I thought it was strange. Ekaterina was standing by it at Euros, but she drank from her own water bottle..."

"That's a clue?"

Inessa shook her head. "If someone has their own water bottle, they would not drink from the water fountain, right? It would be odd if they did."

Mark tilted his head. "Yeah, but it's not exactly criminal..."

"It is if their water bottle's full of poison," Hser Nay snapped, now catching on. "And if that person has a reason to make sure Inessa isn't around to land a Quad Sal in the next year or so." A second later, Huan leaned forward with a lurch, seeing what Inessa was.

"Bottle same color..." She turned to the rest of the group. "Bomb?"

"They were present," Inessa confirmed, and grimaced to herself. "This is it, this is what I forgot! No one would have suspected a thing, while a partner attacked me from a continent away. If two worked together, both would have the perfect alibi."

"That's genius, isn't it?" Mark marveled, eyes still glued to his computer screen. "You can have all the motive in the world, but who's gonna convict you if you're an entire country away? All you need is someone to agree to it."

"So, what now?" asked Hser Nay, barely able to breathe. Things had been going so slowly, it seemed unbelievable that they could actually solve the mystery now. She reached out for Issac's hand and squeezed it, hoping it would hide any shaking that might have sprung up. "It doesn't explain everything, but... Is this enough for the police?" she asked, the gravity of the accusation bearing down upon her. If they said something and were wrong...

But if they were right, and said nothing... "We might not have enough to accuse, but maybe the police can do something?" Inessa said, unsure. But she was determined when she reached for her phone. "It doesn't matter. Satoru needs to know right away!"

37

———

T HE SITUATION with Damien remained complicated. He wasn't unkind to Satoru, but he was distant, and in Satoru's opinion, depressed. Something he'd caused, but now couldn't do anything to fix. It was confusing and cast a shadow over the competition for him.

As if it were necessary. Things were already tense enough at the World Championships with the competition itself, and then all the unresolved mystery surrounding the season. Satoru and Damien didn't need any concerns added, but were reminded of the gulf between them every time they passed. And with them both sharing a coach, both skating in the final group, it was impossible not to cross paths.

But with Competitive Cone of Silence in effect, Satoru couldn't resolve the issue, nor would it have been advisable to open such an emotional can of worms when they had a job to focus on. So Satoru tried to put those issues to the side as he prepared for the short program.

As always, his feelings bled into his skating. When he closed his eyes to visualize the program, to see the story play out, his opposite partner of Giselle was neither Kara Beth nor Inessa, but Damien.

After a few confusing seconds, Satoru stopped fighting it and accepted that interpretation. By the time he took the ice, he felt confident in the story he was about to tell.

Too confident for his tastes. He'd never connected so well to the story of Giselle, or the character of an arrogant Prince who ruined a life in a careless moment. But he saw the first act of the story play out with a different sense of love, one with Damien in the peasant's role with an innocent spirit and a weak body. A common exterior to hide the precious heart within, as well as the fragility. Satoru betrayed that trust, failed to treat it with the necessary care, and watched what he loved descend into madness and death.

Damien was alive and well, but whatever the future held for them would never be the same, and it was too early to say if that change would make them stronger or weaker in the end. There was nothing to do but press on into the woods, searching for absolution and forgiveness, no assurance that anything could be restored.

The despair took over Satoru's footwork, his spins, his jumps. The Quad Toe replaced his previous Quad Flip, and that new stability blazed the path to death's domain. Prince Albrecht didn't fear the Willi spirits and what they could do, and neither did Satoru. Dancing to death could not be more excruciating than the heart he already had to live with. Albrecht could not face the world after Giselle's death; Satoru didn't want to. If he couldn't repair this situation with Damien, a part of his soul would die and be buried under the frozen water.

But was there hope? Giselle forgave and wanted to save the person who'd destroyed her. Perhaps there was still a chance for forgiveness, for a deep friendship to overcome such mistakes. Damien had always been on Satoru's side, whether it was deserved or not. Surely they couldn't lose so many years of friendship in one moment of idiocy!

And yet, Satoru hit that final Triple Axel knowing that this hope could not be. Giselle could love and save, but the Damien of his youth would be forever gone. Satoru had killed that boy with his own thoughtlessness, and that innocent trust would never return.

Things could be good again, maybe, but they would always be different.

For the second time, Satoru finished his short program with tears, though for a much better reason. He took his bows and left the ice with a heart that had found some clarity on his feelings, but still no direction. The ballet didn't provide any insight into what Albrecht did after leaving the forest.

That feeling lingered when Kara Beth didn't join him in the Kiss and Cry. She stayed at the boards long enough to congratulate him, but then had to run off to help Damien prepare. It was a familiar routine in the bigger events where both he and Damien competed, and if Satoru was being honest, he really didn't need his coach once his skate ended.

But it felt a little lonely, even if he had Maureen next to him while they announced his scores. And what scores they were! Not his world record, but so close, and enough to return some of Satoru's good mood. He'd hold onto that lead through the rest of the skaters and be sitting in a nice place when the free program came around.

Damien had a good skate as well, and Satoru felt bittersweet to watch it. Less because of the scores, though those were stellar. Satoru was trying not to think about the numbers. But there was so much about Damien that the world never got to see, things that only came out of his heart while skating, then skittered back into their hiding places like woodland mice.

Perhaps Damien could act distant and unaffected back at the hotel, but on the ice, he was reminding everyone that their Grand Prix Champion knew how to bleed.

They exchanged congratulations after the fact, but where Damien had once gravitated to Satoru, now Satoru seemed to repel him. The press conference after the competition had a noticeable wall between the two of them, though nothing either said was antagonistic. And on the shuttle bus, Damien passed Satoru's seat with barely a glance and hunkered down in the back seat by himself. Satoru debated whether to join him, then decided not to push it. He pulled out a notebook to occupy himself and began flipping through sketches of Inessa's Romeo and Juliet costume.

As he was making a quick note on one of the designs, another skater sat down in the seat next to him, and Satoru did a double take when he realized who it was.

"Hello, there," greeted Derek Donner of Great Britain, with a smile on his face that could have been cheery if it weren't so forced. Satoru's eyes darted around the bus at all the empty seats, then back to Derek.

"Hello?" Why was he sitting there? Why the creepy smile? In just a few seconds, the reminder that he was living under threat of murder slammed back into him with the weight of a bus crash, and Satoru couldn't focus on anything else. "Can I help you?"

"Just needed a place to sit." He could have chosen anywhere else. At any other competition, Derek would have, he'd never sit next to Satoru on purpose! "Is there a problem with that?"

"Um..." He looked around to find the security guard assigned to the bus, but at that moment, the bus pulled away from the curb with a small jerk, and Satoru pitched forward.

Derek managed to catch the notebook before it went tumbling off his lap. His eyes widened when he saw the drawings. "Is that Inessa Levi?" He barely waited for Satoru's nod. "I didn't know you drew."

Satoru collected himself enough to shrug. "I only do for costumes." He was still trying to figure out why Derek cared, and why nearly a full minute had passed without an insult. Was he acting out of character in order to lure Satoru into a false sense of security? Surely no one would try to murder him on a bus with a guard within meters? Then again, they'd managed it in a crowded ice rink in front of video cameras.

It was weird to see expressions like enthusiasm and admiration on his rival's face. "You know, I'm studying art at university," Derek said, and Satoru sagged with relief. Here it came, the declarations of superiority and disdain. The world was about to right itself again. "These are quite good."

That didn't compute. Satoru stared, not confident enough to

blink. He curled his hand around his pencil just in case the situation called for an emergency shank. "Only draw people and clothes. Ask me draw flower or something, I can't do." It was kind of embarrassing, really. He'd gotten decent at drawing the human form and fabrics, even gestures and facial expressions, but the few times he'd tried to make art instead of mere clothing design had ended in abysmal failure. At the same time, Satoru had no real interest in learning how to draw trees or clouds, so the imbalance of skill was his own fault. "And pencil colors all look weird now, so maybe I have strange costumes next season."

But Derek didn't take the opportunity to criticize. "Well, many people think Vincent Van Gogh may have been colorblind." He handed the notebook back with a look that Satoru could almost call encouraging. Was he hallucinating, or was Derek genuinely trying to have a moment here? "Have you thought about going further with it? After retirement, maybe?"

"Not really," Satoru admitted, still amazed that the conversation was even happening. He cast looks around the bus, wondering if Derek had lost a bet. "Is fun, but not like job feeling. Not like..."

"Skating?" Derek finished for him, and Satoru confirmed with a surprised nod. Finishing each other's sentences now? At this rate, he and Derek were going to be engaged by the end of the bus ride. "Then, what is your plan for the future, after skating? No pressure, I'm just making conversation," he said with a wave of his hand, once Satoru gaped like a deer caught in headlights.

No pressure, but for the first time in his life, Satoru didn't feel the weight of dread when thinking about the question. He'd been able to imagine several ideas without breaking into a cold sweat. "Feels far away, but... I think maybe immigration?" he said, though he still wasn't sure why Derek would care. But the other man seemed at least mildly interested for some unknown reason, so Satoru continued. "Like, mentor people in new country. Find belonging and not be scared by paperwork. Like that."

"Huh. Back in Japan, you mean?"

Satoru pursed his lips, having never made it that far in his future plans. A life where he wasn't physically on the ice was a new concept for him. But it was all skating, he realized now, so not as daunting as he once believed. "Maybe. Or wherever. Maybe international work, or like with refugee?" He felt a little embarrassed, suddenly wondering if such speculation was too grandiose for him. "Have to get better at English first. But I think I understand some of the hard feelings. And good with talking to people. Skating doesn't need language and everyone can learn, so maybe start there..." Satoru shrugged. "Is far away dream. Don't really have plan yet."

"A better plan than most have." Derek's response was more positive than Satoru expected, considering he'd never told this idea to anyone before. Strange that his first confidante would be his greatest rival. "I don't know, a part of me just assumed you would go on skating and winning things indefinitely."

"I'm still going to do that," Satoru declared, and earned a bark of laughter. "What you do, in future? You make art?"

"Teach," Derek clarified. "I like sculpture, but it's a hard living. If I could turn into an old, woolly professor at an obscure university, I'll be a happy man."

"Sounds nice." Very peaceful, not the image he'd always had of Derek. Then again, they'd never talked like this before. Neither of them were as they appeared on the outside.

The new perspective was pleasant enough that it masked the unfamiliarity, but only for a minute. "You didn't deserve what happened to you." Derek said, soft and somber. Satoru's head turned so fast he nearly wrenched his neck, but Derek didn't notice, eyes fixed on the seat backing in front of them. "I'm glad you're competing again."

If this kept up, Satoru was going to have a heart attack. "Why you say all this?" he asked, and tried not to make it sound like an accusation. "I mean, thanks. But we don't usually talk..." Politely, at least. If you counted trash talk, they were downright loquacious. But Derek made a face, and Satoru tried to backpedal. "Sorry, that was rude. I'm kind of jerk right now, get nervous and snap at everybody. Sorry."

Derek gave him a sideways look, then sighed. "Well, if half the world thinks I tried to murder you, then maybe I've been taking the banter a little far." He leaned back in his seat and smirked a little. "Truth is, I kind of missed you. How am I supposed to prove I'm better than you if you're not around?"

That sounded more like Derek. It was possible that this was all an act, a string of lies to make himself look innocent. And yet, Satoru felt assurance coming from somewhere, a comfort in old relationships. Even though Satoru wouldn't have called them friends, there was a bond in that rivalry, a connection as strong as it was strange. A proof, providing hope in the unseen. "Thank you. I'm glad to skate with you again."

"Don't you mean against me?"

"No, I mean together." It was how he viewed competition, even if it didn't always make sense to others.

But Derek seemed to understand, much as he tried not to show it. It struck Satoru that he'd never felt personally attacked by anything Derek said. For all their animosity, Derek never struck blood, and might never have meant to. Satoru hadn't either, but he remembered what it felt like to cross the line with Damien and Kara Beth. He liked to play around and be a delinquent in English, something he couldn't get away with in other settings, but to genuinely hurt someone was never his intention.

"If I say something that hurts," Satoru said with a pause, "I'm sorry. Don't mean to make real bother for you."

"Ha! Likewise. But not much bothers me," Derek reassured, stretching his legs a little. "I get mad quickly, but it doesn't last."

"Just like Damien," Satoru laughed, then clapped his hands over his mouth when Derek fixed him with a glare.

"Okay, *that* was a step too far, Miyazawa." But there was a bit of a smirk to his growl that let Satoru know he could press his luck. "I am in all ways superior to that snooty Frenchman." From the back of the bus, Satoru saw Damien straighten at the word, then roll his eyes at the pair of them.

"Not all ways. Damien has better accent. When you speak English, don't understand word you say," he said, loud enough for

Damien to hear. As much as he tried to look like he wasn't paying attention, Satoru saw him trying to hide snickers behind his hand.

"Excuse me?" Derek looked flabbergasted. "*You're* critiquing *my* accent?"

"My English is perfect," Satoru said, drawing out the 'r' sound on purpose. "It's efficient. Only use words I need. You, accent is so weird, other English don't understand."

"I'm just from Northumberland, you twit!" In the back, Damien had given up all pretense and was now cackling. "You are absolutely impossible, you know that?" But he smiled as he said it.

A giggle came from elsewhere on the bus. Satoru looked across the rows and saw Aaron Leval poking Alberto Casal. "And with that, this season is officially back to normal!" He winked when he caught Satoru's eye, and Satoru grinned right back, even while Fujiwara Ainosuke turned to Yukiya and asked, "*Is he always like this?*"

It was a strange definition of normal, but Satoru didn't disagree.

AS THEY ALL stepped off the bus, Damien glided near Satoru. "Everything is all right between you two, yes?" he asked in a subdued tone, head indicating Derek.

"We're fine," Satoru replied, touched and relieved that Damien still cared to check up on him, given the state of things. "You don't need worry, I don't think he's criminal."

"You trust people too much," Damien grumbled as the guard at the hotel entrance looked over their bags. "You trust all the people who hurt you, but not me?"

"Dami..." Satoru wanted to protest, but he had treated Damien differently, and still couldn't say why. Maybe because Damien made it safe to challenge him? Safe to question and release tension, without fear of retribution, just as family did? Or perhaps it was because Satoru was so confident that Damien posed no physical threat, but had felt threatened by Damien in all the ephemeral things? The titles and skating skills that had driven him crazy for so long were as affecting as any poison.

But that didn't make it right. "I'm sorry about-"

But Damien cut him off. "I have to meet someone," he said, looking at his phone. His eyes narrowed and flicked up to Satoru. "Where are you off to?"

Satoru was caught off guard, but if Damien was interested in his plans, maybe there was hope for them. "To room to change clothes. Then meet family. We go to dinner together. You want come with?" he offered, and saw the revulsion flicker across Damien's face.

Well, it had been a long shot. "No, thank you," Damien said with a bit of a shudder. "I have to meet someone. But can we...?" He stopped himself, and Satoru leaned in.

"Yeah?"

But in the end, Damien just shook his head. "Never mind. Just stay safe. Maybe I'll see you around."

Satoru growled out his frustration, but there was nothing he could say to Damien's retreating back.

ALISHA HAD BEEN a podium contender for much of her skating career, but it had been a long time since she was the favorite for gold. There was always some new teenager fresh out of Juniors and armed with some crazy quad or axel combo to put a stop to that. Alisha enjoyed the stiff competition, because it made her feel like she'd earned each of her silver and bronze medals, though the constant narrative from outsiders could overpower the pride sometimes. Or maybe more than sometimes. But whether or not she liked it, that was the reality she lived in. Alisha had grown used to the spotlights pointing at others.

Now, with Inessa Levi withdrawn and Ekaterina Raskolnikova skating like a drunk, Alisha was suddenly thrust into the limelight again. For the first time in years, she had a real chance to reclaim her world title, and she'd forgotten what that pressure was like. All the media attention, all the hopes and expectations that she now had to bear, it was a burden like no other, but one she'd endured before.

Alisha had been at this game too long to crumble under pressure, World Championships or not.

That didn't mean it wasn't exhausting. She pushed her way across the hotel lobby, ignoring the watchful eyes of security, and scurried into the old fashioned elevator. She held the doors to let Satoru Miyazawa in, dragging his skate luggage behind him, and only allowed herself to deflate once the doors closed. She slumped a bit against the wall, feeling worn out. The World Championships had the highest highs and lowest lows, and the extremes seemed wider every year.

Especially this year. Satoru looked much the same as Alisha, though having just finished a short program, he had an excuse. He also looked a little down, and it was only after the noise of the lobby faded away that he seemed to relax. Alisha had to sympathize. The extra security measures at the event had to be putting pressure on him, as it did on everyone. Cameras followed his every move, guards checked every bag and rode with competitors on the shuttle busses. Even at the hotel, there was security monitoring every floor, every entrance and exit.

Except the parking garage. "Is everything all right, Sato?" In hindsight, that was a stupid question. Not much in poor Satoru's life was going right these days. Alisha grimaced to herself as she waited for his answer.

"Yeah, just... weird day." That could cover a lot of things. "It's fine, don't worry, please."

"Okay." They only saw each other at these competitions, it wasn't the basis for a real friendship. And yet, she'd known Satoru longer than the people in Alisha's circle of friends back home, and had gone through more triumph and heartache with him than most of them. She'd looked out for him at international events since he was a little kid, a gesture his older brother welcomed with relief. To see him so obviously upset was tugging at her heartstrings.

Maybe she didn't have the right to call herself his friend, but that didn't mean she didn't care. So she forced a cheerful tone, "Your short program was really great, by the way. Your best Giselle yet."

"I barely do this season," Satoru said with an eye roll. "Not much to compare."

"Aw, you never change. You're supposed to say, 'Thank you, Alisha! That's nice of you to say so!'"

Satoru grimaced. "Sorry. Thank you, Alisha! That's nice... of you say so." He stumbled a little in trying to mimic her. "Sorry, I'm trying to not be, like, angry rude person all the time."

"I wouldn't call you either of those things," Alisha said with a laugh. "We all give you a hard time because we want to see you enjoy yourself a little. You're too lovable to be depressed all the time." Satoru's eyebrows wrinkled a bit at that, he didn't seem to think himself so lovable. That was always his biggest problem, Alisha thought, that Satoru resisted even the idea of liking himself. It went way beyond usual humility, and she could see where having to live with that day after day could wear down the sympathy. Wataru complained about it all the time back when he was following his kid brother around.

But Satoru did seem a little more grounded and content with himself than he'd been at the start of the season. His phone buzzed to interrupt her thoughts, and his eyes lit up when he saw the screen. Honestly, those two were too cute. "You mind I take?" he asked, and Alisha shook her head.

"Not at all."

"Thanks. I ignore phone during press conference, so many missed calls." He swiped his finger across the screen as he asked, "Do you guys find something after I leave?"

"Not that I've heard." Alisha had left the group in pretty much the same place they were when they'd started. Maybe Inessa had finally remembered what she'd forgotten, but Alisha wasn't especially optimistic about their chances of figuring things out. There were too many contradictions, and even if they hit on the truth, there was no way to prove it.

That was the brilliance of the scheme. Alisha dug through her purse while Satoru took his call, eyes bright with a glee that only came from young love. "Hi, Inessa!" Just those two words seemed to drive out some of the clouds he'd been under when he'd first stepped into the elevator. "Really? Slow down, you talk too fast!"

The sight hurt Alisha's heart a little, but she shoved that down with a deep breath. Her hand gripped around the object in her purse as she closed her eyes, and for one second, she didn't see the cute, little Satoru she'd watched grow up into a figure skating titan.

That one second was enough to steel her resolve. Alisha moved, and when Satoru turned around, he found a handgun pointed at his chest.

<h1 style="text-align:center">38</h1>

F OR A MINUTE, silence passed between them. It was difficult to take his eyes off the gun, but Satoru forced them to travel up the arm and all the way to Alisha's face.

"It's Alisha," Inessa was saying through the speaker, and Satoru could have laughed at the irony. *"I was right, the water fountain was a clue! No one with their own water bottle would bother with the fountain, unless there was something wrong with it!"*

As much as Satoru appreciated the information, it felt a bit redundant at the moment. In front of him, Alisha mouthed the words, "Hang up."

"Satoru? Can you hear me?" Inessa's voice grew nervous. *"You must listen! The World Championships will be her last chance to get to you! I am sure she will try to hurt you again! You must get somewhere safe!"* There was a pause, while Satoru's brain tried to catch up with things and Alisha grew more impatient. *"Satoru? Do you believe me?"*

That phrase jolted Satoru into laughter. "I believe, Inessa..." Oh, he definitely believed Alisha capable of murder, as long as that gun was in her hand.

"Hang up," Alisha repeated, and this time there was something frightening in her eyes. She shoved the gun a little closer, and Satoru backed up into the wall. The elevator reached his floor, but Alisha hit a button to shut the door, and then sent them traveling back down the shaft to the parking garage.

"Um, this is real bad time," Satoru said into the phone, eyes drifting back to the gun and staying there. "I have to go…"

"What? But Satoru, didn't you hear? It's not just her. There are two in this scheme! She must have a partner-"

"Inessa, this is real bad time," he said again, stressing as much as he dared. Alisha cleared her throat in a way that definitely wasn't casual. *"Pomogi mne!"* he said in Russian, then hung up the phone and let it drop on the ground, just as Alisha's finger tightened around the trigger. It clattered on the floor and Satoru held his hands up in surrender. "Done, all done!"

Alisha's eyes narrowed. "What did you say?"

"I love you. Seems like time for last words." He wasn't sure if Alisha believed him, but it hardly mattered now. She picked up his phone, using her sleeve to cover up her fingertips, but still keeping the gun trained on Satoru.

He wondered if he could fight her in an elevator booth, but decided not to risk it. Instead, he said the thing at the front of his mind. "You can't let me do Quad Axel before I die?"

That got a painful snicker out of Alisha, and shook her head. "I'm sorry, Sato. Really."

"Sorry enough to put gun away?" It was a distant hope, but worth a shot.

"Look, it's just how it has to be." For what it was worth, Alisha did seem to regret it. "Nothing personal."

"Nothing personal," he repeated. Funny that he didn't cry. Facing death, not a tear in sight, just an eerie calm that threatened to choke him. "But you shoot me?"

"I don't want you dead. It's just the deal. One for one."

The pieces fell into place. "Inessa." Without her, or at least her Quadruple Salchow, Alisha stood a fair chance to win gold at Worlds, an even better chance now that Ekaterina was being blamed for it. She could even take the Olympic title in a year. Was that what Inessa meant by a partner, Alisha would kill him in exchange for someone eliminating her greatest rival? "You'd do that to her?"

"Don't look at me like that." Alisha frowned, but Satoru thought the face was more for herself than him. "I've won the World Championships before, you know. National champion, ten years running. I've only gotten better as I've gotten older. The scores I put up now, people used to think they weren't possible!" She gave him a look that was so heartbroken, Satoru almost forgot there was a deadly weapon in her hands. "How can I be better, but still losing? It's not fair to work so hard and score higher, but place lower in the rankings. How am I losing to these little girls who jump up just long enough to win Worlds and then disappear?"

Satoru wished he had an answer. He really did, but that was just the game. If Kara Beth were here, she'd grab Alisha's ear and march her into her office for a lecture, just like she had Eric. "So you kill?"

Alisha grimaced, but her hand stayed strong. "Let me go out on a high note," she said, a plea in her voice.

Though Satoru wasn't sure why she thought any of this was in his control. "I get it. Crowds, they just see fun. Just see titles we don't get." The damage they did to their bodies, the hopes and dreams of others that piled on their shoulders, all of that went unseen. The personal victories that didn't have medals attached were worthless, even when they won them for their families and their countries. "But you're still good skater. Have many titles. To not be gold now isn't worst thing."

Perhaps that was the wrong thing to say. The elevator dinged out their new destination, the parking garage, while Alisha's face plummeted even further. "That's easy to say when you're the one winning everything, Sato."

As if he'd won anything this year. "But we all have same feeling. I do, too. Lost half a season this year and went crazy, how can I do retire?" He peeked out the door as it opened, and his face fell to see no one there. Just a dark carpark. He sighed and continued. "Right now, gold medal is all we see. But later, when we don't have this life, I think gold medal won't feel so important. You'll regret if you do bad things to get it."

"Coming from anyone else on earth, that speech might be almost believable."

"Maybe I change." He bit his lip as Alisha shoved the gun in his back and marched him out. "What if someone see you?"

"That's why you're not going to make a sound, right?" Did Satoru dare press her? If he screamed and got someone's attention, would she run or shoot?

But running wasn't an option, Satoru realized. Inessa was right, this was Alisha's last chance before the season ended, and her partner had already put themselves on the line by attacking Inessa. Now that Satoru knew what she'd done, if she didn't destroy him soon, she'd be ruined.

And there was no one to hear him scream, anyway. How could a place be so deserted, with what felt like half the world converging on Slovenia? "Friends know it was you. Inessa knows. Stop and you only go to jail for injury. Maybe she forgive you and don't tell anyone if you don't shoot." He wasn't sure about that last one, they'd have to see if Inessa loved Satoru more than she mourned her Quad Sal, but Alisha wasn't moved either way.

"They don't have anything they can prove. Just speculation. No one's going to believe it's me, not when I don't have a single reason on earth to kill you. We're friends."

If that was her definition of friendship, then Satoru was starting to understand why Damien was so close to giving up on it. They took a few steps into the parking garage before Satoru felt brave enough to ask, "Person you make deal with, wants me dead..." The words stuck in his throat. "Who is it?"

Alisha didn't answer him. Maybe she couldn't, or maybe she was too busy looking for a good place to dump his body. "Alisha, why-"

"Look, can you just stop talking?" she interrupted. "This is hard enough as it is."

Satoru grit his teeth. "Sorry, yes, I should make easy for you to kill me!" The gun dug a little harsher into his shoulder blade, but he couldn't help himself. "Canadians supposed to be nice. This don't count!"

He heard Alisha chuckling behind him, but she didn't remove the gun. "Man, I'm going to miss you..."

"Liar. You miss me, you don't kill me."

"If you don't clam up right now..." She trailed off and stopped, grabbing Satoru's arm before he could retort that there was nothing she could threaten him with worse than what she already planned to do. That thought flew out of his head when Alisha stopped by the stairwell, and when he saw two young men waiting there. One with a troublesome face he'd thought he was through with, Henri Petard.

And the other...

"Dami?"

Because it was Damien, standing next to the man who'd threatened him in a grocery store, holding a carryout tray of coffee and muffins, of all things. At Satoru's betrayed tone, he ducked his head. "I am sorry."

Sorry didn't even begin to cover it.

CHEN HUAN WOULDN'T SAY she spoke English. Other people would, and she could muddle her way through a few press questions if she needed to, but there was a big difference between knowing something of a language and being comfortable with it. She secretly thought her dance partner, Song Min, was better at it, but he'd once praised her in an interview for her superior skills, so maybe he only seemed like the more fluent one.

Either way, she understood just enough of the language to want to connect with the people she met as she travelled the globe for skating, and not enough to ever feel like she was in control of the situation. The project to help catch Satoru's attempted killer only magnified that. She and Min did well enough on their own to log times in videos and fill in the names and backgrounds of the people they saw, but when it came time to share that information with the rest of the group, things fell apart. Everything had to be translated, poorly, or exchanged with such juvenile words that Huan sometimes wondered if it was worth the bother.

But with the stakes so high, it was better to try than not. Especially now that Inessa seemed to be saying that Alisha had gotten to Satoru first. The younger girl was gesturing frantically to her phone and repeating the word 'Help', but since no one had run for the door yet, Huan assumed that meant no one knew where Satoru was.

Talking wasn't her strong point, not in this group. But she was just as capable of action. "We split up," she said, dragging Min to his feet. "Tell security. Search hotel, find Satoru." The men's short program had been over for some time, so Satoru and the other skaters had probably returned to the hotel by now. The odds suggested that, and it would be the easiest place for Alisha to cross paths with him, if she were planning something. "All of us go." They were a large enough group, and could recruit more help now that they knew who the perpetrator was. Huan already had her phone out and was typing up an alert to the entire Chinese team. "Others help," she explained when Hser Nay asked about it, and the Canadian ice dancer lit up like a Christmas tree. What she said next was unknown, but Huan was pretty sure they could count on help from all Canadians currently in Slovenia. Her sister took upon the task of calling the police, and Isaac seemed to be calling in reinforcements as well.

But as Huan finished sending her message, she stopped and stared at her phone. An idea occurred to her, one so simple that she was almost embarrassed it had taken her so long to hit on it. She crossed over to Inessa and held out her phone. "Phone!" she declared, shaking the screen a little, but Inessa didn't grasp her meaning.

"I already tried calling him back," she said, and continued on to say something else that went over Huan's head. Satoru wasn't answering, that was the important thing, but not what Huan meant in the first place.

"No, phone sees!" She pantomimed for a few more seconds before Min came over.

"What are you trying to do?" His eyes lit up as she told him in Chinese, and he praised the brilliant solution. *"But can't you just do that on your phone?"*

"I'm not friends with him on any of the apps that do that." Otherwise

Huan wouldn't have bothered with the choppy English conversations. Inessa would be connected to Satoru, but that was useless if they couldn't communicate what she needed to do.

It was a paradox. Min started pulling up a translation app, which would hopefully be more accurate than it had been at any point in the past. Meanwhile, the other skaters were splitting up to canvas the hotel. Huan thought she heard Clara and Mark use the word "outside", and Isaac and Hser Nay mentioned something about the police again.

Huan cursed herself as they left, even though that plan was her idea. Everything she did was a step behind, it seemed. She should have suspected Alisha sooner, too. Especially once the attack on Inessa occurred, they should have looked at all the women singles skaters at with a skeptical eye. But Alisha had been in the perfect position to throw them off the trail if they got too close. They'd let her have that kind of power, never giving it a thought. Someone they'd looked up to for so long had to be trustworthy.

And now that Alisha had found Satoru, every second counted. The time lost as Huan searched for words could be the difference maker.

The time to be polite was over. Huan grabbed Inessa's phone out of her hands and made a few swipes with her finger. Inessa protested, but once Huan handed it back, the words all disappeared. Huan had opened her phone to a popular social media site, where Inessa was linked to Satoru.

One that tracked your friends' locations with GPS. They didn't need a translation for that.

39

————————

I T REALLY WAS SOMETHING, how life could change in the course of one season. Or one evening. Satoru could have passed good time in philosophical thought over that, if he didn't have a gun digging into his back. A part of him wondered if it was just a prop, since Alisha would have had to do some work to get her hands on a gun and smuggle it around Slovenia, but then he remembered that the woman had put a bomb in his car. She wouldn't start playing around now.

As he gaped at the darkened stairwell, a place that perfectly fit the murdering mood, he cast his mind back to Skate America and filled in the gaps in the mystery. Alisha had sat down right next to him while he was stretching, she could have switched the water bottles. He wouldn't have suspected her of a thing, and one turn of his head would be all she needed. She was in Granville the day of the car bombing as well, and as one of the people looking for Satoru's killer, could guide everyone's focus away from her with ease. And as a student, Alisha could obtain arsenic for one of her school experiments without it looking suspicious at all.

It all made sense, except for the part where Alisha was one of his oldest friends. To pretend all that was a lie was impossible. But it was

393

equally impossible to ignore that this crime was premeditated. How many hours had Alisha spent plotting his death while lying to his face?

And then, Damien, appearing here now... Wanting to know where he was going earlier, present at Europeans when Inessa was hurt, meeting with Henri, even with murder suspicion on him? He felt his knees grow weak, and almost didn't register that Henri was speaking. "You pests! You thought you could frame me, did you?"

"What are you talking about?" Alisha asked, at the same moment that Satoru said, "Don't you have restraining order?" 'Restraining order' came out a little garbled, since Satoru could hardly be bothered to focus on that hard 'r' sound when he was at gunpoint, and Henri sneered at the words.

Which was unfair, Satoru thought, given Henri's own thick accent. "You are too devious, trying to keep me away when you have girlfriends of your own! You are not worth the thoughts wasted on you!" The look on his face was murderous, or would have been, if Satoru didn't know that murder looked like a trusted friend. For his part, Damien just grit his teeth and clamped a hand on Henri's arm.

The carryout tray tipped threateningly, but Damien steadied both it and Henri. "There is no need for this. It is over now, see?" After a moment, Henri paused, then smiled.

He linked his hand with Damien's free one. "Yes, it is. We will never see that little brat again, will we?"

"Dami? Why?"

Damien wouldn't meet Satoru's eyes. "He's persuasive. It's for the best." And then he drew himself up, a snobbish air shielding his thoughts. "Why do you care? We just train in the same building, after all."

Satoru wanted to cry. This wasn't Damien. His friend could never hurt him, or anyone. Then again, he and Damien had openly brawled on the floors of the locker room, they'd said cruel things to each other over the years, and now Damien was here with two people who meant Satoru bodily harm...

And yet, for all he'd had doubts and questions, Satoru's heart still refused to accept it. Damien was no murderer. He'd hurt himself before hurting Satoru or Inessa. Satoru knew this, knew it with every logical bone in his body. He had years of evidence to inform him of Damien's true character, and he *knew,* even if all the current evidence pointed to the contrary.

Perhaps this was what Inessa meant by faith being proof, not hope? Either way, Satoru decided to act on it. Damien was not here to kill him, and that being true, his shame must be for some other reason...

"Dami, did you meet him to protect me?" Damien jolted, and Satoru felt more of that hope in the unseen. "Did he threaten? You talk with him, he leaves me alone?"

"Silly fool, you have lost!" Henri crowed, and squeezed Damien's hand all the tighter. "I will be a better fiancé than you could ever be!"

"Fiancé?" Alisha repeated, while Damien just looked up to the ceiling with a quiet, "*Nom de Dieu...*"

But the interaction was enough to reward Satoru's faith. "Henri isn't person who try kill me." He felt Alisha's eyes on him as surely as he felt her fingernails digging into his arms. It prevented him from shuffling away, to stand at an angle to let Damien see the gun.

As it was, Damien wouldn't have seen it if Alisha took the thing out and waved it around. He was too busy trying to look at anything but Satoru. "It's not for you to worry about," he muttered, and while he looked like he was trying to convince himself, Satoru felt pained all the same.

Enough that he almost forgot about Alisha. "Dami, you have stupid friend!" he blurted out, and that got Damien's attention. "Stupidest friend, worst friend! But one bad friend doesn't mean... doesn't mean take risk! Or settle!" He gestured to Henri, and the carryout tray in Damien's hands. "He bring you coffee? You hate coffee! He don't care about feelings! Tell police he's here!"

"Satoru, we don't have time for this," Alisha said in his ear, voice sick and sweet. "You can chat later, you and I have places to be." The hint of a threat was still music to Satoru's ears. Because if she was still trying to hide the gun now, then it was his faith rewarded. Damien wasn't who she was working with, nor Henri.

And he could use that. "Call police," Satoru repeated again, trying to signal with his eyes that he was in trouble.

Henri looked incensed. "What? You brat, why must you always ruin our lives?!"

"Enough, Henri," Damien growled. "He is not worth it. It is you I talk to now, yes?"

That sated Henri for a minute, much as Damien looked like he wanted to be anywhere else. Still, the Belgian stalker turned up his nose at Satoru. "Leave us alone, I'm warning you!"

Or what? Satoru wanted to ask. So many people wanted him dead, at this rate he'd have to set up a queue to handle the overflow. But he kept his eyes locked on Damien, ignoring the harsh steel biting his flesh. "You should call police, Dami. Right now ."

"All right, that's enough interfering with the lovebirds, Sato." Alisha nudged him, trying to get him moving again. "Enjoy your coffee date, you two." The gun was slipping down a little. Maybe Alisha was trying to look less suspicious?

If her attention was divided, that worked for Satoru. And she couldn't shoot him now, not with witnesses. Even if they left the area, Damien and Henri would tell the police they'd seen her with Satoru right before he died! They'd have to look deeper into her, and between that and Inessa's testimony, it would be impossible not to connect all the clues. It was too big a risk for Alisha to take. All Satoru had to do was stay near Damien until he figured it out and called the police, or Alisha gave up and put the dumb gun away for good.

As it was, they were close to that point. "What are you two doing down here, anyway?" Damien asked with narrowed eyes. "It's dangerous for you to isolate yourself."

Maybe the three of them could overpower her? "We look for Inessa, can you call her for us?" Damien raised his eyebrows, hopefully in realization, and Satoru dared to take a step forward, because what could Alisha do, but go along with this?

... Unless she decided that she'd already gone so far, might as well go all the way. The gun that had been sticking into Satoru's back flipped up above his shoulder to point at Damien.

He was shot before the phone even made it to his ear.

FOR SATORU, the sound disrupted his ability to process anything else. Even though the bullet was aimed away from him, the force caused him to jerk to the side, head pounding as his eardrum tried to recover. The sound itself was unlike anything Satoru had heard in a movie, and far, far louder. He could see Alisha had been startled by it, too. But Satoru was looking at her from the ground now, trying to find his balance again.

He wasn't sure if he'd screamed. If he had, he didn't know if he'd have heard himself. But Satoru wanted to, seeing Damien on the ground, blood coating his shirt and the cement of the car park. His phone had bounced a few feet away, along with the muffins and coffee cups.

Satoru's hands were shaking, but so was Alisha. Maybe she hadn't been mentally prepared to kill someone. She'd certainly botched his own murder attempts well enough to suggest a lack of commitment. But even if it affected her, she'd still pulled the trigger.

There was no reason to think she wouldn't do it again. Satoru grit his teeth and tried to think through his blossoming headache, while Alisha turned to Henri with the still smoking gun in her hands. But he had already started running, and her second shot only struck the leg. All the same, it slowed Henri down. The third shot stopped him completely.

Satoru inched away, using the wall to steady himself as he got to his feet. Alisha was distracted, talking into her phone. Closing his eyes, covering his hand over the one ear and trying to focus, Satoru listened... "It's me. We've got a problem here!" It sounded a little garbled, like Alisha was underwater or buried underneath fifteen comforters, but the sound improved with each word. "Well, Saint-Michel showed up, I had to shoot him. That stalker of his saw! ... No, I can't, that's the problem! There's more of them than me! Just get down here!"

On the ground, Damien moaned. Satoru saw it more than heard, but it rattled him just the same. Even so, he saw Damien's arm, the one that wasn't curled with the rest of him in the fetal position, reaching towards Alisha.

Their eyes met, and Satoru knew what Damien was planning. "No," he mouthed, but Damien's face was determined. She wasn't focused on them, hands and attention divided by her phone conversation. And once Damien grabbed her leg like a zombie, she wouldn't have any eyes for Satoru. If Satoru was going to have a chance at escape, it would have to be now.

But if he ran, who would help Damien? Despite the silent objections, Damien made the choice for them. He clamped his hand around Alisha's ankle and dug his fingernails into her skin. Satoru, much as he hated himself for it, decided not to waste the opportunity. Feeling some of his balance recovered, Satoru pushed to his feet and made a break for it. "No! Get back here!" Alisha shrieked, as if Satoru was ever going to listen. His feet pounded against the pavement, chest heaving, but the exit was in sight. If he could just get back to people, he'd be rescued...!

He didn't stop for the next gunshot. It missed and struck a parked car. Satoru heard the wrenching metal in great detail now, though one side of his head still ached and begged for silence. He forced his feet to keep running, and was spurred on by a little bit of hope. If she'd aimed at him, then she hadn't shot Damien, and he heard Alisha's heels on the ground now. Damien might be all right, if Satoru could get to help soon. All he had to do was make it up the stairwell, and he'd be back in the hotel.

But his eyes stung, as Alisha's voice echoed behind him. "The northeast entrance! If he tells someone, it's all over! Are you here yet?" Satoru turned into the stairwell, putting at least some wall between him and Alisha's gun. Just the steps now, he was almost there!

Alisha wasn't far behind. He heard her follow with all her loud chaos, but Satoru had already rounded the corner and bound up the second flight of stairs, his hand was inches away from the door to the hall. She couldn't shoot him from this angle, he'd be in the hallway by the time she turned the corner, within eyes and ears of the lobby! He was free!

And then the door opened and nearly bashed him in the face. Satoru jumped to the side at the last minute, then latched onto the newcomer with relief.

"Big Brother!" he almost cried, then tried to push him back out the door. "Move! Move, she's got a gun!" Wataru moved, but not in the way Satoru expected.

He grabbed Satoru's shoulders and then pushed him down the stairs.

40

———————

WHEN SATORU'S head finally stopped tumbling backwards, his first action was to take stock of his limbs and make sure they were still bending the way they were meant to. Getting back on his feet and running should have been his first priority, but once again, Alisha's gun was staring him in the face.

And his brother was striding down the steps with the tone of one annoyed. "What happened here? How many times are you going to keep screwing this up?"

"Hey, there's no way I could have planned for Henri and Damien to show up! I'm already up to three bodies now! If one of them gets away, it's your skin, too!"

"I'm not even supposed to be here," Wataru hissed at her, then gave an exasperated sigh. "Fine. Where are the other two?"

"Big Brother," Satoru tried, but Wataru was ignoring him, and Alisha didn't care what he had to say, either.

"Damien's just past the doorway, he might still be alive."

"He most definitely is." All of them turned to see Damien leaning against the stairwell, clutching his arms close around him and leaning against the cement wall. The brown leather jacket and the angle obscured much, but Satoru could see a dark pooling around Damien's midsection, a harsh contrast to his white dress shirt. He wasn't sure if the bloodstain or Damien's winces of pain brought him the closer to fainting.

But Damien wasn't dead. Yet.

That should have spurned Satoru on, should have given him hope and courage to keep fighting, but he found himself unable to move or speak. The sight of Damien's blood oozing out of his body stole Satoru's along with it, and he could only stare as those around him decided his fate.

Alisha had a gun, but Damien had retrieved his phone. "Stop this nonsense, you two. I have already alerted the police."

"Your phone's not on," Wataru pointed out, and unfortunately, he was right. Damien's phone was missing its back, and the screen was shattered, emitting no light. A bluff.

Nonetheless, his face was fierce. "Get away from him, or I will tell everyone."

"Even if you could, no one would believe you," Wataru dismissed. A short struggle, and Damien was soon on the ground next to Satoru. It gave Satoru a better view than he wanted of that bloodstain.

It had spread so far... But what could he do about it now?

"If you'd have gotten it right the first time, we wouldn't even be in this mess," Wataru continued to snap at Alisha. "You're the one who keeps hesitating."

"Oh, like Levi isn't still up and around."

Wataru ignored that. He stepped over his victims' sprawled legs and made for the exit. "Let's get this over with. People already suspect Petard and Saint-Michel anyway, we can pass it off as a murder-suicide. Take care of this one, and then we'll move Saint-Michel over to-"

"Take care of me?" Satoru croaked in Japanese, finally able to force sound through his throat. "Get it over with?" Not that any of this was a surprise, after all the bombshells that had been dropped on him, but still... "Why are you doing this? Big Brother?"

Countless thoughts passed through his mind as he waited for an answer. All their past conversations, where he thought they'd been making progress. Did they mean nothing to Wataru? Was it all a ploy to make himself look more innocent?

"Please," he begged. "Why?" Didn't Satoru deserve that much? And maybe Wataru agreed, because he turned around. He walked back to Satoru and the look on his face was not one of cold indifference, or of a furious killer.

It was one of a loving older brother. "Don't be scared," he said, and each sweet word broke Satoru's heart. "I promised things would get better. It's over now."

"But..." None of this made any sense! "I don't want to die!"

"Don't fight it, Satoru." Wataru had the gall to smile at him while saying such things? "You've won everything, conquered all the titles. Take a rest and let the rest of us have our lives back."

"Wait, I-" But Wataru was already leaving. Satoru yelled after him until the sight of Alisha and her gun shut him up. "Don't," he pleaded, but she just looked away.

"I made a deal. He's already held up his end. Mostly." Yes, Inessa. Not dead but certainly out of commission. Ruining two people's lives, now three with Henri and four with Damien, and for *what?* Satoru still didn't understand.

As Wataru left, Damien reached out with whatever feeble strength he still had. He kicked Wataru's leg, for all the good it did. "You..." he growled, and continued in a line of French that Satoru couldn't follow, until Wataru kicked him back. Damien crumpled again, and Satoru gulped to see that dark stain forcing the white shirt to cling to Damien's skin like laminated plastic, hugging each curve of skin with a black grip.

Wataru just turned his back and walked away.

And that was the most infuriating part of all. More than anything he'd said or reasons he and Alisha could give, it burned Satoru from the cells outward that his brother could walk away as if none of this was worth his time. He seethed and would have spit out a vomitus rage at Wataru's back, if Damien hadn't started shifting beside him.

"What are you doing? Stop," Alisha commanded, though without urgency. It wasn't as if Damien was in a position to do anything to her. And Damien didn't listen, just kept pulling himself along with painful grunts, one arm significantly more useless than the other, and spreading his blood everywhere. Satoru noticed a hole in the leather jacket, the same arm that seemed to be in pain, and blood leaking from there, too.

Damien needed a hospital now. "Alisha, don't. He won't tell anyone, promise, just let him see doctor, please..."

"Shut up," Damien wheezed, and now Satoru could see what his purpose was. Damien shifted into position, trying to shield Satoru from Alisha's next shot. It was the most useless gesture, since she was going to shoot them both in the end. But Satoru's eyes filled with tears at the sight of Damien facing Alisha with defiance in his eyes, blocking and defending Satoru until the very end.

Weren't they still fighting? "Dami..." He didn't know what to say, let alone what to do. They were both trapped, Henri was already dead, and Satoru's entire head felt like it was being crushed in a vice. He closed his eyes and let the back of Damien's jacket hide his tears, while he listened to his friend's ragged breathing, the slap of Wataru's shoes as he descended the stairs, the shift of Alisha's weight as she prepared to fire her gun for the final time. Given the choice, Satoru thought it would have been better to die alone on that rink in California. "I'm sorry..."

The door above them flung open with the clamor of a thousand angels, and the voice was just as sweet. "*Yesh!* I found them!"

<h1 style="text-align:center">41</h1>

CHAOS WAS QUICKLY BECOMING the routine of the day. Satoru had all but given up hope the universe would take his side in something and send him a favor, so when he looked up and saw Inessa Levi at the top of the stairs, wheelchair flanked by the Chinese dance team of Chen Huan and Song Min, he couldn't muster an emotional reaction beyond awe. He thought he heard the additional voices of the Bertinelli triplets and Hser Nay Wah somewhere, too.

Heroes in the movies always showed up at the last second, with the wind in their hair and all the spotlights trained on them. Riding a white horse to rescue the damsel in distress, full of action and perfect confidence. Inessa rode a wheelchair rather than a horse, and the light from the hall wasn't quite a spotlight, but otherwise, she made an entrance worthy of any Hollywood movie.

Especially once her eyes lighted on Alisha, and she wrenched her wheels forward to barrel down the stairs. Alisha only had a moment to debate whether to run or shoot before Inessa bounced down the stairs like a derailed train. She didn't stick the landing, but she did bash Alisha in the thigh as she went down, and the gun fell from her hands to slide across the floor .

"Inessa!" Satoru could only stare, stupefied, then rushed forward to try and pick his girlfriend up. Three teams of ice dancers bounded down the stairs afterwards to assist, some of them going over to grab Alisha or aid Damien. It was over, they'd overpowered the danger with sheer numbers, but Satoru couldn't bear to look. "Your knee... that was crazy, is it hurt?"

"Trust me, my knee is so unimportant right now," Inessa said, but with duress. She must have bumped her leg in all the action. He could only hope it didn't delay her recovery even further, and helped her back into her wheelchair with the help of Isaac and Mark Bertinelli.

A thought seized him amidst all the chatter and commotion, a tiny sound that Satoru may have only imagined, rather than heard. But he saw in his mind the perfect image of Wataru walking away, descending the stairs and calmly escaping into the carpark, and he felt something shift inside him. A primal urge that went beyond thought or reason, and he wouldn't have resisted it, even if he had the thought to.

Satoru lunged forward, picked up the gun, and charged down the stairs.

It didn't take long to find Wataru. He hadn't had that long to make his escape, nor had that been the goal. His brother was walking towards Henri, still calm, sliding gloves over his hands as if he was doing a simple household chore. Perhaps he planned to move the body, or tamper with evidence to make up for Alisha's mistakes, but none of this mattered to Satoru anymore. He lunged at his brother from behind and tackled him to the ground.

It gave him too much satisfaction to hear the wind being knocked out of Wataru, let alone the feeling of their bodies smashing into the pavement. Having the element of surprise, there wasn't much struggle before Satoru found himself perched over Wataru, gun pointed to his older brother's chest. "Why?"

It was the only question worth answering, and needed no context. He thought of the nightmarish hospitalization at Skate America, the bribing of a friend in order to hurt him, and the weeks and weeks of suspicion and distrust that followed everyone he knew. He thought of the medical diagnosis, the weeks of arduous physical recovery, the permanent changes to his vision and jacked up kidneys. Inessa sitting by while others were skating, of Damien bleeding and probably dying, all because he had a psychopath instead of a big brother. *"Why?!"*

Wataru didn't look scared, or anything near repentant. "Come on, Satoru," he said, voice as condescending as ever. "You've gotten everything you've ever wanted. Can't you let me have my turn?"

Satoru wasn't sure if it was the shaking, or the tears warping his vision, but the gun in his hands was bouncing all over the place. "I don't understand."

"I know." That look of disgust, Satoru knew that look. He knew that tone well, too. "You never get it. You think you deserve to have the world revolving around you. It never occurs to you that other people have to sacrifice for that to happen!" It did. Satoru thought about that all the time, tried to make those sacrifices worth it. But it seemed it wasn't enough for Wataru.

It never was. "It's not just the skating, it's everything about you. I always take a backseat to my little brother, and it's not going to change unless we do something about it! You hate it, too, don't you? Always pushing yourself, never able to be happy?"

What was he talking about? "I am happy," Satoru said, and hated that it came out as a whisper. Maybe there was once some truth to what Wataru said, but not anymore. He'd gained a new perspective on his life, it wasn't all desperation. Even losing wasn't something to fear. "You said you were sorry. That it was going to get better! You said you were proud..." Didn't Wataru say he liked Satoru? Weren't they family? Brothers didn't kill each other, they worked things out!

But Wataru only gave him a pitying smile. "I am proud of you." Satoru choked to hear those words, but Wataru kept on, "You've overcome everything, had the career most people only dream of."

"Then why?" Satoru insisted, still not understanding, or not wanting to. Behind him, he heard clamoring voices, possibly police sirens. Inessa's voice cut through, calling his name. But he couldn't focus long enough to determine if she wanted him to put the gun down, or shoot.

That thought sent ice down his spine. Wataru had stood in a place similar to this one, with a bludgeon in hand, and beat Inessa so hard she nearly died. His big brother had done that. "What's wrong with you?" he sobbed out, barely holding himself together. "Why?"

"We're brothers. Brothers share." Wataru was so cool for staring down the barrel of a handgun. "I've given up so much for you. Why couldn't you give up something for me?"

42

———————

S T. Bartholomew's Church was one of the oldest buildings in Slovenia. Made from brick and reinforced concrete, it had survived since the 1300s, perhaps longer, and made the Slovenian Cultural Heritage list. It was also right off the bus line, which made it a convenient place for Satoru to flee to.

There was no shortage of historic churches in Ljubljana, Slovenia, or the neighboring cities. It was one thing Satoru loved about that corner of the world, the way history put down its roots and dug in, determined to survive the changing seasons. And like most of Satoru's favorite old buildings, damaged by fire and restored multiple times.

"They could have just built a new church," Satoru said to himself as he approached. He didn't go inside, suddenly feeling unworthy to enter a religious building. He wasn't sure why, since he was still on the fence about the existence of God in the Judaeo-Christian-Islamic sense, but less agnostic towards Shinto's *kami*, and the gods inside all things. If there was a god of old historic buildings, Satoru was sure it lived in this church.

And it didn't want to be walked on by one whose own brother couldn't love him. "I mean, what are they asking of you with that?

408

You're never going to be a shiny new building. And you're never going to get back to what you used to be. Whatever they do, you'll always be something less than perfect. Your prime was 700 years ago." He took a seat on the grass outside and leaned against the tree near the entrance. It was evening now, and Satoru couldn't be sure if the church was even open for visitors. He'd lost track of time between the ending of the men's short program and facing the possible end of his life.

Hopefully, no one called the cops on the depressed athlete parking himself on the lawn. "Would it be better," he wondered aloud, and traced his finger along the tree roots pushing into the ground, "To put you out of your misery and let something new have a chance?" After all, did God care how long these churches stood, when He could build and destroy them in an instant? If Inessa and Damien had taught him anything, it was that the heart was more important. Churches were just a symbol, but personal devotion took place inside. If the old facility crumbled, why not make a new, cleaner, more pristine offering to the high being they loved?

Everything came to an end eventually, right? "You've stood for hundreds of years. The new buildings keep coming, each one more impressive than the last. But you're wearing down and the colors fade. I can see your flaws."

Satoru saw Wataru's face in front of him and shut his eyes. He saw Wataru walking away without a shred of concern and opened them again. "There's a chip right there, but I guess it's just one flaw among hundreds at this point. Too late to fix it. The whole world knows it's there." What were the past six months about if Wataru was planning to kill him anyway? Why go to the Gand Prix with him or meet up in Beijing when he was just waiting for Alisha to get rid of the obvious nuisance? "I guess you'll just keep getting flaws, I mean, you're old. A hundred years, that's going to do some damage. No one really remembers how spectacular you used to be." Even old paintings and photos weren't the same as seeing it in person. People could tell Satoru that this homey and homely building used to be the epitome of achievement and splendor, and all he could do was take their word for it.

"But we still keep coming, don't we?" He leaned his head back and sighed. The whole point of coming here was to avoid thoughts of Wataru, but Satoru kept replaying childhood memories against his will. He remembered one of the few times they'd gone ice skating together, when Wataru could still take pleasure in being the faster one, and forced Satoru to chase him around the rink. Their parents had a home video of that saved somewhere. It had frustrated Satoru to come in second place on all the races, but his face showed elation at playing with his big brother.

Wataru had looked happy, too. Not like that proved anything. "Have you made peace with yourself over that? Does it ever get better?" That was the definition of pathetic, Satoru thought in the back of his mind, to be asking such questions of a hunk of bricks. What did it know about skating? "I guess I always thought I'd someday hit a point and know I could feel good about myself. Something that couldn't be taken away, and I'd never have to doubt again, because I did that one thing..." Never doubt, and never fear that one day someone might spike his water bottle, or that his brother would decide the *entire world* wasn't big enough for the two of them. But he thought if he reached that point, his eventual deterioration wouldn't hurt so much. "I just wanted to feel satisfied."

He never wanted to hurt anyone, least of all his brother. And now, Wataru was going to jail. Inessa might never see her Olympic dreams come true. Henri was dead, and Damien might not be far behind. All because Satoru couldn't be satisfied with where he was, because he always wanted to jump higher, skate better, learn and do more. Wataru had been right when he said everything was skating, and Satoru agreed with him that simply quitting the sport would have never solved the problem between them. If not skating, he'd have funneled all that drive and energy into something else, because the pursuit was all the same in Satoru's mind. Whatever Satoru did, it would have pushed his brother into corners.

Satoru was too much, and still, not enough. "But I guess, if people were satisfied, they wouldn't build you." What was he supposed to have done? Failed less? Not tried at all? Taken himself out of the picture, because how else could he stop himself from trying to grow, how could he see the skyline and not build higher floors, look out over the horizon and expand outward, build awnings to shelter everyone else in pursuit of the same goals?

If this was his life, then fixing the problem had only one solution... *"Je t'ai trouvé!* You talk to buildings now?" Damien's voice took Satoru by surprise, and he whipped his head around at the sound.

"Dami?" The man in question typed a few quick words on his phone before shoving it in his pocket and joining him on the ground. Satoru suspected he was notifying one of the many parties who surely wanted to speak with him, but was too focused on Damien's actual presence to comment on it. His shirt was still dark with blood, and it drew Satoru's eyes like a black hole. He tried not to throw up. "You didn't go to hospital?"

"For this?" Damien laughed. "The bullet only grazed me. Very painful, but not worth so much fuss in the end." He gestured to his arm, the leather jacket gone and left shirt sleeve cut off to reveal the winding of gauze and bandages. "They did not even give me stitches! Or painkillers, I have many complaints about that. My body is covered in skating bruises and pulled muscles, but this tiny surface wound? I cannot bear it."

"You were bleeding." All over Satoru's shoes. Or was that just mud? Who could tell, but the crime scene investigators took them, anyway. They should have taken Damien's shirt, wasn't that important too? Or did they already have enough evidence to condemn Wataru and Alisha?

"I promise, a few patches and then everyone wanted me out of their hair. If it had gone deep enough to hit the artery, well..." He shrugged, and Satoru blanched. "It did not. We have been very lucky today."

Damien's idea of luck needed some revising. "But..." Satoru pointed to Damien's midsection with a shaking hand, to the blood that stained and caked his friend's body like an accusation. "That...

Dami, there's so much blood. You're not okay, we need to go to hospital...”

“What are you talking about?” Was Damien in shock? Satoru had heard about things like this, victims of great injury being so affected by trauma that their brains saved them by imposing denial.

That said, Damien wasn't the one growing hysterical. “That! Blood! Dami, please, we have to go!”

“This?” Damien pointed at his shirt, flabbergasted. Since he didn't make a move, Satoru grabbed his hand and tried to haul Damien to his feet. “What blood? I was barely nicked on the arm, there's nothing there...” He trailed off, then suddenly gripped Satoru's arms with equal force. “Ah, *je comprends*! Calm down, Satoru, that is not blood you see.”

“But...!” How could Damien stand to laugh? Yet here he was, chuckling while bleeding to death, his white shirt blossoming with blood like a three-year-olds attempt at drawing the Japanese flag. “But, there, you...”

“It is coffee, Satoru! Just a coffee stain! I promise, I am not injured!”

“Coffee?” Satoru allowed himself to be pulled back to the grass, suddenly weak. He stared at Damien's midsection, puzzling this out before his brain decided it was just done with the whole day and would like to pass out now, thank you very much.

“Just coffee. Brown and red look similar to you, yes?” He shifted position so that his face came into view, and blocked the macabre sight. “Keep breathing, all is well. I merely spilt my coffee on myself in all the action. But I appreciate your concern,” he said with a twinkle in his eyes, and that's when Satoru finally caved.

“Just coffee,” he repeated, deflating like a balloon. And then, the feelings he'd been trying to suppress for hours boiled over. He launched himself at Damien and gripped his friend's coffee-soaked shirt. “I thought you're dying!” he bawled, aware that this level of waterworks was over the top, even for him. Snot was coming out of his nose, and Satoru didn't care. “Told you leave! Why you stay? You could have...!” He wanted to scream. What if Inessa and the others hadn't arrived when they did, what if Alisha had been more prepared and a better shot? What if Wataru had decided he wasn't satisfied with leaving the rest to Alisha, what if timing and angles hadn't all worked in the way they had?

"We are both alive and well, there is no need to cry." Except Damien was wrong, because so much could have happened differently. Henri was proof of that. One small change, and Satoru could have been having this conversation with a corpse.

"You still mad at me, shouldn't be there, could have been dead, and I..." He pictured Damien, bleeding, kicked and frightened, still trying to protect him. "Mad at me, and..."

"Goodness, stop talking before you hurt yourself." Damien patted his back with gentle, amused care. "Fighting or no, there is no world in which I would not take a bullet for you." With that, Satoru broke a little more, but he accepted Damien's command to shut up, and simply cried for a few more seconds.

When he felt composed enough to uncurl his fingers, he sat back and wiped furiously at his eyes, while Damien continued encouraging pats on his shoulder. "What about you, my bruised little friend? Is this bandage a sign of something serious?" It took Satoru a minute to realize Damien was pointing to his forearm.

He honestly couldn't remember when they'd put that there. "No." He also couldn't remember the word for 'scrape', and gave up. "It's fine."

"I'm glad. We were all very frightened for you." On his behalf? Or because of him? Satoru wasn't sure. His brain couldn't handle English nuance on top of crying and breathing and what felt like heart palpitations.

"I'm sorry."

"Why aren't you with your family? They are most anxious to see you are okay."

Satoru snapped his head around, a rage breaking free of the chains he'd tried to bind it with. "Family just try to kill me!"

The words took Damien aback. "Surely you don't think they were all in on it?"

Now that it was asked, Satoru had to say he didn't. Then again, what did he know? In some ways, it seemed Damien knew more than he did. "No. But don't think brother either. Still don't. Said he liked me, don't know what I did…"

"If you defend him now, I will puke," Damien said. "Goodness, but you are the most frustrating friend!" Satoru winced, but Damien wasn't done. He picked up a small leaf from the ground and twirled it between his thumb and forefinger. "And yet… is this what it is, to love without conditions?" He looked pensive, then tossed the leaf away. "Go to your family. They need you."

"I make trouble," he said, knowing that was true, at least. His parents endured so much grief due to their sons fighting. He didn't believe they agreed with any of Wataru's actions, but their oldest son was getting dragged to jail and it was the problem child's fault. "Family don't want to see me."

"Have you asked them? Because I have." Damien frowned at him. "I can't claim to understand, but it is possible that they are hurting just as much as you." And more guilt. Great. As happy as he was to find Damien alive, Satoru wished he could go back ten minutes to where only old buildings judged him.

With great effort, he got his eyelashes moving at a pace just under a hummingbird's beating wings in order to control the flood. "Then they better without cheer me up. Shouldn't give extra trouble."

"Don't you think it's rather the reverse?" The only word that had any meaning to Satoru was 'reverse', the rest was just a jumble of particle, possibility, vague verb usage and a negative that probably didn't even need to be there. But when he applied the word 'reverse' to his previous sentence, his frustration with Damien's English completely vanished. So did the air in his lungs, and no amount of blinking would bring it back.

Of course. He thought he was being all noble, hiding alone so as not to drag the rest of them down. Never did his self-centered soul consider that his family or friends might need him to cheer *them* up. Satoru tried to restart that whole regular breathing thing, but his throat only gave a shallow wheeze in response. The bricks in the church wall all blurred together, swimming in a mess of gray and dim light from the street.

Damien sighed and scooted a little closer. "Tell me the thoughts swimming around in your head, little duck."

Swimming was the wrong verb. Satoru's brain, once whirring like a machine at speeds too fast to control, now clogged up and ground its gears trying to move forward. "I... don't know how to explain."

"That's okay. I'm very good at listening. Words just help the process along."

Satoru's laugh sounded something like a sob. "Everything is awful!"

"All this, I know. Tell me something I don't."

"I think..." He forced his eyes to focus on the church that was barely perceptible through all his tears. What was he going to do, never talk about this? Keep skating like he hadn't dropped a bomb in everybody's life, like his family wasn't falling apart, like his girlfriend might never compete again, like he hadn't been responsible for the death of some man whose only crime was to aggressively follow his favorite skater around?

"I think that without skating, I'm not so good to know." Was that his voice? When did his vocal cords get replaced with downy feathers? "Like, nothing else to... be important." Damien didn't jump in to deny it, and Satoru wasn't sure if that was something to worry about or if he was just relieved to not be interrupted. "I feel like I'm hiding bad secret. When skating stops, they'll see. Maybe brother sees all along." He poked a little at his shoes. They weren't the ones he'd put on, those had been taken into evidence. He wasn't sure where these had come from. "Thought I was wrong, maybe I learn to change, but..." Why on earth would someone take such great pains to restore the building and not repaint or bleach the stones? This dirty gray was so depressing. He missed the bright, happy church back in Granville.

"You cannot base your worth on the actions of one deranged monster." One? Did Damien mean Wataru, or Alisha? His old coach, or the internet, himself?

His worth wasn't looking so good, no matter what angle you came from. "I'm afraid everyone will see me like I see me."

The quiet descended like flakes of snow on a winter morning, to cling and accumulate on the small church lawn despite the spring air. A chill spread through Satoru's bones as the seconds dragged on. He tried not to shiver, but he couldn't shake the new weight off, and he felt the metaphorical snowdrift building barriers between himself and Damien, flake by flake, fault by fault. He shouldn't have said these things out loud.

When he finally dared to look up, Damien was smiling with watery eyes that had somehow escaped winter's frost. "That's such an odd thing to say. Since I have spent years praying that you will see yourself like I see you."

Satoru felt his sternum crack. All this freezing and melting wasn't good for its integrity. "What do you mean?"

"I mean, colors aren't the only thing you've gone blind to, little duck." Despite the insult, Damien was smiling. "You have grown too used to the muddy pond. I think you see love the way I see food." Satoru was having trouble keeping up with the flow of Damien's words, but latched on to the last sentence.

"Food?"

"Yes. Your brain tells you that you don't want it. It will make you ill, you don't deserve it, all manner of things," Damien explained. "And so you don't see that you are starving. You need someone to shove affection in your face, and learn to trust them more than your own head."

Satoru frowned. "I don't understand... I think is different."

"Is it? You know, my own mother doesn't feed me like you do. She sees me shrinking in front of her and pretends nothing is wrong." Damien braced himself to say more, as if giving up information might get him dragged into an interrogation booth somewhere, while Satoru tried and failed to come up with an appropriate response. Damien *never* talked about his family. "My father is the type to yell at the problem. They are both unpleasant people. The type to make one lose their appetite." He deliberately looked away from Satoru. "Still, they are family. They care in their own way. But they do not cook me food and mend my clothes and nag me to take care of myself. I came to Ohio for spin lessons and instead got a strange little boy to be my mother."

"You make too big a deal," Satoru tried to say, but Damien cut him off.

"No, Satoru. It is the biggest deal. To fight with the only person to ever..." he trailed off and sighed. "You call yourself a duck and keep asking why you are so ugly, when the swans are begging you to see your reflection and know your home is with them." The metaphor was a little much for Satoru to wrap his head around, given all the emotional reactions he was trying not to have, and Damien seemed to sense it. He tapped Satoru's glasses and continued, "Someday you will realize that the only thing wrong with you is your own perception. Until then, I will force affection on you like you force food on me. It is the only way to repay you."

"There's nothing for pay-"

"There is," Damien insisted, suddenly sharp. The smile dropped off his face and he faced Satoru with the same determination as he faced his Quad Loop. "I don't show gratitude well. But if I had not met you, I would not be here now. That is the truth."

Satoru paused, wondering if he was understanding this correctly. Hoping he wasn't. "At World Championships?"

"No."

Satoru had known Damien his whole life, and hadn't known anything. To be honest, he'd kind of hated Damien when he first showed up, still insecure about moving in with Kara Beth. For all he knew, he'd made a bad situation worse. All these nice words, but Satoru couldn't think that he'd done anything worthy of thanks. "I don't..."

"It's ironic, isn't it?" Damien said, interrupting Satoru's directionless pause. "Wataru has a brother he does not want, while I want a brother I cannot have." He twisted his lips into a rueful smirk. "Pity this mess could not have been solved with a simple exchange."

And despite everything, a chuckle forced its way out of Satoru's clogged throat. "You're too nice."

"I have been called many things, none of them nice." Damien stretched a little, then grew serious again. "You are more important than I can ever say, for all my metaphors. Do you understand?"

Satoru nodded, even though he didn't, really. "Call me duck because friends, right?"

"It sounds so banal like that." Damien's smile had a teasing lilt to it. "But it is well. If you need constant reminders of your worth, I am happy to provide them. It is worth it for the moments my sincerity gets through, and I see my friend's face lit like downtown Paris."

Satoru gulped. An impressive feat, since his entire chest cavity had become glass shards that traveled up and embedded themselves in his eyeballs.

"And then, sometimes I overdo it and see his face become Niagara Falls."

That did it. "I run out of tears! Jerk!" He punched Damien in the arm, careful to make sure it was the non-bandaged one. "Always make me cry!" But they were laughing again. It felt like a betrayal, to laugh in the middle of something so horrible. Something so good felt like it needed to come with a price.

As if on cue, Damien paused in his snickering and looked off to the horizon. "Ah. It is time to return." Satoru followed his gaze, and blanched to see a taxi some hundred feet down the road, his sister and parents trepidatiously climbing out of it.

"No, I..." But even as Satoru scrambled, he knew there was nowhere to hide. Not unless he planned to barricade himself in the church and try to claim sanctuary.

Damien followed Satoru as he got to his feet and put a hand on his arm. "Enough. For years, you have believed yourself the ugly duckling. It is time to let that go."

"What you talk about?" Satoru winced, when Izumi caught sight of him and started running over. "Isn't that awful story? No one nice to duck because ugly, until they find he's actually pretty swan, then nice?" Or a world-renowned ice skater, with a brother who felt threatened by his feathers...

Damien made a face of disgust. "How do you get the story so wrong? It is not about the other ducks! Who cares about them?" He poked Satoru on the forehead, as if drilling the point in. "It is about that little swan realizing he is exactly what he was intended to be! Realizing he is looking for acceptance in the wrong place!" Damien gave Satoru's forehead one last tap, then grabbed his shoulders and turned him around to face Izumi. "You can cry that the ducks don't love you, or you can go home to the swans! Enough of this hiding!" And he gave Satoru a light shove forward.

He was forced to face his sister, and her face broke his heart. "Big bro," she said, just short of a sob, and Satoru wanted to dig a hole and die. All of Damien's pretty words, thoughts that he wanted to dare to put hope in, rattled against the storm of emotions like a poorly constructed skyscraper. A building that hadn't taken time to lay the foundations. It couldn't stand against the force of reality, that Satoru's precious little sister was hurt because he wasn't good enough!

Satoru looked over his shoulder, just a fraction of a turn, to see Damien backing away. Making space. Damien, who'd been ready to take a bullet for him, and acted more like a brother than the one Satoru was born with.

"Big bro, please!" Izumi's voice couldn't be ignored. Satoru turned back, but wasn't sure what to say.

"Izumi... I'm sorr-"

"I'm not like Wataru." His sister clenched her fists, trying not to cry, and failing. "I'm not! I've never been jealous, I wouldn't do... any of that, so, please..." She was trying to hold herself together with so much effort that spasms rocked her small frame. "Please, come back..."

Did he have this backwards, too? "Hey, don't cry. I'm not..." He trailed off as his parents arrived, stopping just beside Izumi. "Mom... Dad..."

Maybe the foundation was as strong as ever, just the walls that needed a little restoration. Maybe he was seeing blood in place of a coffee stain. "I'm sorry. I didn't mean for all this to happen." Because he was sorry, whether or not he had cause to be. No one ever meant to put heartbreak on their parent's faces. "How's... uh, is Wataru okay? Do we need to get him a lawyer, or something?" Call the consulate? When this went to trial, his parents would need to defend both of their kids.

He didn't envy their position. "We're doing what we can for him," his father said, after sharing a look with his mother. Neither of them seemed to know what to say.

"You're the one we're worried about right now." His mother came over and inspected the scrape on his arm. "Are you hurt?"

"No, I'm fine..." He wasn't, but that was beside the point. "We were lucky."

"Lucky..." His mother pursed her lips and turned away. "You know, I'm getting a little sick of this family's luck."

Satoru couldn't help himself. "Yeah, me, too." He reached up to take her hand, then took Izumi's as well. Almost unconsciously, his father shifted in and closed the circle. Satoru smiled at the sight. "But at least we are still a family, right?"

Even if the world could see its flaws, some structures were worth preserving.

43

———————

THE WORLD DIDN'T STOP SPINNING on account of Satoru's personal problems. Much as Wataru and Alisha made an impact, the World Championships were still going on, and even a murder couldn't shut them down.

But that wasn't to say the event went without notice. With Alisha taken into custody and Ekaterina so far behind after her disaster of a short program, the women's division felt empty. Some skaters could take advantage of the opportunity to rise in the placements, but Satoru knew the victories would always be bittersweet, and he told Inessa as much while they watched the competition.

"Life is not perfect," she said diplomatically. "We can only do our best." And clutching her collection of flags, she cheered on each skater, including Ekaterina.

The Russian champion did well, considering all she'd had to deal with in the past month. And she finished to an arena of supportive cheers and flags. Satoru was glad to see her exonerated, though it was tinged with sympathy when Ekaterina fell to her knees and cried upon the ice after her skate. He could only imagine that feeling, and wished he could have given her a better experience at her first World Championship. One of the three favorites for the podium, and Ekaterina was going home with a tenth place finish. Vindication was her real victory today .

And with Ekaterina in tenth place, Alisha arrested and Inessa out with an injury, thirty-one year-old Sokonthy Masters, ended up winning the World Title. No one was more surprised than she was. "I'm not even sure how to react to that," she said after the fact, and both Satoru and Inessa laughed at her. "No one expected me to even medal, now I've got to defend a World title? What if I can't find a babysitter?" She was pleased, despite all her protests, but still flabbergasted. Her hard work and skill could not be denied, but it was hard to ignore the circumstances that took down her competitors. Satoru hoped the balance of emotions swung a bit more in a happy direction as the days wore on. Nobody liked a medal with an asterisk beside it.

But the competition wasn't all touched by gloom. Isaac proposed to Hser Nay in the Kiss and Cry, and received both a 'yes' and a nice smack on the lips. To add to that victory, both Bertinelli teams made the world podium, marking a historic achievement for siblings everywhere. Clara and Mark inched just ahead of Isaac and Hser Nay, but there didn't seem to be any resentment in front of or behind the camera. Satoru tried to enjoy that, be inspired by it, but his heart ached to recall their smiles and hugs when he came face to face with his own brother, kept behind a sheet of plexiglass.

There were a million questions to be asked, the when's and why's that started Wataru and Alisha's conniving, but Satoru only had energy for one. "The past six months, getting along and spending time with me. Was that a lie?"

"No."

"Why bother? If you were just going to kill me, anyway?"

"It made you happy, didn't it?" That wasn't the answer Satoru expected to hear, but it came too easily to doubt. "The opportunity was there, and I thought I owed you that much. None of that was a lie, it was... nice."

Satoru tilted his head, not sure why he felt touched. "If you hadn't tried to kill me, we could have had all the opportunities in the world." Maybe they still could, if Wataru was sorry, if he wanted to change.

Satoru could add "murder attempt" to the pile of things he was still trying to forgive Wataru for, what was one more offense?

He really had a problem. Satoru wondered if he should see someone about that.

Wataru had just shrugged. "Yeah, but the opportunity was there. Thought I might as well take advantage of it." And just like that, the moment was gone. A sneer curled at Wataru's lips, taking the place of that smile. "What about your life is so important that you couldn't let me have this?"

Satoru couldn't answer at the time. The inherent rights of all human beings had seemed like a weak response, but he couldn't come up with a better one on the spot. The question followed him for the rest of the weekend, as he remembered his childhood with Wataru. He remembered those times when his brother flew with him to competitions, a chaperone in lieu of their parents. Wataru had grumbled sometimes, but he seemed to like flying to all those exotic countries well enough. And he never seemed to mind hobnobbing with all the famous skaters and coaches in Satoru's orbit, nor utilizing those relationships to advance his career in sports journalism. Like Alisha.

Satoru wondered which one of them thought of murder first.

"I know he's your brother, and we love him in spite of ourselves," his mother finally said, after days of watching her son think himself in circles, "But stop taking his side. There's nothing you did to deserve this."

"Yeah, but it had to be hard for him," Satoru couldn't help but say, even as Izumi was prepared to write her oldest brother off and never talk to him again. She held a makeup compact in one hand as she brushed color over Satoru's face, a lanyard bouncing with every agitated movement as Satoru's competition time grew closer. But even with his sister's demands to hold his face still, Satoru couldn't help but defend Wataru a little.

"I don't care," Izumi finally said. "It's hard for me, too. Hard for Mom and Dad, hard for you. Life's hard for everybody. What makes him think he's special?"

Satoru let Izumi finish his makeup in silence. Rather, he was silent. She kept grumbling about how he should have hired a professional to do his makeup, since everyone was going to see his face in high definition. While her music, her remix of his free program, echoed around the globe on hundreds of networks.

"But there's no one else I'd rather have do this," Satoru swallowed, not sure why he was hesitant to say it. "I'm... I'm really glad you're my sister. I wouldn't change you for anything."

There was a long silence, in which only a brush moved over his cheeks. It wasn't until after he heard the click of the compact closing that Satoru got a reply. "Me, too." Izumi then cleared her throat and added, "You can open your eyes now." Satoru did as instructed, then grinned.

"How do I look?"

"Dead," Izumi replied, and looked a little disturbed by her creation. Satoru just grinned all the wider.

"Perfect."

CONFIDENCE WAS KEY. If it began to lag, Satoru would have to fake it. He marched down the hall to the ice like he owned the arena, like the World Title was his for the taking, but by the time he found himself opposite Kara Beth at the boards, insecurity was settling in.

There was no place for it. "*I can do this,*" he muttered to himself, more an order than a reassurance, and Kara Beth nodded her agreement.

"Of course you can. Trust your training." He wondered if she'd even noticed the language shift, or if she'd just guessed at what he was saying. But there were other things to focus on. "Who's your opponent?"

Satoru pursed his lips and visualized it. "World."

"The whole world?"

"Yes," Satoru said, feeling the anticipation build as he thought about it. "Whole world, everyone who sees."

"Good. It's going to be a war out there. If you want to come back to life, you can't give them a single inch." The tension lingered for another moment before she blew out a huff of air. "Man, but it's so weird to look you in the eyes like this..."

Satoru grinned, knowing that it only increased the eerie effects of Izumi's makeup job. "I look spooky?"

"You look like you just walked out of the morgue." That was the idea. The pale makeup sucked the color from his face and high-lighted dark circles around his eyes. He'd sewed himself a new costume, a white shirt with gray slacks instead of the bright colors he'd used before. And for the final touch, he'd spattered it in what everyone assured him was red, the largest blotch being right over his heart. "Are zombies eligible to compete at the senior level?"

"If they win," was Satoru's cheeky reply, and he was eager to get to that. "You got pom-poms? Come on!"

"Okay, okay." Kara Beth grabbed her red and white pom-poms, and raised them in the air. "A-M-A-Z-I-N-G! You're the best from sea to sea! Go, Sato!"

He grinned back and was about to reply when the announcer finally called out Damien's score. Oh, *wow...* That sobered him for a moment, and he had to grip the boards to steady himself.

"Hey, whatever happens," Kara Beth said, somehow audible over the eruption of noise. "Whatever happens, I am so proud of you. You're going to kill it out there. Your opponent is the world, and there isn't a single person on earth that can stop you."

Right. Satoru was a warrior, once defeated, but back to challenge the earth and sky and life itself. And his first conquest would be Damien's score. He pushed off the boards and took center ice, any gaps in confidence filled with drive. It wasn't every dead man who could find the strength to rise.

He dug in his feet in the few tense seconds before his music started, like a sprinter at the start of a race, a samurai waiting for his opponent's first move. All eyes in the arena were on him, and he could sense the whispers about his costume choice. It was a state-ment, a declaration. They thought they'd killed him, that he'd been shot and buried, and they would have been right, in a sense. But that gold medal was his. And it meant far more to Satoru than first place. His whole season, whole career, everything he ever learned or did was on the line today.

What they broke down could be rebuilt. The first notes of his free skate hit the arena like shattering glass, and Satoru's lips curled in response. Izumi's remix was bursting with confidence and authority, fueling the drama inside him. Dead and buried? No, just scarred. How many new buildings existed because old ones had been restored? How many new heights were achieved after seeing another tall structure do it first? They could try to kill him, but Satoru would live forever.

The music built, a slow, rhythmic kick drum counting up to a cathartic release of tension that would be the Quad Axel. Channeling Axel Paulsen, Satoru pushed low into the ice and came around the corner of the rink with a series of crossovers, each push of his legs driving power and synced to the music.

With each press, he pictured Wataru in front of him. His life was short enough, and his competitive career was even shorter. Like a cherry blossom, it would fall and fade with nothing but a memory.

But what a memory! The seeds would give life to new trees, new trees blossoming with Tano Sals and Quad Axels, double quad combos and still the highest components scores around. Blossoms that people hadn't even conceived yet. There would be new trees, year after year, boughs heavier with more and more stunning flowers, and all because one flower fell down to the mud.

Transience was eternal. But until then, Satoru took no shame in wanting to be the pinkest blossom on the tree.

Maybe he was a little too wound up, or maybe it was just bad luck, but Satoru felt his blade catch on an imperfection in the ice's surface just as he was about to spring into the air. It stole half of his momentum, and he knew right away that he wasn't going to pull four and a half rotations out of that jump. But he tried to salvage what he could.

His foot touched the ice, and he wrenched his free leg around to check the rotation, hoping he'd gotten three turns out of that. Disappointment bashed into him, but only for a moment. He was more than a jump, even that one, and life was long. He could try again, as many competitions as he needed to. The present was a bigger problem. With only a Triple Axel, he'd have to replace the final jumping pass in order to keep from breaking the Zayak rule, not to mention all the points he now had to make up.

But there was time to think about that later. For now, he had the Tano Salchow coming up, his oldest friend. He hoped Wataru would be allowed to see, because this was what Satoru was living for. The balance was precarious, the strength and timing so precise, but he lived in the center of that tornado, one arm trying to grasp heaven. He could be buffeted and knocked off course, always pulled one way or the other by the force of physics, but miserable?

Never. Satoru landed that Salchow with the drop of the bass, feeling the moment that the audience regained their breath and beating hearts. Nothing would kill him today. And what he built on this ice would last longer then Stonehenge, then the pyramids, then the Megalithic Temples of Malta.

Even so, a bit of disappointment lingered in the back of his mind. He'd wanted a perfect skate, to prove himself after so much time away, after everything that happened. Perhaps he wouldn't get a perfect skate, but it could still be a redemptive one. Satoru set up his entrance for the Loop.

Loops were a fun jump, and kind of weird. The takeoff and landing leg were the same, and there was no toe pick assist to get them off that tricky edge. Before his knee injury, Satoru used to love his Triple Loop, but after the injury, it became an impossible feat. By then his coach had moved on to drilling the Flip and the Lutz and unleashing disgusted fury when they inevitably failed, so the Loop took something of a backseat. It was worth less points in those years, less important.

But the Loop jump didn't hurt half as much on the takeoff, and falling on the jump was significantly less painful than landing it, so Satoru had unconsciously let himself fall. The rules were different back then. He still racked up points for rotating a jump, even with a fall, and the deductions were not as steep. His coach grilled him for it, but Satoru continued to fall with the satisfaction of knowing he could keep one secret.

When he'd come to Kara Beth, and been forced to get surgery, it had been a struggle to remember what it was like to land on purpose. His muscles had grown so used to his safer falls that the correct body position eluded him for some time. That was an old problem, though, one that he'd successfully trained out of himself.

Or so he thought. Now, flying through the air and knowing that his body position was off, he wondered if some of that old mentality still lingered. Or maybe he was just having an off day. Either way, things weren't looking good for his Quad Loop.

Satoru drove his landing foot into the ground, knowing that he hadn't completed the full four rotations. The technical panel would be all over that landing, but better to abort than fall, under the current judging system. Better to stand up on the landing than go sliding on his butt, so he forced himself to land while he was still somewhat vertical in the air. He was a warrior, he could adapt, lose the battle but win the war. A silly jump wasn't going to defeat him, not at the World Championships, his best stage!

That pep talk failed. His weight slipped too far over the side, just when he thought he'd balanced, and he went tumbling into the ice. All the preparation, all the hopes and dreams and vindication, undone by two botched jumps. Satoru was seething even before he hit the ice, darkly wondering if this was going to be Beijing all over again. No, this was different. Satoru wasn't going to end his program with shame, though perhaps with a whole bunch of righteous anger. The ice was supposed to be his ally in a fight against the world, a battleground where honor and skill could prove himself. It felt like a betrayal, like a brother with his hand on a trigger, to think the ice wouldn't catch his blades. He slid for a moment and managed to find his feet, but before rising again, he slapped the ice with an open palm. *-How dare you!-*

As soon as he did, he felt stupid. The magic of music and costume faded away for a moment, and Satoru grew vividly aware that he was just a person, with millions of people watching him trip up and then proceed to have a little fit with the ice. Covered in costume and makeup, the whole situation seemed kind of ridiculous.

And he laughed. With a push of his leg, he was on his feet, snapped back into character. Didn't people say he always had his best skates on days he didn't win? Time to prove that. He'd fallen, and popped a jump before that, but this wasn't like previous mistakes. It wasn't failure at all, because Satoru didn't hate himself, World Championship on the line or no. He'd go home and mope for a few days, then jump into training and come back next season like a returning king.

Right now was only about the moment. Beautiful moments that bloomed ever spring, but never the same blossom twice. Each tiny flower was transient and precious, and if some took their time to break free from the bud, it didn't diminish their beauty when they finally revealed their true colors to the world. Each stretch of his muscles felt like the uncurling of a petal, how had he never noticed he was still wrapped in his green cocoon? All these years of skating, and he was only now answering the call of spring.

Izumi's music filled his ears and soul, a firm brace offering support to his old foundation, while the knowledge that his family, Inessa and Kara Beth were watching filled all the cracks like a generous pouring of wet concrete. All the madness and personal heartache, but they chose to come support him in this most important of moments. Even Damien would be watching now from the greenroom, and despite the title on the line, Satoru knew that his friend would never wish for him to fall. It wasn't just a hope, but a knowledge built upon years and years of evidence. Damien was the brother Satoru always deserved to have, and Satoru had as much faith in that as he did in himself.

Spins and steps and choreography, beautiful jumps, Satoru fought for every second with the passion of one denied a chance to live.

-Is this what happens after 'Giselle' ends? Is this the next part of Ablrecht's story?-

The thought was curious, and Satoru let it feed his performance, giving into some abandon as he turned into a pattern of twizzles. The world would always criticize the Prince for his treatment of Giselle, and carry wide and disparate opinions of how he should atone. There would always be judgement and expectations following him, fueling a personal guilt that might never be completely shaken.

But though they'd try, none of them got to tell Albrecht what his life was worth. Giselle had deemed him worthy of breath and forgiveness, and she didn't hold off the forest spirits just to see an animated corpse walking through the village. Albrecht would live, he would find joy, and he would remember that dark dance in the forest until he was brought to Giselle's side again as a redeemed and worthy man.

The world had changed, the colors had all shifted, the Prince had lost some jewels from his crown. Satoru would live on.

More than that, he would thrive. That was the meaning behind this new music, new costume, that Satoru would fight for every inch of his life, even if the world was already nailing his coffin shut. And he could do that amongst failure and defeat, disappointment and betrayal.

And imperfection. He was down to the last jump in the program, the triple axel. Thanks to popping the first 4A into a triple, he'd already done two of the same jump. This last jumping pass would be invalidated if he didn't do something else.

There were other jumps in his arsenal. But a plan began to form in his mind, and a delicious grin took over his face at the thought. He'd drilled that jump with Kara Beth so many times, until his legs were jelly, just to be sure he could land it under *any* circumstances...

This was what he'd trained for. Satoru lowered himself, utilizing the bend of his knees and building speed for all he had. Some of the transitions felt a little wild, not used to being performed at such velocity, and Satoru cut some of the more difficult steps out in favor of efficiency. It wasn't ideal, doing the program as planned would have been ideal, but Satoru felt the reward would be worth it.

-No way am I ending the season without that Quad Axel!-

Sometimes flowers bloomed late in the season. And sometimes the last blossom fell with all the power of a mic drop. Satoru felt the anticipation of the crowd build, realizing what he was up to, and then, shoving those whispers out of his mind, took that first step.

It was a little rough, a little off kilter, but he persisted. One rotation. Two rotations. Three. -*Yikes, is that the ceiling?*- Four...

-*One half.*- Wow, he was lucky his landing knee didn't explode on impact. Forget plushes and roses, the fans would need to throw him painkillers. But he held on, checking the jump and doing his utmost to make sure he ended on his feet, even as it felt like his femur was splintering.

How could a handful of seconds could mean so much? But after those agonizing seconds were over, Satoru was still on one blade, riding backwards with his arms out to the side, shaken but strong. He'd landed his favorite jump in the very moment that mattered most.

And he screamed.

The audience screamed with him, and Satoru launched himself into the last of his program with a glee and vigor he'd never had the freedom to share before. He was imperfect; he was magnificent; he was loved and loved himself and probably wasn't even going home with a first place medal, but already held the greatest trophy inside his heart. This was why he skated, what he lived for, the chance to catch lightning in a bottle.

His final spin sequence awaited, a flying sit spin. It had the same takeoff as an axel, and the image of Surya Bonaly's Olympics came into his mind, whispering to him, "*why not?*"

He did a double axel, before dropping into the spin. No extra points for that, in fact it might get invalidated. No reason to do so much extra effort except that it looked cool and today's skate was about his statement to the world, the declaration of his life and legacy. A promise of all he had yet to conquer, because a few delusional voices didn't get to tell him when his life had exceeded its worth.

His blades spun and carved up the ice, like roots burning deep into the ground, finding new life for the tree that would grow higher and wider as it reached for the light. New flowers, new skyscrapers with higher and higher floors, lasting for centuries because of all they meant to the people who dared to crane their necks back and dream. An ocean of rising suns burst forth in his periphery, a swirling radiance despite the colors being different than he'd always remembered.

But he didn't have to see the color red to know that richness in his heart. In one final motion, Satoru broke the spin and spread his arms to receive it.

Leaving one boy with a glass jar, who'd just caught lightning.

HE WAS STILL giddy when he finished his bows and made his way over to the boards. He'd heard Kara Beth screaming over the roars of the crowd, and she was still screaming now.

Happy and exasperated, his favorite expression on her. "What in the grass-loving *earth* was that?" She roared at him while he was still at the center, and Satoru giggled as he skated back to her.

"You said you'd trust me!"

"Not the point!" She chucked a pom-pom at him, and it missed him by a good five feet. "You just went YOLO on a Quad Axel! You were horizontal in the air!"

"Please, Dami's loop is horizontal! I was maybe forty-five degrees!" He closed the remaining distance and launched himself into her arms. "I'm so excited!"

"Good job. I can't even..." Kara Beth sighed, and her hair tickled Satoru's ears. "You're something else..."

A Quad Axel, and in the second half of the program, no less. First in his country to do it. And unplanned. The weight of it was hitting him. He hadn't just made history, he'd patented, set up a factory and mass-produced it.

"And I probably won't even win," he said, suddenly dizzy with the awe of it.

They broke their hug, and Kara Beth hit him in the shoulder before handing him his guards. Once they got to the Kiss and Cry, she whacked him again. "What were you thinking?"

Satoru couldn't help but wink. "Well, I was thinking, 'Oh no, what should I do', and then the voice of Surya Bonaly came into brain and say 'do the awesome thing'."

"Oh, shut up," Kara Beth snorted.

"I'm serious! And then God Hanyu comes down in vision to say I must not ignore voice of angel, do the axel!"

He could see her trying not to laugh. "And did Axel Paulsen appear next to complete the Holy Trinity?"

Satoru clasped his hands together. "Doesn't need to, for he is always living in my heart."

"Oh, my actual Lord," Kara Beth put her head in her hands. "You're too much." They laughed together for some time, waiting for the scores. The jumbotron cut to the green-room, and Damien waved at him. Satoru waved back, ridiculously excited, even knowing that his fallen Loop put him at risk to overtake Damien. It would be close, he'd left himself too vulnerable.

But next season... and that was a warm thought. There would be a next season, if he wanted it. "Are you happy?" Kara Beth asked, breaking into his thoughts. Her voice was low, head tilted to the side, trying to gauge him.

Of course she was. A season ago, she'd be dealing with someone who might hang themselves with their own skate laces over such mistakes. But that was another lifetime. Satoru passed through the forest of death. He'd earned his right to live again.

He didn't want to say so where microphones could pick it up, or where cameras could have fans devoting the next twelve hours of their lives to reading his lips, but for once in his life, he didn't feel shame or regret. "I'm happy."

"Even if you fell on the Loop?"

"Yeah." He couldn't stop the laugh. What else could he do? But it didn't hurt like it had in the past. "Yeah, I did."

"And you're okay?"

"Is freaky mistake. I'll get right next time. More worried about first Axel. But I know how to fix. It's... not a big deal." He paused, wondering if he should be so cavalier in front of his coach. He was supposed to take his work, and hers, seriously. "I mean, would have been better to get it right, I don't mean..." He clapped his hands together in a show of contrition. "I'll work very hard in practice, I promise! But I think it's okay to..." he paused. He couldn't say it was okay to make mistakes. It wasn't. But it wasn't worth beating himself up over. It wasn't... dire. "It's okay to... keep living over."

Kara Beth burst into laughter and Satoru wondered what he'd actually said, but gave up when she patted his knee. "Yes. *Please* keep living over this."

And in that moment, he felt in a perfect state of grace, despite everything waiting for him when he unlaced his skates. He wanted to tell her, but it would have to wait. Some things were too intimate for the Kiss and Cry. So he forced his face into a devious grin. "Besides, if I'm perfect, you have nothing to teach. Mistakes mean you keep your job."

"You're such a brat," she laughed again, then quieted when the music on the intercom cut out. "Whatever the score, that was a brilliant skate," she said, all serious now. "I've never been more proud of you."

Satoru swallowed and offered a thank you before the fate of his World Title was revealed. "Wow..."

"Oh man, and that's with the fall deductions..."

He could only nod in a daze. Personal best. Season's best. And still... "Good day for France..." He saw Damien again, and clapped. His opponent gave a gracious bow back. "Silver is beautiful color. I can see silver. And I get to put *Hinomaru* in the sky." That was something. A bittersweet victory.

But with that, reality came back. The season was over. A weight of finality settled on him, even though he knew his problems hadn't come to an end. He'd be dealing with the aftereffects of Wataru and Alisha for months, at least.

The benefits would linger, too, though, and he thought of Inessa. Of Damien, who would remain in Ohio. Izumi and his parents, ready to receive him at home, and Kara Beth keeping the other door open. It wouldn't do to forget that.

"You'll be with me after this?" he asked of Kara Beth in a quiet voice, suddenly feeling thirteen again.

He was rewarded when she squeezed his hand. "Of course. Long as you want me. You're the boss," she added with a wink, and Satoru shook off his melancholy. It had no place here.

"Good, 'cause I was thinking about quintuples-"

"No."

ABOUT THE AUTHOR

Anne Werner is a writer, actor, podcaster and incorrigible fangirl. Her love of axel jumps is only exceeded by her love of storytelling. She grew up in Medicine Hat, Alberta, and studied both Theatre Arts and Japanese Language at Utah State University, during which she was able to study abroad at Kobe University in Japan. Anne currently lives in Ogden, Utah.